Soth's fist struck the tabletop like a dwarven hammer hitting the finest elven crystal. At the blow, the worm-eaten wood broke into hundreds of fragments. "On Krynn I am a favored servant of the dark goddess, Takhisis," the death knight said, taking a step toward Strahd. "There she is my master. In Barovia, I recognize none as my better."

Soth lashed out at the vampire lord, but Strahd caught his wrist. The vampire held him fast, and the two dead men locked gazes.

"No one—not even your dark goddess—has the power to challenge me here." The vampire smiled viciously. "All who dwell in Barovia serve me, as you will soon learn, Lord Soth."

Ravenloft is a netherworld of evil, a place of darkness that can be reached from any world—escape is a different matter entirely. The unlucky who stumble into the Dark Domain find themselves trapped in lands filled with vampires, werebeasts, and worse.

Each novel in this series is a complete story in itself, revealing the chilling tales of the beleaguered heroes and powerful evil lords who populate the Dark Domain.

Books

Vampire of the Mists
Christie Golden

Knight of the Black Rose
James Lowder

Dance of the Dead
Christie Golden

Heart of Midnight
J. Robert King

Books

Knight
of the
Black Rose

James Lowder

KNIGHT OF THE BLACK ROSE

Random House and its affiliate companies have worldwide distribution rights in the book trade for English language products of TSR, Inc.

Distributed to the book and hobby trade in the United Kingdom by TSR Ltd.

Distributed to the toy and hobby trade by regional distributors.

Cover art by Clyde Caldwell.

RAVENLOFT, FORGOTTEN REALMS, and POLYHEDRON are registered trademarks owned by TSR, Inc.

The TSR logo is a trademark owned by TSR, Inc.

First Printing: December 1991
Printed in the United States of America
Library of Congress Catalog Card Number: 90-71507

9 8 7 6 5

ISBN: 1-56076-156-3

TSR, Inc.
P.O. Box 756
Lake Geneva, WI 53147
U.S.A.

TSR, Ltd.
120 Church End, Cherry Hinton
Cambridge CB1 3LB
United Kingdom

To Debbie, for her patience and support, even when the death knight took over the apartment.

Many times, Lord Soth threatened to drag me into the Dark Domain with him, and I owe lots of people thanks for pulling me back: my parents and in-laws, who understood why I spent the summer at the computer; John Rateliff, whose knowledge of fantasy literature and gracious criticisms helped immeasurably; and my editor, Pat McGilligan, whose enthusiasm and hard work made the plot move and the characters breathe—those that were supposed to, anyway.

Thanks especially to Mary Kirchoff; your confidence in my abilities made it possible for me to write about Soth, and your wit and friendship made it easier for me to survive months of living with vampires and ghosts.

 **PROLOGUE**

From the *Iconochronos* of Astinus of Palanthas

One name recorded here, in these scrolls that make up my history of Krynn, has become a byword for corruption and monumental evil throughout the continent of Ansalon: Lord Soth of Dargaard Keep.

The Knight of the Black Rose.

Such was not always the case. Once, in the years before the gods punished mortals with the Cataclysm that shook these lands to the core, Lord Soth was a great and noble soldier for Good, a member of the renowned Knights of Solamnia. In that most famed of famed brotherhoods, Soth attained their highest honor, the Order of the Rose. For a time, he fought for justice and freedom. His heart remained pure then, his soul unspotted. When it came time to build his castle, Soth designed it himself to resemble the symbol of his order—the flawless red rose.

Yet it was not long after Soth married and brought his wife to Dargaard Keep that darkness settled upon his life, a darkness so profound he has never escaped it, a corruption so complete it made the once-proud knight a willing agent of Takhisis, the Queen of Darkness.

Some claim that pride undermined Soth's will to do good, others say lust, and still others greed. Of those who still walk beneath the triple moons of Krynn, only Soth himself knows for certain the cause of his own doom. The world is left to construe what it will from skeletal bits of history.

Soth's wife befitted a man of his station and potential. A noble's daughter and only child, she offered the young knight much in the way of worldly goods. That love had little traffic in Dargaard in those days was apparent to all who visited the keep, if they found Soth there at all. The lord of the castle spent much of his time traversing the Solamnic countryside in search of suitable wrongs to right, accompanied by thirteen knights loyal to him above all others.

The summons to Palanthas, most beautiful of all cities, came to Soth early in the spring. He and his retainers set off for the Knights' Council to be held in that unconquered city, but before they reached its perfectly planned streets, temptation bested the Knight of the Rose. He and his men came across a mob of ogres attacking a small band of elven women. The knights easily defeated the brutes, save one who had snatched up an elfmaid and dashed off into the woods.

Lord Soth himself battled and conquered this, the strongest of the ogres. The woman he saved, a young elfmaid on her way to take her vows as a Revered Daughter of Paladine, dazzled him with her innocent beauty. Soon after, they became secret lovers, though in doing so Soth broke both his sacred marriage vows and the Code of the Knights of Solamnia.

It seemed as if the lord of Dargaard Keep believed this blot on his soul would remain hidden forever, for he went to the Knights' Council as if nothing had transpired between him and the elfmaid. Yet two things conspired to bring the Rose Knight's shame to the pure light of Krynn's sun. The first was the news that Soth's wife had disappeared from Dargaard Keep. The blood found in her chambers cried foul play, and the nobleman's almost casual reaction to this shocking news made many in his order wonder for the first time if they had judged Soth too highly.

The second incident that shouted Soth's guilt to those gathered at the Knights' Council was the elf-maid's sudden illness. When it was discovered she was with child, many suspected Soth, for he had kept company with her even before his wife's disappearance. The other elven women who had been rescued by the Rose Knight and his followers that fateful day confirmed those suspicions and revealed Soth's faithlessness.

The minutes of Soth's trial are recorded elsewhere in this history. Here I will note only that he was found guilty of many crimes, sentenced to death, and dragged through the streets of Palanthas in shame. Death would have been a kinder fate than the one eventually claimed by the fallen knight.

The nobleman's thirteen loyal followers rescued him from his prison on the night before his planned execution. Accompanied by the elfmaid, the dis-graced band slunk from the walls of the city and made their way to Dargaard Keep. The true Knights of Solamnia pursued the renegades, but Soth reached the safety of his castle before they could capture him.

In the months that followed, the lord of Dargaard attempted to build a new life within the walls of his besieged castle. He married the elfmaid and went through the motions of honoring his order's rituals. Though none who stayed within Dargaard's walls for long lived to tell the tale, legend has it Soth grew moody and violent. Not even his wife, heavy with child, was spared the disgraced knight's mailed fist.

The gods granted Soth enough self-knowledge to see how low he'd fallen, and the realization fanned the few sparks of honor left in the weave of his besotted soul. In Dargaard's long-unused chapel, Soth prayed to Paladine, Father of All Good, and his elf-maid bride offered her hopes to Mishakal, the Light Bringer. Again the gods favored Soth with the ability to see, though this time it was a vision of the Kingpriest of Istar, who some named prophet and others labeled madman. Paladine himself charged Soth with a sacred task: prevent the kingpriest from demanding power from the deities who oversaw Krynn.

Had Soth succeeded in this quest, Ansalon—nay, all of Krynn—would be a much different place today. Yet the fallen knight never reached the city of Istar. The elven women he had once rescued now poisoned his mind with intimations of his wife's infidelity, and Lord Soth returned to his castle before his quest was done. Raging like a lunatic, he confronted his elf-maid bride, mother of his newborn child, with the imagined transgressions of their vows; at that very same moment, the kingpriest raised his voice to the heavens, demanding the power to eradicate all evil on Krynn, ordering the gods to bow down and serve those mortals who offered them worship.

In their fury at this affront, the gods hurled a mountain at the prideful city of Istar. The destruction wrought by that most terrible of heavenly messengers is known to all as the Cataclysm. Yet few who know how that catastrophe twisted the land realize the manner in which it altered Lord Soth's destiny, as well.

As the flaming mountain struck Istar, a fire engulfed Dargaard Keep. Soth's elfmaid bride, trapped in the blaze and dying, held out her infant for the fallen knight to rescue. Still possessed by jealous rage, he turned away.

For failing in his quest, for letting his own child burn to death before his eyes, Soth's elfmaid bride called a curse down upon the once-noble knight. "You will die this night in fire," she wailed, "even as your son and I die. But you will live eternally in darkness. You will live one life for every life your folly has brought to an end!" Some say the elfmaid's curse still echoes through the mountains around the castle. Others claim Lord Soth repeats the words to fill the silence of his long and sleepless nights.

The flames took Soth's life that night, but he did not die. Blackened and burned, he was reborn as an unliving, undead creature of evil. He still wears the charred armor of a Knight of Solamnia, but the rose emblem that once told of his honor was scorched and twisted by the fire. It is by this corrupted symbol—the black rose—that many know Soth; and for more than three hundred years he has walked the earth, doing the bidding of the most evil of evil deities, Takhisis, Queen of Darkness.

Though the Knight of the Black Rose has appeared in the pages of my history before, I write of him now because he is once again coming to Palanthas. We await him here in fear, in this city that has never been conquered. We have received word he brings a frightening force to stand against us. He and the dragon highlord, Kitiara Uth Matar, will be at the walls before sunset.

The future remains hidden from men, and with good reason. On this day, however, I would not refuse knowledge of the morrow.

 **ONE**

With each strike of its burning hooves, Lord Soth's monstrous steed left flaming tracks on the arrow-straight streets of Palanthas's New City. The creature was a nightmare, a denizen of Hades that evil beings such as the undead knight could summon for use in battle. One look at its coat of most profound black, eyes of sulphurous red, and nostrils brimming with orange flame revealed the steed's unearthly origin.

Lord Soth was unconcerned with his mount's reputation for treachery. His mind was wrapped around thoughts of his own traitorous plans.

The death knight served as vanguard for the armies of the dragon highlord, Kitiara Uth Matar, who coveted the city of Palanthas for a single magical building sheltered within its walls. In the Tower of High Sorcery, near the city's heart, lay a portal to the Abyss, and through this portal Kitiara's power-mad half-brother Raistlin had ventured to confront the evil goddess Takhisis. The dragon highlord planned to raze Palanthas to reach the tower. From it she would present the defeated city to whomever emerged victorious from the portal; Soth cared for none of this. He wanted Kitiara, preferably dead.

Though he now led the armies of Highlord Kitiara,

the death knight had warned Palanthas of her coming. Soth knew the Palanthians were not powerful enough to stop the evil troops, but the guardian of the tower had magic enough to bring Kitiara low. After retrieving her corpse and trapping her soul, Soth planned to abandon the fight and return to Dargaard Keep. In the shelter of that hellish place, he could perform a rite that would make the highlord his unliving companion for all eternity.

Soth banished these thoughts as he drew near the twin minarets that framed the main gate. The death knight could see scores of men, some armored, others clad only in cloth, lining the ancient wall. Their gazes were locked on the flying citadel that had just dropped from the clouds and now moved steadily over New City. As Soth stopped before the gate, many turned in horror toward the undead herald come to deliver the attacking dragon highlord's demands.

"Lord of Palanthas," he called, his hollow voice echoing from the walls. When the noble Lord Amothus moved to the fore on the battlements, the death knight continued. "Surrender your city to Lord Kitiara. Give up to her the keys to the Tower of High Sorcery, name her ruler of Palanthas, and she will allow you to continue to live in peace. Your city will be spared destruction."

A pause followed in which the soldiers around Lord Amothus evidenced panic. Though frightened himself, Amothus ran a hand through his thinning hair and glanced with forced casualness at the death knight, then at the flying citadel approaching in the sky.

Lord Soth sat astride the nightmare, clad in ancient armor. The fire that had taken his life had also blasted the mail and obscured its intricate carvings of kingfishers and roses. The lone image still visible—a rose on the breastplate, charred black—had become the dead man's symbol.

A flowing cape of royal purple waved in the breeze behind Soth like a ghostly banner of challenge. From his helmet, his eyes glowed with an orange fire of their own. He sat stiffly in the saddle, one mailed fist gripping the reins. His other hand rested on the hilt of his sword, a blade dark with the blood of hundreds of men. As the citadel passed overhead, a shadow covered the death knight and he faded from view slightly, as if the darkness welcomed and engulfed him as part of itself.

The flying citadel was a masterpiece of evil sorcery. A dark-stoned castle rested on a mammoth rock, which was itself surrounded by boiling, magical clouds. The shock of being wrenched from the earth had toppled a few of the keep's walls, but the citadel remained intact enough to house an army of foul creatures. And as the citadel came close to the walls protecting Palanthas's Old City, evil dragons dropped from the clouds. They flew in looping, chaotic patterns around the fortress as they awaited the order to attack. Even now evil creatures lined the edge of the rock, waiting to drop into battle. Formations of good bronze dragons sped into the air and clashed in defense of Palanthas with the blue and black swarm. The great dragons dove through the sky at terrible speeds, their screeches resounding through the almost-silent streets.

"Take this message to your dragon highlord," Amothus said at last, forcing steel into his voice. "Palanthas has lived in peace and beauty for many centuries, but we will buy neither peace nor beauty at the price of our freedom."

The citadel was even then gliding over the wall surrounding Old City as Lord Soth shouted his reply. "Then buy them at the price of your lives!"

Softly the fallen knight uttered a magical command. From the darkness around him there appeared thirteen skeletal warriors, all mounted, like their lord, astride nightmares. Behind them banshees from Dargaard Keep rode low over the ground in chariots wrought of human bone. Wyverns pulled the ghastly chariots, but it was not those broadwinged, lesser dragon-kin that thrust fear into the Palanthians' hearts. The banshees were wailing and swinging swords of ice as they circled before the gate. It was the sound of their shrill cries that froze the souls of men on the battlements.

Again Soth spoke a word of magic, pointing a gauntleted hand at the massive gate before him. A gorgeous pattern of frost spread like lace across the iron bands that held the gate together. The frost rapidly grew thicker and thicker until it covered the entire gate. At another command from Soth, the frozen gate shattered.

Faintly the death knight heard the frantic cries of the city's defenders as he rushed forward, his skeletal warriors and banshees trailing in his wake.

"The gods of Good save us!" one man shouted.

Another soldier fired an arrow at the undead warriors. "Stop them! By the Oath and the Measure, we can't let the monsters inside!"

This last exclamation—uttered by a Knight of Solamnia—caught Soth's attention, but only momentarily. The knight's words and the various other cries were drowned out by horrified gasps as the army began to plummet from the floating citadel onto the walls and into the city. Their leathery wings spread out to slow their fall, draconians leaped by the hundreds from the fortress. The creatures looked

in many ways like men, but their flesh was reptilian
and their hands and feet savagely clawed. As they
lowered, the draconians shouted out their battle
cries. Inhuman, lisping voices swore allegiance to
Highlord Kitiara and Takhisis, the dark goddess she
served. Other draconians called out for human blood
and licked their lips with long, snaking tongues.

One such creature landed next to Soth as he entered Palanthas's Old City for the first time in three
and a half centuries. The draconian hit the ground
next to the death knight's horrible steed and cringed
in fear at the demonic horse and its inhuman rider.
Even the lizardlike soldier, with its tough, scaly skin,
felt the cold radiating from Soth. Like the human defenders of the proud city, the draconian fled before
the fallen knight.

"Kitiara is planning to race to the Tower of High
Sorcery on her dragon once the battle begins. Kill
everyone standing between us and the tower," the
death knight said. Magic carried his words to the
skeletal warriors and banshees, even over the din of
battle.

The undead minions began their slaughter, but
Soth's attention was drawn to the defensive line
forming far down the street. In the middle of the
broad, stone-paved way was a group of mounted Solamnic Knights, waiting for Lord Soth and his undead warriors. The assembled Knights of the Rose
interested the death knight only marginally, however. His attention was drawn to their leader.

Tanis Half-Elven.

Lord Soth headed straight for Tanis. The death
knight had faced the heroic half-elf before, and Tanis
had survived the conflict through luck—or so Soth
believed. Then the half-elf had killed the dragon
highlord Ariakas and taken the mighty Crown of

Power from the body, stealing the artifact out of Soth's very grasp. But that defeat had little to do with the overwhelming hatred the death knight felt for the young hero. Tanis had been one of Kitiara's many lovers, and the half-elf held a powerful influence over the ruthless general.

Now, by the armor Tanis wore, it seemed the Knights of Solamnia had granted him some honorary rank for his help in defending Palanthas. Soth scoffed at the sight of the half-breed wearing the armor of a knight; in his day, the Order would not have allowed such a travesty. Tanis had surely never faced the necessary tests for advancement. He had proved neither himself nor his family worthy of such ranking. Smiling foully, Soth told himself that he would prove the half-elf unworthy in battle before the day was through.

The death knight's eyes blazed as he watched a small figure leap at Tanis. A kender, one of the much-maligned, mischievous race of beings known for their penchant for "borrowing" things not their own, clung to the half-elf like a sorrowful wife at her husband's departing. After a brief struggle, Tanis caught the kender around the waist and dumped him unceremoniously out of harm's way. As the child-sized kender landed, Soth recognized him as Tasslehoff Burrfoot, one of the half-elf's longtime companions.

"Tanis!" the kender wailed from the mouth of a nearby alley, "you can't go out there! You're going to die. I know!"

The half-elf glanced once at the kender, then ran back to the knights. "Fireflash!" he shouted, looking to the sky. With an audible rush of wind, a young bronze dragon swooped out of the air and landed in the broad street next to Tanis. Close at hand, the other knights' chargers whinnied and shied away from the good dragon.

From the alley, the kender ran a few steps down the street, his blue leggings pumping frantically. He stopped, then screamed, "Tanis! You can't fight Lord Soth without the bracelet!"

Bracelet? The death knight pondered the kender's words for an instant, then he concluded that Tassle-hoff must be referring to some magical trinket meant to aid Tanis against the undead. "Imposter," Soth murmured maliciously. "No real knight would ever use wizardry in a duel of honor."

The death knight was close enough now to see that the half-elf wore the insignias of a Knight of the Rose on his armor. At last, one of the mounted riders pointed at Soth and called his commander's name. Tanis turned, his brown-red beard framing a fright-ened scowl. His gaze met the flaming orbs glowing from Soth's helmet, and an expression of fear spread across his tanned face. The death knight reined in the nightmare and slowly dismounted.

"Run!" Tanis croaked. He gazed at Soth. The ban-shees and skeletal warriors were right behind the death knight, and behind them, the shattered main gate. Taking a step backward toward the bronze dragon crouched in the street, the half-elf shouted, "There is nothing you can do against these!"

Lord Soth drew his sword and took a deliberate step toward his foe. At that instant a draconian from the citadel landed in front of Tanis. The half-elf smashed the creature with the pommel of his sword, kicked it hard in the stomach, and leaped over its scaled back and leathery wings.

"The kender!" he yelled to Fireflash.

The dragon took to the air. With an easy elven grace gained from his mother's people, grace not hampered even by the heavy armor he wore, Tanis trailed Fireflash at a steady run. The other knights scattered and raced off into the nearby alleys.

Revulsion battled a dull self-satisfaction as Soth watched Tanis flee in disgrace. The undead knight had dismounted in order to face the half-elf in accordance with the Measure, the strict code of the Solamnic Knights; in the pages of the Measure it was deemed unfair to battle from horse against an unmounted opponent. Such an honorable act was not unusual for Soth. Although he held the Measure in contempt, he followed it whenever possible, proving that the supposedly honorable men of the Order should not be esteemed for their rigorous principles.

Yet Tanis's cowardly retreat had surprised even the fallen knight. He had expected the half-elf to fight, or at least to attempt to delay his charge into the heart of the city. The surprise was tempered by the loathing he felt for a man wearing the badges of a Rose Knight who had chosen to flee from battle. Once that armor had symbolized all that was dear to Lord Soth, and seeing someone sully it by cowardice reminded him that he'd expended his life pursuing the phantom of honor. The knighthood may not be the group of pure-hearted paladins that they pretended, but knowledge of their failings was never sweet to the death knight.

Having cleared the street, the skeletal warriors subservient to Soth now gathered around him. After watching the bronze dragon disappear around a building, Tanis following swiftly behind, the death knight turned to his minions. Farther into Palanthas, down the long, straight road, a group of poorly equipped merchants were erecting a barricade against the evil army. Armed with old, battered swords taken from pawn shops or from their places of honor over family hearths, the Palanthians were piling crates and overturned tables in the path of the advancing enemy.

"Those nuisances block the way to the tower," Soth growled, pointing to the doomed group. "Remove them."

The skeletal warriors pulled hard on their reins, and their nightmares bolted down the road. At the mounted skeletons' approach, a few of the merchants scattered, but those who stayed at the barricade fought hard. At first it seemed they might succeed in holding the undead at bay, until one of the banshees joined the fray. As the unquiet spirit raced above the street, her bone chariot rattling fearfully, she brandished her swords of ice. She smote the trees lining the way, trees whose beautiful leaves resembled fine gold lace year round. With each blow, one of the rare trees withered and died.

"Up!" the banshee shrieked to the wyvern pulling her chariot. "Over the barricade."

Flapping its wings, the wyvern pushed higher into the sky. The great flying lizard barred its yellow fangs and twitched its scorpion's tail as it drew close to the barricade. Then, with a shriek, the creature grabbed one man from atop the redoubt in its two taloned feet. The banshee in the chariot sliced through another defender. Before the two halves of the man fell to the street, many of the other merchants fled. Those who remained to fight were swiftly overwhelmed by Soth's minions. The battle was brief and bloody.

Neither complimenting his servants nor even acknowledging them, the death knight mounted his nightmare and rode through the gap they had cleared in the barricade. Most of the skeletal warriors chased the fleeing Palanthians. Others shuffled mindlessly from body to body, beheading the wounded. The banshee stood in her chariot, waiting for her wyvern to finish with the body of a fat fletcher. Though the unquiet spirit had control over the dim-witted dragon-kin, she knew better than to deny it a well-earned feast.

The forebears of these men lined these same streets once and pelted me with garbage on my way to prison, Soth mused as he passed the headless corpses. My vow is now fulfilled. They have been made to pay.

Yet the death knight felt no joy at that realization; like many emotions, joy was denied him by his curse. Anger, hatred, jealousy—those and many other destructive impulses still had power to make Soth's unbeating heart flare. He could destroy, but never know anything but a dull, ash-gray pleasure from it. Like a tepid glass of water, such a reward did little to slake his thirst for relief from the monotony of unlife.

So it was, under a pall of impotent dissatisfaction, that Soth rode through Palanthas. All along his route draconians were slaughtering people dragged from their hiding places. The victims' blood colored many a white facade of home and shop bordering the road to the city's second ward, where the Tower of High Sorcery lay. The feral screams of evil dragons, fighting against warriors mounted on their good-aligned brethren, reverberated all around the city. Blood from one of these battles rained into the street, drawn from some fatally wounded dragon. The eerie shower created pools of gore that evaporated with a hiss under the burning step of Soth's nightmare.

With his hellish mount's reins in his mailed fist, the death knight caught a glimpse of the flying cita-del. The floating mountain lumbered almost drunk-enly across the sky. Though it appeared to be free from attack, the fortress lurched as if it had been stricken. After puzzling over this strange occurrence, he realized that the citadel had stopped and was hovering unsteadily over the Tower of High Sorcery.

With the arrogance of one inured to mortal threats, Soth dismissed the citadel's odd movement and raced off in the direction of the tower. He found the rest of the city empty of challengers; the few who saw the death knight charging through the streets fled at his advance. Soon Soth saw the avenue widen, then open into the courtyard surrounding the Tower of High Sorcery. The citadel hanging over the ancient structure blotted out the sky overhead, but the darkness that hung around the accursed tower was omnipresent, as was the twisted grove that stood sentinel around it.

Soth urged the nightmare closer to the picket of massive oaks known as Shoikan Grove, but the creature shied back. An intense cold radiated out of the dark trees, making the nightmare's hooves burn less brightly, its hot breath steam in the air. With a frightened snort, the mount pawed at the stone pavement and reared.

After letting the nightmare retreat a few paces from the Shoikan Grove, Soth dismounted. "Go, then. Return to the infernal flames that spawned you." Again the nightmare reared, then vanished in a burst of foul-smelling smoke and ash.

As he crossed the empty courtyard to the grove, the death knight studied the ancient structure guarded by the oaks. The Tower of High Sorcery had once been a vaunted seat of magical learning, a place where mages stored their books and underwent the dangerous tests to determine their place in wizardly society. But many years past, when Soth himself had been mortal, the Kingpriest of Istar had launched a crusade against magic; the religious zealot branded sorcery a tool of evil and directed the people of Ansalon against the towers. The wizards destroyed two of the five existing strongholds rather than let the peasants assume control of the secrets they housed, then agreed to retreat to a single tower far from civilization. The tower in Palanthas was supposed to have been abandoned.

On the day the mages planned to leave the Palanthian tower, a wizard of the black robes, a servant of evil, cursed the structure. He swore the tower's gates would remain closed and its halls empty until the vague prophecy he uttered came true. To seal the curse, he leaped from the tower's highest balcony onto the spiked fence surrounding it. Instantly the gold and silver gates turned black, and the once-beautiful structure darkened. Now the Tower of High Sorcery was a pool of shadow within the radiance of Palanthas; its ice-gray marble stood in stark contrast to the pure white stone that made up the city's minarets.

The only way to enter the Tower of High Sorcery was through the Shoikan Grove; not even powerful spells of teleportation could gain someone entrance. The twisted oaks that had grown up around the tower housed dreadful supernatural guardians. The grove radiated fear as well. The terror the place inspired was so overwhelming that even kender, whose curiosity almost always overcame their fears, could not pass within the grove without their resolve crumbling.

Such threats held no sway over Soth, and he stepped into the bleak grove as if it were any ordinary wood.

Yet as he moved into the trees, the death knight

dimly felt the chill that would have made a mortal
shiver uncontrollably. An eternal darkness hung like
moss on the grove's twisted roots and branches, and
no wind stirred the ragged, shriveled leaves. Indeed,
there was a presence in the grove. Soth recognized
the pulsing that permeated the cursed wood: the
aura of souls caught in tormented unlife. It was a
feeling with which he was quite familiar.

The ground, spongy with decaying leaves and
mold-covered from the lack of sunlight, trembled
with each silent step. When Soth was surrounded by
the tall trees, the trembling stopped. Covered with
grime, a pale hand burst from the dirt and reached
for Soth's leg. Another bony hand, then another,
pushed through the soft earth to clutch at the death
knight. Still more dead hands closed around Soth's
ankles and tried to pull him down.

"You have no cause to bar me, brothers," the death
knight said calmly. The pale, decayed hands hesitated. "I wish to take nothing from the tower that you
have been sworn to guard, but I will destroy you if
you delay me."

From inside the ground a voice came weakly, "We
know you, Soth, as one of us. What do you seek in
the Tower of High Sorcery?"

"The mortal woman—Kitiara Uth Matar—half-
sister to the dark mage, Raistlin. She passed through
the grove a short time ago, did she not?"

"She attempted to brave the Shoikan Grove,"
came the disembodied reply.

"Attempted?" Soth asked, anger edging his voice.
"She possesses a black jewel granting her power to
pass through your grasps unhindered. I was with her
once when she used it against you."

"The jewel grants her protection . . . unless she
shows fear," the voice murmured from deep in the

ground.

Tensing at the guardian's implication, Soth snapped, "Where is she?" The hands fell back and withdrew into the spongy earth.

"Surrender her body!" the death knight shouted, furious. His hollow voice echoed through the silent trees.

The oppressive feeling in the grove grew stronger, and a quiet moan of despair floated from deep underground. A single hand pushed through the matted fallen leaves. It held a fragment of night-blue dragonscale armor. "We wounded her, shattered her armor, but we did not claim her body. She is alive, in the tower."

The death knight stormed toward the iron fence that surrounded the tower. He wrenched the rusted gate open, then forced the rune-covered door that barred his path into the tower itself. Like the guardians of the grove, the shapeless, shadowy things haunting the ancient halls of the Tower of High Sorcery cowered before Soth.

Once inside, the death knight stood at the foot of a long stair that ascended to the tower's upper floors, its length lit sparsely by globes of feeble magical radiance. The room that held the portal to Takhisis's domain, the room that had been Kitiara's goal, lay far above him. Without hesitation, Soth stepped into a large corner of shadow, away from the magical globes. Using a power granted him by his nether-life, the death knight melted completely into the darkness.

A moment later, Soth emerged from a similar shadow that darkened the door to the tower's laboratory. This was the room that housed the portal. Noting with a dull satisfaction that the wards had not prevented his magical travel within the tower, the death knight pushed the heavy wooden door. Its battered hinges creaked a loud complaint as it swung open.

The outcast elf, Dalamar, gazed at the open door, but at first Soth hovered in the shadows, hidden from sight. The mage sat in an uncomfortable chair, reflexively crumpling, then smoothing his black, rune-covered robes. "No one can enter," he said softly to an armored man who knelt with his back to the door. The mage's hand dropped to a parchment scroll in his belt. "The guardians—"

Soth stepped into the room just as the armored man turned to face the door. It was Tanis Half-Elven. "—cannot stop *him*," the half-elf said, completing Dalamar's sentence.

A look of horror came over Tanis's face at the sight of the death knight. Dalamar smiled grimly and relaxed. "Enter, Lord Soth," he said. "I've been expecting you."

When the fallen knight did not budge, Dalamar repeated the invitation. Soth remained in the doorway a moment longer, his orange glare locked onto Tanis's visage. The death knight didn't care how his foe had come to be in the tower—perhaps he'd flown over Shoikan Grove on the bronze dragon and dropped onto the roof. All that mattered to Soth was that Tanis Half-Elven stood between him and his prize.

Tanis lowered his hand toward his sword, a move that surprised Soth after his earlier cowardice. Dalamar placed slender fingers gently on the half-elf's arm and said, "Do not interfere, Tanis. He does not care about us. He comes for one thing only."

Dim candlelight illuminated the laboratory, revealing rows of black-bound spellbooks, ominously hissing vials and beakers, and huge stone tables reserved for larger, more frightening experiments. The portal through which Raistlin had already passed to encounter Takhisis stood on the opposite side of the room, away from Soth. The great circlet of steel was covered in gold and silver runes, and five carved dragons' heads snarled around its edges. In a corner away from the portal, covered in a cloak, was the object of the death knight's search. Kitiara! Soth's undead heart leaped as he crossed the room with forceful steps. He drew back the cloak and knelt beside the corpse.

In death Kitiara Uth Matar appeared as beautiful to Soth as she had in life. Her bright brown eyes were frozen open in an expression of horror. Her nightblue dragonscale armor had been stripped away by the tower's guardians, and her black, tight-fitting doublet was shredded, revealing her tan skin. The death knight hardly saw the bloody gash in her leg or the long scratches, purple from poison, that the guardians had inflicted. The charred hole burned into her chest, undoubtedly from some magical attack of Dalamar's, troubled him for only an instant. The wounds mattered little as long as Kitiara's body remained intact enough to house her revived soul.

The last embers of Kitiara's mortal life were flickering out, yet her soul still hung over her body. A small, ghostly image of the general writhed in torment, attached to her corpse by a thin, yet brilliant cord of energy. "Let go of this life," Soth murmured to Kitiara. The cord brightened as the soul clung desperately to mortal life. The cause was not fear, but love.

Soth turned to face his most hated adversary. "Release her to me, Tanis Half-Elven," he said, his voice filling the laboratory. "Your love binds her to this plane. Give her up."

The half-elf screwed a look of resolve onto his face and took a step forward. His hand was on the hilt of his sword. Before he could move closer to Soth, Dalamar warned, "He'll kill you, Tanis. He'll slay you without hesitation. Let her go to him. After all, I think perhaps he was the only one of us who ever truly understood her."

The words of the outcast elf fanned the blaze of hatred in Soth's heart; Kitiara was being kept from him by cowards and lackeys! The death knight's orange eyes flared. "Understood her?" he rumbled. "Admired her! Like I myself, she was meant to rule, destined to conquer! But she was stronger than I was. She could throw aside love that threatened to chain her down. But for a twist of fate, she would have ruled all of Ansalon!"

Tanis gripped his sword more tightly. "No," he said softly.

Dalamar grasped the half-elf's wrist and met his gaze. "She never loved you, Tanis," he said without emotion. "She used you as she used us all, even him." As Dalamar glanced toward Soth, Tanis started to speak. The dark elf cut him off. "She used you to the end, Half-Elven. Even now, she reaches from beyond, hoping you will save her."

As Soth grasped his own sword, ready to strike Tanis down, the half-elf's face went slack. It was as if he had been granted a vision of Kitiara's selfish soul. Tanis met the death knight's fiery gaze as he released his grip on his sword. Lord Soth considered killing the half-elf anyway, just for giving Kitiara up without a fight; such a lapse proved again to Soth how unfit Tanis was to wear the armor of a Knight of the Rose.

He will have to live with this cowardice, the death knight decided as he turned to retrieve Kitiara's corpse.

Her soul was gone.

Though Soth had hoped Kitiara would not try to escape him, he had foreseen this possibility long ago. Even as the death knight gathered her corpse up in Tanis's bloodstained cloak, his seneschal journeyed across the Abyss to the domain of Takhisis. There the ghostly servant would capture the highlord's soul and return it to Soth's home.

Stepping into a shadowed corner of the laboratory, the body in his arms, Soth called a spell to mind that would transport him to his castle. With a single word, he opened a dark chasm at his feet. The void belched a blast of icy air into the room. With one withering glance at Tanis Half-Elven, who had shielded his face from the numbing cold, the death knight stepped into the gate and disappeared from the Tower of High Sorcery.

* * * * *

The dusty plains stretched infinitely in all directions, parched by a hell-born vermilion sun that never set, never moved in the sky. Siroccos that smelled of burned flesh pushed spinning clouds of grit across the blasted landscape. Occasionally these whirlwinds would merge into a shrieking tornado and reach up into the air. Such disturbances never lasted long. The sun beat them down with the same brooding might it used to oppress everything entering the domain of Pazunia.

"Forty-nine thousand and thirty-eight. Forty-nine thousand and thirty-nine."

A lone being trudged across the wasteland, his shoulders hunched, his head cast down. Caradoc, for that was the poor soul's name, did not need to lift his eyes to know that spread around him was an endless plain of dust. He had been walking for hours, perhaps days, through this netherworld that served as the threshold to the Abyss. Only three things broke the monotony of the place, and none of them were particularly welcome diversions.

Far from Caradoc, almost at the horizon, the river Styx crawled sullenly across Pazunia. Its banks were as treacherous as the rest of the land, for the river was by nature a thief, not a benefactor. Simply touching water drawn from the Styx robbed a man of all memory, and its swift currents had swept many a traveler in the netherworld to his doom.

"Forty-nine thousand and fifty-four." Caradoc put his hand to his forehead. "No, wait. Forty-nine thousand and *forty*-four."

Weird fortresses wrought of iron jutted from the dead earth in places, too. These were the forward outposts of the most powerful tanar'ri lords that dwelt in the six hundred and sixty-six layers of the Abyss, camps from which they could launch forays into the world of mortals. Horrifying guardians stood watch over these fortresses, protecting them from fiends serving rival tanar'ri lords. Still, attacks were frequent. Sounds from these bloody battles—metal ringing against metal, shrieks of the wounded fiends, and curses vile beyond belief—carried on the wind in Pazunia. Luckily for Caradoc, the fiends involved in the conflicts had little interest in a single traveler on the dusty plains, especially one who was already dead.

"Forty-nine thousand and sixty-eight," he murmured kicking a small stone in his path.

Glancing down at his high black leather boots, Caradoc shook his head in disgust. The source of his unhappiness was neither Pazunia's heat nor its stench, but the state of his clothing. His boots had kept their shine for the three and a half centuries he'd been dead. Now they were dull and covered with grit. The heels were worn to nothing from the long march. Caradoc felt his silk doublet plastered to his sweat-soaked back and shook his head again. No doubt it would be stained when he left the Abyss and went back to Krynn.

Before he counted his next step aloud, Caradoc straightened his tunic and brushed off his boots. Then he paused and squinted into the distance. "I should be close," he said, if only to hear his own once-human voice.

The weary traveler expected to see a hole yawning ahead in the ground, but nothing out of the ordinary was evident. Gaping portals in the ground were a regular feature of the landscape, the third type of landmark that broke the monotony of Pazunia. Caradoc had passed dozens, perhaps hundreds of such holes on his trek. Some leaked thin mist onto the plain. Others spewed forth tortured, anguished screams. Those portals had been unwelcome because they did not lead to the level of the Abyss where Caradoc's business awaited him.

"Forty-nine thousand and sixty-nine," he sighed and started off again. He did not hurry. Neither did he cease his counting. Lord Soth, his master, had given clear instructions about that. Ten thousand steady paces should be named for each head of a chromatic dragon, Caradoc repeated to himself. Only then would he stand before the portal that snaked down to Takhisis's domain.

At last he announced, "Fifty thousand paces."

As he named the last of the steps he had been ordered to make across the plains, he stopped. No portal stood before him. Caradoc shielded his eyes against the sun and looked into the sky. Perhaps the portal lay above the ground, for such things were not unheard of in Pazunia.

Nothing.

Caradoc stood in utter consternation. The wind gusting around him sounded like mournful moans, and the dust hissed like a dying man's last breath.

"Fifty thousand," he repeated. "Where's the damnable portal?" He grabbed the chain around his neck, pulling the medallion of his office from under his doublet. A twisted rose—once red, now dark with rust—shone on the badge. "I am seneschal to Soth of Dargaard Keep. I seek entrance to the domain of the Queen of Darkness."

Without warning, the parched plain cracked open, swallowing Caradoc. For a time he was lost in darkness, falling through a lightless void, but that soon passed. With dreamlike slowness, he floated past level after level of the Abyss. The sensation of flying was not so strange to him. The sights, smells, and sounds assailing him most certainly were.

A place of ice followed the layer of absolute darkness. Frozen rain slashed across the air, borne on bone-chilling gales. Cracked floes of ice stretched to the horizon, broken now and then by huge pillars of snow-encrusted rock. The wind howled and curled around the monoliths, making them as smooth as the ice at their feet. The outcroppings stirred. A pair of cold blue eyes slowly opened on each pillar, and the malevolent gazes followed Caradoc as he passed to the next level.

On a plain of rusting steel two armies were arrayed. They met at a vast front where bodies and parts of bodies tore at one another. The air was filled by a low, sickening moan of despair, and the sharp smell of rusted metal overpowered even the stink of blood and decaying flesh on the battlefield.

A multitude of gaunt, squat creatures with rubbery bodies massed on one side of the field. Beings twice their size herded the squat creatures toward the fighting. These larger tanar'ri appeared as giant snakes from the waist down, but they had the faces, shoulders, and breasts of human women. There the similarity ended, though, for they brandished razor-bladed weapons with each of their six arms.

Across the field of metal massed an army of equal proportion. Caradoc shivered as he recognized these pathetic creatures as manes. Mortals who spread chaos and evil while they lived became such things in the afterlife. Their skin was pale white, bloated like corpses left in a fetid river, and tiny carrion-eaters crawled over them. Vacant white eyes staring ahead, the manes were herded toward their enemies by a monstrous general. This towering tanar'ri had deep, dark red skin and wings made of uneven, scabrous scales. Its yellowed fangs dripped venom as it shouted commands. In one hand the general waved a whip with twenty thorny tails, in the other a sword of lightning.

Caradoc knew that, had his evil deeds in life been more heinous than the murder of Lord Soth's first wife, he might now be part of that army. For the first time in three hundred and fifty years, he was glad he was damned to spend eternity as a ghost on Krynn. He closed his eyes and moved on.

Through places of darkness and places of light he passed, domains of fire, of air, of water. Once Caradoc entered a hot, humid realm. At first it was too dark to see anything, then his eyes adjusted. The world was filled with dripping, slimy fungus. Mushrooms climbed a thousand feet into the murky air, trailing ropes of leprous white vegetation. Puddles of gray slime oozed along the spongy floor, and purple masses sent forth long, groping tendrils. The realm was silent, but the decay filled Caradoc's nose and mouth. Worst of all was the sense that some magnificent but perpetually evil power was watching from the silence. Though Caradoc never saw a glimmer in the murk, he knew some great being had watched him pass.

At last the seneschal ceased his descent. He stood upon the roof of a shattered temple, its columns broken, its walls blackened from fire. The temple had once been the home of the Kingpriest of Istar on Krynn; now, Takhisis, the Queen of Darkness, used this fragment of the building as a portal to Krynn itself. From the temple she worked to defeat all that was good in the world of mortals. The irony of that was not lost on Caradoc; the kingpriest had wanted desperately to destroy all evil. Now his temple was a base for the most malevolent of gods.

"Perhaps the kingpriest is somewhere nearby, too," Caradoc mused as he studied his surroundings.

Around the temple a mass of lost souls thronged, pushing to get close to the building. "Dragonqueen!" the masses cried. "We are your faithful. Let us aid you!"

Caradoc knew Takhisis would not answer, not just then, anyway. As Lord Soth had told him before his journey to the Abyss started, a mortal mage from Krynn was planning to challenge Takhisis in her own domain. Such a conflict was unprecedented; few mortals had power enough to contest a god in her home plane, especially one as mighty as Takhisis. Still, the conflict would divert the Dark Queen's attention just long enough for Caradoc to locate the soul of a newly arrived woman named Kitiara Uth Matar.

He smiled in anticipation. Once he had recovered

the soul and brought it to Dargaard Keep, Lord Soth would reward him. The death knight was a powerful servant of the evil gods, and he could petition Chemosh, Lord of the Undead, to revoke Caradoc's curse. He could be alive once more. At least that was what Soth had promised.

A sudden thought awoke in Caradoc's mind. What will I do if Soth refuses to honor the bargain? After a moment of contemplation, the smile returned to his face. There were ways to force the death knight into keeping his word.

The seneschal took his medal of office in his hands. "Reveal to me the shade of Highlord Kitiara," Caradoc said.

Soft magical light radiated from the black rose on the medal's front. The seneschal held the disk before him, and a sliver of radiance lanced out into the throng before the temple, revealing the woman he sought.

 **TWO**

"Where is that fool?" Lord Soth growled impatiently. He clutched at the warped, worm-eaten arms of his throne. "The task was simple enough. Caradoc should have returned long before now."

A transparent figure with long, flowing hair and gently pointed ears hovered before Soth. *He has cheated you as you have cheated all who ever trusted you,* the banshee keened.

The betrayer is betrayed! another unquiet spirit shrieked as she slithered through the air.

The banshee closest to Soth threw back her head and laughed. Her twelve sisters picked up the cackle. They whirled about the large entry hall that served as Soth's throne room. Their howling echoed from the stone walls of the circular hall, up the twin stairs that climbed to the balcony, even up to the vaulted ceiling. Anyone within a mile of the keep could have heard the terrifying cacophony through the hall's shattered doors, but few mortals ever ventured close to Dargaard Keep and the banshees' wailing would drive even the fiercest creatures from the rocky cliffs.

A banshee moved closer to Soth, her fine-featured visage twisted with hatred. *The gods penned the book*

*of your punishment in the blood of two murdered
wives and the tears of your own dead child.*

The banshee was close enough that Soth could
have reached out and struck her if he'd wished. Her
face was fleetingly that of a beautiful elven woman.
Though her eyes were pale, a slight hint of purest
blue shone in them. The wild hair wreathing the creature's head had been golden long ago. Even the banshee's lithe movements belied a grace that was
granted to elves alone. That flash of beauty passed
quickly, though, and the elfmaid was once more a
spirit without substance, a luminescent, perverted
image of the lovely being she had been.

Your fate is written in that book, Soth of Dargaard,
the banshee hissed. *It is set down in those pages. You
will know treachery!*

The ranting of the unquiet spirit had little effect
upon Lord Soth, for he no longer felt the sting of con-
science or the unsettling fear of the future that
plagued some men. The conflagration that had long
ago blackened the walls of Dargaard Keep had taken
his life. Those on Krynn who'd had the misfortune to
cross paths with the lord of Dargaard called him a
"death knight," and the title carried more terror than
that of ghost or ghoul or banshee.

"No such book exists—on Krynn or in the heavens. I have made my own destiny." Soth dismissed
the banshees with a wave of his hand. "I gladly take
both credit and blame for all the evil I have done."

And you have done great evil, the nearest banshee
wailed. *For you were first dark in the light's hollow, expanding like a stain, a cancer.*

Another added her inhuman voice. *For you were
the shark in the slowed waters beginning to move.*

A third and a fourth sang their affronts over the
words of the others. *For you were the notched head of*

a snake, sensing forever warmth and form; the inexplicable death in the crib, the long house in betrayal.

The words circled back on themselves, weaving a deafening volume of infamy. At the point when the sounds became an unintelligible scream, a single banshee's voice rose over the others. *For you were once the bravest of the Knights of Solamnia, the most noble in the Order of the Rose. Your heroic deeds were told in song throughout Krynn, from the dwarven halls of Thorbardin to the elf-wrought spires of forest-cloaked Silvanost, from the sacred glades of Sancrist Isle to the temples of Istar's kingpriest.*

Soth scowled beneath the helmet he wore. "You do your task badly," he said in a voice that sounded as if it came from deep within the earth. "Paladine made you banshees and sent you to haunt my castle. Every night for seven times fifty years, you have been the Father of Good's accusing mouth, telling me of my failings."

Suddenly the death knight stood. His ancient armor did not creak. His long cape swirled behind him, but did so in absolute silence. "Your vapid accusations bore me. Only memories cause me pain, and your prattle does nothing to return the most welcome past to life in my mind."

One of the banshees screamed. The twelve other spirits took up the screech, adding their own weird voices to the chorus. *You desire to remember your sins? You must be growing to enjoy the pain!* the spirits wailed. *We are undone even in this!*

"I desire only diversion," the death knight said at last. He gestured to something hidden in the shadows next to his throne. "After all, that is why I brought Kitiara here."

With surprising gentleness, Soth pulled aside a shredded, bloodstained cloak. There, half hidden in the mist now drifting in patches across the floor, was the corpse of Kitiara Uth Matar.

Impatience washed over Soth again. "I will have you with me again soon," he said to the corpse, his voice strained. He bent down and caressed a bloodless cheek. "You will be able to break the pall hanging over this ruined keep, dark heart."

You will tire of her as you did your other wives, the banshees began. *Her end will be—*

"Enough!" Soth rumbled, and the banshees backed away. The death knight looked around the room, noting the weak sunlight that bled through the ruined doors, the lengthening shadows that crept across the scorched hall. Those things, along with the mist that was growing thicker with each passing moment, told Soth the day was near its end. "Caradoc has been gone for hours. He will rue this delay!"

Perhaps the battle between the Dark Queen and Raistlin ended before Caradoc could capture the soul, a banshee offered softly. *Both Takhisis and Kitiara's half-brother have reason to keep her in the Abyss.*

Clasping his mailed hands together before him, Soth paced across the throne room. His footfalls made no sound on the stones. Neither did his boots stir the mist that curled in through the shattered doors and cloaked the blackened floor. The banshees withdrew into the shadowy corners of the hall as the death knight made his way to the stairs and began to climb. "I go to look for signs of the battle's outcome," he proclaimed without looking at the spirits. "Let no one disturb the highlord's body."

No windows allowed sunlight entrance to the keep's hallways, but the death knight could see quite clearly in the darkness. He saw the ancient stone walls and the cracks climbing them like ivy. Even a small rat—thin from starvation and deaf from exposure to the banshees' constant keening—that ventured meekly from a hole did not go unnoticed. The creature fled when Soth got close, driven away by the unnatural cold radiating from the undead knight.

Stiffly Soth marched down the pitch-dark corridors, thinking aloud about suitable punishments for his tardy seneschal. "Perhaps I should change his clothes to rags," Soth said. "He was a fop in life, more concerned about brocades than blades, and death has not changed him a bit."

A warped door on rusted hinges marked the end of the hallway. It groaned long and loud as Soth shoved it open. The room beyond was small but seemed the larger for the gaping hole where the wall had crumbled long ago. Playful breezes swept in from the breach, stirring up the dust and dirt that covered the floor. Because of the view it afforded, this place had been a guard post once. Dargaard Keep no longer had real need of sentries. The reputation of the castle's lord was more effective at keeping people away than the strongest, dwarven-built walls. Nevertheless, a lone figure walked a post in the rubble-strewn room.

"Ah, Sir Mikel," Soth said distractedly. "Stand aside."

The armored figure ceased its pacing. Sir Mikel's rusty armor was as ancient as Soth's and hung loosely on his skeletal body. Scabrous yellow ribs shone through the gaps in the knight's breastplate, and his worn boots hissed and thumped across the floor as he walked. An eyeless, fleshless skull stared out from a raised visor. As the skeletal warrior studied him, Soth wondered if some tiny part remained of the knight's soul. Mikel, like all thirteen of the Solamnic Knights who had aided Soth in his crimes, had been damned to serve the death knight for eternity. The flesh had abandoned their skeletons long ago, and their individuality had fled them as well. Now, unless Soth gave them orders to follow, the knights ceaselessly walked the posts where they had died.

After a moment, Mikel seemed to recognize his master. He inclined his head and stood aside as the death knight crossed to the breach. Before Soth reached that vantage, he turned to Mikel. "Have you seen Caradoc this day?"

A painfully long pause followed the question, then Sir Mikel nodded haltingly. His bones rubbed together with the noise of stone grinding against stone.

"You saw him this morning, before he ventured into the Abyss on my errand?"

Again Mikel nodded.

"Have you seen him since I returned from Palanthas with the dragon highlord's body?"

Another pause, and the skeletal warrior shook his head. No spark shone in the voids that were his eye sockets; no expression broke his petrified rictus.

The death knight looked to the sky, darkening by degrees into night. The three moons that watched over Krynn were just beginning to reveal themselves in the heavens. Solinari, the silver-white moon of good magic, was but a sliver in the sky. The symbol of neutrality, Lunitari, shone fully, casting an eerie, blood-red radiance onto the mountains surrounding Dargaard on three sides. The third moon was visible only to creatures of evil like Soth. Nuitari gave off a sort of negative light, a black, putrid glow that shone most fully upon things of darkness.

The stars, too, were beginning to twinkle to life against the velvet sky that stretched from horizon to horizon. Each of the twenty-one gods of Krynn were represented in the heavens by a constellation, a planet, or a moon. The stars denoting Paladine, the Father of Good, were seen as a brave silver dragon. These pinpoints of light, called the Valiant Warrior, stood in opposition to the five-headed dragon known as the Queen of Darkness. In the past, these avatars of godly power had mirrored the deities' struggles, their triumphs and their defeats. Soth looked to the five-headed dragon now for some sign of the battle that had occurred—or was still occurring—between Takhisis and Raistlin Majere.

The Queen of Darkness was spread across the sky, coiled and ready to strike the Valiant Warrior. Nothing had changed.

"The battle must be over," Soth rumbled. "Takhisis has defeated the mage." He turned away from the breach and faced the skeletal Sir Mikel. "I order you to watch the stars, especially the constellation known as the Queen of Darkness. Do you understand?"

The undead knight shuffled to the breach. With preternatural slowness he presented his eyeless sockets to the heavens.

"If the stars break from their natural course, you are to find me," Soth added and stormed from the place.

The death knight started back through the musty, darkened hallways. With each step he rued the fact he'd trusted his seneschal to retrieve Kitiara's soul. None of his servants possessed the power to defeat the guardians at the Tower of High Sorcery, so Soth had been forced to go after the highlord's corpse himself. And of his minions, only Caradoc was intelligent enough to survive a trek across the Abyss. Now it appeared the ghost had either failed or had double-crossed the death knight.

Soth roughly pushed a door from his path, the

blow splintering the ancient wood. "Caradoc will regret that his curse requires him to return to Dargaard Keep," the death knight hissed.

He paused and pondered that truth. There was one place to which the seneschal must return, whether he had succeeded or not with his errand. Soth decided to wait for Caradoc there. His pace quickened as he moved up the stone stairs, higher into the tower that served as the keep's main building.

Caradoc had been caught up in the curse that doomed Soth to unlife. In life, the seneschal had been a grasping, ambitious man, who had helped his master's career in any way necessary. He had spread scandalous rumors about any rival who challenged Soth's position in knightly society. When the Knights' Council had questioned his master's claims to certain good deeds, the seneschal bore false witness to uphold Soth's version. He had even murdered for Soth, taking a dagger to the lord's first wife while she slept. Even as the fire struck Dargaard, Caradoc had been forging financial records in Soth's private study. It was there that his bones still rested.

After climbing a number of steps that would have easily winded a strong, mortal man, Soth came upon a landing. The platform was broken away from the wall, and a rift in the stonework floor revealed empty air. The hole plunged downward a dozen feet to the next landing. The frame that once housed the door to the study was partially collapsed. Soth had to step over a large, shattered block of masonry to enter.

Compared to the disarray of the rest of Dargaard, the study was clean, even tidy. The layer of dirt, broken stone, and dust clinging so thickly to the other rooms' floors was strangely absent. Missing, too, were any fragments from the missing door or the heavy wooden furniture that had once filled the room. A single tapestry covered one wall. Upon the broad, bright field of the cloth, elves clashed against elves. The tapestry depicted the Kinslayer Wars that had rocked the elven nations hundreds of years past. On the floor below the tapestry lay a skeleton.

The room's single window admitted light from the moons. Red as new-spilled blood, Lunitari colored Caradoc's fleshless remains and pushed pools of darkness into the study's corners. Soth walked to the skeleton and frowned. Like the rest of the room, Caradoc's bones were clean. The decaying flesh had been carefully pulled from them, not gnawed away by the few vermin that inhabited the keep. Its arms had been folded across its chest, giving the skeleton a deceptive look of peace that none of Dargaard's other inhabitants ever possessed.

Soth knew it must have taken his seneschal years to compose the corpse and clear the debris from the room. Part of Caradoc's curse—like that of most ghosts—was that his wraithlike body allowed him little contact with the physical world; to move even the smallest pieces of stone would require intense concentration. As in life, though, the ghostly seneschal was overly concerned with his appearance, and it was clear he wanted his remains to be presentable. He had even covered his skull with a silken cloth in the fashion of ancient Solamnic funerals. The death knight bent to pick up the veil.

"That cloth once belonged to Kitiara herself, my lord," came a trembling voice from behind Soth. "I stole it from her one night when she stayed at the keep."

The death knight spun about. There, in the shadowy corner near the doorway, cowered Caradoc. "Where is she?" Soth asked quietly.

The seneschal floated from the darkness. The

moonlight painted him crimson. "My lord . . . " he began, then paused as the death knight took a step toward him. "As you can see, I made the journey you requested."

Caradoc spread his arms wide, gesturing at himself. Though the ghost's form was transparent, Soth could see that his garments were rumpled and stained. Phantom dust still clung to his boots. "The plains of Pazunia seemed to stretch on forever, and the portal—"

"Where is Kitiara's soul?" Soth growled impatiently, again moving toward his servant. "Where is your medal of office?"

Bowing his head, Caradoc replied, "We had a bargain, my lord. You promised you would plead my case with Chemosh, that you would convince the Lord of the Undead to make me human."

"I have not forgotten my promise," the death knight said, the lie coming easily to his scorched lips. He pointed to the ghost. "The promise will be revoked unless you tell me where Kitiara's soul is."

The ghost knew that, had his legs been flesh and blood, they would have crumpled beneath him at the fear he felt. Caradoc looked at the fiery gaze of Lord Soth, forced steel into his voice, and stood tall. "Forgive me, my lord, but I have seen you break your word too many times in the last three and a half centuries. I want—"

"You will demand nothing of me!" Soth shouted and lunged forward.

The ghost evaded the death knight's mailed hand as it reached for him. He flew across the room to the open window. "Harm me and you will never have her."

Forcing the fury swelling inside him to subside, Lord Soth faced his seneschal. "Fly out the window if you'd like, Caradoc. I know your curse requires you to return to your corpse eventually." He raised a hard-soled boot over the skull beneath the tapestry. "Your next threat brings my heel down."

The ghost froze. He valued nothing so much as the bones that had once housed his soul, and the hope that he might one day be raised from undeath had impelled him to keep his corpse clean and intact. "Wait! Please!"

Soth stood perfectly still, his boot resting lightly on the veiled bones. "Come here."

Reluctantly the ghost floated toward his master. "I reached Takhisis's domain as the battle still raged between the Dark Queen and the mortal mage," he noted as he drew close to Soth.

The death knight placed his foot on the floor once more. "Good," he said. "Did you locate the soul of Kitiara Uth Matar?"

"Yes. The spell you cast upon my medallion made it easy."

Soth nodded, and the orange globes of flame that were his eyes flickered in anticipation.

The ghost paused. A look of indecision crossed his face, and he nervously glanced away from the death knight. "She . . . struggled, my lord," he continued at last. "Luckily, her spirit was still disoriented from the plunge into the Abyss. As you instructed, I trapped her soul in the medallion."

The death knight could bear the suspense no longer. His hand darted out and locked around Caradoc's throat. Before the ghost could react, Soth shredded the neck of his seneschal's doublet with his other hand. "The medallion's not here! Where is it?"

The death knight struck Caradoc. No mortal could have done the same, for the ghost's noncorporeal form protected him from physical attack. To Soth, another undead creature, Caradoc was as solid as the skeleton that lay preserved in the room. "In Pazunia," the ghost gasped. "I left the medallion in Pazunia."

"And Kitiara is trapped inside of it?"

"Y—Yes."

The steel in Soth's voice was more threatening than the cold emanating from his unliving form. "What do you hope to gain from this, traitor?"

"I—I made a bargain with a powerful tanar'ri lord on my way back from Takhisis's domain," he said. "Unless you—" The ghost swallowed hard and forced himself to continue. "Unless you honor your word and see to it I am made mortal again, you will never have Kitiara's soul."

Nonchalantly, Soth kicked Caradoc's remains, shattering the rib cage of the skeleton and splintering both arms. The ghost, still trapped in the death knight's grip, cried out in anguish. Next, Soth crushed the skull at his feet. Ancient bones fractured and skittered across the floor in the moonlight, disappearing into the thin fog spreading unnoticed on the stones.

"You have no idea how angry you've made me," the death knight said coldly, his voice level.

Soth dragged Caradoc toward the shadowed corner of the study. When he and the whimpering seneschal were covered by the murk that lurked in the corners, the death knight spoke a word of magic. Both creatures disappeared into the darkness. An instant later they emerged from a patch of shadow in the keep's throne room.

The banshees were hovering near the hall's high, vaulted ceiling. When the death knight stepped from the darkness, still clutching Caradoc by the throat, the unquiet spirits broke into a mad fit of howling. The thick fog now covering the floor swirled and pulsed, as if it responded to the chilling call of the banshees.

See how he treats his trusted servant! one of the unearthly voices shrieked.

Another of the banshees streaked across the room. *I do not see Kitiara's soul.*

The highlord has eluded the death knight's grasp! Can it be that the book of his fate is correct? Has the master of Dargaard found a traitor in his ranks?

"Do not mock me," Soth said chillingly, "or I will deal with you after Caradoc."

The threat quieted the banshees but a little. As the death knight moved to the hall's center, the spirits floated out of his reach, whispering taunts and barbs. All the while, Caradoc tried in vain to pull free from Soth's iron grip. "Mercy, my lord," he cried.

Abruptly Soth marched to his throne, dragging the ghost behind him. There he grasped the hem of his long, purple cloak and fanned the mist away from Kitiara's still, rigid form. The fog parted for an instant, revealing a corpse covered with tiny drops of water condensed from the ivory mist. On Kitiara's cheeks, the beads of moisture looked like nothing so much as tears gradually working their way from her deadened eyes.

The death knight gazed at the general's beautiful face, then he lifted his servant off the ground with one strong arm. "You buy my mercy with Kitiara's soul. Tell me where to find it."

During the long return journey from Takhisis's domain, Caradoc had carefully calculated his bluff. He knew that it was unlikely that Soth would fulfill his promise . . . unless the death knight believed the seneschal had an ally of greater or equal strength. The substance of the lie had come easily to the seneschal, for even Lord Soth respected the tanar'ri, the terrible fiend-lords that populated the Abyss. Now, though, the thought of maintaining the charade terrified the ghost. His only option was to reveal the true location of the medallion and Kitiara's soul, however, and that would certainly mean the end to the ghost's hopes for resurrection.

"On my way back across Pazunia," Caradoc stammered, "I came to an abandoned fortress. I left the medallion—and the highlord's soul—there."

"I will open a portal to the Abyss, and you will take me to this fortress."

"I—I cannot."

"Why?" Soth snapped. He tightened his strangulating grip on the ghost's throat.

Caradoc flailed at Soth's arm, desperate to break away. "A tanar'ri lord arrived at the fortress and took the medallion," he gasped.

"A tanar'ri lord," the death knight repeated flatly. He lowered the ghost to the floor.

"Yes, I made a bargain with a very powerful denizen from a place of rotting fungus in the Abyss," Caradoc said with some relief. He was surprised to find his voice did not quaver now, as if, somehow, the lie gave him strength. "Highlord Kitiara's soul is trapped in the medallion, and the tanar'ri lord will hold it until I come to collect it . . . in an unharmed mortal body."

The banshees hooted with malevolent glee at Caradoc's words. *He has outsmarted you, death knight,* they taunted. *His new master will shield him from his old. You are undone!*

Caradoc looked into the death knight's glowing eyes, hoping to read something of his intent there, but found them barren of expression.

"Your ploy is clever, Caradoc," Lord Soth said finally, his voice surprisingly calm. "Though it means I will have to fight this tanar'ri master of yours, I cannot let your cleverness go unrewarded."

That said, the death knight tightened his grip on the ghost's throat once more. Caradoc squirmed and clutched at Soth's mailed hand, but the fingers dug slowly, painfully into him. Soon enough the seneschal found he could not speak, then he heard a high ringing in his ears. Soth's voice broke into his consciousness.

"After I destroy this form, your soul will return to the Lord of the Undead. He will jail you in the void he reserves for ghosts that are no more," the death knight said.

Caradoc's vision faded for a moment, then mist rose to block his view of Dargaard's throne room. He heard the banshees screaming from a place very far away. Only Soth's voice remained clarion.

"Perhaps Chemosh will resurrect you once again, traitor, but this time as something more mindless— rather like Sir Mikel and the other knights who are condemned to serve me."

A loud snap sounded from Caradoc's neck. His head lolled to one side, unsupported by his broken spine. Yet even that did not end the seneschal's life, so the death knight continued to exert pressure. "Or you may end up as a mane, caught in the army of some monstrous general. I think—"

Abruptly the death knight stopped speaking, his grip faltering. Around him a bank of mist had risen high off the floor, obscuring the throne room, muffling the shrieks and taunts of the banshees. "Is this some kind of trick, Caradoc?"

The ghost, nearly senseless, grunted a reply, but Soth did not comprehend it. Caradoc would tell the death knight where the medallion was if only he would deign to stop the torture. Perhaps if Soth knew that Kitiara's soul really lay within Dargaard's walls. . . .

Swirling mist closed in on the death knight and his seneschal. The ivory fog swelled in every corner of Dargaard's throne room, permeated every stone. The wailing of the banshees faded in Soth's ears and then stopped.

The mist streamed out the hall's shattered door into the night as if it had been summoned away. It flowed like water over the cracked stone of the floor, around the charred, worm-eaten throne that was the hall's only furniture, past the still form of Kitiara Uth Matar, and beneath the thirteen banshees hovering near the ceiling.

Sisters! one of the unquiet spirits cried in astonishment, pointing to the spot where Soth had been standing but a moment earlier.

The death knight and the ghost were gone.

 **THREE**

The sheer whiteness of his surroundings caused Lord Soth's unblinking eyes to smart. The mist pressed thickly in from all sides. It crept through the gaps in Soth's armor and rubbed against him like a monstrous cat. Tendrils of the milky stuff ventured into his ears and mouth and nose, but soon retreated from the corrupt being of the death knight.

"Caradoc," Soth uttered as he scanned the brightness around him.

The mist swallowed the word, leaving him to wonder if he'd actually said it. Perhaps he'd only imagined calling his seneschal. He repeated the name more loudly. "Caradoc!" No reply.

Soth did not know how, but he had lost hold of the ghost when the mists had flooded the throne room. He felt certain the cowardly seneschal had fled. No doubt he's cowering in some corner of the keep, Soth decided. Or he's floating around the study, trying to pretty up his shattered skeleton.

After listening for a moment, Soth cursed with frustration. The fog was even damping the banshees' wailing. Yet that seemed incredible to the death knight; the high keening of the unquiet spirits could be heard from the keep's highest tower, even through floor after floor of stone. Soth listened again. Nothing. The banshees were silent.

"This is some ploy on their part," he rumbled. "Or perhaps they fled when I attacked Caradoc."

But Soth knew that the banshees would not have missed out on the entertainment of Caradoc's punishment. The elven spirits were spiteful creatures, and the seneschal's pain would be nectar to them. Recalling that his throne had been just behind him when the mists had obscured everything, the death knight turned slowly. Step after careful step he took, but more than three dozen paces brought him to neither throne nor wall.

Two things became obvious to Soth: he was no longer in Dargaard Keep's throne room and the fog that had engulfed him was born of magic, not nature. "This is far beyond your power, Caradoc," he hissed. "But there are others . . ."

The death knight let the sentence trail off as he considered the source of his predicament. Perhaps it was Takhisis. Had he angered the Dark Queen by plotting the death of Kitiara, one of her favorites? No. In-fighting and murder were common amongst the inner circle of her faithful. She would not punish a minion for acting upon the evil urges she herself championed.

This sort of indirect torture was unlike Paladine as well. The Father of Good preferred to torment his enemies with more blatant hells. The same was true of the self-appointed Heroes of the Lance, Tanis Half-Elven and the motley group of mortals who fought against Takhisis's forces on Krynn. Like Paladine, they eschewed subtlety in favor of direct confrontations with their foes.

"Ah!" Soth exclaimed at last. "Caradoc's tanar'ri ally!" He looked into the mist, searching for some sign of the evil creature. "Show yourself, dark one."

The mist curled before Soth's glowing orange eyes, but no creature appeared. The death knight frowned beneath his heavy helmet. Again he listened intently. No sound penetrated the fog.

"Have you brought me to the Abyss, then?" Soth asked of his unseen tormenter. "If so, this is a place I have not yet visited."

Soth expected no answer, but he was no longer speaking in hopes that someone might reply; he was talking for his own sake. Mortal terrors held no sway over the death knight, yet absolute silence was as frightening to him as the grave to most living men on Krynn. It was in silence that Soth felt himself slipping into oblivion, losing memory, losing the pain that reminded him he still existed. For the last three hundred fifty years the banshees had filled Dargaard Keep with their screams. Now Soth found himself surrounded by silence, utterly alone, absolutely adrift from Krynn.

The death knight momentarily considered using magic to escape from the fog. He had a few spells at his command and many supernatural powers granted him by his unlife—he could journey from one shadow to any other of his choosing, for example. But there were no shadows in this mist, and Soth was wise enough to know that attempting any other incantation when he was still unsure of his surroundings would tempt disaster.

"If you will not show yourself, I will explore your domain and find my own way out."

This said, the death knight marched off at a steady pace. To keep his mind occupied, he concentrated on moving in a straight line and counting his steps. Such a tedious task could not make up for the lack of sound, lack of smells, lack of sights in the mist. Soon a numbness washed over Soth, sapping his will to proceed.

When he ceased his march, the death knight drew his ancient sword from its scabbard. What should have been a sharp hiss, metal scraping against metal, came to Soth's ears as a dull, flat sound. "You will not break me!" he said, raising his sword high into the air. "I defy you, whoever you are!"

With a start, the fallen knight realized that he could see the sword he held in front of himself, its blade sharp but stained dark with old blood. The mist had ebbed at least that much. Looking from left to right, Soth saw that other things were revealing themselves as well.

It appeared as a looming shadow at first, but soon a large, barren tree became visible. Its withered branches were twisted and gnarled, reaching into the mist like an old miser's hand clutching after a pile of gold coins. Soth held his sword before him and studied the tree for a moment.

The small hill upon which the death knight stood revealed itself next. Patches of weeds struggled for purchase in the rocky soil. Small bushes and stunted plants huddled away from the tree at the hill's crest. Near those tangled, white-flowered privets and scrawny belladonna, swirls of mist still covered the stony ground. Most of the fog was rolling steadily downhill toward vast stands of drooping firs and barren oak.

"I am far from Dargaard," Soth whispered.

The rest of the scene became clear to Soth as the mist retreated completely. The death knight stood on a low hillock, which was itself surrounded by a dense forest. To the south a turgid river, swollen with spring runoff, meandered through the trees. Distant mountains stood in almost all directions, their snowcapped peaks pushing high into the air. As Soth watched, the sun touched the range to the west, setting the horizon alight with subtle shades of crimson, gold, and purple.

After the monotony of the mists, he was overwhelmed by the vista unfolding around him. The sound of small birds heralding the end of day, the pungent smell of nearby flowering bushes, and the brisk touch of the evening breeze now stirring the trees—all these prodded the undead knight's slumbering senses. To one who had long tasted the world as only ashes, the sudden burst of sensory input was almost maddening.

Again Soth faced the tree at the hill's crest. What the knight saw there momentarily blinded his glowing eyes to the wondrous sights and struck his ears deaf to the marvelous sounds. Beneath the gnarled tree thrust up from the rocky earth stood his seneschal, Caradoc.

The ghost was obviously dazed. He hovered beneath the black-barked tree, his head resting painfully on his shoulder. Blankly, through pupilless eyes, Caradoc stared at the world around him. The wisps of mist that clung to the seneschal's clothes made them seem even more ragged than they were.

Soth smiled grimly. "The tanar'ri lord betrayed you," he said, pointing the tip of his sword at Caradoc for emphasis.

The seneschal stood as if caught in a trance. His eyes remained rolled back in their sockets, his lips moved in rapid bursts. He didn't raise his hands to defend himself. In fact, he acted as if he could not see Lord Soth at all.

"I will break each of your limbs before I send you back to Chemosh," the death knight vowed as he approached the ghost. "You will beg for mercy, beg to reveal the hiding place of Kitiara's soul."

Soth took another step closer to the ghost, then paused. He was but an arm's length away from Caradoc, and still the seneschal hovered mindlessly beneath the tree. Now, however, the death knight was close enough to hear the low utterances coming from the ghost's lips.

"The void," Caradoc muttered. "Death for the undead. White. Nothing. The void!"

Travel in the mists has unhinged the weakling, Soth decided scornfully. He looked to the lowering sun and addressed it. "Tanar'ri lord! This insect is broken. Any pact you forged with him is null." He watched the sky and the earth for some sign of the monster. "Give me the medallion containing the human woman's soul and transport me to my castle on Krynn, and I will consider this matter settled. If you do not, I will hunt you forever. I must have Kitiara's soul!"

"Kitiara?" the ghost mumbled. " 'Retrieve her from the Abyss,' he commanded, and so I did."

Savagely the death knight grabbed the ghost's arm and shook him. "Yes, Caradoc, you retrieved her. Which tanar'ri lord did you leave her with? Where is Kitiara?"

A spark of consciousness flickered in the ghostly seneschal's blank eyes. "Tanar'ri lord?" he asked, confused. With a shudder, Caradoc pulled away from the death knight. A panicked look had replaced the vague one on his face, and he held his hands straight before him. "Enough, my lord. I have seen the white void that waits for the undead banished from the mortal world. You have tortured me enough."

"Then tell me where Kitiara rests," the death knight said. In anger he slashed at the tree, and the withered trunk oozed black pus. Before the death knight could press the seneschal further, a low moan split the air.

The sound was sepulchral, like Soth's voice, but it rattled with the noise of wind blowing dead leaves. Both Soth and Caradoc stared at the gnarled tree. The oozing gash the death knight had caused by his blow had opened into a mouth. Thick black liquid still dribbled from the hole, but now it passed over twisted wooden fangs before seeping onto the trunk.

The moan grew louder, ringing with power over the hillock and shadowed forest. Soth lashed out at the tree to silence it. The sword opened another gash, which became a second drooling, moaning mouth. Now two hollow voices sent their mournful cries of pain into the gloaming.

"Only in the Abyss," Soth growled quietly as he stepped back from the tree. "Creatures such as this reside only in the Abyss."

The death knight let the hand holding his sword drop straight at his side. With a slow, stiff gesture, he held his other hand out before him. The incantation he spoke was brief, its effect instantaneous.

A small dot of blue light appeared on the moaning tree, near its two wounded mouths. Thin tracers of azure radiance burst forth from the dot, then wound around the trunk and even into the fanged maws. A delicate lace of sizzling power soon covered the entire tree, thickening into a blanket of light. It filled the mouths, choking off their cries. The black ooze froze in ridges down the trunk to the tree's knotted roots.

With the same inexorable strength that had crushed Caradoc's neck, Soth closed his outstretched hand into a tight fist. The blanket of radiance tightened with it. A high-pitched whine sounded as the first cracks snaked around the trunk, then the tree shattered into a thousand shards of black wood. A low stump marked where the tree had been. Dark liquid pulsed and bubbled from the stump for a moment, then stopped.

An instant of silence followed the destruction of the tree, then a throaty howl echoed in the forest to the east. The long, low cry mimicked the shattered tree's mournful call. To the west, where the sun had almost dropped behind the mountains, creatures hidden in the twilight forest howled their replies.

Caradoc had not moved since the eerie mouths had first cried out. Fragments from the tree lay scattered on the stony ground at his feet. Some chunks were covered with blue light; others, from deeper inside the trunk, were coated with obsidian ooze.

When howls sounded to the south and north, closer to the hillock, the ghost looked up suddenly. "Master, return us to Dargaard Keep," the ghost said. "I have seen enough of this place."

"What? Afraid of your tanar'ri ally's minions?" Soth said. "You shouldn't feel threatened here, in his abode."

A puzzled look crossed the ghost's face. Tanar'ri ally? Caradoc thought. Soth still believes my story about the tanar'ri lord! Then another realization hit Caradoc like a bolt of lightning: the death knight had not transported them somewhere through magic. Soth, too, had been taken against his will. Soth, too, was lost.

A growl rumbled from the drooping firs at the base of the hill. In the darkness there, a pair of blood-red eyes stared intently at the knight and the seneschal. The orbs were all Caradoc saw, but Soth saw more.

With his unblinking gaze, the death knight saw a monstrous, shaggy wolf crouched behind a thin cover of brambles. The gray-furred creature was twice the size of any wolf Soth had ever seen on Krynn. Its gaze met the death knight's, then the wolf drew back its lips in a snarl. To Soth the gesture showed contempt, not fury, and seemed almost motivated by a greater-than-animal intelligence.

A second beast moved stealthily through the forest and joined the first behind the brambles. As soon as it arrived, it threw back its head and yowled. From a dozen places nearby, on all sides of the hill, similar calls erupted.

The death knight crouched into a loose fighting stance, his sword held before him. He knew that, though the creatures appeared to be large wolves, they might actually be more dangerous monsters in a lupine guise. After all, the gnarled tree had seemed mundane at first.

"Come on, then," Soth challenged. A dozen or more pairs of glowing eyes now shone in the trees all around the hill. "If your master has ordered you to attack, curs, get it over with."

The wolves remained at the bottom of the hill. Some crouched in one spot. Others paced back and forth, crossing the ground in steady, loping strides. Occasionally one of the great beasts would howl into the night, and the cry would be answered from the distance. And after each such call, another wolf would join the pack ringing the hillock.

Soth studied his adversaries. They showed no signs of immediate attack, so what were they up to? Brandishing his sword before him, the death knight took a few quick steps down the hill. The wolves close at hand rushed as one to block his path. They crowded before the death knight, yellow teeth bared in snarls. Soth took another step forward, and the beasts braced for his charge, but did not advance up the hill.

Letting his sword drop, Soth stood still and listened for sounds of other movement in the trees. "They are intelligent, after a fashion," he noted aloud, not taking his eyes off the wolves. "They have orders to keep us here. Something else is in the woods, too. It's coming this way."

The death knight turned toward the shattered tree, expecting to see his seneschal hovering over the stump, as before. "Caradoc?" He scanned the hill and the tree line, but the ghost was nowhere to be seen.

A hiss of pine needles rubbing against something large and the snap of sticks under the tread of something heavy revealed movement in the trees. That can't be Caradoc, Soth decided instantly, for his body has no substance here.

A strange creature broke out of the trees and lumbered up the hill. At first it appeared to be a man dressed in rags, protected by a few pieces of ill-kept armor. A rusty helmet hung low on its brow, almost over its eyes. Its chest was protected by an ancient and battered breastplate, but only one leg was covered by a greave. It shuffled barefoot through the thorny privets as if it wore the finest dragonleather boots.

The smell of rotting flesh reached the death knight before the feeble moonlight revealed anything else about the creature coming toward him. "Zombie," he said to himself.

As the dead thing got closer, Soth saw that it had gray-green skin. The flesh looked to be smeared onto its body like soft clay and was covered with welts and sores. The stench grew stronger; Soth knew it would have choked a mortal. Yet the odor of corrupt skin and stagnant blood was nothing new to the fallen knight. Though his flesh had never really decayed, his loyal knights had slowly decomposed over the years, filling Dargaard Keep with the thick charnel smell of unburied corpses.

"Turn back," Soth ordered, though his tone was more patronizing than commanding. "You have no quarrel with me. Go on your mindless way before I am forced to dismember you."

The zombie didn't pause in its halting march up the hill. Soth repeated his order. "Turn back now."

The undead creature continued its advance. Soth was baffled. He had some modicum of control over all the lesser forms of undead on Krynn; zombies were unthinking masses of reanimated flesh, but on some instinctual level they had always recognized the death knight's power. Until now.

Soth planted his feet, waiting for the shambling corpse to get close to him before he lashed out.

One step closer, then another. The moon revealed the zombie's features to Soth. Beneath the rusty helmet, dark voids filled the creature's eye sockets, and only the barest fragment of a nose clung to its face. Pasty skin, pocked from maggots feasting upon it, pulled tight over its cheekbones and chin. Lips and cheeks had been torn away to reveal a set of large, crooked teeth. Slowly, mechanically, the shambling undead took a few more steps. At last it thrust out its hands toward Soth. The bony fingers ended in sharp talons.

Soundlessly Soth's blade cut through the air. The blow knocked the zombie off balance, and its left arm dropped to the hard earth with a thud. Grunting, the creature straightened and reached for the death knight with its remaining arm. Soth calmly swung his sword again. The zombie's right arm followed its left. Yet the mindless creature pushed closer to the armored man. Jaws opened wide, it leaned forward to use the only weapon left to it—its sharp, yellowed teeth. With a curse, the death knight struck the creature in the face with his sword's heavy pommel.

The zombie reeled backward, its skull caved in, the fragment of its nose gone. Before it could shamble any farther forward, Soth lashed out with his blade. The creature's severed head rolled through the air and landed faceup in a thorny bush. Headless and armless, the zombie's body stumbled drunkenly on the hill, then toppled into the dirt. A small gout of blood dribbled from its neck, staining the rusted breastplate crimson.

"Pay heed to this!" Soth shouted into the darkness, pointing at the corpse with his sword. "I've passed your test!"

As if in response to this boast, the wolves around the hill released their voices into the night. The baying rang through the forest. More sounds of creatures crashing through the underbrush came just as the howling ceased. Six more zombies, clad in armor and rags like the first, shuffled up the hillock.

"Bah!" the death knight scoffed. "One or six or six hundred, I will slaughter these mindless things like sheep before a feast."

When Soth took a step forward, however, he found his movement hampered. He looked down and, there, clinging to his armored right ankle, was one of the defeated zombie's arms. Even without a body behind it, the limb was holding Soth fast, anchoring him in place. The zombie's other limb was dragging itself across the ground, its fingers resembling nothing so much as a spider's legs as it moved closer.

"What madness is this?" the death knight exclaimed.

He glanced at the severed head caught in the bush. Its mouth still chewed at the air, and the bush's thorns dug long, deep scratches into its cheeks as it moved from side to side. The gruesome sight distracted the death knight's gaze for just a moment. The other zombies had almost reached him by the time he looked up again. Soth did not raise his sword at first; instead he called to mind a spell and pointed.

A small flame burst from the tip of Soth's finger, then sped toward the lead zombie. The flaming ball swelled quickly, leaving a dancing trail of fire and smoke in its wake. The half-dozen undead climbing the hill did nothing to avoid the missile, almost as if they dimly realized they were doomed.

The fireball struck. Hissing as it was engulfed in magical fire, the first creature fell to the ground, an unmoving, charred husk. The lethal attack took in the shuffling things around that one as well. Suddenly, the flaming corpse exploded, showering all the remaining zombies with fire. Three more of the monsters were soon burning, their bodies covering the hillside with dark, foul-smelling smoke.

Of the two remaining undead, one wore no armor whatsoever. This zombie was clad in a long robe, one like those worn by some priests or monks on Krynn. The death knight dispatched this one first. He raised his sword high and swung it down in a two-handed blow. With a sickening sound, the blade tore through the zombie's shoulder, continuing through bone and desiccated flesh before exiting from the hip on the other side of the body. The robe-clad zombie managed one more step before its body split into two writhing halves.

The howl of wolves sounded over the hillock once more as the last zombie stopped, just out of sword's reach from Soth. This one wore no helmet, but the rest of its body was covered in ancient armor. Emblazoned on the breastplate was a raven, its wings spread wide in flight. Wisps of long blond hair hung in places from the zombie's rotting scalp, and much of its face was covered with skin, making it look far more human than any of its compatriots.

Soth, his feet still held by the two disembodied arms, presented his sword in a defensive stance. Yet the expected attack never came. The wolves cried out again, then the zombie turned and shuffled down the hill. Passing its burning kin, the creature repeated a single word over and over again. "Strahd," came the strangled hiss. "Strahd."

The zombie waded into the forest. The monstrous wolves also faded into the trees one by one until only a solitary beast remained. This wolf glared at the death knight, and the small fires on the hillside made its eyes sparkle malevolently in the night. Soth met that savage stare with his own unblinking gaze.

At last the wolf turned and retreated. As he hacked the clutching hands from his ankles, Soth could hear the wolves barking and yelping as they spread out in the forest, heading west. The death knight knew their noise was meant for him. "Follow," they were saying.

The death knight tossed the writhing limbs and bodies onto a pyre. He bolstered the fire with chunks of the shattered tree, though the wood did not burn even half as well as the undead flesh. The blaze sent even more thick, pungent smoke into the night sky.

A few stars winked against the carpet of black, but their positions seemed random to Soth. Gone were the Dark Queen, the Valiant Warrior, all the constellations that defined the night sky of Krynn. Gone, too, were the black and red moons. Only a single gibbous orb, its light reflecting brightly, hung overhead.

"I am far from Krynn," Soth said. After a pause, he added, "But I will not return there until I find Caradoc, until I know where he has hidden Kitiara's soul."

To the west, a wolf howled long and low.

The death knight sheathed his sword. "Your master lies at the end of your trail, and he might be of aid to me in finding my wayward servant," he said. "I will follow and let you take me to this 'Strahd.'"

* * * * *

Bony, age-spotted hands caressed the crystal ball like a lover. The milky white glass glowed slightly under their touch. The ancient artifact would reveal nothing to the casual observer. To the scarred fingers weaving intricate patterns upon it, however, the crystal ball had much to say.

"Urrr," the ancient mystic groaned pensively. He closed his blind eyes and rubbed his fingers over the globe with more urgency. The light from the crystal grew more intense, casting ominous shadows over his wrinkled face.

The old man removed his hands from the glass suddenly, almost as if he'd been burned. With jerky movements, he reached for the parchment and the feathered quill pen that lay nearby. He turned his sightless eyes, as white as the crystal orb, to the paper and started to write.

The lines wandered across the page, some sentences crossing over others, some curling almost in a circle around the parchment's edge. Yet the mystic's hand never strayed from the yellowed paper, and, for those used to reading his scrawl, the message was quite legible.

When the old man finished writing, he swayed for a moment, then lowered his head to the rutted tabletop. "Let us see what you have learned," came a silken voice from the other side of the room.

With a word of magic, a half-dozen candles burst into flame. A slender hand gloved in kidskin lifted the candelabra that held the wax sticks. Warmly their light flowed across the stone floor and onto the table where the mystic lay, exhausted. The possessor of the voice reached into the pool of light and gently lifted the parchment.

Two have arrived, the message began, *one of great power, both of great use. The sins of ancient wrongs unforgiven bring them to your garden, though they know neither the Dark Powers nor the place to which they have been brought. Boarhound and boar, master and servant; do not hope to break their pattern. Honor it instead.*

The graceful man placed the candelabra on the table, the parchment held absently before him. His eyes bore a vacant, distant look, and his lips were turned down in a slight frown. His dark clothes and his long black cape swallowed the light striking them, but the large red stone that dangled on a chain of gold from his neck reflected the candlelight sharply. Tracing his high cheekbone with a single finger, he stood elegantly, lost in thought. At last he reached down and stroked the old man's snowy head.

"It is a shame your visions cannot provide you with more specific messages, Voldra," Count Strahd Von Zarovich said, though he knew the mystic could not hear him. The old man was as deaf as he was blind. "At times like this I almost wish I hadn't torn your tongue out. Ah, well, it cannot be helped. We could not have you revealing my secrets to the villagers if you escaped, could we?"

The count crumpled the parchment and tossed it into the empty fireplace. The paper burst into flames. "Boarhound and boar," Strahd repeated as he opened a hidden panel in the stone wall. In the tiny alcove he placed the pen, ink, and crystal ball. "Intriguing."

The mystic stirred and reached out for the crystal ball. "Urrr," he groaned plaintively when he found the table empty before him.

The globe was Voldra's only means of contact with the world. It provided the old man, who had been deaf and blind from birth, limited glimpses into life beyond his sheltered mind. The orb granted other gifts, as well. The mystic had never learned to write; in the farming village where he'd lived much of his life, there was little need for such skills. The crystal ball allowed him to join pen to paper and make meaningful, if somewhat vague, statements.

The wordless, strangled cries of his prisoner hardly touched Strahd's consciousness as he crossed to the iron door and left the barren cell. His mind was coiling itself around the notion that the two strangers might prove useful to him. The count had known one of them was quite powerful even before Voldra's scribbled message; no being with strength of will or spell entered the duchy without Strahd's knowledge.

Strahd knew that the zombies he'd sent to test the newcomers' strength had been destroyed. He knew, too, that the weaker of the two strangers had fled into the forest before the battle. The wolves were following that one, herding him toward the castle.

The other would prove more of a challenge. The thought excited Strahd; it had been a long time since a problem worthy of his serpentine intellect had presented itself. The thing to do now, he decided as he paced with stately grace down the lightless corridor, past the sobbing prisoners in their filthy cells, was to gather more information.

 **FOUR**

The tearful keening of a violin filled the clearing and twined with the moonlight in the forest. The man playing the sad, rustic melody tapped his foot in time with his bow's movement. Nearby, two dozen men, women, and children sat in the glow of a campfire. The small crowd swayed to the music as if they were cobras mesmerized by a serpent tamer's flute.

Seven caravans were drawn into a semicircle around the forest camp. Ornately carved, brightly painted creatures and designs covered the large wagons, and these now served as a backdrop for the young man playing the violin. The multicolored scarf tied around his head and the similarly dyed sash girded about his thin waist blended in with the garish wagons. His tight black pants and the white shirt hanging open at his neck were in contrast to them.

As the song wound to its conclusion, the musician picked up the tempo. He played the last few bars boldly, in defiance of the piece's somber tone. Three notes plucked, *pizzicato*, from the strings concluded the tune. After, all was silent in the midnight forest save the crackling campfire. The musician expected no applause, for these were his nephews, cousins, and grandparents who were listening to him play. Their thoughtful silence told Andari his music had touched them, and that meant almost as much to him as the coins that sometimes rewarded his performances for strangers.

The young man wrapped his violin in a thick, embroidered cloth, stolen yesterday from a village nearby. He took meticulous care of the instrument. It had been handed down from father to son for five generations now, and he intended to give the violin to his own eldest boy when his fingers were too cramped to play.

"No! Leave me alone!"

The woman's shout startled Andari into dropping the precious heirloom. Had the violin not been covered by the cloth, the stone it struck may well have gouged a hole into its exterior. A small chip was the only damage the instrument sustained, yet it was enough to send Andari into a rage.

"Magda!" he shouted, cradling the wounded violin in his arms like a child.

The sound of glass shattering erupted from inside one of the wagons. "Get away from me!" Something heavy thudded against the wall of the caravan, and the door flew open. "Go back to your fat wife!"

A young woman stood framed by the lantern-lit doorway. Her raven-black hair fell in loose curls to her shoulders, and she shifted a lock of it away from her eyes with a defiant toss of her head. High cheekbones lent her expression a hard edge, despite her full, soft lips and inviting green eyes. With those eyes she cast an angry look back into the wagon as she gathered her long skirt in one hand, revealing slender legs. The way she leaped down the wagon's three wooden stairs told of her skill as a dancer.

"Damn you, Magda," Andari cursed. In two long-legged strides he was at the woman's side. With one hand the musician clutched the violin to his breast, with the other he grabbed Magda's shoulder. "Look what you've done! Your screeching made me drop my violin!"

A short, balding man peered from the noisy wagon. His face was pale, and drops of sweat worked their way down his forehead into his beady eyes. With a shrug, he straightened his shirt. As he did up the expensive silver buttons ornamenting the white cotton, he said, "She's not for me, Andari, not unless I want to be murdered in my bed."

Violently Andari shook the young woman. "I told you to be friendly to him, didn't I?"

Magda slapped her brother across the face. The men and woman nearby paid no attention as they wandered away from the campfire toward their own wagons. They had seen similar scenes between Andari and his sister before; there was no need to interfere. "You can't make me bed such a lout—not even for my keep," Magda said, her voice low and taut with anger.

His shirt buttoned tightly over his sizable paunch, the balding man emerged from the caravan. "I would have paid handsomely for a wench as comely as you," he offered. He scowled and rubbed the back of his head. "For hitting me with that bowl I ought to have the constable whip you. You're lucky I'm an affable fellow."

Andari smiled obsequiously. "Indeed, Herr Grest," he purred. "Have no fear. We will see Magda is punished for her ill treatment of you."

"Whatever," the little man replied absently. He looked the beautiful woman up and down. Anger flushed her tan face, and her green eyes flashed like a storm at sea. Even after her insults, the boyar found those large eyes inviting. They were the kind of eyes a man could drown in. . . .

Grest shook his head. "I could have made you a wealthy woman." That said, he sighed and turned to Andari. "My horse, boy. I should get back to the village right away."

The young musician's false smile dropped. "Are you certain you do not wish your fortune told, Herr Grest? Or perhaps you would prefer the company of one of my cousins?" He eyed the purse tied to the merchant's belt; it wasn't often the tribe allowed strangers, who they called *giorgios*, into camp. To let this one escape with his purse intact would be a shame.

"Just get my horse," Herr Grest said drily. He looked away from the semicircle of wagons into the darkened forest. "I'm a fool to be traveling at night . . . but I thought the journey would be worth the danger."

"Go get the gentleman's horse," Magda snapped. Andari tensed to strike his sister. She dropped her hand to the wide sash that bound her waist, and he paused. Andari knew from experience that she had a dirk secreted there.

"My sister does not understand the ways of the world," Andari noted as he turned to retrieve the boyar's horse. He rubbed a long, white scar on the back of his hand. "Do not think we Vistani are all so naive." The musician ran to his wagon, placed his cloth-wrapped violin on the steps, and disappeared behind the caravans.

An uncomfortable silence settled between Magda and Grest, then the young woman smiled. "There may be something I can offer you, after all," she said coyly.

Magda walked to the family wagon and, careful to

avoid touching Andari's violin, grabbed a small burlap sack that lay near the opening. The bag's contents jingled as she returned to the *giorgio*'s side.

"There are subtle ways to make you irresistible to young girls," she murmured, pulling a tiny pouch from the sack and holding it up for inspection. "Slip a pinch of this into a beautiful woman's wine and she will be at your command. Of course, it does not work on we Vistani."

Herr Grest considered the pouch. "Rubbish," he grumbled. "Love philters are for those too old or ugly or poor to have a woman they want."

Smiling thinly, Magda dropped the item back into the sack. Better that he didn't buy it, the Vistani thought. Grest is the type who would hunt for the tribe once he'd discovered that the powder was only so much ground bone. "Perhaps this charm, Herr Grest. You are a brave man to travel through Barovia after sunset, but even the boldest would be well advised to carry one of these."

She held up a long leather cord, and the silver charm at its end glittered seductively in the firelight. On the shining teardrop, a single eye was engraved, half-lidded and malevolent. "It's a ward against the dark things that prowl these woods by night." Magda lowered her voice to a conspiratorial whisper. "Zombies, werewolves, even vampires cannot see you when you wear this."

From the way Grest's beady-eyed gaze locked onto the silver amulet, Magda knew that she had a prospective sale.

"How much?" the *giorgio* asked, his hand gliding toward his purse.

"Thirty gold."

"Rubbish," Grest countered. "Fifteen at the most."

Magda shook her head, setting her raven-dark hair

dancing around her face. The charm did have some power, even if she was exaggerating its strength. "I'm only offering it to you at that price because of my unfortunate rudeness before. If you won't pay what it's worth, though, I—"

"Thirty it is, you charlatan."

As the transaction was being completed, Andari returned with the horse, saddled and ready to go. Grest had snatched the silver amulet from Magda's hand, and after dropping two handfuls of gold coins into the dirt, mounted. "I would have paid twice that for a night with you," he said to the beautiful woman as he wheeled his horse about and headed down the narrow path leading into the forest.

As Grest's mare reached the edge of the wood, it reared nervously, reluctant to leave the safety of the campfire. The balding man angrily kicked his heels into the horse's flanks. "Come on, you bastard. Get moving." The mare stared into the bushes at the clearing's edge, its eyes wide with fright. Grest kicked it again. After pawing the ground a few times, the horse bolted forward.

A figure, even darker than the darkness in which it was hidden, shifted slightly. The death knight turned back toward the Vistani camp, resuming his watch. He had pursued the wolves through the forest for hours, over dark-watered streams and through brush as tangled as a madman's mind. Some miles back, the monstrous guides had ceased their howling, which was replaced by the faint sound of music. Soth had followed that sweet sound here to the small camp.

At first he had assumed the gypsies gathered around the campfire to be an illusion or the human guises of the foul denizens of the Abyss. During the hour or so he had spent watching the men and women, the death knight had abandoned this notion; it seemed clear these were merely humans. Now Soth waited for someone to reveal himself as leader of the ragtag troupe—perhaps even this "Strahd" of whom the zombie had spoken. The young man named Andari obviously had some power over the others, but no one seemed to fear him. No, he was not the one who kept the tribe together.

Unaware of the glowing eyes that watched him, Andari continued to berate his sister. "You won't steal. You won't dance for strangers. Your stories are worth nothing to the tribe." The young man kicked Magda in the side, and she fell to the ground. "You are lucky Grest bought that amulet or you would be sleeping in the woods tonight."

"Magda's fate is not for you to decide."

The young man spun around to face the shriveled old woman who had made that terse pronouncement. "Madame Girani," he said, color rising to his cheeks in embarrassment. "I do not presume to speak for you, but Magda—"

"Heeds my word, not yours." Madame Girani set her cold gaze upon Andari, and her blue eyes leeched the heat from the man's soul. Cowed, he extended a hand to his sister. "Good," the old Vistani said as the young woman stood and brushed the dust from her skirt. "Now, what is the trouble?"

Magda moved to the old woman's side. She placed a gentle hand on Madame Girani's stooped shoulder. "Andari wanted me to sell myself to a wealthy boyar from the village. When I said no, he left me in the caravan alone with the pig. I had to break a crystal bowl over the man's head to convince him to leave me alone."

Madame Girani sighed and clutched her gnarled walking stick more tightly. "I have told you before,

Andari, I have plans for your sister. The tribe is large enough to support a storyteller, and I want Magda to be the one to fill that role."

"I only thought to gain the tribe a little more gold from a *giorgio*'s fat purse," he replied sullenly. Andari dropped to one knee and gathered up a few of the gold coins scattered in the dirt. "This is for you."

The old Vistani woman did not reply. Instead she stared at the armored man who had appeared at the edge of the clearing; it was as if he'd materialized out of the darkness, so abrupt was his coming. As the tall man drew closer, the firelight revealed him to be a knight clad in ancient armor. The damage from many battles marred the delicate ornamentation on the breastplate, which was also blackened from the touch of intense heat. Yet those scars could not hide the beauty the armor had once possessed.

A long purple cloak hung heavily from the stranger's shoulders and draped behind him almost to his knees. A tassel of long black hair topped his helm, which was as ancient and as ruined as the rest of his armor. Of the man himself, only his eyes shone from beneath the plate mail. He entered the camp with the haughty self-assurance of a wealthy boyar, his tread slow and confident, like the relentless progress of fall into winter.

"Welcome," Madame Girani said. "This is the camp of my tribe, and I offer you its shelter."

Lord Soth bowed slightly and rested a hand upon the pommel of his sword. "I accept that offer."

Andari gawked at the stranger. At his side, Magda stiffened at Soth's sepulchral voice. Like all Vistani, she knew that unnatural creatures stalked the forests of Barovia after sunset, and this might well be one such monster. She reached for the silver-bladed dirk hidden in her wide sash.

"He is under the protection of the master," Madame Girani whispered, placing a bony hand on Magda's arm. The young woman relaxed, though her eyes did not leave the death knight.

The two women, standing side-by-side as they were, appeared to Soth as age-distorted reflections of one another. Both Magda and Madame Girani were dressed in long, flowing skirts and snow-white blouses with billowing sleeves. They wore colorful sashes wrapped about their hips. Large bracelets circled their wrists, and glittering gold rings dangled from their ears. And, even though Madame Girani's hair was silver and pulled back from her face, the death knight could see that once it had been as dark as Magda's halo of curls.

The similarities went beyond their physical appearance. In the eyes of both Vistani women Soth saw determination and fearlessness. Whereas Andari was clearly frightened by the death knight, Magda and Girani appeared to accept him for what he was. These women know much, Soth decided, but they are not to be trusted completely.

"The night is growing chill," Magda noted after a moment. "Come, giorgio, warm yourself at our fire." She moved toward Soth, but the death knight held up a gauntleted hand in warning.

"I have no need of such comforts. I want only information."

"You will have that," Madame Girani offered as she turned her back on the death knight. With slow, deliberate steps, she made her way to a chair set close to the dying fire. "Andari, you will play for our guest. And, if we are so honored, Magda will dance."

Andari balked at the suggestion. "Magda never dances for—"

"Of course I will," the young woman interrupted.

"Get your violin, Brother. I will dance a tale of Kulchek the Wanderer."

With obvious dismay, the musician unwrapped his instrument and tuned the strings, running a finger mournfully over the slight damage inflicted earlier. Magda stood at Madame Girani's side, helping her settle a fringed shawl around her thin frame. Soth remained at the clearing's edge. When Andari appeared ready to begin, the old woman motioned to the knight. "Enjoy the dance, then we will talk."

The death knight crossed the clearing to stand near the fire, away from Madame Girani. When Magda gestured to a chair near the old woman, Soth shook his head. "I am quite comfortable here," he said flatly.

The song Andari chose started slowly, but it seemed to take possession of Magda from the first note. Eyes closed, she swayed to the music, her body writhing with a grace known only to the elves of Krynn. Her lips moved as if she were speaking to some unseen lover, and Soth tensed, expecting some sorcerous attack.

"She speaks some of the tale that goes with the dance," Madame Girani offered reassuringly from across the fire. "It is long and she does not know the entire tale yet."

As the tempo increased, the words were forgotten. The Vistani beauty whirled with greater speed and started to circle the fire. Magda's skirt spread and swooped as she twirled, and her bracelets jangled together, adding their rhythm to the violin's.

Despite his suspicions, the death knight found himself mesmerized by the woman's dancing. Long ago, when he'd been alive, Soth had loved little as much as music and dance. Of course, Magda's wild flamenco was quite unlike the stately, formal ballroom steps of which he used to be fond. Still, the fallen knight found himself missing the mortal life that had been stolen from him by his curse.

The fire flared. At its center, the flames took on the shape of a man. In one hand the man-image gripped a club, in the other a dagger. A hound of smoke was at his side. Soth's sword had cleared its sheath before Madame Girani had a chance to say, "That is part of the storytelling, a shadow play for those who don't wish to watch the dance."

Magda continued to whirl, blithely unaware of the weapon in the death knight's hand. Soth stared at the fire, watching as the man and his hound battled a giant formed from a gout of blood-red flame. It was then that Soth noticed how the shadow play mirrored the young woman's dance. When Magda whirled faster, the combatants exchanged furious blows; they circled each other warily when her movements slowed.

The spell Magda had cast with her grace was broken when she danced too close to the knight. The unearthly cold that always radiated from Soth's long-dead body washed over her, even through the heat of the fire, chilling her to the core. The woman did not stop her dance, but for an instant her steps were clumsy and out of time. The thread of the tale was lost. The fire engulfed the flame-born hero and his hound.

Luckily Andari finished the tune then, and Magda could hurry to Madame Girani's side. Because Soth had been watching Magda so intently, he had not noticed the old woman studying him closely all through the dance. "Good night, children," Madame Girani said. The other two looked surprised by the abrupt dismissal, but did not argue. Magda bowed to Lord Soth and smiled as graciously as she could—

though her concern for the old Vistani was clear on her face. Andari hurried into the caravan, his precious violin in his arms.

When they were gone, Madame Girani stood stiffly and headed for a wagon at one end of the semicircle. "We will talk elsewhere," was all she offered as an explanation to the death knight.

The caravan she entered was the largest of the tribe's seven. The old woman had a wagon to herself; a single, small bed—no more than a pile of blankets, really—was crammed into the crowded interior. The rest of the space was filled with jars and vials of every description, some filled with powders, others with liquids. Animal skins hung from the ceiling, blocking much of the light from the single oil lantern dangling in their midst. A few books with tattered, chipped pages and greasy leather covers lay piled in one corner. Cups filled with dice, bones, and other assorted small items were scattered everywhere.

A gilt cage, large enough for a young child, stood near the Vistani's bed. The gap between its bars was narrow, and the bars themselves sturdy. Serpents wrought of silver twined around the base, their heads merging with the bars. The cage's top was a single bloated snake, coiled around and around until its mouth opened at the very pinnacle. Soth had seen similar cages used on Krynn to house exotic birds. The thing trapped in this one was nowhere near so mundane.

"I see you are admiring my pet," the old woman said. She picked up a broom handle and ran it along the bars.

The creature's squeal sounded like a pig's, but the string of half-finished words that followed were definitely in some exotic human tongue. The thing gripped the bars with brown fingers and toes that curled completely around the metal, like a monkey's tail around a branch, shaking the bars hard enough to make the cage dance in place. Small wings, feathered like a dove's, beat the air in the cramped prison, then folded against the thing's scaly body. The face it pressed into the gaps was round with fat, but it had no nose, no ears—only a single red-rimmed eye and a large, slobbering mouth.

"A wizard traded it to me long ago for some information." Madame Girani shrugged. "I still don't know what it is, but every now and then it murmurs things in its sleep—secrets and spells and words of power. I learned the sorcery you saw tonight, Magda's shadow play, from its rambling."

Again she rattled the bars, and the creature spit out a string of words that sounded hateful, even if Soth did not comprehend the language in which the thing spoke. Madame Girani chuckled at the tirade, then dropped a heavy blanket over the cage. The creature's muffled squeals continued for a moment, then the wagon subsided into silence.

In the center of the squalor, directly under the lantern, rested a small table bracketed by two chairs. Madame Girani hobbled through the mess, deftly avoiding the bundles of clothing and packets of feathers cluttering the floor. She took a seat on one side of the table and motioned to the other chair, opposite her. "I will tell you what I can, Lord Soth of Dargaard Keep," she said in a whisper that sounded like tearing paper.

The death knight nodded, showing no reaction to the old woman's use of his name. He'd purposefully neglected to reveal it when he'd entered the camp; it was obvious now such precautions were futile in this strange land. "You may find sitting so close to me uncomfortable. The cold of the afterlife clings to me like a sickness."

The old woman laughed mirthlessly. "The chill of death seeps into my old bones with every sunrise and every sunset," she said, knitting her fingers together on the tabletop. "Your aura can do nothing to me that time has not already accomplished. Please, sit."

Soth accepted the invitation. "The wolves in your forest are quite large," he noted without preamble.

Madame Girani nodded. "The wolves are but half as ominous as the other creatures that prowl these woods, but little in this land could harm you, Lord Soth."

"And what land is this?"

"The duchy of Barovia."

"Barovia," Soth repeated pensively. "I have never heard of this place. Is it part of Krynn? A level in the Abyss, perhaps?"

"Though I have traveled much with my tribe, I know nothing of either of those places," the old Vistani said. "Barovia is simply . . . Barovia."

The death knight fell silent as he considered the reply. Madame Girani smiled and toyed with one of her bracelets. "The Mists brought you here, did they not?" she asked after a time.

"Yes. One moment I was in my castle on Krynn, the next I was surrounded by a fog. When it receded, I was on a hill a few miles from here."

"Were you alone?"

Secretly, Soth frowned beneath his helmet. "I am alone now. That's all that needs concern you."

Madame Girani took the rebuke mildly. Her smile never faltered as she sank back in her chair. "I promised to answer what questions I could, Lord Soth, but I am an old woman who needs her sleep. Is there anything else you wish to ask?"

"Who controls the Mists?"

"I do not know," came the answer. "Some say the Mists are a mindless force, pulling people from different places and bringing them to Barovia. Others claim that there are dark powers directing the Mists."

"Dark powers? Is Strahd one of those beings?"

The question seemed to surprise the old Vistani, Soth thought, but she did her best to conceal it. "Where did you hear that name?"

"Can't you read minds?" the death knight asked. "You knew my name when I did not offer it to you, so why do you not know this information as well?"

Madame Girani scowled, and the folds of wrinkles on her face knitted together, almost obscuring her dark eyes. "I had my grandchild dance for you, had her call up the shadow play, to show you we are a magical people. It was easy enough to discover your name."

Folding his arms across his armored chest, Soth repeated his earlier question. "Who is Strahd?"

"Some information comes at a high price in this land," Madame Girani answered.

Soth slammed his fist onto the table. A pattern of fine cracks snaked across the wood like a slowly expanding spiderweb. "I do not carry gold, and I have nothing to trade with you."

"Ah, but you do," the old woman said slyly. "We Vistani travel a great deal. Over the centuries my people have learned that there is one universal currency: information."

She stood, grabbed one of the worn books lying in the corner, and tossed it onto the table. It flipped open of its own accord. Two columns of cramped script marked each page. "This is a list of the true names of all mages in the faraway land of Cormyr, magical names that can be used to control those men and women. No magic-wielder in that country would dare harm a Vistani of my tribe, because I could give that true name to an enemy."

"I will never part with any knowledge that would grant you power over me, old woman," Soth said, brushing the book away from him. It closed with a thump as it landed on a pile of feathers.

"I would be foolish to expect you to, Lord Soth," Girani said soothingly. She returned to her seat. "But you realize I must have something in return for what I can tell you."

"What do you wish to know?"

Count Strahd had dispatched a vague set of orders to the Vistani camp: learn what you can of the knight, but do not anger him or reveal too much about me. The Vistani often served Strahd in such matters, and they were skilled in gathering information from unwary travelers. The undead warrior was far from unwary, however, so Madame Girani had to consider her answer carefully.

"Tell me what you will. A heroic deed you once performed. How you came to be as you are now, perhaps," she said. "And I will relate to you what I can of Strahd."

The death knight scanned his memory for a suitable story—one that would satisfy the Vistani but tell her nothing that could be used against him later. "In the three and a half centuries I have walked as one of the undead, I have forgotten many proud moments from my life," he began. "But I can tell you this. I was once the bravest of the Knights of Solamnia, the most noble in the Order of the Rose. My heroic deeds were told in song throughout Krynn, from the sacred glades of Sancrist Isle to the temple of Istar's kingpriest.

"My fall was long, and it started the day I set out from my home for a Knights' Council in the city of

Palanthas, the most beautiful city on Krynn. Along the way, my thirteen most loyal knights and I rescued a party of elven women from some brigands."

The memory washed over Soth, and the shabby caravan faded from his sight. "I was married," he continued, his voice sounding almost mechanical as he related the remembered events unfolding in his mind, "but my eye was drawn by the beauty of one of their number, an elfmaid named Isolde. On the long journey to Palanthas, I seduced the beautiful, innocent elf. She was to become a Revered Daughter of Paladine, a priestess of Krynn's greatest god of Good, but I corrupted her!"

An image flickered to life in Soth's brain: in a sunlit glade, he held Isolde close, her long, golden hair streaming over his arms, her face radiant. Though he could no longer feel the stirring of lust, the death knight was overtaken for a moment by remembered desire.

"My bonds to another," Soth noted, "did nothing to lessen my desire for her. I offered to give up everything for Isolde—my status as a knight, my place in Solamnic society . . . my honor."

"Honor was important to you?" Madame Girani asked, breaking Soth's concentration and scattering the memories gathered before his mind's eye.

Forcing away his annoyance at the interruption, Soth said, "One oath was sacred to all who filled the ranks of the Knights of Solamnia: *Est Sularus oth Mithas*. My honor is my life."

The death knight clenched his hand into a tight fist. "I gave up my honor for Isolde," he noted. "Before I reached Palanthas, I sent orders to my seneschal, who had remained at the keep to look after my affairs. He was to murder my wife, slit her throat in our bed, and dump her body into a chasm that lay

near the castle. The deed was done. It seemed that I
had solved my problems in ridding the world of my
shrewish wife, but Isolde fell ill in Palanthas. She was
pregnant with our son."

Waving his hand to dismiss the matter, Soth concluded quickly. "The elven women revealed my
crimes to the Knights' Council, and they tried me as
an adulterer and murderer."

The death knight leaned forward across the table
menacingly, but the old woman did not shrink back.
"Now," he said, "who is Strahd?"

"Count Strahd Von Zarovich is ruler of Barovia,"
Madame Girani replied without hesitation. "His castle, called Ravenloft, stands on a mountainside. It
overlooks the village of Barovia, from which the entire duchy takes its name."

Soth nodded. "This Strahd is a powerful necro-
mancer, is he not?"

"Strahd does not control the Mists that brought
you here, if that's what you mean," she said. A worried look crossed the old Vistani's face again. The
death knight pressed too hard for information she
was forbidden to offer. "Some say he dabbles in the
arcane. He is shrouded in rumor and mystery."

"It takes more than a dabbler to raise zombies that
repeat a name and fight on after their limbs have
been severed!" the death knight shouted. "I am not
some naive farmhand for you to bilk with vague pre-
dictions, old woman. Tell me everything you know
about Strahd!"

Overcome with fear, Madame Girani got up slowly
from her chair. "The villagers call him 'the devil
Strahd,' and he has earned that title." Soth stood as
well and took a menacing step toward her. "When
Vistani pass through Barovia, they are under
Strahd's protection, so the villagers do not dare

harm us," she concluded, edging backward.

Soth's evil laughter filled the wagon, setting the thing in the cage to squealing again. "You said before that little in this land could harm me, gypsy. If you were telling the truth, I have no reason to fear you or Strahd."

Before the death knight could make another move, the Vistani snatched up a jeweled dagger. The death knight laughed again as she held the weapon before her. "You think to harm me with that?" he asked. He reached for the old woman.

"I told you that we are no strangers to magic, death knight. This is an enchanted blade, one ensorcelled to deal with one such as you." Madame Girani flicked her wrist, and the dagger bit through the mail on Soth's fingers. Though the wound was not deep, it burned as if the dagger were coated with a powerful acid. The death knight gasped at the pain, for he had not had such a feeling in many years.

Soth wasn't foolish enough to draw his sword, for a long-bladed weapon like that would prove a disadvantage against a properly wielded knife in the close confines of the wagon. Instead, he acted swiftly, lifting up the cage and tossing its blanket aside. The thing inside shrieked and clawed at Soth's hand; its pointed nails ran harmlessly over his armor.

Madame Girani turned for the door, but not before Soth split the cage open as if it had been made of reeds, not metal. The creature launched itself at the old Vistani, its angel's wings unfurling, its hands and feet clutching the air before it. Futilely the old woman tried to hold the thing at bay, but it landed on her outstretched arm and scrabbled up it toward her face.

Soth reached up and pulled the lantern from its hook. "My regards to your dark powers," he said before smashing the lantern on the floor.

Flaming oil splattered onto the feathers and cloth and paper strewn at the old woman's feet, igniting them all. The blaze leaped from one stack of baubles to the next. Still struggling with the thing as it tore at her shoulder, Madame Girani managed to scream out one final curse.

"A pox upon you, Soth of Dargaard Keep! You will never return to Krynn again, though your home will always be in view!"

The thing raked one of its brown-fingered hands over the woman's face then, leaving bloody ribbons of flesh in its wake. It opened its mouth wide, and its single eye rolled back in its head as its teeth sank into her throat. A sheet of fire obscured Madame Girani from Soth for a moment, then a horrible shriek filled the wagon. The stench of charred flesh was added to the foul smell of scorched animal skins and burning wood. Soth turned and kicked the caravan's door from its hinges. The rush of night air fanned the flames, and the death knight left the wagon surrounded by a cloud of thick black smoke.

"Fire!" someone shouted. "Everyone awake."

"Help us here!" came another voice. "I heard Madame Girani scream."

The tribesmen had left their beds and were now rushing around the campsite, gathering water to put out the blaze. They heard the screams coming from the wagon and saw Lord Soth walk from the inferno. The death knight was untouched by the flames. When ashes landed on his cloak or his helm, they cooled instantly. When a cloud of thick, choking smoke covered him, he passed through it as if it were a gentle spring breeze.

"He's murdered her," someone whispered, though no one dared move toward him.

The Vistani stood, clutching buckets of water, faces paralyzed in expressions of terror. This man with the glowing orange eyes had to be a messenger from Strahd. Perhaps he served the shadowy powers of evil that ruled over all, even the count himself. That thought sent most of the Vistani fleeing into the forest.

There were others, younger and not so superstitious, who saw Soth as nothing more or less than a *giorgio* who had possessed the nerve to attack one of their own. Two of these, boys no more than fifteen winters old, rushed at the armored man. The unwritten code of the Vistani demanded revenge upon the stranger, and these boys took up the charge with all the unthinking enthusiasm of youth.

One wielded a long sword, the other a dagger. Both appeared to be skilled fighters, but the death knight could see that anger and fear had made them reckless. With little effort, he drew his sword and dispatched the two. Their blood ran into the dirt, coloring it red.

The death knight stood with the caravan at his back, his sword resting in his left hand, point down before him. The flames licking hungrily at the wagon cast a wild, dancing shadow of Soth across the bodies at his feet and over the entire clearing. A small explosion rocked the camp as Girani's jars and vials of exotic spell components fell to the blaze. The caravan's roof, already burning, shattered into a thousand fragments and blew across the clearing. The few Vistani who had not fled were tossing buckets of water on most of the smaller fires ignited by the fragments, but the wagon nearest the old woman's soon burned steadily, too.

From the screaming children and panicked adults left in camp only one other person dared to near

Soth. Magda, the beautiful dancer, rushed across the clearing toward the conflagration. "Madame Girani!" she cried, tears streaming down her cheeks.

Soth grabbed the young woman as she tried to pass. The unearthly cold from his hand raised blue welts on her thin wrist. "She is dead," he told her.

Magda stood rigid with fear and pain. She tried to pull away from the death knight, but found his grip like an iron vise. Falling to her knees next to the corpses of her tribesmen, the young woman looked out at the remaining Vistani as they fled into the forest. Her brother, Andari, paused at the clearing's edge and met her gaze. Unashamed at his cowardice, he turned away and ran, his violin clutched to his chest.

The death knight scanned the clearing. The Vistani had all scattered into the night, and only the crackle of the fires and the quiet sobbing of the young woman at his feet broke the silence. Loosening his grip on her wrist, he said, "Your name is Magda, is it not?"

Without waiting for a reply, Soth continued. "You seem an intelligent woman, Magda, so do not think to lie to me or try to escape." He released her wrist and sheathed his sword. Rubbing her wrist, Magda did not look up at her captor.

"Madame Girani said your tribe has traveled throughout Barovia, so I think I will make you my guide," the death knight said at last. "Castle Ravenloft is the first place we will visit. Take me there."

 **FIVE**

Magda stumbled over a twisted branch hidden by the half-light of dawn and dropped to her knees. After five hours of walking through the tangled forest, she was exhausted. "Please," she begged, "let me rest. We've been walking all night."

"Get up," came the reply from behind her. The voice was emotionless.

The young Vistani rubbed her eyes, then struggled to her feet. She looked down at the holes torn into her skirt, the patches of grime splattered onto her white blouse. Her leather shoes were wet from crossing a stream, and deep scratches crisscrossed her legs from passing through thorny bushes. She'd lost all her gold bracelets hours ago. "We can meet up with the Svalich Road near here," she said hopefully, straightening the small burlap sack tied to her waist. "The going won't be so hard then."

Soth did not consider the comment before he replied. "We keep to the forest. The roads in most lands are patrolled, and I do not wish the count to know I am coming." He extended a hand toward the woman. In another place the same gesture might have been seen as one of support. Magda knew it was a threat: Walk or I will burn you again with the frost of undeath.

Magda did more than walk. She ran.

As fast as her cramped legs could carry her, the young woman raced through the trees. Thin branches whipped her face and arms, and vines seemed to curl purposefully around her ankles. Her breath came in heavy, wheezing gasps after a time, but she did not slow her pace. The road is ahead, she told herself over and over. Reach the road and you might escape him.

Magda dared not glance back, for she was certain the dead man was right behind her, reaching out with his freezing hands. Her pulse thundered in her ears, blocking out the sounds of her own feet stumbling through dead leaves and clinging brambles. Yet no hand closed on her shoulder, no blade pierced her back. Magda dared to hope that she, unencumbered as she was, had escaped her armored captor.

Through a gap in a stand of fir trees, she could see the broad Svalich Road. The rising sun broke through the forest in places, casting long shadows everywhere, and it was through these alternating patches of darkness and light that the young woman now raced. I'm free! she shouted silently. Safe!

Two orange eyes flickered from the pitch-dark shadow of the firs. Magda screamed and slid to a stop. Her muscles taut after the long march and the sudden, frantic run, she tumbled. Ignoring the pain from a wrenched shoulder, she got to her feet and ran again.

She couldn't tell if she was nearing the road or not. That didn't matter any longer. Somehow the dead man had gotten ahead of her, between her and the road. Just keep running, she told herself. He can't keep up with you forever.

Directly in front of the woman, Lord Soth emerged

from the shadow of a large, moss-covered boulder. Magda fell to the ground at his feet, wheezing and sobbing. "It is good that we have this out of the way," the death knight said in a calm voice. "Now that you know escape is impossible, we can continue."

Sadness in her green eyes, Magda struggled to her feet and resumed the march.

The death knight had stayed in the Vistani camp only long enough for the woman to wrap her frost-bitten wrist in strips torn from her skirt and collect a few things from her wagon. He'd not even allowed Magda time to say a simple prayer over the ruin of Madame Girani's caravan.

For the first few hours, it had all seemed like a terrible nightmare to Magda. She often hoped that she might awaken in her bed, Andari snoring loudly nearby, and find it so. The distant howling of wolves or the grunt of something more sinister and much closer in the dark always brought her back to reality. Then she would turn to see the dead man walking behind her, his orange eyes glowing like will-o'-the-wisps. His heavy boots made no sound as he walked through the undergrowth, and he rarely spoke. Still, by dawn it had become clear to the young woman that Lord Soth did not intend to kill her—at least not until they reached Castle Ravenloft.

The idea of seeking out the home of Count Strahd Von Zarovich frightened Magda almost as much as Soth himself. Rumors of the bloody crimes inflicted upon unwelcome visitors by the devil Strahd circulated freely in the duchy, and Magda herself had seen the ghastly remains of two such hapless victims on display in the village of Barovia. They had been would-be adventurers, thieves who had attempted to sneak into the castle after dark. Hope for quick riches had blinded their common sense, and Strahd had presented them to the other villagers as an example of his justice.

The young Vistani shuddered now at that memory of the bloodless, decapitated corpses dumped in the village square. To dispel the grisly images she tried to focus on the bird song trilling through the forest around her, the bright slants of sunlight breaking through the canopy. It was to no avail. The memory of the dead men pushed to the forefront of her thoughts.

But Madame Girani had said that Soth was under Strahd's protection, Magda remembered with a start. Perhaps the count wished them to arrive at the castle safely. That thought kept hope alive in the young woman for the next few hours.

The sun was almost directly overhead when three riders charged along Svalich Road, their horses kicking up chunks of packed earth. They led a fourth horse behind them, a man slung over its saddle. The road was far enough away that neither Soth nor Magda could make out any detail of the riders, but similar groups of mounted men, as well as lone farmers with wagons full of supplies, had become a more frequent sight in the last hour.

"We must be nearing the village," Soth said once the riders had passed. "If we continue at this pace, when will we arrive there?"

Magda looked around. She noted that the road was beginning a steady curve to the southwest; the village and Castle Ravenloft were little more than four miles away. "Midafternoon," she answered, "but only if we press on at the same rate."

After considering that for a moment, the death knight ordered Magda to sit. "That is too soon," he noted. "I wish to reach the castle well after dark. It will be easier to breach its defenses then."

The stories told by the natives of Barovia made it clear that, day or night, Castle Ravenloft seldom welcomed guests. And the hulking stone fortress had a more sinister defense than walls or thick doors—if the local rumors were to be believed. Still, Lord Soth was more than a sneak-thief intent on pilfering a few of the count's treasures.

"You may sleep," the death knight said, though it was more of a command than an offer.

Magda studied the wounds Soth had caused by grabbing her wrist at the camp; the frostbitten welts were still sore, but healing. Her shoulder was feeling better, too. The grueling march had taken a much worse toll on her feet, however. After examining the blisters and scrapes covering her heels and toes, the Vistani took out her silver dirk and shredded part of her sash into bandages. Pausing in that task, she glanced at Soth. He stood a few yards away, his arms folded over his chest. "Aren't you going to sit?"

"I need no rest," Soth answered shortly.

" 'The living tire easily, but the dead never sleep,' " she murmured, reciting part of an old Vistani saying. She wrapped her feet, tied the remainder of her sash around her waist, then leaned back against the tree. "What do you want with the count, dead one?"

"Do not be coy with me, girl," the death knight rumbled. "I am Lord Soth of Dargaard Keep. If you must address me, use my title."

Magda had not intended to be disrespectful, but exhaustion had made her forget her fear momentarily. "Forgive me, Lord Soth," she said, her voice betraying no hint of anxiety.

The silence that followed was full of tension. "You Vistani are a bold lot," Soth said at last. "You must have great faith in Strahd. Do you think he can protect you from me if I decide to kill you?"

For a horrifying moment Magda wondered if the dead man could read her thoughts. All Vistani—not only those of Madame Girani's tribe—served as Strahd's eyes and ears in Barovia, as well as the duchies that bordered it. In return for this service Strahd granted them freedom of movement in and out of his domain. "Why do you think I am a servant of the count?" she asked nervously.

"Your mentor warned me the Vistani were under Strahd's protection," Soth replied. He waved his hand, dismissing the matter. "What happened in the camp should prove how little that means."

The young woman met Soth's gaze directly for the first time. "Strahd has great power, but so do the Vistani—after a fashion. There are many Vistani tribes in Barovia and the duchies nearby, and word of your crimes against my people will spread to them all."

"Bah!" the death knight snapped. "Your gypsy brethren can do nothing to harm me."

Magda settled back against the tree and closed her eyes. "There are dark powers greater than you, greater even than Strahd, who listen to the pleas of the Vistani and make our curses come to pass." She rolled onto her side, her back to her captor. "Even Strahd respects the Vistani, Lord Soth. There is no shame in that."

Anger was the death knight's first reaction, but as he considered Magda's words he realized that they were merely a statement of rote belief by a tired, beleaguered woman. As Soth stood over the Vistani, watching the dark-haired beauty drift off to sleep, he found himself comparing her to Kitiara. The same fierce desire to survive burned in both women. The highlord had courage the Vistani lacked, though. She would never have submitted to the march the way Magda did. Perhaps the young gypsy was biding her time. Perhaps she possessed greater patience than Kitiara could have hoped to muster. . . .

Thoughts of Magda and Kitiara turned to thoughts of Caradoc. Soth wondered where his traitorous seneschal had hidden himself, where in Barovia he would seek asylum—for the ghost must have known his master would succeed in killing him when next they met.

"There is no one powerful enough to shield you," the death knight vowed. "And once I am certain you have been destroyed, I will escape this hellish place and resurrect my Kitiara."

*   *   *   *   *

The Svalich Road emptied of travelers well before sundown, and not a single rider traversed it after dark. Soth woke Magda when daylight started to fade. "It is time," was all he needed to say for the Vistani to hurry to her feet. As she trudged along, Magda ate the last of the food she had managed to gather before leaving the ruined camp. Even though a river crawled within a few hundred yards to the south, Soth did not allow her to get any water to drink with the crusty bread.

The land rose and fell dramatically as they crossed the last few miles to the village of Barovia and Castle Ravenloft, and the road was forced to twist and turn around huge outcroppings of granite. Overhead, a large flock of bats dove haphazardly through the air. The soft flutter of their wings in the cloud-covered sky heralded the coming of night.

"They're a bad omen," Magda said, making an arcane sign over her heart.

Soth felt a twinge of . . . *something* when the woman performed the superstitious gesture. Perhaps the ritual had once been part of a spell intended to protect the caster from evil, he decided. As Madam Girani had said, the Vistani were no strangers to magic.

At last they reached the top of the final rise. Below them lay a valley, a small village huddled in its embrace. In the lessening sunlight, the place looked grim and uninviting.

The Svalich Road passed through Barovia's center, bisecting the tiny collection of two- and three-story buildings. A squat, dilapidated mansion stood just outside town, and a sagging church of stone and wood, its bell tower shattered, rested away from the village to the north. Forest pushed in on the houses and fields from all sides, and the river that earlier had come so close to the road now bordered Barovia to the south. Both the road and the river continued to the west. The river formed a large pool before snaking into high, craggy hills. The road led to a castle that crouched on a massive spire of rock overlooking the village.

"Castle Ravenloft," Magda whispered. She wrapped her arms around herself, but Soth was unsure whether she did so to stave off the chill night air or because of the sight of the ancient, brooding fortress.

It wasn't only the castle that drew Soth's attention as he looked out over the valley. In a band several hundred feet wide, a ring of fog circled both Barovia and Castle Ravenloft like a protective wall. "More fog," he hissed. "So Strahd *is* the one who brought me here from Krynn."

"No," Magda said. "The ring of fog is a defensive barrier for the village and the castle. Strahd uses it to detect and control who enters or leaves the area."

She rummaged in her sack and withdrew a stoppered glass vial. A thick purple liquid filled the small container.

After drinking the bitter fluid, she continued. "The fog is a powerful poison. If you do not drink an antidote—one only we Vistani have permission to create—the poison works into your lungs and your heart. Then, if you try to leave the village without Strahd's permission . . ." The Vistani let the sentence trail off.

"It is fortunate I do not breathe," Soth said as he started toward the barrier.

Magda hurried after the death knight. When they reached the edge of the fog, Soth hesitated. "Tie your sash around your wrist—tightly." When Magda did not jump to the task, he added, "If you do not, I will be forced to hold your arm as we pass through the fog."

The death knight had to say little more. Soth took the other end of the cloth and said, "Keep this tight between us. If I feel it loosen while we are in the fog, I will grab you by the throat and hold you that way until we are in the village."

They emerged from the fog to the north of the village and kept to the trees as they made their way toward the high, steep hill that held the castle. Just as the sun was tossing its last feeble rays over the mountains to the west, Soth and Magda heard voices close at hand.

"Hurry!" someone shouted, panic making his voice shrill. "The light is almost gone!"

"Get the rope over that branch!"

The death knight moved silently through the trees, Magda at his side. At the forest's edge, near the sagging church Soth had observed from the rise, a group of ten stout men milled. One tried time and again to toss a rope over a high, sturdy branch of a gnarled tree that stood in front of the abandoned building. Most of the men had dark hair and dark eyes, and sported long, drooping mustaches; Soth himself had worn a mustache like that once, as did all the Knights of Solamnia on Krynn. Their rough wool vests and heavily accented speech marked these men as rustics, however, not noble-born warriors.

"Give me that," one of the villagers snapped, taking the rope from his compatriot. This man, unlike the others, had blond hair and blue eyes. He was also clean-shaven, and, instead of heavy work clothes, wore long red robes faded with age and in a size too small for his bulk. He held the rope in his pudgy fingers and looped it over the branch with a single throw.

Hidden in the trees, Magda closed her eyes. "A hanging," she murmured. "Probably someone caught stealing from a boyar."

The men had turned expectantly toward the village. Being near the forest as the sun set obviously upset them, for they continually glanced into the woods. Gloaming had not yet turned to full night when a man mounted upon a spirited chestnut gelding charged up the dirt and cobblestone road leading from the main cluster of buildings. A small figure was tied behind the horse, and he bounced and rolled painfully.

"At last!" one of the villagers cried, and the group raced toward the rider. The gelding came to a stop not far from the tree, and the unlucky prisoner was pulled to his feet.

He stood four feet tall, from the tip of his bald pate to the iron heels of his boots. The rough treatment had torn his pants to ribbons, and bloody scrapes covered his bare chest and steel-muscled arms. His hands were tied behind him with enough rope to bind several men. The captive struggled against the bonds like a madman being dragged toward captivity.

"You are making a very, very large mistake," the little man growled. He took a deep breath and stopped struggling. "Let me go now and we can forget about this whole stupid misunderstanding."

"Ah, a dwarf," Soth said softly. "This world is not so unlike my own."

Magda looked puzzled. "Do you mean there are more of those freaks where you come from?" she asked. "There are few like him in Barovia."

As Soth pondered this, the chubby villager in the red robes struck a torch and held it toward the captive. "You must pay for your crimes."

By the light of the torch, Soth saw that a swollen bruise held one of the dwarf's eyes shut. His face was as scratched as his chest, and a steady stream of blood ran from his flat nose. The gore matted the close-cropped brown mustache that dipped beneath his nose and joined with his muttonchop sideburns. Oddly, the dwarf was smiling at the man in the red robes. "Really," he advised, "we'll all be happier if you let me go now."

"Let's just get this over with," one of the other villagers said, glancing nervously at the bats darting overhead.

The rest of the group murmured their assent, and the dwarf was pushed toward the hanging tree. As the villagers draped the noose around the criminal's neck and tied the other end to the horse, Soth turned away from the spectacle. "Come," he said to the Vistani. "I've seen enough."

Magda gladly followed the death knight away from the clearing. As they made their way deeper into the forest, the ominous sounds of the hanging were replaced by the gentle chirping of crickets. Magda let the familiar sound calm her.

"By all that's holy, no!"

A scream split the air, then a growl rolled, loud and low, in the night.

"Run, you fools, run!"

A snarl echoed from the scene of the hanging. Screams, first of one man, then of two more, cut through the darkness. The sound of a horse shrieking in pain came hard upon these awful cries, followed by the awkward crashing of someone running blindly through the woods.

Without a word, Soth turned back toward the commotion. Magda stayed close to him as he moved through the darkness. Both the death knight and the Vistani were surprised when the man in red robes burst toward them from behind a huge fir. The man waved a torch in front of him.

The scene in the forest froze in a weird tableau. Magda crouched in a defensive position. Soth, his head cocked slightly, stood stiff and still, though his cloak flapped silently behind him. A few feet away, the red-robed man leaned forward, off balance but motionless, staring at the death knight with panic-filled eyes. Soth saw something else in those eyes: recognition. The red-robed man was not just startled, but horrified because he recognized the death knight.

Just as suddenly as the villager had burst upon Soth and Magda, he fled into the forest, his torch bleeding a trail of light.

The death knight considered chasing the robed man, but the terrifying yowl that came from the clearing pushed that thought away. Instead he turned in the direction of the hanging.

A surprising scene greeted the death knight and his guide. The horse and five of the villagers lay near the hanging tree, their corpses shredded and bloody. The other rustics were nowhere in sight. In the center of this carnage sat the dwarf, bruised and battered but free of the ropes that had been wrapped around his hands and coiled around his throat. As he pulled on one of his iron-soled boots, he whistled tunelessly.

With the slowness of one just awakened from a long nap, he stretched and reached for his other boot. He stopped moving abruptly and wrinkled his nose in disgust. "More farmers?" he muttered, letting his boot drop to the ground. The dwarf crouched low, almost onto his hands and knees, and sniffed the air. "Come on out of there so I can see what you are."

He was looking toward Soth and Magda, though they were quite well hidden by the thick-needle firs around them. The Vistani tried to shrink back into the forest, but the death knight stepped forward.

"And the other one," the dwarf said, squinting after the Vistani.

"Now, Magda," Soth ordered when the woman hesitated. She moved from her hiding place, her hand straying to the dagger in her sash.

"Vistani!" the dwarf hissed as he saw the olive-skinned, dark-haired woman. He growled deep in his throat and tensed as if ready to spring. "I should have known you'd be agents of the count."

Magda drew her dagger, and the dull moonlight pushing through the clouds made the metal blade glow. The dwarf took a wary step forward.

"Enough," Soth said. "The girl is my prisoner, and I am no servant of Strahd Von Zarovich."

The dwarf snorted and shrugged his shoulders. "A

Vistani woman and . . . hmmm." He studied Soth, taking measure of the death knight with his one good eye. His face betrayed his interest in the new-comer. Not a hint of fear showed in his stance.

Nodding toward the castle, the dwarf said, "You certainly aren't one of *his* walking corpses, Sir Knight. They can't say much other than his name. Shows his ego, don't you think—having zombies that can only groan or say 'Strahd'?"

Soth watched the dwarf closely as he sat back down and struggled with his other boot. "Did you do this to the villagers?" the death knight asked.

Wiping some blood from his brawny arms, the dwarf smiled. "Not all this is mine, if that's what you mean," he replied. "I warned 'em, though. 'If you try to hang me, you'll be sorry,' I said." He glanced at the dead bodies. "And so they are."

"How?" the death knight asked emphatically.

Having finished with his boot, the dwarf was now doing what he could to straighten his tattered pants and daub away the blood. "You're new here." He laughed and looked up at the Vistani. "I'm right—er, *Magda*, wasn't it? He's new to the duchy, isn't he?"

The Vistani, her silver-bladed dirk still clutched tightly in her hand, remained grimly silent. Her gaze wandered from corpse to gruesome corpse, and whenever the dwarf made a sudden movement, she brandished the weapon before her menacingly.

Not fazed in the least by either Magda's hostility or Soth's silence, the dwarf returned to the task of cleaning himself up. After doing what he could for his clothes, he walked from body to body, looking for anything worth stealing. Most of the villagers' rough-woven clothes were shredded beyond use, but the dwarf managed to salvage a sleeveless wool vest from one of the corpses and a brightly patterned blanket from the horse. As he draped the latter around himself like a cloak, he turned to the death knight. "Is there something else I can do for you? I mean, you're not hanging around here just to watch me rob corpses."

"You said I was a newcomer to this land. Why do you think that?"

The dwarf moved closer to the death knight. When he got near Soth, he pulled the blanket tighter around his shoulders. "Look," the dwarf said in a conspiratorial whisper, "there are two things I've learned about Barovia in the time I've been here. First rule: Don't ever ask strangers about themselves. Most of the people I've met here have dark secrets they'd rather keep hidden. They've done things worse than you or I might ever think of doing—well, you anyway. And some, maybe even most, don't like people prying into their business."

He stood back and glanced around as if someone might be listening. "For example, I know you're not mortal—don't ask how, 'cause I won't say—but I'm accepting that for what it is. I've seen stranger things than you around here. Not many, of course." When Soth did not comment, the dwarf shrugged.

"Why are you telling me this? Are you so certain I am not a spy for Strahd Von Zarovich?" Soth asked.

A smirk crossed the dwarf's face. "The second thing I learned about Barovia is: Don't have anything to do with the Vistani. They tell the count everything they learn about strangers, and harming 'em is like insulting Strahd to his face." He nodded toward Magda. "If she's learned anything about you, Sir Knight, you should take her back into the forest and make certain no one sees her again. Just a suggestion, mind you. Free advice from someone who's been stuck in this hell for quite some time."

Magda, who still stood a few feet away, nervously gripping her dagger, took a step back toward the forest. "Something's coming," she hissed. "From the direction of the village."

"Can't be the yokels," the dwarf said. "They never leave their homes after sundown if they can help it. Too many things like you and me roaming about."

A distant clatter of wooden wheels and the roar of horses' hooves pounding steadily on stony ground sounded from the direction of the village. Two lantern lights flickered in the darkness, and the clatter grew louder.

"It's a carriage," Soth said, staring into the night with his glowing eyes. "Two horses, dark as pitch." He peered down the road. "I do not see a coachman."

"Oh! Bloody—" The dwarf started for the trees. "I told you, didn't I? Bloody Vistani!" With a burst of incoherent cursing, he disappeared into the forest.

Soth drew his sword and turned to Magda. "What is it?"

The woman did not have the time to answer before the carriage came to a stop in front of the broken-down building. The black horses stamped in agitation, snorting and tossing their heads. No coachman had directed the horses along the road from the village, and no hands touched the carriage door as it opened invitingly.

"Strahd's carriage," Magda managed to say at last. "Just like the stories! He sends it for you!"

"For *us*, Magda," Lord Soth corrected. "Don't think I would leave my charming guide behind."

 **SIX**

Strahd Von Zarovich stood before a massive fire-place, one arm resting on the mantel. A few logs burned in the hearth, but the light they gave off scarcely illuminated the count let alone the cavern-ous room which he now occupied. The lord of Baro-via leafed absently through a book of poetry. As he turned each time-worn page the smile twisting his cruel mouth grew wider and wider.

"Ah, Sergei. You always were a hopeless roman-tic."

The book had been penned long ago by Strahd's younger brother, Sergei, and the verses it contained were all dedicated to a single woman, his beloved Ta-tyana. The cause of the count's smile was not the poems themselves, for they were like everything Ser-gei had created in his tragically short life—beautiful and full of heartfelt sentiment. No, it was knowledge of the futility of those exclamations of love that amused him so. Sacred vows had never bound the lovers in wedlock; Strahd knew this because he him-self had murdered his brother on the day he was go-ing to wed Tatyana.

An all-consuming desire for the girl had made it so that Strahd could think of nothing other than the gentle, loving Tatyana. The thought that she was to be wed to his hopelessly naive sibling had only fueled Strahd's hunger for her; he had spent his days in a foul temper, roaming the halls of Castle Ravenloft, hoping to catch a glimpse of his beloved. At night he had pored over arcane tomes, hoping against hope to discover some charm that would win Tatyana's heart for him.

At last the unrequited desire had driven Strahd to forge a pact with the forces of darkness, a pact to be sealed with an act of fratricide. He had concluded his bargain on the day Sergei was to be married, with an assassin's dagger sharper than any he had ever seen. With his brother's murder, Strahd had gained powers that could be imagined only in nightmares, but even those new strengths could not sway Tatyana's love.

When Strahd had revealed his desire for her, Tatyana had ended her life rather than spend a single moment in his embrace.

Strahd closed the book sharply. Tatyana had no idea that now, almost four hundred years after her death, he still inhabited the castle . . . still desired her.

He tossed the book onto the fire, and its ancient, dry pages flared and burned. Impatiently the count paced the stone floor.

Yes, the dark powers Strahd had bargained with so many years past had given him much in return for Sergei's death. He never felt the pall of sickness or the weight of old age. In fact, he had ruled Barovia for the lifetimes of five men. The count had devoted much of that time to arcane study, and the dark secrets he had uncovered in that pursuit granted him sway over the living and the dead.

Barovia, the duchy over which the Von Zaroviches had ruled for many years, had paid for the count's bloody deeds, balancing Strahd's triumphs with its suffering. Soon after Sergei's murder, the duchy was drawn into a netherworld of mists. Strahd soon found he could not cross the borders out of Barovia, though he gained the ability to prevent others from leaving the domain. He became absolute master of the land, yet that victory soon grew hollow. Few of the peasants and boyars who populated the scattered villages offered Strahd much of a challenge; that was why the count anticipated the times when beings such as Soth would appear in Barovia.

"I wonder if my guests are comfortable," Strahd said softly as he approached a window. The count looked out at the road twisting and clawing its way up the mountainside to his castle. Near the bridge that crossed the River Ivlis, the carriage, marked by the twin lamps on its front, moved steadily onward.

The master of Castle Ravenloft closed his eyes and concentrated. Just as the driverless carriage obeyed his will, the minds of those within the coach stood as open to him as Sergei's book of verse. He considered the Vistani woman first. As he had expected, terror clouded her mind, yet a part of her intellect resisted the fear, a core of bravery she bolstered by repeating ancient tales of Vistani heroes. The stories couldn't block out the terror completely, though. That fear would be useful to Strahd, especially when it was heightened by the little shock he had in store for Magda.

In comparison to Soth, the Vistani held no real interest for the count. After all, she was merely a pawn. On the other hand, the death knight demanded careful study, so Strahd let his mind clear, then pushed into the newcomer's consciousness.

The surface of Soth's mind appeared as cloudy as the wall of choking fog surrounding the village.

Many of the usual emotions that colored the
thoughts of men—love, desire, respect—were gone
or deadened. Strahd ventured further, and a wave of
seething hatred and impotent lust broke around
him. The intensity shocked the dark lord, and his
mind recoiled for an instant.

What surprised Strahd most, as he resumed his
journey into Soth's consciousness, was the absolute
lack of fear. Every other newcomer who had known
anything of the count had shown apprehension
about meeting him, but not this undead knight. The
master of Castle Ravenloft cast no ominous shadow
over Soth's mind. Is he foolhardy? the count wondered, but the power he sensed told him otherwise.

Thinking he knew all there was to know of the
death knight's turbulent thoughts, Strahd readied
himself to leave Soth's mind. He backed slowly away
from the swirling chaos of violent emotions, but a
flickering impulse made him hesitate. The ride in the
carriage had stirred up some ancient event in the
death knight's mind.

With the perverse joy of a voyeur, the lord of Barovia settled back.

Soth's knees ached as he kneeled in a huge hall.
The room was packed with members of all three orders of the Knights of Solamnia—Crown, Sword, and
Rose—and every man craned to see their fallen fellow. Their gawking faces angered Soth, and he
forced himself to meet the eyes of many of the
knights. It gave him a little comfort to see them turn
away before he did. To him, their murmuring voices
sounded like women gossiping in the marketplace,
and their polished armor smelled like the scented
handkerchiefs favored by courtiers in Kalaman.

At the room's front, he saw the highest-ranking
members of each order. A long table lay before

them, covered with a blanket of black roses. The dusky flowers proclaimed the council's sentence, but Soth knew the Solamnic Knights would follow the trial's ritual to the last. They weren't kneeling in armor, though. Their knees weren't cramped and almost numb from pain.

"You have failed to defend yourself with regard to the charges brought 'against you, Soth. We have found you guilty of adultery with the elfmaid Isolde, the murder of Lady Gadria, your lawful wife, and a dozen other less hideous infractions," Lord Ratelif said sadly. The high warrior of the Rose Knights picked up one of the black flowers and hurled it at the prisoner.

The rose struck Soth in the face, but he refused to flinch. I will not even give them that much satisfaction, he thought vindictively.

Sir Ratelif stood, then pronounced the fallen knight's doom. "In accordance with the Measure, Soth of Dargaard Keep, Knight of the Rose, will be taken through the streets of this city in disgrace. He will be jailed until highsun tomorrow, then executed for crimes against the honor of the Order."

Rough hands grabbed Soth's shoulders, and a sergeant jerked the knight's sword free of its scabbard. The burly soldier then handed the prisoner's weapon to Lord Ratelif. The high warrior held the bright sword before him, its blade toward Soth. "The means of execution shall be the guilty party's own sword."

The memory grew vague in Soth's mind as the knights pushed toward him in the room. Strahd had to strain to follow its thread.

His armor was pulled off, but still Soth remained silent, refusing to lend legitimacy to the proceedings. Dressed in only a padded doublet, he was dragged to a cart and paraded through the streets of

Palanthas. The day was cool, and the smells of the
port city were everywhere—the taunting aromas of
meats and vegetables cooking in the open-air mar-
kets, the sharp tang of smoke from crafters' forges,
the smell of salt air from the harbor. Scribes and
butchers, priests and bureaucrats, all had come out
to see the fallen knight, the man of honor brought
low. To Soth they appeared as nothing so much as
sheep, round-faced and bleating.

"You knights are no better than any citizen of Solamnia," one woman shouted from the throng.

A grocer hurled an overripe melon at the cart.
"The kingpriest is right! Even the Knights of Solamnia are corrupt!" The crowd cheered when the missile hit Soth.

Calmly wiping the smear from his eyes, he looked
back at the grocer. In the man's jowled face, made
red from standing in the sun to hawk his wares, the
knight saw more hatred than he'd seen from most
foes he'd faced at sword point.

I'm no innocent, Soth told himself as the cart
lurched through the crowded streets. His inner resolve cracked, and a coiling thread of self-doubt
wound around his heart. Now I've given the
kingpriest proof that corruption exists everywhere—
even in the knighthood.

A woman emptied a bucket of filthy water from an
open window. As the shower soaked Lord Soth, he
lost all thoughts of his own guilt. The people of
Palanthas were acting like a mob, and the knights
meant to guard him were doing nothing to shelter
him. "You are all as guilty as I!" he shouted.

Something struck Soth in the face, a blow that
made stars appear before his eyes. When the haze
cleared, he saw a young Knight of the Crown standing over him. The youth had his mailed fist raised,

ready to strike again.

Cold resolve took hold of the fallen knight's soul
once more, sealing his heart against any self-
recrimination. For the rest of the humiliating ride
through Palanthas, he closed his eyes and shut out
the insults. Somehow I will make them sorry for this,
Soth told himself over and over. Somehow I will
make Palanthas pay.

*　*　*　*　*

A draconian, its curved blade coated with blood,
stands over a fallen woman. His face frozen in horror,
a young man holds his ground against one of Soth's
own skeletal minions, only to have his head severed
from his body. Tanis Half-Elven flees down arrow-
straight streets, showing his true soul at last. . . .

Something tugged at the edges of Soth's consciousness. Amidst the clear scenes of victory a
shadowy thing lurked. Yet, when the death knight
tried to concentrate on it, the shadow-thing slipped
away. Something powerful was intruding upon his
mind.

The death knight scowled. I will destroy any who
betray me, any who prevent me from returning to
Krynn, Soth repeated to himself again and again as
the carriage rattled along its way through the night.

Magda gasped, and the sharp sound drew Soth out
of the near-trance into which he had lapsed. He had
lost track of their progress, for now the carriage was
high in the foothills. "What is it?" the death knight
asked, but the answer was obvious.

They had reached Castle Ravenloft.

Twin gatehouses of crumbling, turreted stone
slouched in the darkness like drowsing sentinels.
Their charge, a wooden drawbridge that spanned a

chasm of frightening depth, swayed in the wind, and the rusted chains holding the planks in place chimed and groaned. Across the bridge lay the keep, protected by a moss-covered curtain of gray stone. Gargoyles with hideous, tortured faces stared sightlessly from the wall.

The rickety, weathered planks protested as the pitch-black horses charged across. Their complaints were so much idle threat; the carriage crossed the bridge without mishap. At the horses' approach, the ancient portcullis that sealed the entrance to the keep lifted sullenly off the ground, clearing a path to the courtyard. Once inside the massive wall, the horses slowed, then stopped.

"We have arrived," Soth said as the carriage door opened. The death knight slid from the coach into the empty courtyard. He took in his surroundings with a glance.

Castle Ravenloft must have been gorgeous once. Its subtly peaked roofs and lofty towers still gave testament to the builder's skill, but wild vegetation left unchecked and weather damage left unrepaired had long ago marred the virgin beauty of the place. The castle's huge double doors stood open now, and soft light bled into the courtyard.

"Come," Soth ordered. Magda hesitated, then shrank back into the plush red velvet seat. His voice cold, the death knight added, "Your master awaits."

Steeling herself, the Vistani climbed from the carriage. As soon as she was clear of the coach, its door slapped shut and the horses shot forward. The carriage disappeared back across the drawbridge and into the night.

Magda led the way into the castle. A small entry hall, no wider than the main doors, greeted them. Near the ceiling, four dragons carved from red stone crouched. They seemed ready to pounce on unwelcome visitors, their gemstone eyes glittering menacingly.

"Your Excellency?" the Vistani called.

With a creak, the doors to the courtyard closed.

"Parlor tricks any jester could rig," Soth said disdainfully. Without waiting for a further reply, he boldly entered the next room.

The room was large, and torches in iron sconces provided barely enough light to banish the darkness. No furniture filled the hall. No tapestries covered the walls. The domed ceiling and the leering gargoyles squatting around its rim were festooned with cobwebs. The gray sheets danced and fluttered, casting fantastic shadows over the ruined frescos that graced the dome. An arch opened onto a small room to the right, doors of solid bronze sagged on their hinges straight ahead, and, to the left, a wide stair of dust-covered stone climbed from the hall.

"Count Strahd?" Magda said, shuddering. There was an oppressive feel to the castle, an air of subdued mystery that reminded her of nothing so much as the mausoleum from which she'd rescued Andari when they were children. He'd gone in to rob the dead, but all he'd gotten for the trouble was a broken ankle from a falling stone.

"Ah, Lord Soth, Magda. I am Count Strahd Von Zarovich, ruler of Barovia. Thank you for accepting my invitation."

The Vistani started at the smooth voice, but the death knight turned with an air of disinterest to the man who had appeared at the top of the broad flight of stairs. "You must forgive me for not greeting you at the door," the master of Castle Ravenloft said evenly. "I was in one of the tower rooms when you arrived, reading some tomes of . . . sentimental value."

The count took the stairs slowly, with a studied elegance. His long black cape floated behind him. Yet
the cloak could not hide the strength in its wearer,
strength possessed only by great warriors.

The lord of Barovia was tall, just over six feet. A
tight, formal jacket hugged his lean frame. He wore
black pants and polished dark leather boots. A chain
of gold links hung from his neck and ended in a large
red stone that sharply reflected the torchlight. His
white shirt stood in stark contrast to the rest of his
attire, and the count wore its pointed collar turned
up. The white cloth framed his strong chin like
dove's wings.

As he reached the foot of the stairs, he bowed to
the death knight. His face was pale, with high cheekbones and dark hair brushed back from his forehead.
Black, arched brows rested over probing eyes. He
rested his gaze on the armored dead man and waited
for him to bow in return.

Soth scowled. "Let us not waste time with pleas-
antries, Count," he said. "Why have you brought me
here?"

Strahd held up a gray-gloved hand in lieu of an-
swering, then turned his hypnotic eyes to Magda.
"The trip has not been an easy one for you, my dear.
I'm sure Lord Soth meant to cause you no discomfort
in taking you through the forest, but—" he pulled his
thin lips into a smile "—like me, he is a soldier. Soldiers tend to forget everyone is not as disciplined as
they themselves must be."

The woman looked down at her mud-splattered
legs and her torn skirt. "My apologies, Your Excellency, I—"

Again Strahd smiled, this time more unctuously.
The expression was every bit as frightening to see as

a wolf's snarl. "Think nothing of it," he said, his voice a mesmerizing purr. "However, I do think it would be best for you to change out of those ragged clothes. There are some dresses in the next room, old but in good condition. One might fit you. Please go and try them on."

To emphasize the invitation, Strahd extended a hand toward the small room across from the stairs. Magda walked shyly to the vaulted room. "The doors to your right," the count noted patiently. "Modesty will demand you close them behind you. Take your time changing. We will be waiting here when you are through."

Strahd kept a smile plastered on his pale face until the doors clicked shut behind her, then he looked to the death knight. The polite facade had vanished. "Your question is a bit vague, Lord Soth, but I will answer it anyway. I do not, as you suspect, control the mists that brought you to Barovia." He waited for some reaction from Soth. When it was obvious none would be forthcoming, he added, "I brought you to my home as a gesture of politeness. It is my way of apologizing for the unfortunate treatment you received from Madame Girani."

"You admit the Vistani are your spies?"

"Nothing so formal as all that," Strahd replied. "I grant them certain privileges, and they offer me information about visitors to my land. It's all very casual. Still, I will admit that I asked Madame Girani to discover what she could about you."

"Why? What interest am I to you?" Soth's hand drifted threateningly to the hilt of his sword.

A flush of anger passed over the count's face, and his dark eyes took on the character of burning embers, red-hot sparks. "You are a guest in my home and in my land," he said with forced calm. "Let us assume you had good reason for attacking the gypsies. They have paid for whatever slight they may have given you. But do not think I will allow you to threaten me. Even with your curse, I am still your master in experience. Do not underestimate my wrath."

Soth smiled inwardly at the count's attitude. Had Strahd not taken offense, the death knight would have assumed him a fool or a weakling. Either conclusion would have precipitated an attack.

"My apologies, Count," Lord Soth said, relaxing his hand. At last he returned Strahd's courteous bow. "My journey to your land was quite unexpected and quite unwelcome. I desire now only to find my seneschal and travel back to my home."

Strahd arched one jet-black eyebrow. "Seneschal? Do you mean the ghost who entered the land with you?"

"What news do you have of him? Is he here?"

"Alas, no," the count replied. "He made it to this castle and attempted to enter without my permission. My home is protected by certain magical wards—quite ancient and deadly, even to the undead. This . . . seneschal of yours was destroyed utterly by one of those wards." After a suitable pause, he added, "My condolences, Lord Soth. Were you close to the man?"

The death knight didn't hear the count's question. Caradoc destroyed? The notion was almost impossible to believe. Had he been robbed of his revenge against the traitorous ghost? And what about Kitiara? This would make finding her soul all the more difficult. Ah, the death knight cried inwardly, it would be worth almost anything to have had my revenge upon Caradoc. Frustration boiled within him, but something about the tale wasn't quite right.

"How do you know he's dead?" Soth asked.

Strahd shrugged as if the question wasn't of the least importance. "As I said earlier, the wards that destroyed him were magical. While I did not witness his demise as it occurred, the enchantments on the castle are such that I can recreate almost any event that transpires on the grounds."

"Then I, too, wish to see how Caradoc expired. Call upon your enchantments."

"Now?" Strahd asked, incredulous at Soth's audacity.

When Soth nodded, the count rubbed his chin. "I do this because you are my guest, Lord Soth, and because I wish to be open with you."

With a slight gesture, Strahd called up a reduced image of the keep's huge portcullis. The gate appeared faintly at the room's center, and as Soth watched, Caradoc crept toward it. The ghost's neck was broken, his gait slow and labored. There was no sound from the phantom scene, but the death knight guessed that something followed close on Caradoc's heels; every few steps he looked back, his eyes wide with fear. He tried to pass through the portcullis, but a bolt of bright light struck him the moment he touched it. The grim result was over quickly. Caradoc stiffened under the violent lashings of the magical bolt, then opened his mouth to scream. Finally, he faded away, leaving no trace.

As the image faded, the count turned from his guest and studied the ruined frescos overhead. "This keep is well over four hundred years old. It's hardly the luxurious place it once was, but—"

"You are obviously a mage." Soth motioned toward the spot where Caradoc's demise had played itself out. "Is that how you learned my name, how you kept track of my movement through the countryside—

magic?"

Strahd sighed and faced the death knight once more. "I know a great deal about you, Lord Soth. More than you might imagine. As you have guessed already, the Vistani are but one source of information for me. However, it would hardly be prudent of me to reveal all my secrets to you. In time—"

At that instant Magda entered the room. A sleek floor-length gown of red silk flowed from her bare shoulders. The fabric hissed along the stone floor, stirring up dust. Magda's bare feet peeked out from under the hem. "Thank you, Your Excellency," she said. "It's a beautiful gown, far more lovely than anything I've ever owned."

The count watched her cross the floor, his attention ensnared by her beauty and simple grace. She had obviously found the pitcher of water he'd left out; the mud on her cheeks had been replaced by a rosy blush of modesty. She'd also put her hair up in a style that emphasized the curve of her neck. "A dress is a collection of cloth snippets sewn together. It is made lovely by the person who wears it."

Magda curtsied in response, proud to wear the count's gift and certain she had been given the gown as a reward for bringing Soth to the castle. Then her eyes spotted the death knight. She shuddered visibly. "Lord Soth," the woman began. Her words trailed off into uncomfortable silence.

"The knight is still on edge from his journey," Strahd said amiably. His eyes remained locked on the woman, on the soft white flesh of her shoulders. "Let us retire to the hall for a little food and some entertainment."

"I do not require food," Soth noted hollowly.

Strahd placed a hand on the death knight's shoulder. "But the young lady does," he said. "And I am certain you will find the entertainment to your liking."

With a single, long stride, Soth stepped from the count's grasp. The fact that the nobleman's hand, though gloved, looked none the worse for its contact with his form did not escape the death knight. "I do not see the need, Count. I want information, not diversions."

Magda froze, afraid to disturb the tense silence that settled on the room. Strahd and Soth remained a few feet apart, their gazes locked. Without raising his arm, the count secretly traced a pattern in the air with his fingertip. Neither the knight nor the Vistani noticed the casual movement.

A high keening rang out in the next room, the sound of a violin played masterfully. The music crept into the hall where Strahd and his guests still stood. "Ah, he's started without us," the count noted, feigning mild surprise.

As the mournful music continued, a look of puzzlement crossed Magda's face. "There was no one else in there a moment ago . . . and there is no way into the room except through here." She moved to the open door and peered into the massive hall where she had changed clothes.

Three crystal chandeliers of enormous size lit the room. Pillars of stone stood at attention along the white marble walls. The long wooden table dominating the hall was covered by a fine satin tablecloth, as spotlessly white as the ceiling and walls. The clothes Magda had tried on—and the rags she had discarded—covered the table close to the door; place settings for three, along with steaming dishes of meat, soups, and vegetables, lay at the opposite end.

The food and the dishes had not been there when

Magda had changed clothes a few moments earlier, yet the Vistani barely noticed the roast or the red wine, even though her stomach was quite empty and her head light from eating so little during the day. No, her attention was riveted by the lone figure at the other end of the hall.

The musician stood before a massive pipe organ, framed by two mirrors that ran along the wall from the floor to the ceiling. A multicolored scarf covered his head, a black scarf protected his neck, and a sash girded his thin waist. His black pants were torn and dotted with blood, as was the billowing white shirt he wore. His head bowed, the man moved stiffly as he played his ancient violin, for all the world like a mechanical toy Magda had seen once in the village.

His song ended, the musician lifted his head. Magda screamed, "Andari!" then staggered a few steps forward.

The Vistani was at her brother's side before she saw how sickly he looked. His usually dark skin was pale, his eyes watery and unfocused. "Andari?" When he did not respond, she placed her hand against his cheek. It was cold and bloodless.

"Your brother barged into the village late this afternoon, warning everyone about the creature that had destroyed Madame Girani," Strahd said from the doorway. He turned to Soth. "As I told you earlier, I am quite disappointed in that tribe's treatment of you. Girani's kin will be hunted down and destroyed for the insult. Andari is only the first."

The room swam before Magda's eyes. She reached up to steady herself against her brother, who had just lowered his head to begin another tune. "Do not be concerned, Magda," she heard Strahd say. "Because you have cooperated with Lord Soth, I will spare you." The voice seemed to come from far, far away.

With a soft cry, the woman crumpled to the floor, unconscious. As she fell, Magda jerked the violin from Andari's grasp, but the being who was once her brother failed to notice. He moved his bow over the air just as if he were still holding the heirloom once so dear to him.

Strahd sighed. "My surprise seems to have exhausted her completely."

"Why do this?" Lord Soth asked, though he was unmoved by the woman's plight.

"Exactly as I have said. Andari came into the village, trumpeting what transpired at the Vistani camp. He was eavesdropping on the old woman's caravan, so he knew all that was said between you and Madame Girani. I learned of this, decided you had been insulted, and chose to make reparations for that slight in the manner you see before you." Strahd strolled casually into the hall. "Is the payment sufficient?"

Soth followed his host. "Yes. It will do."

Strahd's mood seemed to lighten greatly. "Fine," he said. With a flourish, he tossed his cape over one shoulder and bent down to take the Vistani in his arms. He lifted the unconscious woman easily. "I will see to Magda. There are empty rooms upstairs where she can rest. Remain here, if you don't mind, and I will return shortly. There is much for us to discuss."

Without waiting for a reply, the count walked away, the girl held firmly in his arms. "I believe you will find the wait worthwhile, Lord Soth," he added as he reached the door. "I have something very valuable to offer you."

The sound of Strahd humming the tune Andari had played came from the adjoining room, then from the spiral stairs. When the noise had grown faint, the death knight crossed his arms over his chest and gazed around the room.

The death knight studied one of the large mirrors towering to either side of the massive pipe organ. For the first time in many years he saw himself—scorched armor, flowing cape, burning orange eyes—yet his own reflection was not what interested Soth. A moment earlier, Strahd had lifted Magda and walked past that same mirror. As the count had passed the silvered glass, he had cast no reflection.

Soth pondered this as he walked to Andari's side. The Vistani was still fingering the air where the strings should have been and moving his bow mechanically back and forth. With care, the death knight removed the black scarf covering the man's neck. His throat had been torn open, and the flesh around the gaping wound hung in tatters.

"Yes," Soth said softly, "the count is a man of many surprises."

Gently the death knight replaced the scarf, then retrieved the fallen violin. After placing the instrument in the Vistani's hands, he sat at the long table. In a room filled with melancholy music, the death knight waited for his host to return.

*   *   *   *   *

The door to the bedroom opened of its own accord as Strahd approached. Like everything else in Castle Ravenloft, it recognized its lord and master.

A single four-poster dominated the room. The white sheets were musty and moths had damaged the gauzy cloth that hung from the canopy, but in the light from the room's single torch the bed looked luxurious. The count lowered Magda onto the mattress. His face half in shadows, he stood back to admire the woman.

The Vistani's hair had fallen loose. The raven curls spread around her head in a stark contrast to the whiteness of the pillow. Strahd's eyes followed a line from her cheeks, pale from shock, to the gentle curve of her neck and bare, tanned shoulders. He ran his tongue over his cruel lips. An involuntary hiss escaped those lips as a wave of lust swept over him.

The woman's eyes fluttered open, and the sight that greeted her was far more horrifying than the one that had sapped her strength earlier. Strahd loomed over the bed, surrounded by sheets of moth-eaten gossamer. His eyes were closed, but his mouth was open wide enough to reveal sharp white fangs.

Magda screamed when Strahd grabbed her. "I should kill you for what you know," he hissed. His eyes were open now and glowed red.

With the discipline of hundreds of years of existence as a vampire, Strahd Von Zarovich fought the urge to drink deeply of the Vistani's blood. Plenty of other unfortunates filled the larder the count kept in the dungeons; he would sup on one of them before the night was through.

"The dark powers smile on you this night, girl." Strahd let her go. "I have a use for you. Listen closely."

Magda scuttled backward on the bed, her dress riding up her legs as she moved. When she had pressed herself against the wall and drawn her knees up to her chest, Strahd continued.

"Now that you are comfortable," he said smoothly, the mesmerizing purr coming back into his voice, "I can state my generous offer." Strahd smiled. "I want you to continue as Lord Soth's guide. In return for this service, I will allow you to live."

"W—Where am I to lead him?" Magda managed at last.

"The death knight will be undertaking an errand for me," the count replied. "You will lead him to his destination and report back to me each day through an ensorcelled brooch I will give to you."

As best she could, Magda forced the fear from her eyes and stilled the trembling of her hands. "We Vistani live to serve you, Your Excellency," she said evenly, letting her body relax. The lie was spoken with the same practiced air that had served her well in selling useless trinkets to boyars in the village; Strahd was no uneducated shopkeeper, however.

Strahd was amused at her false humility. He took her chin in his hand and looked deeply into her eyes. "I think you realize I am a man of my word, Magda. Serve me well, and you will be rewarded."

The count crossed the room. "Do not leave here until I call for you," he said. "I will tell Lord Soth you are resting after your long trek."

Strahd closed the heavy door but did not lock it. This could be a test of sorts for the Vistani, he decided. If she followed his command and remained cloistered until the sun set tomorrow night, she could be trusted to carry out further orders. If she disobeyed . . . well, the castle was very well guarded, and the creatures that patrolled the halls during the day would tear her to bits.

Content with the plan, Strahd paced quickly through the halls. He entered a small room without knocking, startling the lone figure who occupied it.

"My lord," Caradoc said. The ghost bowed, but his broken neck made the gesture look more comic than courtly.

Strahd gestured for the seneschal to rise. "Lord Soth has arrived," the vampire murmured, a hint of malicious glee in his words. "He is everything you said he would be."

 **SEVEN**

The sound of the count's voice flushed a rat from its hiding place on the landing that spread out just ahead of the vampire and the death knight. The bloated, mangy creature squinted at the pair in the stairwell. Its beady eyes shone red in the faint light from Strahd's candelabra.

"Ah," the count said, genuinely pleased, "you do your job well."

After a long, wavering squeal, the rat waddled ponderously to a crack in the masonry. Strahd, satisfied with the report he'd just received, continued walking into a small hallway off the landing. "The rats are but one of the things that guard my home," he said to Lord Soth casually.

Soth had become increasingly aware of quiet, steady sobbing as he followed Strahd. At first it seemed like one voice, but as they moved through the castle he realized it was people crying out together.

The noise emanated from the corridor that branched to Soth's left. Pools of putrid water fouled its floor, and black beetles the size of the pommel on the death knight's sword scurried everywhere. From behind the decaying wooden doors lining both sides of the hall, weeping and pleading melded into one mournful chorus.

These were the first signs of human life the fallen knight had detected in his tour through Castle Ravenloft. The place was huge but seemingly as bereft of people as Soth's own keep. If Dargaard had its collection of banshees and skeletal warriors, Strahd's keep was home mostly to rats and spiders and very little else—at least little that the death knight had seen.

In all, the place struck Soth as a monument to decay. Paintings and statues filled many rooms, but all the artwork had been ravaged by time. Strahd had pointed out the keep's chapel, a huge room that once had housed a magnificent collection of stained glass windows. Now the windows were broken or boarded over. The chapel itself was littered with shattered benches, its altar unused.

Strahd looked behind him and saw his guest staring into the hallway that contained his larder. The vampire frowned and unlocked the iron-braced door before him. "This way, if you please, Lord Soth. I want you to meet a man who holds information you'll find most intriguing." The death knight forced his attention away from the pleading of Strahd's victims and followed his host into a large room. The door closed with a resounding thud.

"Good evening, Ambassador Pargat," the vampire lord said. He held his candelabra up high, but its light was too feeble to illuminate the entire room. "I have brought you a visitor."

Wary of treachery, Soth tensed and gripped the hilt of his sword. There was no telling what the room housed.

Strahd frowned. "He must be sleeping." When he saw the death knight's militant stance, he added,

"Have no fear, Lord Soth. The ambassador can do no one harm as he is now."

At a word from the vampire, torches all along the walls of the large room burst into flame. Apart from the doors standing at the center of three of the chamber's sides, nothing man-made adorned the cold stone walls. Lichen and green-tinted ichor oozed from between the blocks and pooled on the floor. A few spider webs, as big as Soth and as geometrically precise as Palanthas's streets, clouded the corners. If the spiders were larger than normal, the death knight could not tell, for they remained hidden. That the unseen web-builders were unusual seemed confirmed by the good-sized rats that hung in the webs, paralyzed and encased in silk.

The ambassador lay at the room's center, surrounded by a framework of metal as intricate as the giant spider webs. The device squatted on eight legs wrought of thick steel. Bands of silver stretched between these legs, suspending the man above the floor and holding his limbs fully extended. A series of weights, pulleys, and counterweights hung over the prisoner, attached to a bronze axe blade and a bristling array of daggers, some silver, some bronze.

"I repeat: Good evening, Ambassador Pargat."

The prisoner started awake and mumbled something incomprehensible. Again Strahd frowned, hard lines creasing his face. "Is that the best you can do? I'm afraid it's not good enough by half."

Ambassador Pargat began to whimper pitiably as the lord of Castle Ravenloft glided to his side. The vampire placed the candelabra on the floor, then stroked his chin in thought. "Ah," he exclaimed at last. "We've damaged your tongue, have we?" He idly fingered the razor-edged silver blade that hung over Pargat's face. "I should have foreseen this problem."

As the vampire removed the bloodstained silver blade and exchanged it for a fresh bronze one, Lord Soth came forward to examine the torture device. When the ambassador saw the newcomer standing over him he pleaded and cursed and whined. Soth could not understand the man's garbled words, but his meaning was clear by the desperate panic in his eyes.

Strahd absently gestured toward the prisoner. "Lord Soth, this is Ambassador Pargat. He is a messenger from Duke Gundar, who rules a bordering duchy called—creatively enough—Gundarak."

A thin man and not very tall, Ambassador Pargat seemed, nonetheless, quite strong; the metal framework groaned when he pulled against it. The manacles Strahd had placed around his wrists, waist, and ankles were composed of an odd sort of webbed steel, more flexible than chains, but just as effective. Pargat's buttonless white shirt was shredded, and its blood-rimmed holes revealed a few wounds, pink, healthy skin elsewhere. The same was true of his ravaged leather boots and breeches. All the holes were aligned with the blades that hung threateningly from the frame.

"I do not enjoy torture," Strahd said apologetically. He stood back and seemed to reflect.

Soth was certain the count was admiring his own handiwork. "It looks to be an ingenious creation," the death knight said.

With a ragged sigh, Ambassador Pargat stopped pleading.

"It is quite simple, really," the count began, warming instantly to the topic. "The weights and pulleys move the blades. They can keep the machine in operation for hours without anyone here to maintain it."

The vampire circled the metal frame, fussing over the blades and adjusting the tension on the weights. "You may have noticed some of the blades are silver, others merely bronze. That is because Ambassador Pargat is a lycanthrope, a wererat to be precise." He shifted to the prisoner's head and ran a gloved hand along his cheek.

Soth touched one of the ambassador's wounds, making the man flinch and choke back a scream. "The silver blades cause him pain, the others cannot because of his unnatural healing abilities as a were-creature."

"Just so."

Now Soth circled the machine. "And you take a silver blade away for every piece of information he gives you?"

A smile slithered across Strahd's features. "Just the opposite. For every item about his master he reveals, I *add* a silver blade. Sooner or later the pain or the sheer number of wounds will kill him." He stroked the prisoner's blood-caked hair. "I'm certain Pargat would like it to be sooner. This gives him . . . *incentive* to reveal all he knows quickly. Correct, Ambassador?"

Pargat's words were incomprehensible, but the tone identified them as a string of curses. "How rude," Strahd said with mock indignation. Pointedly he replaced the bronze blade over the prisoner's left eye with a silver one.

Soth studied the man's features. Pargat's pale blue eyes were watery, his thin face taut with pain. His nostrils flared, making his thin nose look deformed and his wispy mustache bristle like whiskers. A large, gaping slice in his cheek revealed white, broken teeth and the remains of his tongue. Whenever the man tried to speak, the wound bubbled with saliva and blood. "What information does this man have that might interest me in the least?" Soth asked.

Placing a hand on the death knight's arm, Strahd smiled. "There is but one way for you to escape this hellish place, and that is through a portal—a rare gateway between this and some other world. Ambassador Pargat knows the location of one of these rare gateways."

"This man knows of a portal back to Krynn?"

"He knows the location of a portal that leads *from* this netherworld," Strahd corrected. "I do not know what lies on the other side of the gateway. Still, a being of your resources should have little trouble getting back to Krynn—once you escape the duchies, that is."

The vampire ran a finger along the edge of the bronze axe blade that hung over Pargat's throat. It swung back and forth on a well-oiled track. "I know the portal stands somewhere in Duke Gundar's castle. When the ambassador sees fit to tell me its exact location, I will replace this blade with one of silver. His life and his torment will be ended almost instantly."

"How long has he been here?" Soth asked.

"Three days," Strahd answered. He watched his prisoner's features, scanning them for signs of weakness. "Gundar sent him to deliver an ultimatum regarding some mundane mercantile matter—freedom of movement for tradesmen or some similar drivel."

The death knight shook his head and turned away. "If he has not revealed what you want to know after three days of torture, he will not break."

"You are too hasty, Lord Soth," the count said, picking up the candelabra again. "On the first day, the machine ran for only a few minutes. The second, for an hour. Tonight, I will let it run for several hours."

The vampire turned to the prisoner. "Then you will probably fall unconscious from the pain, but have no fear, I will not let you die."

Without looking at Pargat, Strahd pulled the lever that set the machine in motion. "Come, Lord Soth. We will return in a little while to see if the blades jog his memory."

The death knight stole a glance over his shoulder as he followed his host from the room. With a shudder, the frame began to move, lowering and raising the blades with clocklike precision. The axe head swung like a pendulum, slicing into Pargat's throat, and the newly placed silver blade dug into his eye. The prisoner screeched and arched his back, not to avoid the blades, but to push them deeper in hopes of causing himself a mortal wound.

As the door closed behind Soth and Strahd, the vampire smiled. "I let Pargat sleep because sleep is very much like death. If he yearns for sleep's respite from pain, he will tell me what I want to know all the sooner so he can rest eternally."

"Can't you cast a spell to read his mind?"

Shaking his head, the count started down the hall. "Duke Gundar, or his son, to be more precise, is a mage of no small skill. They've never been foolish enough to send anyone here without magical protection from such spells." He shook his head. "The first ambassador exploded most unfortunately when I tried to question him magically."

As the count turned down the door-lined hallway, Soth asked, "Is Magda in one of these rooms?"

"She rests comfortably upstairs," the vampire replied. He studied the death knight, a hint of surprise in his dark eyes. "Why do you ask? Is she important to you?"

"Hardly," the death knight replied emotionlessly.

"Curiosity only."

"Of course," Strahd said, a bit too quickly. He moved to the last of the doors and stopped.

Soth followed, stepping over the puddles of filth and masses of beetles that covered the floor. Since Strahd and Soth both moved silently, the pitiable cries of the cell's inmates were all the more clarion in the hall.

"Why have you forsaken me, Gods of Light?" one woman cried.

"No," a man with a low, gravelly voice called out. "We'll find a way out. Only one of us needs to escape. Let's work together." When no one responded to his call, he futilely repeated it over and over.

From behind another wooden door, a man sobbed uncontrollably. Every few seconds a burst of words erupted from the room, spoken in a language the death knight had never heard before.

"In here, Lord Soth," the count said from the open door at the hall's end.

The tiny room beyond was barren save for a small table, a stool, and an empty fireplace. Strahd placed the candelabra upon the rickety table, revealing a wizened old man, his sightless white eyes searching the cell in vain. He sat upon the stool and probed the air with scarred, bloody fingertips. His parched lips moved soundlessly.

"You asked earlier how I came to know so much about you," Strahd began as he entered the cell. With stately elegance he moved to one dripping wall. "This is Voldra, a mystic of some competence, though mute, deaf, and blind to the mundane world around him."

The vampire whispered a command, and a small door opened in the stone. A crystal ball, as milky white as Voldra's eyes and long, scraggly beard, rested inside the secret alcove. "With this," the count explained, lifting the ball gingerly with one gloved hand, "Voldra can tell me things about those who serve me and those who work against me."

"Can he tell us more about this Duke Gundar or the portal that lies in his castle?"

"Urrr," the mystic moaned when the crystal ball came in contact with his bony fingers. He began to weave a pattern over the crystal, smudging the glass with blood from his fingers.

"He is starved for contact with the outer world," Strahd said, then added matter-of-factly, "The wounds he gained during his latest attempt to claw his way out of the cell."

The death knight and the vampire watched Voldra as he traced an intricate design upon the glass. After a time, Strahd retrieved a quill and parchment from the hidden alcove and placed them on the table. "He will answer your question, though he did not hear it. I don't quite understand how his powers work, but I am usually quite pleased with the information he provides."

Shuddering violently, the old mystic grabbed the pen and wrote a brief message. His hands shook, and the effort of penning each word seemed to tax his whole frame. When Voldra finished, he slumped forward in exhaustion.

The count pulled the paper out from under the old man's thin arm and read it aloud:

" 'The blood of a child who was never an innocent opens the door in Castle Hunadora. Madness is not weakness, so beware the undying son.' "

Strahd crumpled the parchment. "This is hardly useful," he sighed and lifted the old man from the stool. Voldra hung limp in the vampire's grasp like a rag doll in the hands of a small child. "Let us try again, shall we?"

The count set the mystic in front of the crystal ball, and the man wearily set about the task of calling forth a better answer to his captor's query. "This is the same message Voldra offered the last time I had him search for information regarding the portal," Strahd explained, tossing the parchment into the empty fireplace. "It tells me nothing new. The problem is distance, I believe. The farther Voldra is from the object or person he's attempting to divine, the more nebulous and rambling the message he produces."

Soth walked to the fireplace and retrieved the message. After reading the note, he let it drop to the filthy floor. "Is the child the mystic mentioned known to you?"

Glancing at Voldra, who was still weaving his pattern over the orb, the master of Castle Ravenloft nodded. "The child is Gundar's son. To open the portal, one must enter the duke's home—the Castle Hunadora to which Voldra referred—and spill his or his son's blood. The blood is the key somehow. The important question is: Where in the castle does the gateway stand?"

"How do you know their blood will open the portal?" the death knight asked.

"Legend, information gained from ambassadors and refugees from Gundarak, Vistani lore, Voldra's rambling." The vampire wrapped himself in his cloak and stretched luxuriously, like a bat waking after a long day's sleep. "So many sources cannot be wrong."

A silence covered the room as both the count and the death knight considered the rewards the venture against Duke Gundar offered. For his part, Lord Soth wondered if this might truly be his road back to

Krynn, back to Kitiara. With Caradoc dead, he would need to search for the tanar'ri lord who held the general's soul, but that did not matter. Nothing would prevent him from recapturing her life force and resurrecting her as his immortal consort.

The vampire's mind curled around evil plans, too. For many, many years, Strahd and Gundar had exchanged unpleasantries. The count made it a policy to murder every ambassador sent by the duke, and the duke returned the insult in kind. It had become a perverse sort of challenge to the dark lords to offer up an envoy who would not die too easily; of course, they sent men on these journeys with whom they were fatally displeased. That coy game was growing stale to the count.

The cries of the prisoners and the sound of Voldra's fingers rubbing along the glass underscored his thoughts. For a time, the mystic continued to create his pattern with steady, mechanical movements. Suddenly his hands slid with urgency over the orb. He fumbled for the pen and began to scrawl a note. Like before, Voldra's thin frame shook as the answer forced its way through him to the blank page.

"His answer is much longer this time," Strahd noted. The vampire and the death knight hovered over the old man, waiting for him to complete his scribbling. When Voldra at last sank to the tabletop, drained of energy, the count lifted the parchment.

" 'Success will cost you everything,' " the vampire read. He squinted at the page, unable to decipher a few words. "There are a few unreadable scribbles, then it continues: 'End at the beginning, and . . .' "

Strahd again turned the paper so the light from the candelabra illuminated the scrawled message. The paper cast a huge shadow against the far wall, but the vampire—like all his kind—did not. "I fear a second reading with no rest wore Voldra out. Most of this is impossible to read." He glanced at Soth and added, "The only other thing I can make out is the last line: 'The general with the crooked smile is lost to you forever.' "

The death knight stiffened and, without preamble, snatched the page from Strahd's hands. He read what he could of the message, and, as the count had foretold, it ended with a clearly legible conclusion. The general with the crooked smile, he fumed. That was Kitiara!

"You said he could divine something about the duke's castle, about the location of the portal?" Soth rumbled as he tore the paper in two.

Strahd leaned against the table with feline grace and steepled his slender, gloved fingers. "Voldra answers whatever question is most pressing to the people close at hand. I take it, then, you know this general?"

With a lightning quickness, the death knight snatched the crystal ball from the table. He raised it over his head and dashed it against the filthy stone floor. A brilliant flash lit the room, and a thunderclap shook the table, rattling the door on its iron hinges. When the twisting, noxious cloud of multicolored haze dissipated, Soth and Strahd stood face to face.

"You fool!" Strahd shouted. "That crystal cannot be replaced!" He gestured to the old man. Voldra's beard and hair had been burned away, and much of his right side was blackened from the explosion. "Without the crystal, he's of little use to me."

Soth folded his arms across his chest. "I do not approve of others plumbing my thoughts," he said flatly. "I killed the Vistani witch for that offense. The old man is no different. If you say he's unable to scry without the crystal, then he's of less use to me. I would enjoy killing him."

"Your enjoyment means nothing," the vampire hissed. He dropped to one knee beside Voldra and curled his long fingers around the old man's neck. A wheezing breath escaped the mystic's lips, then the count twisted Voldra's head savagely, breaking his neck. Strahd never took his eyes from Soth.

When the lord of Castle Ravenloft stood again, his face was flushed with fury. "I am the master of this domain, Soth, and I hold the key to your escape. If you want to return to Krynn, if you wish to see your crook-smiled general again, you should remember who your betters are."

Soth's gauntleted hand struck the tabletop, and the worm-eaten wood shattered into hundreds of fragments. The candelabra clattered to the floor, the candles extinguished. "On Krynn I am a favored servant of the dark goddess, Takhisis," he said, taking a step toward Strahd in the darkness. "There she is my master. In Barovia, I recognize no one as my superior."

The death knight swung hard at the count's head. Before Soth's gauntlet rose halfway to its target, the vampire caught his wrist. Strahd held Soth fast, and the two dead men locked gazes. From the corridor, the prisoners' voices howled at the disturbance.

Soth's left hand began to move in a quick, rhythmic pattern. "Do not even think to use a spell against me," Strahd hissed, tightening his grip on the death knight's wrist. The armor buckled slightly at the pressure. "I have studied magic for many mortal lifetimes, and I know spells that will cause you great suffering."

After a moment, when the tension had gone out of Soth's arm, the vampire released him. Strahd pulled his cloak around himself again, and the angry color faded from his cheeks. "There have been other trav-

elers from Krynn in these halls," the count murmured, a trace of amusement in his voice. "In fact,
Voldra and four others arrived in Barovia twenty-
five—no, thirty years ago. They came from a city
named Palanthas."

Soth stood numbly, listening to the count. He had
been human the last time he'd been equally matched
by a foe, and that awareness chilled him to his soul-
less core.

"Voldra called himself a 'Mage of the Red Robes',"
Strahd continued, his eyes glittering in the darkness,
"and he said he was a servant of the great god Gilean,
Patriarch of Neutrality. This Gilean must be a rival to
Takhisis, eh?" The vampire's cloak flowed behind
him as he swooped down on the mystic's corpse.
"Gilean did not send his hosts to punish me when I
ripped out Voldra's tongue. His bearers will not come
to Castle Ravenloft to carry the dead man's body—or
his soul—away to his eternal reward."

Strahd stood, then uncovered the candelabra and
candles in the debris. At a word the stubby pillars of
yellow wax burst into flame. "The gods of Krynn
mean nothing here, death knight. You will serve me,
or you will never escape this place."

In the silence that followed, the cries of the prisoners could be heard again, distinctly.

"Why have you forsaken me, Gods of Light?" a
woman shouted hoarsely.

"Only one of us needs to escape," a man called in a
low, gravelly voice. "Let's work together."

The vampire stifled a sudden yawn. "I will take
your silence as a sign of your consent. A wise
choice."

Shaking off his shock at the vampire's power, the
death knight kicked Voldra's corpse absently. "What
did you do with the other four from Palanthas? Are

they in your larder, too?"

Strahd tilted his head. "Voldra was the only one of any use to me. The others I let wander in the duchy as they wished." He rubbed his chin pensively. "One of them is still alive, a fat cleric named Terlarm. He lives in the village."

The master of Castle Ravenloft glided to the door. "I am afraid we will have to continue our chat this evening, Lord Soth. It is getting close to sunrise, and I'm afraid I am a bit fatigued by our . . . discussion." He turned his back on the death knight and disappeared into the hallway.

The stench of Voldra's burned flesh filling his nose and the wailing of the captives pounding in his ears, Lord Soth remained in the tiny cell. He was indeed far from home, cut off from Takhisis, cut off from the banshees and skeletal warriors who had always done his bidding in the past. Yet the death knight had never been one to accept servitude easily.

A rat peered tentatively into the room from the doorway. It watched Soth with black, beady eyes and twitched its nose probingly at him. As Soth moved toward it, the carrion-fattened creature crouched slightly but did not run.

"Does Strahd think me so beaten his vermin spies do not fear me?" Soth whispered softly. He raised a boot and crushed the rat with a single kick. The creature's death squeal was echoed by a dozen of its kin in various parts of the hall. That attack, the death knight knew, would be reported to Strahd as an act of defiance. It would matter little; Soth intended to do far worse before the sun set.

 **EIGHT**

Magda stood before a torch, watching its steady flame. A product of magic, the wood feeding the fire replenished itself as quickly as it was burned up. She had been in the small bedroom for a long time—hours, perhaps.

"If I stay here, the count will make me one of his slaves," she began, repeating the argument she'd been having with herself since Strahd had left her. She pictured her brother, his eyes as blank as a corpse's, playing sad music in the hall. The image made her shudder anew with fear and revulsion.

Old Vistani tales often concerned vampires, and Magda knew quite well the horror that awaited her if the count chose to feed upon her. A wretched, starving thing, she would be forced to do Strahd's bidding. She would stalk the night, drawing others to their doom so that she might live on their blood. It was a terrible fate.

If only there were a window in the room. Daylight was the enemy of vampires. Shielded by the light of day, she might find the courage to venture into the hall. At least she could be certain Strahd would be asleep in his coffin then.

"The count is not foolish enough to leave the halls

unguarded while he sleeps," she countered, closing her eyes. "But day or night, Strahd will kill me if I stay. If I try to escape, at least I have a chance."

Magda looked once more into the torch's flames. In camp, with Andari's music compelling her to dance, she would have been able to call up an image of ancient Vistani heroes. But even without the shadow play, as Madame Girani had called the flame-borne images, she still remembered the stories—tales of great heroism, of daring escapes and heart-stopping rescues.

A smile crossed her face as she called one such tale to mind, the story of Kulchek and the giant. The tales concerning Kulchek were Magda's favorites. This particular yarn told how the wily hero had out-smarted a giant, stole his beautiful daughter, and escaped from a trap-laden castle. Andari had always hated such tales, for they were too fantastic for his liking or his limited imagination. His taunts had never lessened Magda's love for the stories, however. Andari would take back those jibes now if he could, she thought darkly.

Her resolve strengthened, Magda tied her long red dress into a knot at her waist. She was surprised to find her hands shook only a little. Perhaps I am braver than I thought, she decided. After all, I survived the journey to the castle in the company of an undead knight. Why shouldn't I be able to escape back to the forest? Taking the torch, she went to the door and opened it cautiously.

The light sent a few rats scurrying for their hiding places. From fissures in the stone walls, the bloated vermin watched the Vistani creep from the bedroom. On the ceiling, centipedes the length of Magda's arm pulsed forward on hundreds of thin, clutching legs. The woman flinched at the sight but pressed on.

Such mundane creatures were certain to be the least frightening thing she would encounter.

A single cobweb-covered stair led from the hall. There were no windows, no doors. Magda quietly crept toward that narrow staircase, holding the torch before her in much the same way a cleric presented a holy symbol to a creature of darkness. Before she mounted the first step, she heard something shuffling down the stairs toward her.

Without hesitating an instant, Magda headed for the bedroom. She reached for the brass doorknob, but it resisted her attempts to turn it. The sound of the creature's heavy footfalls grew louder in the hallway as it neared the bottom of the stairs. A scream of panic welling in her throat, Magda tried the door again, but again it would not open. Somehow, the door had locked behind her. She held the torch to the right and left, but the walls appeared solid save for the few cracks inhabited by vermin and insects. She was trapped.

"Somethin's out o' place," came a voice from the darkened stairway. The words were hissed in a voice that sounded like metal grinding against stone. "Somethin' that needs light t'see."

Magda threw her back against the solid wooden door in an attempt to break it open. The footfalls stopped, and two glowing blue eyes appeared in the darkness at the foot of the stairs. "It's a she somethin'," the creature said gleefully.

With a shaking hand, the Vistani held the torch at arm's length. The creature chuckled crassly from the shadows. "Want t'see me, do you?" it asked and stepped into the circle of light.

The creature was manlike and stood about four feet tall. Rough, obsidian skin covered its thin frame, from the tip of the single twisted horn that jutted from its forehead to the end of the long, spiny tail that ran from its lower back. Its eyes were wide and staring, its nose little more than two holes, its mouth a wide, drooling chasm. With a flutter of movement, the creature folded small, leathery wings tight against its shoulders, then crouched and let its three-fingered hands scrape against the floor. As the guardian studied Magda with its blue eyes, it ran a gray, forked tongue over its pointed teeth.

"Master'll be wantin' you, I think," it said. The creature spoke slowly, as if moving its jaw caused great pain. With a start, Magda realized she had seen this creature, or ones similar to it, all around the castle. It was a gargoyle, animated by sorcery, that stood before her.

The obsidian creature leaned forward and thrust a hand at Magda's leg. With a small shriek of surprise, the woman leaped back and swung at the gargoyle with the torch. A resounding crack echoed through the hall. The flaming club rebounded off the stone-skinned arm, jarring Magda's shoulders. The light from the cracked torch dimmed a little; the torch was magical, but obviously not indestructible.

"Want t'play, do you?" the gargoyle hissed. It crawled out of the light's reach, rubbing its arm where the magic flame had singed it. Its blue eyes shone malevolently in the darkness.

Keeping the torch between her and the creature, Magda edged toward the stairway. She attempted a prayer to the spirits of her ancestors, but a lump in her throat held the words back. Only a strangled gasp escaped her lips.

One step, then another. The Vistani watched the gargoyle's ice-blue eyes as it retreated from the torchlight. A hope flared in her heart; the creature was leaving! That hope was crushed almost the instant it sprang to life. Without warning, the gargoyle rushed into the torchlight. Its face held a horrifying expression—eyes bulging, fangs bared, and mouth gaping wide. A terrible, grating scream split the air as the creature lurched past the Vistani.

With speed Magda had no hope of countering, the gargoyle raked one taloned hand across the woman's shoulder. Three thin lines of crimson appeared almost instantly, marking the path of the claws. The shoulder began to throb, but the pain was nothing compared to the sickening smell of offal and decayed flesh coming from the creature's hot breath. Gagging, Magda brought one hand to her mouth and fell back against the wall.

Taunting laughter sounded in the hallway, as the creature circled Magda with deceptively heavy footfalls. The Vistani, disoriented from the pain in her shoulder, stumbled along the wall. Her hand brushed across a centipede, and the creature curled around her arm before dropping to the floor and pulsing into the darkness. Magda barely noticed.

"Don't want t'play no more?" the gargoyle hissed facetiously.

Magda had her gaze fixed on the creature's bright blue eyes, so she almost ran into the end of the hallway. Somehow she'd gotten turned around and, instead of the stairway, she'd reached a dead end of stone and mortar. Her shoulders slumped in defeat, and the torch nearly dropped from her hand.

Seeing its opponent drop her defenses, the gargoyle burst into the light. Magda reacted swiftly, though, and thrust the torch into the creature's ice-blue eyes as if it were a long-bladed dagger. A look of horror flashed across the monster's face as the magic flame licked at its eyes and insinuated itself into its nose and gaping mouth. A stench of burned flesh and corrupted earth erupted in the hallway.

"What, no more playing?" the Vistani shouted as the gargoyle careened off the wall next to her, its talons tearing at its scorched, bubbling eyes. Magda found herself laughing uncontrollably at the howls of torment that erupted from the darkness as the creature ran away. When she realized what she was doing, the laughter stopped and tears began to stream down her face.

"I will not let them do this to me," she whispered. "I will not go mad. I will not be like them."

Magda pushed herself off the wall as a low, grinding sound caught her ear. She held the torch low, close to the noise. There, where the stone met the floor, was a short space scraped free of dirt and dust. The wall had moved! Carefully placing the torch at her feet, Magda pushed with all her might. The sound of stone grinding against stone grew louder as a section of wall slid backward.

After retrieving the torch, the Vistani ducked through the low portal into the short corridor that lay beyond. Two sets of double doors lined this hallway, and weak daylight seeped under the doors to Magda's right. Relief and hope made her heart beat faster. With renewed vigor, she clutched the torch and started for the doors.

"Tryin' t'get away," a voice slurred.

Magda turned to see the gargoyle crawling from the secret door. The gray tongue lolling from its mouth was blistered. The obsidian skin around its nose had cracked open, and gray liquid oozed from the wounds. Its eyes had sustained the most damage. One socket gaped empty, though the deep scratches seemed to indicate that the gargoyle itself had clawed the organ out. The other eye was no longer blue, but rather clouded and milky white. The gargoyle could plainly see well enough, though, for that one remaining eye was trained squarely on the Vistani.

Magda ran and pushed through the ornate double doors. The room beyond was huge. Sunlight filtered into the hall through cracked and broken windows, their iron frames hanging askew. There was no furniture there save for a huge throne sitting atop a raised platform. Magda looked desperately from right to left. Two sets of stairs, separated by a narrow wall, ran down from the throne room.

The sound of the gargoyle shuffling down the hallway had just reached the Vistani's ears when she bolted toward the stairs. Her bare feet kicking up little swirls of dust, Magda raced across the grimy floor. It shouldn't be hard to outrun the gargoyle, she told herself as she stumbled down the first steps. She had injured it enough to slow it down.

But the creature's grating, shrieking voice called out from the throne room, much nearer than Magda had figured it would be. "Worse awaits you down there," it shouted. Magda dared a glance over her shoulder and saw the gargoyle floating across the room on its batlike wings.

Luckily the ceiling was too low and the walls too narrow for the creature's wings to be effective on the stairs. Magda leaped down the stone steps three and four at a time, through sheets of cobweb and over the omnipresent rats. After a small landing, the twin sets of stairs joined together and widened into a broad, gentle curve of stone, then emptied into a domed room.

The Vistani recognized the place as the room where she and Soth had first met the count. Torches still lined the walls in iron sconces. Cobwebs hung from the ceiling in gray sheets, obscuring the ancient, peeling frescos high above. Only the leering gargoyles were missing. Their stations around the dome's rim lay empty.

Magda wondered if she should try to recover her dagger and her belongings from the dining hall but abandoned the idea almost as soon as she had thought of it. The gargoyle clomping down the stairs sounded dangerously close. She turned toward the open double doors that led to the entryway and the outside. As she took a step toward that portal, however, something red and scaly moved from the entryway's shadows and blocked the woman's path.

"None may leave without the master's permission," a small red dragon warned from the doorway, its voice sibilant.

The Vistani had never seen anything like the wyrm. It matched her height with the length of its body, and smoke rose menacingly from its nostrils as it spoke. Wings lay folded against its back. They flexed from time to time as the guardian tensed its muscles. Catlike it crouched, studying her with bright, slitted eyes. With mesmerizing slowness, the dragon's head moved back and forth on its long, ridged neck. Magda had seen a snake charmer in a marketplace once, and the hooded serpent dancing to that old man's flute had moved in a similar fashion. The effect was the same, too. The Vistani found herself as captivated by the wyrm as she had been by the serpent in the market.

"Worse t'await you," came a voice from behind the Vistani, followed by a gleeful chuckle. Magda didn't have to look to know the gargoyle had reached the bottom of the stairs. The torch dropped from her suddenly numb fingers. The cracked wood split when it hit the floor, and the torch broke apart into a dozen useless, burning fragments.

* * * * * *

The huge spider chittered as it hopped sideways across the floor. Tufts of stiff black hair covered its body and spindly legs, and its fanged mouth moved reflexively, dribbling poison in sticky threads. It reared back on four of its eight limbs and lurched forward.

Lord Soth paid the creature little mind; the three other monstrous arachnids that had attacked him lay squashed like so many mundane fleas. The sole remaining spider had challenged him repeatedly but had not moved close enough to be a threat. All the death knight needed to do was draw his sword, and the spider would scuttle back to the corner where its web had been destroyed and now carpeted the floor as ashes.

Soth returned his full attention to the thing strapped to the torture device before him. The were-rat was dead, a silver dagger in his heart, another planted firmly in his skull. As the death knight watched, the hairy, elongated snout melted to human features and the pointed ears shrank and rounded. The hunch disappeared from Pargat's back, and the corpse rested flat on the silver bands once again. The ambassador had transformed into a ghastly man-rat just before Soth drove the silver daggers into his vital organs; in death, he returned to his mutilated human form.

"Go to whatever hell awaits you," Soth rumbled as he stepped away from the terrifying bronze and silver device.

The death knight had tried to force the ambassador to reveal the location of the portal in Duke Gundar's castle, but to no avail. Soth was convinced Pargat had told the truth in the end—he could not talk of the portal because of an enchantment Gundar's son had placed upon him. To negate such a spell lay far beyond Soth's skill with magic, so out of irritation he had killed the unfortunate ambassador.

The giant spider edged closer, but Soth turned his back on it and crossed the room. The arachnid waited for the death knight to reach the door, then it hopped forward and loomed over the dead man trapped in the torture device. "Enjoy your dinner," Soth said as he disappeared into the darkened hallway.

A group of rats that had gathered in the hallway housing the vampire's larder scattered when Soth passed by. The death knight crushed the vermin-spies whenever they got underfoot, and word had obviously already passed along their network to avoid the newcomer. The rats found easy escape routes from the larder hall, for the doors to all ten cells had been shattered. Upon leaving Voldra's room, Soth had methodically smashed each door and slit the throats of the unlucky peasants who were being held captive. One man struggled against the blade; the others went to their deaths almost willingly.

Soth watched the rats flee. "The corpses and spilled blood are my gifts to you, in return for your cooperation," he called after the last whiplike tail to slither into a room. "Keep careful track of all that I do this day and report it to your master when he awakens."

The stairs were empty and silent as the death knight made his way to the main floor. As he walked, he considered what further damage he could wreak upon the count's home; Strahd could not be allowed to forget what a mistake he'd made in ordering about Lord Soth of Dargaard Keep as if he were a common servant. And when he'd caused enough havoc, Soth would head for Gundar's castle. He needed no torture-borne confidences to find the gateway back to Krynn.

"None may leave without the master's permission."

The words came from the room beyond the stairs, and Soth paused, waiting for the sibilant voice to speak again. Instead, a different voice—this one high and grating—announced something the death knight could not interpret. Base laughter filled the room and staircase, then something wooden struck the floor.

"Ah, more of Strahd's minions to destroy," the death knight said and walked from the staircase.

A crumbling archway partially obscured the chamber, but Soth saw that Magda stood at the center of the domed room, the flaring fragments of a torch at her feet, a gargoyle crouching to her left. This hideous creature, with its scarred face and razor-sharp talons, laughed again. The braying reminded Soth of the drunken brigands he had often dispatched in his days as a Knight of the Rose.

"Lord Soth!" The Vistani locked her green eyes on the death knight. When she spoke again, the words came haltingly, choked off by fear and uncertainty. "H—Help me."

Like some stone-skinned ape, the gargoyle loped toward Magda. Its hands scraped noisily over the stone floor. "Help me," it mocked. "Ha! Nothin' t'help you now!" It circled the Vistani, eyeing the remains of the torch.

Magda kicked the embers at the gargoyle, and the creature scurried back a few paces. Soth saw her glance to her left, then she said, "Strahd has plans for you, Lord Soth. I know what those plans are."

"Silence!" something hissed from the doorway,

hidden from Soth by the archway.

The death knight stepped into the room, his cloak billowing behind him. What he saw in the doorway astonished him.

A dragon! It was only a small red, but the death knight well knew that any wyrm could prove a deadly opponent. He studied it closely, taking in its stance and its strength. The dragon had raised itself out of its crouch, standing stiff-legged in defiance of the newcomer. Claws as white as sun-bleached bones scraped against the stone as it pushed forward a step. Tail twitching in irritation, the wyrm probed the air with its forked tongue. That's a good sign, Soth noted. It is uncertain how powerful a foe I may prove to be.

The death knight had dealt with red dragons on Krynn; at one time, the evil fire-breathers had been a keystone in Takhisis's evil army. With age, such dragons gained the ability to study spells like any mage. Soth hoped the young red hadn't lived long enough to acquire such enchantments.

"Greetings, Soth of Dargaard," the dragon said. Though its tone was pleasant, smoke puffed in noxious clouds from the dragon's nostrils as it spoke.

The death knight replied coldly, "I am at a disadvantage. Strahd told you who I am, but he failed to mention your name to me."

"Names have power, Soth. Pardon me if I do not offer you mine." The twitch in the dragon's tail grew more insistent, and the beast slithered a step toward the Vistani. "Perhaps if you lower the blade you brandish . . ."

Soth turned to Magda. "Quickly, girl! To my side!"

The Vistani took only a single step forward before a black, three-taloned hand wrapped around her ankle. She hit the floor hard, face-first, and her breath exploded from her lungs. Through tearing eyes, she saw the gargoyle gripping her leg with one hand. The creature ran its blistered tongue over its lips.

At the same time, the dragon shot forward, cutting the woman off from her would-be savior. The wyrm lowered its head and brandished its set of short horns. When Soth stepped toward the woman, it spread its red, leathery wings. "Do not interfere with us, Soth," the dragon hissed.

The show of strength did not impress Lord Soth. With an overhand swing, he slashed his reply to the dragon's warning. His ancient sword bounced harmlessly off the wyrm's crimson scales, though the creature screeched in anger at the fallen knight's impertinence. Still growling, the dragon sprang at Soth, its mouth open wide.

Needle-sharp teeth clamped down on the death knight's wrist. Pain shot up Soth's arm as the teeth tore a jagged-edged hole in his armor and bit into his flesh. Had Soth been mortal, the attack would have torn his arm off below the elbow.

The blow also knocked the sword from Soth's grasp. The ancient weapon bounced pommel-first off the floor, then slid with a high-pitched whine of metal on stone out of the knight's reach. Soth paid little attention to the lost weapon as he balled his free hand into a fist and battered the dragon's snout.

The gargoyle lay on top of Magda, pinning her legs and one arm. With her free hand the Vistani pummeled the stone-skinned creature's face. It was soon clear, however, that she could do the thing little harm with her fist, so she frantically groped the floor nearby for something to use as a weapon. When her hand closed on the sword's grip, made icy from Soth's grasp, she did not hesitate.

Magda was no stranger to such weapons. The villagers in Barovia and the duchies surrounding it had no love for the gypsies, though they greedily bought the foreign goods they sold. Some even frequented the Vistani fortune-tellers, a practice that cost dearly. Still, a gypsy caught away from her people was an easy target for the superstitious peasants, so at an early age all Vistani learned how to handle a blade.

Gripping the weapon tightly, Magda lashed out and landed the pommel against the gargoyle's temple. The creature howled, clutching its head as it fell sideways. That gave Magda the time she needed to scramble to her feet.

The gargoyle eyed the woman and the weapon slyly. "Blade can't hurt me, 'less it's enchanted. Give up now 'fore you make me really mad."

Tentatively, the gargoyle extended a hand. Magda hesitated. Creatures born of sorcery were often immune to weapons of steel or iron. If the gargoyle were such a beast, it was true—there was little she could hope to do without an enchanted blade.

The gargoyle sidled closer, its arm still extended. "Give it t'me."

Magda struck with all the strength desperation could grant. The bloodstained blade glowed blue, and the weapon cut deeply into the gargoyle's shoulder. One wing hanging limp upon its back, the ebony-skinned monster tried to lope away, but Magda swung again. One of the gargoyle's hands fell to the floor. Its taloned fingers contracted twice, then lay still.

Gray pus dripped from the gargoyle's wounds as it hopped up the stairs, yelping in pain. Magda let the sword slip from her fingers as the creature disappeared. At last her heart slowed its pounding, and the throbbing in her ears died away. She turned and faced a sight more awe-inspiring than any she had ever seen in the netherworld.

Lord Soth stood, his right arm held high. The dragon still had its jaws locked onto the death knight's wrist. Its tail coiled around Soth's legs, and noisily its clawed feet scraped against his breastplate. The wound on Soth's wrist brought no blood, but pain burned up his arm like red-hot splinters. Though he knew spells that might harm the creature, the death knight could not use them; magic required concentration and free movement, both of which had been denied him. Soth bore the pain silently and continued to hammer at the dragon with his fist.

The sight of the two evil titans locked in battle was the stuff of legends, the sort of thing that could form the basis for an epic tale one day. But if I don't escape the castle, the Vistani told herself, there will be no one to tell the story.

Magda kept glancing at the battle as she hurried to the pillar-lined dining room. Andari was nowhere to be seen, and no music echoed from the front of the dining hall. The small sack she had filled at her wagon before setting out with the death knight lay hidden beneath a corner of the table. She retrieved her silver dirk from the sack and used it to rip a few inches off her dress's hem and cut away any frills.

She left the room just as Soth and the dragon toppled to the floor. The crimson wyrm's tail entangled the death knight's legs, and Soth had to use his free hand in an attempt to force apart the creature's jaws. The entire right side of the dragon's head was a bruised and bloody pulp; its eye had swollen shut, and many of its scales had been battered away. Still the creature clamped its teeth down upon the knight's wrist.

The attack was beginning to show upon Soth. The death knight's right hand had curled painfully into a fist, much the same way the hand of a paralytic froze into a clawlike pose. The dragon's teeth had shredded much of the armor on his wrist, exposing skin that was translucent and charred.

With a grunt of pain, the death knight wedged his left hand into the dragon's mouth. He pulled back its lips, stained a dark red from its own blood, and shattered three of the creature's teeth. The needle-sharp teeth remained lodged in the death knight's arm. Slowly Lord Soth pulled the dragon's mouth open. A cracking of bone sounded in the room.

Suddenly the dragon released its grip and rolled back from Lord Soth. Both the dragon and the death knight were slow getting to their feet, but neither appeared ready to acknowledge defeat. "The master will not be pleased I had to destroy you, death knight," the crimson guardian growled, its missing teeth adding even more hiss to its already sibilant voice.

Arching its back, the wyrm inhaled deeply. There was a shrill hiss, like rushing air, then the dragon breathed forth a jet of smoke and fire. Magda dove back into the dining hall, but Soth let the liquid fire wash over him. The death knight's long purple cloak burst into flames, and soon he appeared as little more than a pillar of smoke and fire.

A deep, rumbling laughter filled the room. "Magical fire wrought by the gods themselves took my life three and a half centuries ago," Soth said. The cloak fell from the death knight's shoulders in flaming rags as he stepped forward. "Your spittle is nothing to me, little wyrm."

A preternatural calm came over Soth, and he cleared his mind for an instant. A single word, terrible in its intensity, flashed into existence in his brain. Those on Krynn who studied the darker paths of sorcery knew and feared such magical words of power, for they could be used to blind or stun or kill most living things. Not even dragons were immune to the fearsome effects of these ancient sorceries.

Soth pointed with his uninjured hand and spoke the most deadly of these words. The dragon recoiled at the sound, then opened its mouth to breathe fire again. Before the wyrm could exhale, a crackling ball of black energy formed around it. The sparking bands contracted, and searching tendrils wove their way into the dragon's eyes and ears and mouth. The wyrm shuddered once, then again, and black light began to stream from cracks in its crimson scales. The death knight, his armor still glowing red from the dragonfire, stood over the dying creature as agonizing spasms racked its body. At last the dragon lay still, its eyes bulging from their sockets and smoke seeping from its nose.

"Come out, Magda."

The Vistani emerged from the dining hall, her dagger in her hand. Soth kept his back to her as he examined his wounded arm; his flesh had been shredded by the attack, his bones scarred. The pain still pulsing along his arm oddly fascinated the death knight, for it was rare that an adversary caused him any harm. "I am leaving Castle Ravenloft."

After retrieving his sword, Soth scanned the room for a shadow, one large enough that he and Magda could use to escape the keep.

Gibbering and howling began to sound from the stairway the Vistani had descended earlier. The woman looked from the staircase to the door. "Let me leave on my own," she pleaded. "I'll not tell the count what you did."

Soth smiled beneath his helmet as he turned to her. "I want Strahd to know what I did. Besides, you owe me an explanation of the count's plans. . . ."

The noise from the upper floor grew louder, and a hunchbacked form emerged from the darkness at the top of the stair. It was a gargoyle, similar to the one Magda had fought earlier, though this one had four arms and a double set of horns atop its slate-gray head. "Here they are!" the creature shouted. A half-dozen other gargoyles appeared on the stairs.

Lord Soth stepped toward the shadowy corner and extended his hand. "Well, Magda?"

The Vistani rushed to the death knight. She closed her eyes as she held out her left hand, for she knew Soth's icy grip would be painful.

"A wise choice," Soth murmured, gently closing his mailed fingers over her trembling hand. Together they disappeared into the darkness.

Shouting threats and curses, the gargoyles raked their talons through the air where the knight and the gypsy had stood but a moment before. "The master will not be pleased," the four-armed creature wailed. "He will surely destroy us all."

A small gargoyle the color of old rust cowered at the leader's feet. "Perhaps we can run away," it suggested meekly.

The four-armed creature shook its head and slumped to a sitting position. "There is nowhere in Barovia to hide. Strahd is master of this land, and he would find us before the sun rose tomorrow."

Sadly nodding their agreement, the other gargoyles crouched statuelike in the main hall, waiting for the sun to set and their master to rise from his coffin. Their punishment would be terrible but quick.

Strahd Von Zarovich would offer the death knight and the Vistani no such mercy when he found them.

 **NINE**

The cracked, weather-beaten sign above the tavern read Blood on the Vine, and it creaked as the wind pushed through the square. The building holding up the sign, a tavern, had seen better days. Sun-bleached wooden shutters framed smudged windows, and whitewash clung to the walls in a few places. The tavern's closed door seemed to warn that only regulars were welcome.

Not that many people passed by the shabby place. Though it was almost noon, the village square remained subdued. A few tradesmen delivered their wares, and the scarecrow of a man who held the job of tax collector for the burgomaster shuffled from shop to shop.

"Looks like a storm. With luck, the bastard'll be hit by lightning," one of the patrons of the Blood on the Vine noted sourly, eyeing the tax man through a small clean spot in the window. The words sounded like thunder in the low-roofed room, for the only other noise came from the gently crackling fire in the hearth.

Taking a swallow of watery wine, he looked to his fellows for support. "I said, with luck he'll be blasted by lightning."

The two other men in the tavern weren't up to the task. Arik, the barkeep, murmured something incomprehensible in a dull voice and went back to cleaning glasses that would not be used for days. Thin as he was, he might have been a brother to the scarecrow tax man, but he was as well liked as the burgomaster's man was despised and resented. Most older villagers, both men and women, had been served by Arik or his father—who had also been named Arik. The family that owned the Blood on the Vine thought it best to keep the name of the barkeep the same, and the townsfolk found it convenient.

The other man ignored the invitation to rail against the tax collector altogether and stared intently at the pattern of rings and chips worn into the tabletop before him. His blue eyes betrayed the nagging dread that welled inside him, and his pale face held a haunted expression. Unlike the other two in the tavern, he was clean-shaven and his blond hair was neatly trimmed. The straight bangs over his wrinkled brow emphasized the plumpness of his features, making him look younger than his fifty winters.

"Hey, Terlarm," the man at the window called. "Are you too busy praying to answer me?"

"Leave him be, Donovich," Arik said from his place behind the bar, in front of the shelf full of glasses. "If you'd witnessed a beast of the night slaughter your friends, you'd not be so boisterous either."

Donovich downed the last of his wine, wiped a dirty hand across his drooping mustache, and swaggered to the open cask set at one end of the taproom. "True enough, I suppose, but it was my brother the damned Vistani murdered the other night, wasn't it?" To emphasize the point, he slapped the black arm band he wore, a symbol of grief that told all Barovians the bearer had recently lost family. "You don't see me moping around."

Raising his blue eyes at last, Terlarm noted, "Grief is not so easily forgotten where I come from."

"You've been in Barovia long enough to have learned our ways," Donovich snapped. Like most villagers, he had little tolerance and less patience for outsiders. He refilled his cup and took a place at the table in front of the fireplace.

Terlarm swallowed a caustic reply, then tugged at the sleeve of his tattered red robe. The boyar's words were true enough; he'd been in Barovia for almost thirty years now. Long ago, he and four others had become lost in a bank of fog, only to emerge from the mists in the village of Barovia. Melancholy washed over the cleric as he remembered his home and the four others who had become trapped in the godsforsaken netherworld with him. "I'll return to Palanthas some day," he murmured, half to himself. "It's the most beautiful city in Ansalon. Its walls have never been breached, its white towers have never—"

The door swung open suddenly, interrupting Terlarm's morose reverie and eliciting a curse from Arik at the dust spewed into the room by the wind. When they saw the young woman framed by the doorway, they stared, slack-jawed and amazed. The Vistani's dark curls danced in the wind, and the frayed hem of her blood-red dress swirled up, revealing scratched but shapely legs. She stepped inside, looking over her shoulder as if worried about some unseen pursuer, then closed the door.

Arik picked up a broom, which looked almost as spindly as his arms, and started to sweep up the dirt. "Your kind's not wanted here."

Magda swallowed hard. She knew it was dangerous for a Vistani to travel alone anywhere near the village; Barovians blamed much of their misfortune on the wandering tribes. "I wish no trouble, friend," she said, pouring on the charm with practiced ease. "I'm looking for a villager, a priest named Terlarm. Perhaps you gentlemen know where I might find him."

Donovich stood, knocking over a bench. The clatter startled Magda, but she maintained her pleasant facade as best she could. The burly man took a step toward the Vistani. "Do you know Boyar Grest from this village?" he asked, his voice even and deceptively calm.

Her scuffle with the obnoxious landowner who had tried to buy her virtue already seemed like ancient history. She studied the heavyset man who now stood before her. His mustache and shaggy, dark hair marked him as a local, but his beady eyes and the set of his jaw warned Magda that he might be a relative of Grest's. And the black arm band the man wore told of a recent loss.

"Many know him," she replied cautiously. "He is a great man and a friend to my people. But, please, I am—"

Sneering, Donovich pounded a table with his fist. "Your people *killed* him." He fished into the pocket of his rough woolen pants and recovered a silver charm on a long leather cord. The teardrop pendant winked in the firelight. "When they found him, dazed and dying by the side of the road, he kept muttering about the Vistani's promise. He said the pendant should have made him invisible to creatures of darkness."

The red-robed priest stepped between Magda and Donovich. "Go outside," he said to the woman. "I'm Terlarm. I'll talk to you outside."

A glimmer of recognition dawned on Magda. The fat cleric was the same man who they had seen at the hanging near the ruined church, and who they had encountered in the forest after the dwarf had broken free of his bonds. But before the Vistani could respond, the rugged boyar cuffed Terlarm soundly with a meaty hand. The cleric sprawled on the ground, dazed.

"Mind your own damned business," Donovich growled without looking at Terlarm. He grabbed Magda by the throat and pushed her flat on a table. The Vistani struggled against the grip, but the boyar was very strong.

Arik went about his business. With Herr Grest dead, Donovich was the head of his family now; it wouldn't do to thwart the vengeance of an influential landowner. Besides, he mused as he resumed cleaning the glasses, the Vistani are never very good customers anyway.

Magda kicked Donovich hard in the shin and clawed at his face with her fingernails. It may have been the many cups of wine or the stupor of rage that dulled his senses, but whatever the cause, the boyar didn't seem to feel the blows. The Vistani struggled for the dirk still hidden in the small sack tied to her waist, but Donovich had unwittingly pinned the weapon beneath his bulk. She gasped futilely for air.

"Leave the woman alone."

The voice that echoed hollowly in the room did not startle Magda as it did Arik. The barkeep spun about, for the words had come from the shadowed corner right behind him. There an armored figure stood, orange eyes glowing from inside his helmet. The stranger stank of charred cloth, and sooty ash clung to his ornate armor. Holding an obviously wounded right arm close to his chest, the knight grabbed the barkeep's forehead and twisted his head sharply. The snap of Arik's neck breaking was followed by the shattering of glass.

Intent on his victim, Donovich didn't hear the commotion. Neither did he loosen his grip or turn his beady eyes away from the choking, red-faced Vistani pinned beneath him, even after the wave of cold had settled on his back. In fact, the boyar never saw Lord Soth raise his gauntleted left hand and lash out. Donovich's skull caved in at the blow, and he collapsed, bleeding, on top of Magda.

The death knight lifted the boyar's corpse and dropped it onto the floor. When Magda began to choke, her hands at her throat as if that might bring more air to her tortured lungs, Soth paid her little mind. Instead he knelt by Terlarm's side.

The cleric came to slowly, but when his eyes could focus again, the death knight's ancient, ruined armor—the armor of a Solamnic Knight—filled his vision. "Gilean preserve me!" he gasped.

"You know who I am?" Soth asked.

Nodding weakly, Terlarm raised himself on wobbly arms. Few on Krynn, especially those who lived in Palanthas, did not know the story of Lord Soth, the Knight of the Black Rose. Glancing about the room, Terlarm saw the bloody corpses of the villagers.

The cleric stuttered a few nonsensical phrases, then Soth held up a hand and silenced him. "You and four others were brought here from Palanthas thirty years ago," the death knight noted. "In the time you have been in Barovia, have you ever heard tales of someone returning to Krynn?"

"They're all dead," he mumbled numbly. For a moment, Soth wasn't certain if the cleric meant his four friends or the other patrons of the tavern. "There were five of us, all clerics or mages devoted to the

Balance." Spreading his arms, he glanced at his worn red robes. "One night we went for a walk by the harbor in Palanthas. A fog rolled in, a thick mist swallowed us, and when we stepped out of it, we were in this village."

He smiled, then a mad giggle escaped his lips. "Keth and Bast and Fingelin, they all were killed by the watcher, the thing at the end of the dark tunnel. And Voldra . . ." He made a ritual symbol of blessing over his heart. "The castle took him. Now there's only me."

After a moment, Terlarm leaned forward and studied the death knight closely. "You are trapped here, too?" he asked, his eyes filled with tears. "Then I was correct all along! This place is a hell!" The cleric looked to the grimy ceiling and raised his hands. "Gilean, Master of the Balance, forgive me for my sins. At least tell me what crimes I have committed so I may atone for them. Perhaps then you'll let me through the gate, past the watcher—"

There was an edge in the cleric's words and a wildness in his eyes. The mention of a gate made Soth suddenly take notice of his rambling. "Gate?" the death knight repeated. "Have you discovered a way back to Krynn?"

Fear filled Terlarm's eyes. "The Vistani told us of a way back home. They sold us the information for all the gold we had." The madman frowned. "The gate was there, all right, but the *watcher* wouldn't let us by. Only Voldra and I escaped. It killed all the others."

"Where is it?" Soth growled.

"At the fork of the River Luna," the cleric said softly, shrinking back from the death knight. "But the watcher—"

Soth laughed. "The watcher means nothing to me!"

"Lord Soth?" a soft voice said from behind the un-dead warrior. He turned to face Magda. The woman rubbed her bruised throat, and the claw marks on her shoulder from the gargoyle were bleeding again. Her voice hoarse, she added, "I can lead you to the fork in the river. I've heard stories about the gate that's sup-posed to lie there."

Soth studied her for a moment. Once free of Cas-tle Ravenloft, Magda had revealed Strahd's intention to use her as a spy. After what had happened in the keep, the woman was in danger from the count, so she had her reasons for aiding the death knight. She was set against Strahd, or so her battle with the gar-goyle seemed to show, but that was not the main rea-son Soth believed her.

Magda had proven herself far stronger than the death knight would have suspected on the night he destroyed the Vistani camp. She had defied Strahd, defeated one of his minions, and now she had even overcome her fear of Soth. Such strength meant a great deal to the death knight. He had always found weaklings to be untrustworthy—like the treacherous Caradoc—but Magda was far from weak-willed. Still, he had learned enough in Barovia to know trust should never be given fully. "Go on," he said guardedly.

"The storytellers in a few of the local tribes speak of a gate to other worlds," she began. "It's been there for a long time. One of my ancestors—a hero named Kulchek—escaped from Barovia through the same gate. Legend has it that some horrible guardian watches over it now, some . . . *thing*."

The cleric shook his head. "It had eyes and mouths, and it made us all see visions. Nothing we did could hurt it." He hugged himself tightly. "First it bit off Keth's arm. Blood. Oh, gods, blood everywhere . . ."

As the man rambled on, the death knight turned to Magda. "Does the River Luna run between here and Duke Gundar's castle?" When she noted that it did, Soth said simply, "Let us start on our way, then."

Before the death knight had even reached the exit, Magda had stripped Donovich and Arik of their purses. She took the barkeep's shoes, too. The boots' worn leather would offer little comfort, but the Vistani knew better than to begin a long trek barefoot. Finally, she retrieved the teardrop-shaped charm from the boyar's pocket and slipped it into her sack. One never knew when such charms might come in handy.

"Please," the cleric said, his hands knit together in supplication before Soth, "take me with you. Perhaps you will defeat the watcher." He got to his knees. "Take me back to Palanthas."

"Palanthas is gone," the death knight noted. "I led the armies that sacked it a few days ago." He turned his back on the cleric and pushed open the door.

The priest whimpered and tugged at the hem of his red robes. "It can't be gone," he said. "I won't believe it. Palanthas has never been invaded. Its beautiful walls have never been breached, its towers . . ."

The death knight strode unimpeded through the streets of the village. Shutters banged closed and mothers hustled their ragged children inside their homes. Even the trade road into the mountains to the west remained strangely empty as the dead man and the Vistani left the village behind. Only once, a few miles along the Svalich Road, did Magda think she saw something following them, but when she stopped and studied their trail, nothing seemed out of the ordinary.

* * * * *

Soth sat crosslegged at the mouth of a small cave, watching the rain fall in cold, swollen drops. It beat a jarring, staccato rhythm on the ground around the mouth of the cave. The death knight silently cursed the weather. The noise would make it difficult to hear anything creeping from the rocky crevices or scattered copses of trees nearby. It might even prevent him from hearing if the traps he'd set up were sprung during the night.

Turning his orange eyes to the nighttime forest, Soth scanned the inhospitable landscape for any sign of the trio of wolves that had begun to follow them almost immediately after they'd left the village almost two days past. The shaggy beasts had always remained just out of sight, exchanging piercing howls. Something else was tracking the duo as well. Magda had glimpsed it once, outside the village, and the death knight, too, had spotted a hairy, child-sized thing loping through the underbrush on the following day.

"Are they still out there?" Magda asked from deeper inside the cave.

"Yes," Soth replied. "But the wolves will not attack me, and the other thing . . . We shall see."

A pause followed. "Why hasn't Strahd come after us?"

The death knight did not respond at first, for he truly did not know why the count had failed to chase them. The wolves were clearly his spies; they had led Soth toward the Vistani camp his first night in Barovia. "His reasons do not matter as long as we reach this portal near the river or the one in Duke Gundar's castle."

A wolf howled long and low in the distance. Closer

to the cave, another answered, and a third yelped its response from an outcropping of rock above the cave entrance. As Soth scanned the trees and blisters of granite for some sign of the beasts, another sound came to his ears: music.

Magda half-sang, half-hummed an ancient Vistani bardic song. The death knight caught snatches of the story—a strangely familiar tale of love gained and lost. It was not the fact the gypsy was singing that caught Soth's attention; he'd been in enough battles, awaited enough tense confrontations during his time as a Knight of Solamnia, to recognize an attempt to calm jangled nerves.

No, it was the tune itself that tugged at the corners of his subconscious. The song insinuated itself into the death knight's mind and curled up like a cat before the cold hearth of his memories. At this prompting, images buried by hundreds of years of disregard shrugged off their ashes and flared to life. Soth marveled at the memories, even as he attempted to smother them. The images would not be damped, though, and soon he was lost in the past, remembering. . . .

Music filled Dargaard Keep. Five minstrels in the gallery overlooking the large, circular main hall played a light air on dulcimer, horn, flute, and drum. The spritely notes seemed to leap over the railing, down the twin curving stairs running along the walls, then prance around each reveler in the room. Six men and women, attired in their finest silks and brocades, hose and silver-buckled shoes, twirled by pairs. The music twirled with them, then rose higher and higher toward the room's massive chandelier and vaulted, rose-colored ceiling.

As the dance went on, booming laughter twined with the music. The laughter came from the thirteen renowned knights clustered around a table at the room's edge. Their hands cupping goblets that were brimming with sweet wine from the vineyards of Solamnia, the men loudly saluted the wedding couple who hosted the revelry. This done, they returned to telling stories of heroic deeds and fair maidens.

The song reached a crescendo, sweeping the dancers in breathless haste around the room, then ended suddenly. The three couples clapped for the minstrels, but their polite appreciation of the musicians was overwhelmed by a burst of loud boasting.

"There was never a man in Solamnia, nay the entire continent of Ansalon, who could best Sir Mikel in a test of wit!" one of the knights shouted. He gestured with his cup to the smiling man on his right. "Why, in Palanthas that night—"

Anger swelled in the breast of one of the dancers. Before the knight could elaborate on his boast, this dancer, Lord Soth, took a single step away from his partner. "My loyal retainers," Soth proclaimed, his voice silencing the boasts and laughter. "You do a disservice to minstrels who visit us."

The thirteen knights lowered their wine cups as one. Soth could see the shame in their eyes, though he could not tell if it was feigned or genuine. The men put leather-gloved hands together in gentle applause, but kept their contrite faces upon the man who had pointed out their breach of etiquette.

After a moment, Soth dismissed the minstrels with a wave of his hand. He gave his men the briefest of glances, but they knew from his slight frown that they were to moderate their revelry. Finally, he returned to his lovely partner.

"Sincere apologies, my dear," Lord Soth said, taking his new wife's hand. He gazed into her pale blue eyes and ran his fingertips gently across her lily-white cheek. The warmth of her skin made desire stir within him. "My knights sometimes forget themselves. They are quite happy for me, knowing my marriage to you will make this keep a joyful place." He laughed softly. "Perhaps they celebrate in hopes your fair temper will soften my hand in ruling the lands surrounding Dargaard."

The elfmaid smiled sweetly. "There is nothing we cannot overcome together, you know." She nodded her fine-boned chin, and her long golden hair stirred, revealing the daintily pointed ears of a high-born elf. "Perhaps even Paladine, given time—"

"Indeed," one of the other dancers chimed in, moving to Soth's side. "Lady Isolde is correct. The great god Paladine, Father of Good, Master of Law, will light your way from this, er, time of tribulation. That you brought me here to officiate over your union is a good step, of course. We of Paladine's faithful are certain that such a fine knight as yourself will come to see . . ."

The speaker, a fatuous cleric of little reputation, let his comment trail off and grinned obsequiously when Soth turned his gaze upon him. The knight could feel the tension drawing his mouth into a grim line and draining the happiness from his heart. His desire for his wife fled in the face of boiling anger, a desire to strike the man before him. Soth found it difficult to banish these thoughts of violence, thoughts that were so familiar to him of late.

"Disciple Garath," the knight murmured, taking his hand from his wife's grasp, "we value your presence at the ceremony. Yet even your position as celebrant at this wedding does not give you the right to offer comment on our private problems."

The priest straightened the few wisps of hair remaining on his shining pate and swallowed nervously. His wife, a sour-looking woman twice the age of the young cleric, hurried to prevent her husband from doing any more damage.

"Your Lordship is correct, of course," she offered. With a mongoose-quick grab, she snatched Garath's hand. "We are honored to be at this splendid occasion. The musicians are fine, are they not?" Before Soth could answer, she turned to Lady Isolde. "That is a lovely dress, by the way. I understand you made it yourself."

The elfmaid blushed. "I made do with what we had in the keep. I'm glad you find it pleasing." She raised her arms, and the gossamer shawl of the snow-white dress wafted gently in response. Isolde gazed down at the floor-length gown, and the slightest veil of sadness crept over her eyes.

Soth gritted his teeth. In Silvanost, the land of Isolde's people, the wedding gowns of the high-born were strewn with pearls and other precious gems; hers was but a slight imitation of the beautiful garb her sisters and friends would wear upon their wedding days. Soth could see the unhappiness marring her beautiful features as she looked up, and that expression cast a shadow across his own heart.

Wandering to various other subjects, the conversation let the knight and his bride, the priest and his wife, put the tension behind them. The other couple that had joined them in the dance, a minor bureaucrat from the nearby city of Kalaman and his mistress, came to listen to the discussion of hunting and court fashion, but they said little. They were not used to the company of the rich and powerful.

Though Soth remained polite, the inane chatter galled him. These four were the only ones who had responded to his invitation; the other knights, politicians, and merchants from Kalaman and the smaller towns near Dargaard Keep had found any excuse not to attend. Many had not even responded to Soth's missives.

An hour passed slowly, then the great hall rang with the footsteps of self-importance. Soth, like the others, turned to the spotlessly attired young man who made his way toward the matrimonial gathering. Caradoc was seneschal of Dargaard Keep, the man in charge of the day-to-day operation of the fortress-home. This night he wore a pair of white velvet breeches, high black boots, and a doublet of the finest elven silk. Dwarven-smithed bands of purest gold clasped his wrists, and an ornate medallion proclaimed his office. The servant carried himself with an acquired grace usually denied one of such low birth and spotty education.

Yet the servant's presence was a slap to the master of Dargaard. From the day Soth had ordered the murder of his first wife, Caradoc had used his knowledge of the crime for blackmail; the Knights' Council had condemned Soth for suspected involvement in the mysterious disappearance of his wife, but no one could prove any crime—unless Caradoc revealed what he knew. The seneschal was wise enough to limit the freedoms he bought with that knowledge, for Soth would surely kill him if he pushed things too far. Still, he flaunted his position just enough to make Soth uncomfortable.

Caradoc moved to Lord Soth's side as if unconscious of the attention his entrance had attracted, then asked to speak to the nobleman privately, on a matter of the household. "The knights encamped outside have sent word that the red moon has now risen," he said meaningfully, when they were apart from the others.

Lord Soth sighed. "Then the feast must end, as we

agreed yesterday." He looked around the room and found concern on all faces, creasing even the unwrinkled brow of his elven wife. He forced as convincing a smile as possible to his lips and gestured broadly. "Our keepers tell us the time for celebrations is at an end."

A few of the knights rose, but Soth motioned them back to their seats. "We need not man the battlements again—" he turned to his four guests "—until our friends leave. The men of the army outside are to be trusted. They will not harm you."

A flurry of half-sincere congratulations to the bride and groom followed, then the two couples gathered their cloaks and left, guided by Caradoc to the keep's main entrance. At the door, the priest of Paladine stopped and uttered a prayer, spreading wide his arms as if to encompass all of Dargaard Keep. The gesture struck Soth as pathetic somehow.

"This is not the wedding I would have wished for us," Lord Soth said sincerely, turning to his wife. "The lords and ladies of Kalaman feared to come to a feast in a castle under siege—even if the knights offered a truce for the day. That toadie and his—"

Softly the elfmaid put her fingers to Soth's lips. Her touch was light, carrying the gentle, alluring fragrance of her perfume. "My darling, your men remain loyal to you. And Caradoc. And the servants who man the stables and the kitchen. I, too, will stand beside you always." She cast her eyes down and placed a slender hand on her stomach. "Neither can we forget our child, my lord. He will need you and love you most of all."

The pair stood in silence for a moment, then the wide, main double doors to the hall swung wide. A blast of chill air curled into the room from outside, setting the candles on the chandelier guttering.

Broad shadows warped across the floor and walls, and for a moment it seemed as if the light would vanish altogether. Caradoc closed the doors behind him, however, and the candles sputtered back to life.

"The siege party has seen the musicians and your guests across the bridge and to a safe distance from the keep," the seneschal announced, but not before he straightened his short black hair and settled his chain of office on his chest. "Perhaps it's time to man the towers and draw up the bridge."

"All right," the nobleman said curtly. "Go see to the servants, Caradoc. Make certain the craftsmen have plenty of water stored near their houses in case our foes try to lob burning pitch into the keep again tonight."

With a flourish the seneschal bowed and went his way. Soth faced his wife one last time. "Good night, my love," he murmured. Gently he kissed her hand. "I must prepare our defenses, and you need your rest."

Isolde returned her husband's kiss before she moved up the stairs to her quarters in the keep's upper floor. Only when she had been gone for several minutes did Soth order his knights to arm themselves and take their defensive positions. Then he stood alone in the main hall, which now seemed cavernous and lonely. For an instant, the echo of the minstrels' song wailed ghostly in the back of Soth's mind. With a frown and a shake of his head, he dismissed it and made his way to the stairs.

At the first landing, he passed a full-length mirror, a gift from the cleric and his wife. Such items were rare and quite expensive, though it didn't surprise Soth that the priest could afford it. Churchmen, at least those Soth knew, rarely went without luxury.

Looking into the glass, Soth stood as if on military

review—his broad shoulders squared, his back straight. His golden hair shone in the light of a nearby torch, framing his face like a heavenly glow. His mustache, long but neatly trimmed, hung to either side of a small, expressive mouth. A doublet of black velvet hugged his muscular frame to his waist, its darkness broken by a fiery red rose embroidered on its breast. This, the symbol of the order of knighthood to which Lord Soth belonged, was the only ornamentation he wore.

Soth was satisfied with the man he saw reflected in the silvered glass. Though the Order had stripped him of his rank and official title, they could not take away his nobility. He was still more worthy of respect than all the hypocrites who had condemned him. Isolde knew that. So did his loyal retainers. Given the chance, he would prove his worth to the rest of Solamnia, too.

Self-satisfied, he resumed his march to the keep's upper floors. The interior stairs wound in a circle, tighter and narrower as they reached up. Soth was not even winded by the climb. In fact, he barely noticed as the number of steps passed one hundred, then two hundred. The knight's mind was on other matters, more weighty than purely physical discomfort.

As Soth pushed open the trapdoor marking the stairs' end, a brisk wind tugged at his mustache and ruffled his golden hair. Ignoring the chill that surely signaled the coming of winter, the knight stepped onto the keep's highest vantage. From a thin walkway bordered by a low and ornate wrought iron railing, he surveyed his domain.

The main structure of Dargaard was a large, circular castle—more a tower, really—hewn from the mountain that eternally protected it on all but one side. The castle narrowed as it climbed high into the air and tapered to a blunted peak. Stairs circled the exterior of the keep, flowing into landings at strategically important heights, all the way to the top. It was there, at the very pinnacle of Dargaard, that Soth now stood.

The knight watched as servants rolled cartloads of weapons onto the four main terraces that jutted from the keep just above the fourth story, crossing the courtyard high above the straw-and-wood cottages of the castle's craftsmen. From the terraces, Soth's knights moved the arrows and spears, torches and barrels of pitch across latticework bridges to the hexagonal outer wall. From there the defensive weapons were being transferred to the twin gatehouses standing sentinel to either side of the massive iron portcullis and iron-strapped wooden doors that barred entry to Dargaard. Beyond this single entrance to the keep lay a wide drawbridge that, when extended, spanned the thousand-foot-deep chasm gaping for miles in either direction.

The bridge, however, was being noisily withdrawn. Soth could picture the cavernous room below the gatehouses, where five or six sweat-soaked men grunted and cursed as they turned the giant wheels that reeled the bridge back into the side of the mountain. Greasy black smoke from the men's torches would be swirling around the low ceiling, staining everything dark. Long shadows, like creatures wrought only of darkness, would be playing upon the walls as the men heaved against the wheels. It was like a small window into the Abyss in his mind, though Soth knew the hells must be far worse than that.

The reason for all these defensive precautions lay on the other side of the chasm, patiently huddled around a dozen campfires: a party of knights, fellows of Lord Soth's order, were arrayed before Dargaard, ready to take up the siege they had so graciously delayed for the wedding celebration. Ballistae and catapults stood at the ready, threatening to toss their missiles at the keep's rose-colored stone. Armored knights, their bright cloaks flapping in the wind, stood close to campfires to fight off the cold.

Soth himself had been part of such sieges. He knew the men would be tired, sick of their bland trail rations and the hard ground that served as their bed each night. Yet they wouldn't lift the siege, though they had too few catapults to batter down the walls and winter was coming on fast. Knights of Solamnia never gave up easily.

The whole situation reminded Soth of an old ram he'd seen in the mountains. It must have been blind with age, for it mistook a chunk of rock for a rival. The ram smashed itself bloody and senseless against the stone. Wolves tore it to shreds that night as it lay dazed.

And here is the head of the ram now, Soth thought scornfully, for he could see the leader of the siege, Sir Ratelif, as he broke from one of the group of knights.

Sir Ratelif walked to the edge of the chasm, then waited for the grinding squeal of the retreating bridge to cease. When all that remained of the noise was the echo from the gaping split in the earth, the armor-clad man held his hands out, palms up. To Soth, the gesture looked like pleading, and his scorn for the knight grew.

"Soth of Dargaard Keep, you have been found guilty of crimes against your family and the honor of the Order. In the name of Paladine, Kiri-Jolith, and Habbakuk, surrender yourself to the lawful army arrayed against you," Sir Ratelif cried, repeating a ritual declamation used by the Knights of Solamnia for centuries.

Soth raised a defiant fist. "This keep can withstand your siege for months," he shouted. "And winter is not so far off that you can stay there forever."

Sir Ratelif ignored the nobleman's reply and continued with the ritual, repeating phrases he had said once a day to the besieged Lord Soth for the last two weeks. "Your crimes are many, so I will name only the most grievous offenses. Know first that you stand guilty of breaking your marriage vows by dallying with the elfmaid Isolde of Silvanost while still married to Lady Gadria of Kalaman. Know next that you are guilty of lying to the elfmaid, of misrepresenting your intentions, of getting her with a bastard child." The knight pursed his lips, as if trying to expel some awful taste from his mouth. "Know finally that you stand suspect of plotting and achieving the murder of your lawful wife, Gadria."

His jaw clenched, his hands held in tight fists, Soth turned away from the army. From below, Ratelif's voice rang out once more: "You stand atop a tower wrought in the likeness of the red rose, Lord Soth. Never has there been a greater stain upon that blessed symbol of our Order."

The words bit into the nobleman's heart. He had chosen the sight for Dargaard Keep because of the abundance of rose quartz in the mountains near at hand, had drawn plans to the keep himself so that its tapering tower would resemble nothing so much as that incomparable flower. That a fellow knight would denigrate his monument to the Order . . .

Lord Soth gazed up at the two moons visible to him in Krynn's sky. Solinari, only a sliver in the night, cast its silver-white light over the ground wanly. It was Lunitari's red glow that colored the world, bathing the night in blood. There was a third moon, Nuitari, but that black orb could be seen only by those corrupted by evil.

By the white moon, symbol of good magic, the Knight of the Rose uttered a vow. "I will make them see, by the light of Solinari, how wrong they are, how foolishly they try to expel me from their ranks. My honor is my life," Soth whispered, "and I will have my life back once again."

A sharp snap, like a bowstring breaking, made the remembered image waver in the death knight's mind. His eyes focused on the drab cave and the bleak landscape beyond. The early morning sun flared through breaks in the swirling clouds. The rain had stopped. Silence shrouded the copses of hardy trees and stolid outcropping of granite, then the noise came again—a quick, sharp cracking sound.

Soth got to his feet, his injured sword arm dangling at his side. The noise came a third time. It's the traps, the death knight realized. Something has stumbled across the traps. "Wake up, Magda."

The Vistani came awake instantly and snatched up her silver dagger. Without a word, she followed the death knight out of the cave and into the dawn.

Cautiously they approached the first trap, a simple snare Soth had rigged near the largest copse of firs. A wolf, its throat torn open, its mangy fur matted with its own blood, lay sprawled over the trap. The scenes at the other two snares were the same. The bodies of the wolves that had been following them lay butchered over the deliberately disturbed traps.

The death knight examined the third beast's wounds; the ragged, gaping tears in its throat had been made, not by a blade, but by another animal's teeth and claws. Yet no mindless beast could have purposefully set off the traps so.

"Lord Soth," Magda called, kneeling on the other side of the dead wolf.

She pointed to a muddy patch near the snare. A set of small boot prints trailed through the muddy ground up to the wolf's corpse. Next came an area of watery muck where any prints had been obliterated. "The footprints lead up to the wolf, but I can't find any leading away from it," the woman said, puzzled.

Soth searched the ground, then pointed something out to the Vistani. Another set of prints did indeed lead away from the slaughtered wolf, but ones not made by boots. After leaving the body, the creature had walked away from the area on two legs, but legs that ended in paws with long, curled claws.

 **TEN**

"I never believe anything told to me by bards or historians," Lord Soth said. "For every sentence of truth they proffer, they demand you accept a dozen lies." He marched off down the rain-washed road, his boots leaving no prints in the muddy ground.

Magda sighed with exasperation and hurried after the death knight. The boots she'd taken from one of the dead men at the tavern were soaked with water and covered in muck. "The tales told by Vistani storytellers are different," she said when she reached the knight's side. "Not every word is true, of course, but often they hold more truth than fiction. There might be some fact that could aid us in defeating the guardian and passing through the portal."

Without even bothering to look at his companion, the death knight said, "Where I come from, I am the subject of many tales. I have been told, too, that historians often chronicle my life in great detail." He shook his head. "Never have I revealed my soul to a storyteller or a scribe, and long dead are any who shared of the adventures I lived when the heart still beat within my chest. How, then, can anyone claim to know my story?"

"There are ways for stories to pass from father to

son," Magda noted, her voice full of resolve. "And if
you were once a mortal man, you likely shared a tale
or two with friends or fellow knights. You—"

The death knight stopped. "Yes, I once shared stories of my knightly adventures with my fellows," he
rumbled. "In fact, my order required knights seeking
advancement not only to achieve a feat of great heroism, but to relate that worthy deed before his peers."
Laughing bitterly, he added, "If one story out of ten
told by warriors seeking higher rank in the Knights
of Solamnia were true, Krynn would have been a par-
adise beyond compare from their great works."

Magda was quiet for a time, seemingly cowed by
the death knight's cynicism. At last, though, she
gathered her courage and asked, "Was there no truth
in the tales *you* told?"

It was Soth who now fell silent. The exchanges between the death knight and the young woman had
been marked by such sparring since early the previous day. The discovery of the wolves' carcasses had
put them both on edge. A full day and a night had
dragged past since they had discovered the corpses
in the death knight's snares, and neither he nor
Magda had seen any further sign of the foe or benefactor who had slain the beasts.

As Soth and Magda walked on, the late morning
sun appeared from behind a thundercloud, covering
the landscape with a blanket of bright sunshine. A
few mammoth, gray-hued knots still rolled across
the sky, threatening to plunge the day into the half-
darkness of a storm. In the gnarled trees lining the
path, a few small birds took up their songs, though
the throaty cawing of crows was a more frequent
sound along the trail.

The rutted, muddy road wound deeper and deeper
into the foothills of Mount Ghakis. The snowcapped

mountain loomed always on the left, and far, far to the right the River Luna sparkled silver and blue on its way through the thick, tangled forest. Few traveled the lonesome byway Magda had chosen for their trek, and Soth was glad for that. Only a single group of Vistani, though no kin of Madame Girani's, had appeared on the road. At the sight of them, Magda had hurried into the trees more swiftly than Soth. After the caravans had passed, she told the death knight that Strahd's intention to slaughter those in her tribe would be known by all the gypsies in Barovia by now. She had as much to fear from the Vistani as from any of the vampire lord's more horrific minions.

A mile, then twice that distance, passed as the morning dragged into afternoon. While he walked, the death knight flexed his hand to exercise his wounded wrist. The bones had knit some, and flesh was beginning to fill in the gash from the dragon's bite.

"Tell your tale," Soth noted softly.

"What?" Magda said. "You want me to tell the story now?"

"There might be a kernel of truth in it. That fragment could help us overcome the guardian, if indeed there is such a creature." The words were spoken as fact, without apology, without conceding that Magda had been correct. "Tell your tale," Soth repeated.

The young woman cleared her throat, and anyone studying her carefully would have seen that she stood a little straighter, walked with more of a spring in her step. It was not that the death knight had been swayed by something she'd said, though the weight of that victory was not lost on her. It was the ancient Vistani tale itself that lent her pride. "Kulchek was a wanderer," Magda began, "a subtle thief and great lover who held the reins of his destiny tightly in his own hands.

"He traveled through Barovia in the days before he bested the giant and won the hand of the giant's daughter, before he passed through the corridor of blades to steal the goldsmith's wares, even before he killed the nine boyars who tried to enslave him." The young woman smiled warmly. "He is a great hero of my people, you see, my lord? Madame Girani shared Kulchek's bloodline. So I do, too."

"What does this have to do with the portal?" Soth asked irritably.

"It has been a long time since you heard a bard tell a story," she noted, unoffended by her audience's impatience. "If you don't understand Kulchek, you won't get anything out of his trip through the gate."

The Vistani took Soth's silence for an acceptance of that fact, so she started off again on her circuitous tale.

"As I said, Kulchek traveled through Barovia in the days before his famous feats. It was his curse, you see, that he could never sleep in the same spot twice. In lands he favored, he moved his bed each night, until there was nowhere new for him to rest. Then he had to move on. In that fashion, he lived in many lands and wandered through many countries.

"At his side was Sabak, the faithful hound whose feet left burning prints in solid stone when he was on the prowl. In his hand Kulchek carried Gard, the cudgel he had fashioned from the tree at the peak of the highest of all mountains. Because the tree grew so near the gods themselves, its wood could not be cut by any blade but one. That blade, the dagger Novgor, Kulchek secreted in his boot."

By now Magda had fallen into the pattern of the tale as it had been taught to her by the storytellers who went from tribe to tribe amongst the Vistani.

That the tale had been meant to be repeated to travelers on the road quickly became apparent to Soth, for its language possessed a rhythm that mirrored a slow but steady walking pace. Occasionally the woman would add a personal comment or ask a rhetorical question, breaking the rhythm. In his time the death knight had heard enough bardic stories to know this was meant to keep the sound of the tale from becoming repetitious or plodding. Practiced bards knew well that easily bored audiences seldom lavished rewards on storytellers who didn't hold their interest.

The tale Magda told was simple, though she filled most of the afternoon with its telling. After Kulchek had slept one night in every spot in Barovia, he tried to move on. At first he could find no escape from the duchy; mists surrounded the borders and brought him back to the dark domain whenever he tried to leave. For twenty nights he did not sleep. Neither could he stop to rest, for if he dozed off, terrible winged creatures would come to tear him to bloody shreds. Such were the terms of his curse.

Late on the thirtieth day, when Kulchek was certain he could keep sleep at bay no longer, his faithful Sabak spotted a large, horned rat. The flesh-eating rodent was of a type Kulchek had seen before in his wandering, albeit in a land far from Barovia. The natives of that faraway place claimed the rat lived only there and nowhere else. Since he believed that claim, the wanderer set his dog after the creature. If it lived locally, it would head for its lair; if it had traveled from its home somehow, it might lead him to whatever gateway had brought it to Barovia.

Exhausted from lack of sleep, Kulchek could not keep pace with the hound, but the burning prints Sabak left in the stone as he chased his quarry were clear enough markers in the growing twilight. From high on the slopes of Mount Ghakis they followed the rat, down to the River Luna. At the place where the river forks, the horned rodent shot down a hole and disappeared. Sabak bayed in frustration as his quarry escaped. The Vistani, Magda took time to note, still claim the mournful sound could be heard at the river's fork, just at sunset.

Kulchek finally reached the spot where the creature had disappeared into the earth. In his anger, he struck the ground with Gard, his cudgel, shattering stones and knocking huge welts into the soil. Then, from deep inside the ground, voices came to the wanderer's ears, the voices of one hundred men or more, laughing and shouting in merriment. Realizing the rat's burrow must lead to the scene of this underground revelry—and perhaps a portal, as well—Kulchek used Gard to clear a huge swath of dirt from the area. There, a dozen feet below the ground, lay a pair of huge iron doors. They were parted slightly, but a massive lock and chain of ancient, rusted metal kept them from opening farther than a rat's width.

Such obstacles meant little to a thief of Kulchek's skill. Using the never-dulled, needle-pointed dagger, Novgor, the wanderer opened the lock as quickly as if he'd held the key. The hallway crawling from the gates deep into the earth was dark and damp. Carefully Kulchek crept toward the voices, Sabak at his heels. After treading mile upon mile of corridor, he came to a massive chamber, lit by more torches than he'd seen in his entire life. The light from the flames was almost blinding.

One hundred men sat at long tables, eating and drinking. A horned rat crouched at each man's feet, gulping down the scraps of flesh and lapping up the pools of ale spilled from the table. Past them all, on the other side of the room, stood a doorway wreathed in flames of blue and gold. Through the flickering fires, Kulchek could see a strange landscape. Here was the portal he had sought for so many sleepless days and nights.

The hundred men leaped to their feet, ready to slay Kulchek, for their lot in life was to guard the portal against any who sought to use it. The wanderer knew his lack of sleep would weigh heavily upon him in the battle, so he plumbed his quick mind for a way to win swiftly.

Before the men could even draw their swords, Kulchek held his never-dulled dagger before him, its side toward the guardians. The light from the dozens upon dozens of torches flashed off the bright silver of the blade and blinded fifty of the warriors. These the wanderer slew before they had advanced another step. With each death, one of the horned rats leaped through the portal. Though the blue-and-gold fire licked at their fur, the rodents passed unscathed from Barovia into the strange landscape.

The slaughter of the fifty made the odds more to Kulchek's liking, and he stood against the charge of the remaining warriors. Against these he wielded Gard. With each blow, the cudgel shattered another man's skull, and the bodies soon piled up around the wanderer. Sabak dragged these bodies away so the corpses would not hinder his master in the fight.

"And so it was that Kulchek the Wanderer defeated the one hundred men and found his way from Barovia," Magda concluded, her voice rasping from the long tale.

The sun hung low in the sky, making long shadows trail behind Magda and Soth as they trudged along the road. The river ran close at hand now, and the steady, soothing rush of the water had underscored the end of the Vistani's tale. High reeds partially blocked the Luna from view. From time to time the travelers noticed slanted, reptilian eyes watching them cautiously from those dark-thorned reeds. More often, larger shapes moved in the trees that lined the opposite side of the river.

"Well?" Magda asked. "Was the story any help?" She shielded her eyes and glanced toward the lowering sun. "If nothing else, it helped to pass the afternoon."

The death knight did not answer. Slowing his pace, he cocked his head as if to listen.

Sullen, the Vistani took a slow swallow from her water skin. "At least you could—"

"Silence," Soth hissed, raising his hand. He appeared ready to strike the woman, but then lowered his mailed hand. "Do not turn around. Something is following us. It has been for some time."

From the expression on her face, Magda clearly had to battle her curiosity to stop herself from looking over her shoulder. "Is it another alligator-man?"

The death knight shook his head. "It is a small beast, child-sized, perhaps the thing you saw back near the village." A note of savage pleasure crept into Soth's voice. "I do not like being toyed with, and this mysterious tracker has at last moved close enough for us to discover its identity. I must trust you to do as I ask, Magda."

Trust? The word startled the Vistani. "Of—of course," she replied.

"Do you see that bend ahead, where the trees cover the road in shadow?" he began. "When we reach it, I want you to keep walking, no matter what I do. I will tell you when to stop."

* * * * *

The trail wasn't difficult to follow, not with the death knight leaving a set of scent-prints stinking of the grave in his wake. No, even though his feet did not disturb the ground as he walked, the dead man was much easier to follow than the Vistani who served as his guide. All gypsies knew sufficient wood lore to make their paths difficult to detect, and this one was no exception. What was her name again? Ah, yes. *Magda*.

The beast curled back his thin, leathery lips and grinned ferally. If the knight doesn't mind, I'll leave her hanging by the side of the road for Strahd. That will curb the vampire lord's anger a little. Everyone knows by now that killing one of Girani's brood is enough to win Strahd's gratitude, and only a fool could underestimate the power of that.

In the road, Lord Soth raised his hand to the girl, ready to strike. The beast's heart quickened. The death knight had tired of her prattling at last!

He moved through the reeds a little more quickly, though the sound of the river masked what little noise he made. The soft mud accepted his clawed feet willingly, further muffling the sounds of his passing. Sniffing the air, he leered.

If he's angry, the beast noted to himself with glee, then he might even let me eat her heart. And it's been so long since I've tasted the blood of a Vistani.

Lost in a reverie of victims past, the beast's mind wandered. When he looked for his quarry again, they'd passed around a bend in the road. He hurried to catch them; the knight was ever wary, and more than once since leaving the village he had attempted to lay a false trail. That never threw the beast off the scent, though.

His eyes searching the shadowy roots of the trees for an ambush, the mysterious tracker loped into the copse. Nothing moved in the darkness. No creature hid in the murk. Sniffing, he picked up the scent— first the knight's, then Magda's. They had both passed into the copse.

Warily he crept through the undergrowth, watchful for some flash of silver that might expose a hidden blade or the stench of fear and expectation that meant someone was waiting to strike from the shadows. But the scent continued uninterrupted. It seemed they had both passed through the copse without even pausing.

At last the beast could see the road again, if the muddy path the Vistani had chosen to travel could be called that. Magda walked slowly in the sunlight, but the knight was nowhere to be seen. Panic gripped the beast, and he looked frantically from left to right. A sudden breeze carried a strong stench of decay from behind him, but before he could turn around, an ice-cold hand clamped down around his neck.

"Where is your master?" the death knight asked, stepping from the murk beneath a twisted oak. The ability to enter the darkness and travel from one shadow to another had served Soth well. He had remained hidden within the copse's darkness, shielded from the beast's extraordinary senses.

"Where is Strahd Von Zarovich?" Soth rumbled.

Stunted fingers ending in thick claws scraped against Soth's armored hand. With little effort, the death knight lifted the short, bulky creature from the ground and tossed him from the trees and into the road. The light of the setting sun revealed the hideous nature of the beast that had been tracking Soth and Magda. His frame was heavy, but he stood no more than three feet from head to toe. The beast crouched on legs unfit for great speed but obviously superb for digging and climbing. Short arms, round with corded muscles, stood out from his broad shoulders. Upon his back hung a battered pack, covered with mud and prickling with brambles.

The thing's head rested upon a neck small enough to be almost invisible. He possessed features similar to a man's, but flattened until they resembled a wild animal's. The creature's eyes were set wide apart and were so absolutely black they seemed to belong to a doll. A caninelike muzzle supported a wet black snout, whose nostrils were even now distended from tracking the death knight. Rounded ears lay flat against the beast's broad skull, and sharp, pointed teeth lined his mouth. Over his face, as well as the rest of his body, short hair grew in a thick coat. For the most part, this fur was brownish gray, but the hair ran in bone-white stripes below the creature's muzzle and in a broad stripe running from his snout to the nape of his neck.

In all, the beast resembled nothing so much as a horrifying mating of a small man and a badger.

"I am no servant of Strahd, Lord Soth," the beast said, the utterance sounding like the growl of a bear. "I am here to help you."

"You have been spying upon us since we left the village," the death knight said, studying the strange creature carefully. There was something familiar about the beast, though Soth could not say what. "Those are the actions of a spy, not an ally."

The creature barked a laugh. "The wolves you had on your trail—*those* were spies, Sir Knight. The fact I killed 'em—and I did—should be enough to prove to you I'm a friend." He stood and rubbed the back of his neck with a pawlike hand. "Besides, we've met before."

Shudders racked the beast for a moment, then he doubled over in pain. The hair covering his stocky frame melted away, seemingly drawn back into his skin. His limbs lengthened, and his features took on a more human—or, to be precise, a more dwarven—cast. The snout became a flat nose, the bristling hair a mustache and muttonchop sideburns. A brown tint, the color of freshly turned earth, seeped into his eyes, giving them a deep, thoughtful appearance. He rubbed his bald pate, always the last thing to return to normal, and nodded with satisfaction.

Magda, who despite Soth's orders had turned back to see the thing that had been tracking them, gasped and drew her silver dagger. "Werebeast!" she cried. "I should have known you were a cursed thing when first I saw you!"

The naked dwarf took the pack from his shoulder. He faced the woman, unconcerned with his lack of clothes, and snorted. "Put the blade away, little girl. Even if it is silver—and I know from the way it reflects the light that it is—you won't get a chance to strike me with it more than once before I split your skull open." He pulled a bright red tunic from the pack and shrugged it on over his head, then gestured toward three long scars crisscrossing his stomach. "And believe me, one blow isn't enough to kill me."

Folding his arms over his chest, the death knight said, "Even if you are an ally, why have you been following us?"

"Not *us*," the dwarf noted as he stepped into a pair of ratty leggings. "*You*. I'm following you, Sir Knight. I'd just as soon see the Vistani dead—and I'm willing to act on that, too, if you give the word."

Magda cursed and moved to Soth's side. "He's a spy, my lord. Why else would he follow you?"

With a sigh the dwarf removed his iron-soled shoes from the pack, sat on a stone at the road's edge, and slipped them on. "I'd much rather wear these than carry 'em," he noted. Fully garbed in a motley collection of ill-fitting clothes, the dwarf approached the death knight. "I am Azrael," he offered, as if that information alone was a great concession. "I follow you, Sir Knight, because you are very obviously a being of great power—greater than me, I'm more than willing to admit." He smiled slyly. "Perhaps even greater than Strahd Von Zarovich himself."

The death knight nodded to acknowledge the compliment. "I am Lord Soth of Dargaard Keep. What do you hope to gain by trailing me?"

"First," Azrael said, "let me tell you what you can gain by accepting me as a follower." He jerked a thumb over his shoulder, gesturing toward the east. Darkness had begun to settle on the horizon there. "I can help you to deal with the count's minions—like those wolves I killed a few days back. They were following you and reporting back to Strahd each sunset. That's their howling, you see? Messages. Haven't heard any howling at night lately, have you?" He puffed out his chest pridefully.

"I fear neither the count nor his servants," Soth replied. The dwarf exhaled like a balloon stuck with a dagger. "In fact, there is nothing you can offer me, little man. Be glad I am letting you live." Turning on his heel, the death knight started down the road again. Magda, trailing behind him, brandished her silver dagger at the werebeast as she left. The gesture was not so much threatening as insulting.

A look of puzzlement crossed the dwarf's face. He tugged at his mustache and smoothed his sideburns as he considered his plight. At last he sat down by the side of the road.

He hadn't expected the death knight to turn down his company so quickly or so completely. Yet, when it comes right down to it, Azrael realized sadly, there's little I can offer Lord Soth . . . except my loyalty—not that my loyalty is a worthless commodity. The knight just doesn't realize how valuable I could be. I've got to prove myself.

Smiling, the rag-clad dwarf stood and brushed himself off. Whistling tunelessly, he set off down the road after the death knight.

* * * * *

"None of these stones bear the mark you described," Lord Soth said angrily. He looked out across the Luna, flowing red in the dying light of the sun. "Is there another fork to this river?"

"Yes, but this is the spot where Kulchek found the tunnel into the earth," Magda replied. She overturned a large stone and peered beneath it, searching for the Vistani trail marker that was rumored to show the way to the portal. "The doors blocking the tunnel were buried beneath the ground, remember?"

"In your children's story, perhaps," Soth began, "but I—"

A mournful cry rent the air just as the sun's last glow faded in the west. It wasn't the low howl of a wolf, but a high, sorrowful cry of anguish. The sound echoed over the river and rattled through the foothills for a time.

Magda looked stunned, as if some deity had granted her insight into the workings of the world. "Sabak mourning for his lost quarry!" she gasped. "Did you hear it, my lord? We're in the right place!"

After scanning the area for some mundane source

for the cry, the death knight nodded. "Perhaps, Magda, perhaps. But where is the entrance to the tunnel?"

Cursing vilely, Azrael barreled out of a clump of bushes, his hands clutching at the rabbit that zig-zagged across the ground before him. The dwarf's presence hardly startled Soth or Magda, for he'd made no secret of following the pair. And when they'd refused to reveal anything about the object of their search, he'd set about capturing dinner for the party.

The rabbit proved too quick for the dwarf, and it soon disappeared into a knot of brambles. Futilely Azrael yanked the bushes apart, their thorns doing little damage to his rough, callused hands. The only thing he uncovered was a large, lichen-covered stone, but when he turned that over, a small burrow presented itself. The dwarf considered transforming into his full badger form—for his curse granted him the ability to hold one of three forms: dwarf, giant badger, or horrifying cross of the two—but before he could decide, Magda called out.

"He's found something," the Vistani cried. She was at Azrael's side in a flash, her loathing of the were-creature momentarily forgotten. With a trembling hand she pointed to the stone the dwarf had over-turned. "His paws burn into stone when he's on the prowl," she whispered. "Sabak's print!"

The mark of a single paw, made by a wolf or very large dog, glowed from the stone. Azrael reached down. The track was warm to the touch.

"Perhaps you can be of use, dwarf," the death knight noted, staring with glowing orange eyes at the stone.

The death knight briefly explained what it was they were hunting for, and Azrael offered to dig down from the stone to search for the iron gates. As before, pain shot through the dwarf's body as he transformed, but this time the creature he became appeared as nothing more than a badger, very large but otherwise ordinary. With a nod of his flat head to the death knight, he lunged at the ground and proceeded to tear into the earth.

The rabbit's burrow provided a head start for Azrael's excavation, and in very little time he had disappeared completely. Dirt and stone shot from the hole in bursts, then that, too, stopped. Magda paced back and forth, gnawing at her fingernails, watching for any sign of the werecreature. For his part, Soth appeared to calmly watch the Luna flow past, though he was actually scanning the area, watching for any sign of Strahd's minions or the strange beasts that lived in the river.

At last the badger trundled out of the hole, his fur coated with dirt. Ignoring Magda completely, he went to Soth's side. Letting the transformation flow over him once more, Azrael shifted into his beastlike form. "The wall of iron lies not far below the surface," he reported, brushing the large clumps from his fur. "Little more than your height, mighty lord."

"Then begin to uncover it," Soth said, a hint of excitement creeping into his voice. He turned to the Vistani. "Help him."

Azrael, still in his half-badger form, shredded the hard-packed layer of dirt and stone on the surface. Magda trailed behind him, clearing the loose earth to the side. Like a statue, Soth stood motionless as the pair opened a wide swath of ground. Hour after hour wore past, with the death knight observing the toil of his allies. Yet Magda and Azrael did not complain; the Vistani wanted escape from Barovia, from Strahd's wrath, more than anything, and the dwarf wished to prove himself a worthy servant.

The moon had reached its zenith before the death knight ordered them to stop. "You have uncovered enough of the door for me to open it now," was all he said.

As the werecreature and the young woman fell back, their hands caked with dirt and cut by stones, their hair matted with sweat, the death knight held his closed fists toward the earth. A blue light wreathed his gauntlets, spinning and growing in intensity as he chanted. Slowly Soth opened his hands, palms down, and the energy flowed from them to the newly broken ground. The earth trembled as if some long-dead leviathan were waking and shrugging off the mantle of soil that had settled over him in his millennium of slumber.

The blue light flowed from Soth's hand in crackling bands now. The bands spread out like fingers, working their way into the ground. His arms shaking, the death knight began to turn his palms face-up. The fingers of energy responded, tightening their grip on the still-hidden door.

It became clear why so much of the ground had needed to be cleared. Even with but a foot or two of earth to displace, the strain of magically forcing the doors open showed on the death knight. Soth arched backward, straining to move his hands.

The swelling, trembling ground made a sound like thunder, and as the fingers of energy pulled the door open, another noise was added: the groaning of the metal gate. The cacophony reminded Soth of the cries made by tortured souls in the Abyss. Anything within a mile of the fork would undoubtedly hear the racket.

A dark crack shot across the bulge, swallowing stones and dirt. Deftly the fingers of energy slipped into the crack and forced it wider. With one final surge of effort, the death knight turned his palms to the midnight sky. The doors burst through the ground and swung wide, showering the area with debris.

The blue light disappeared as Soth walked to the edge of the stone-lined tunnel. "Come," he said wearily. "I long to be free of this accursed place."

ELEVEN

The tunnel sloped steeply at first, and the going was treacherous. Water dripped from the stone walls and ceiling, then ran in foul rivulets down the floor. Patches of pale, rank-smelling lichen grew everywhere. More than once Magda slipped and nearly fell, and even Azrael, in half-badger form and moving on all fours, lost his footing twice. Only Lord Soth traversed the corridor as if it were level ground.

"It looks like it goes on forever," Magda whispered, holding high the torch she had fashioned out of driftwood and reeds. The guttering flame showed that the slope gradually evened out and the walls narrowed so that the trio would soon have to go single file.

The death knight walked more quickly. "If the portal at the tunnel's end will take me to Krynn, I will gladly cross the breadth of the Nine Hells to reach it."

Azrael followed close behind Soth as he entered the narrow section of the tunnel. Magda came last, the flame from her torch licking the ceiling. Although the death knight had closed the massive doors behind them and they had passed no holes big enough for anything but rats along the way, Magda had a nagging suspicion that something followed

them just beyond the reach of the torchlight. Time
and again, a sharp crack or low gurgle made the Vistani spin around and hold her torch out like a talis-
man. But if anything lurked in the corridor, it
contented itself with following the trio at a distance.

At length the hallway grew wider, and soon the
werebadger and the young woman flanked Soth
again. The tunnel veered sharply to the right, and
halfway around the bend Azrael skidded to a halt. "I
smell bones," he growled. He stood up as tall as his
stumpy legs would allow and sniffed the fetid air.
"Bones but no meat."

At the end of the curve yawned an arch of jet-black
stone, and beyond that, a vast chamber. The room
was huge, lined with black stone columns that rose
higher than Magda's torch would illuminate. Every
few paces along the walls, torches hung in iron
sconces. The wood was shriveled and warped. After a
few false starts, the Vistani succeeded in lighting a
dozen or so of these, and their combined light
washed over the chamber.

Magda looked up and saw row upon row of filled
sconces climbing toward the ceiling. "The room of
the torches," she said in awe, "where Kulchek fought
the guardians of the portal." She looked around.
"There's no guardian here now, though."

Bleached bones lay scattered in heaps toward the
room's center, the piles broken by the rotting remains of wooden trestle tables. The bones were surrounded and partially covered by patches of filth.
Magda was disgusted by the sight, but the grisly remains drew Azrael like a tavern drew layabouts. The
werebadger lifted a brittle leg bone and studied it
carefully.

"Human . . . male . . . not too old. That's my guess."
He turned the bone over and over in his hairy

paws. After sniffing it once, he bit down upon the end. The thing crunched unpleasantly, and Azrael chewed it, his mouth opening noisily with each bite. "Feh. Ancient, too. Not a bit of marrow left in 'em."

Soth paid little attention to his companions. The death knight carefully studied the walls, running his gauntleted hands over the cold stone. Once he stopped and traced a long, straight crack in the masonry, but when it turned out to be nothing more than a fissure in the wall, he moved on. Both Magda and Azrael were caught up in their study of other things in the room—a store of rusted swords having captured the Vistani's eye, and a few bones of newer vintage having aroused the werebeast's senses.

But Magda and Azrael offered little of interest to the sinister eyes that opened only a slit to study the intruders. One eye, then two, then a dozen, blinked away a cover of filth and dust, then stared up at Soth from the dirty stone floor.

"Aiyeee! Look at this!"

Pleasant surprise made Magda shriek, and her smile told of a wonderful discovery. Pushing aside a broken sword, one that was as old as Strahd's ancient castle, the Vistani grabbed a gnarled wooden club. It was short, only as long as Magda's forearm, but the knob on its end was twice as large as her fist. "A cudgel. It's very old. Do you think it might—"

"There's nothing here!" Soth shouted from across the room. "No portal. No door other than the one through which we entered."

Azrael dropped the skull he was toying with and looked up sharply. "Perhaps I could help you search, mighty lord. My senses are quite keen, you know."

As the werebeast stepped away from the scattered bones, the pile of dirt that lay between him and the death knight heaved up from the floor. As the filth fell away from the thing, its true form was revealed. A cloudy, viscous glob made up its body, and its shape shifted constantly, like something made of water. Tentacles of ooze flailed around it, disappearing from one part of the creature to reappear somewhere else on its body. It had no face to speak of, though it had the features of dozens.

Two hundred eyes, some large and staring, others small and heavy-lidded, covered the creature. Only a few of these were fixed on the intruders. The rest scanned the room and peered into the darkness that filled the corridor, looking for other foes. Around the eyes gaped dozens of mouths. These held a myriad of expressions, most contrary to each other. One opened hungrily, running a black tongue over pointed incisors, while another smiled sweetly. A third, a handsbreadth away, drooled like the maw of an idiot.

From each of these mouths came a constant babble, a cacophony of screams, curses, laughter, diatribes, and pleas. The stone walls echoed the waves of sound, doubling them, then doubling them again. Azrael, who was closest to the thing, threw his clawed hands against his ears. His muzzle rippled with a snarl of pain, but he remained rooted in place.

The voices called to the dwarf. They exploded in his mind and summoned his most vivid fears and dreams. Through a vague haze of pain, images flashed through his consciousness, one after another.

Azrael looked down at the blood on his hands and smiled. It was his brother's blood—or was it his mother's? He couldn't tell any longer; the murders had blended together in his mind. The fact that the screams of his kin had all been surprisingly similar didn't help matters. Azrael wondered if his death-scream would be very much like theirs.

Without warning, the door burst in, the shattering of ancient wood sending fragments across the modest dwarven home. Azrael glanced once at his brother, his neck broken, his face covered in gore, then saw the city's chief constable standing in the doorway. The fat *politskara* was frozen in shock, his jowls quivering with fear or, perhaps, anger. Azrael felt a rush of energy pulse through him, and he charged past the constable.

He was free! Rushing into the courtyard of his family's small home, the dwarf felt the cool air of the city flow over him. Dwarves bustled everywhere, and the clink of hammer upon metal, chisel upon stone, filled his ears. A disgust for all the inhabitants of the Crafter's Quarter—faint-willed lackeys like his family—threatened to overwhelm Azrael. He had to fight down the urge to attack anyone who came near. But, no, he had to escape, had to reach the dark tunnels that led even deeper into the earth.

The cry of "Murder!" rang out from behind him. The constable was shouting out Azrael's crimes at the top of his lungs. The young dwarf pushed a stonecutter out of his way and ran.

A sea of faces watched Azrael pass, eyes staring in shock and horror, mouths agape with strangled shouts. For a moment, the dwarf thought they were going to let him go, that the blood covering his arms, the scratches and bruises on his face, would hold them in terror.

Then the arrow bit into his arm.

Pain flashed from his elbow to his shoulder, and the world turned red in his eyes. The dwarf cursed the unknown archer who'd shot the arrow, then fletchers and arrowsmiths in general. He'd never liked bows; they were a coward's way to fight. No threat of blood on your hands if you shoot someone from a rood away, he thought, stumbling in pain.

The crowd closed in, and Azrael found his way blocked. The eyes of the dwarves stared at him, but those eyes held a different emotion now. Anger, not fear, colored the faces of the craftsmen as they tightened their circle around Azrael, and the threats they murmured filled his ears as he tumbled to the ground.

In the underground chamber in Barovia, the gibbering creature loomed over the fallen dwarf, one of its mouths locked on to his arm. The eyes nearest Azrael bulged with a hungry look, and the thing's body throbbed forward to bring another gaping mouth close to its ensorcelled victim.

Soth and Magda stood mesmerized. They, too, were caught up in paralyzing visions.

Magda found herself once again creeping down the long tunnel toward the underground chamber. A large hound, its head standing almost as high as her chest, followed at her heels.

"Come, Sabak," she said. "We must find a way out of this land." The strain of so many days without sleep had changed her voice to a husky whisper.

Light from a room up ahead bled into the tunnel, and the noise of a celebration filled the air. Magda edged along the wall until she came to the open doorway. The room was bright from the light of thousands of torches, and their dancing flames illuminated a scene of savage revelry. One hundred men crowded around trestle tables piled with raw red meat and dark ale. At their feet, rats with twisted horns fought over the bloody scraps that fell to the ground, squealing and biting their kin. Across the room stood the object of her quest, the portal that would take her from Barovia.

Boldly Magda stepped into the room. She was a

hero, the stuff of legends, and mere mortals would not stand between her and freedom. As one, the guardians of the portal turned to face the intruder, drawing their swords. Uncertainty gripped Magda for a moment, then a plan of action formed whole in her mind: *Use your dagger to reflect the torchlight and blind half of them, then lay into the others with Gard.*

The weight of her cudgel, Gard, felt reassuring in her right hand, and with her left she reached for her dagger. She patted her high leather boots, but the handle didn't jut over the boot top. Panic gripped her, and she looked down. Novgor, the ever-sharp dagger with the point like a needle, was gone.

The hundred men closed in, and Sabak leaped to protect its mistress. A dozen of the guardians lashed out at the faithful hound, striking it down. As the dog lay bleeding, the horned rats scurried over its body and burrowed into its chest, seeking its still-beating heart. The sight made Magda loathe her own weakness.

She rushed forward and lashed out with Gard, shattering one of the guardian's skulls. His teeth rained to the floor, and his staring eyes closed for the final time.

In the chamber, the gibbering thing shuddered at the blow. It released the huge, fanged mouth it had fastened to Azrael and hissed at the woman. She bashed the gaping maw in with the club. Keeping a grip on the fallen dwarf with three other mouths, the thing lurched in the Vistani's direction. Tentacles appeared all over the side facing her. The dripping arms lashed out and tried to snatch the ancient cudgel from her grasp. One struck her across the face and sent her sprawling.

Soth did not see any of this, though his eyes still stared ceaselessly into the chamber; like the others, he was caught up in a vision brought on by the guardian's myriad voices. The scene that lay before the death knight was one that had not welled up in his mind for many, many years. Goblins filled a dank, dismal cavern. Their flat faces—hundreds of them— all turned to look at him, and their grins of victory revealed small fangs eager for his flesh.

Along with two fellow knights, Soth had entered this, the most remote section of the Vingaard Mountains, on a quest. He and his fellows sought a relic of the greatest of the Knights of Solamnia, Huma Dragonbane. Legends claimed Huma himself had entered the mountains, searching for a minion of the evil goddess, Takhisis. The hunt took one hundred days, and during the long trek, the great knight's spurs were lost. Huma had cherished these spurs, for they had been presented to him by the church of Majere for his good deeds, but he did not stop to recover them. The quest was always foremost in Huma's thoughts.

It was for these spurs, symbols of Huma's devotion to the cause of Good, that Soth and his companions quested. Like the other two warriors, Soth had hoped the adventure would present a chance to prove his bravery—for that was the only way he would ever advance from Knight of the Sword to Knight of the Rose, the highest honor of the Order.

The trappings of rank held little interest for the young Sword Knight at the moment. A goblin horde guarded the relics, keeping them hidden from agents of Good, and the evil creatures had succeeded in isolating the knights and capturing two of them. Now Soth stood alone, all thoughts of glory gone from his mind.

I am a Knight of the Sword, he told himself, brushing the sweat from his forehead. Paladine, Father of

Good, teach your servant not to fear.

Although the young knight repeated the prayer over and over in his mind, his hand still shook slightly as he raised his sword. "Release my fellows," he heard himself say, surprised at how clear and commanding his voice was. He pointed to the two wounded knights that hung on one wall of the cavern, heavy chains holding their wrists to the dripping stone. "I will ask once for their freedom. If you do not comply swiftly, I will cut a swath through your ranks and free them myself."

Both captive knights were battered and bloody, and Soth wondered if either of them still lived. The notion was dismissed quickly; his duty to them, dead or alive, was clear. He must rescue them or die trying.

The goblins became a jabbering mob. Some slapped their short, flint-tipped spears against their shields. The leather ovals thudded dully as they were struck, but, added together, they sounded like thunder rumbling through the cavern. Others shouted and cursed in their harsh, guttural tongue. The mob moved forward, the red skin of their faces making them look demonic in the cave's torchlight. Their slanted yellow eyes glowed with malevolence.

Soth gripped his sword tightly and said a prayer to the gods of Good. "You have been warned," he said to the mob, but the goblins came closer.

A command shouted from the rear of the press halted the creatures' advance. Many of the mob turned to face the goblin that had given the order, and fell aside. Down the wide path cleared for him came the goblin king, his armor clanking with each step.

Whereas his subjects were short, perhaps half of Soth's six-foot stature, the king stood almost as tall as a normal human. His skin was bright red, like the rest of his tribe's, his face gaunt. The armor he wore heightened his muscular appearance, and he moved with the steady step of one used to treading unopposed through even the most chaotic battlefield. Soth had seen creatures like this before, had even faced a few in combat. They were proud and skilled and deadly. Defeat with honor was a foreign idea to such warriors, as was mercy for bested foes.

"Throw down your sword, knight," the goblin king shouted. He lifted the studded mace he carried and shook it menacingly at Soth. "Let me split your skull and be done with it."

The young Knight of the Sword swallowed hard. "I am glad to hear you speak the tongue of humans," he said, "for I can inform you that the path of surrender is one I will not tread. Release my friends and give me the artifacts your tribe unlawfully holds. Only then will I leave."

"And if I don't turn these things over to you?"

Unbidden, the teachings of one of the elder knights flew into Soth's mind: *When facing tribes of goblins, a direct challenge to the king or leader can prevent greater bloodshed. If the king is defeated, the tribe will often disperse, for they hold such deaths to be a sign of displeasure from their gods.*

Soth straightened and held his sword point-down, a clear sign of disdain for the goblin king. "If you fail to release my friends or do not give me the things that rightfully belong to my Order, I will face you in individual combat. It is my right as a knight to demand this of you, and it is your duty as a warrior to accept. Unless, of course, you fear me." Soth forced a smile. "If that is so, I will face your champion."

For a moment the goblin king stood in shocked silence. "I do not fear you, human." He sneered. Raising his mace high over his head, the king barked a command. The mob rushed forward. Over the cries of the charging soldiers he added, "But I am not foolish enough to send only one of us against your blade."

Soth slashed the first goblin to come close enough, then cut a second from shoulder to stomach. As the soldiers died, the blood pooled around the knight's feet, making the stone floor slippery. Panic gripped him just long enough for a spear tip to slip past his guard. The flint bit into his leg. As he struck that attacker down, another goblin stabbed him in the back. His left arm went numb, and his head began to swim.

This isn't how it happened, Soth realized as another goblin fell before his blade. On the day I entered the cavern, the goblin king accepted my challenge. I killed him and a dozen more of his kind. The others fled. I won. My courage earned me the right to petition the Knights' Council for advancement. . . .

Another jolt of pain lanced through Soth's sword arm, making it difficult for him to grip his weapon. He looked down and saw a yawning hole in his armor. The wrist beneath the hole was almost translucent, and the flesh that barely covered the bone was pale and scabrous. The skin of a dead man, he realized, though the gibbering voices in his mind tried to push the thought away. Goblin voices? No. Something else, something in a bone-filled room at the end of a long tunnel. And the wound on his arm wasn't the work of goblin spears, but the dragon in Castle Ravenloft.

Lord Soth's fury silenced the voices in his mind. He looked out across the room and saw the gelatinous thing. A half-dozen of the creature's mouths were biting into Azrael's flesh. The werebeast lay curled on the floor, howling in pain, partially buried beneath the monster's bulk. Magda was on her knees a few feet from Azrael, swinging wildly at the thing with a wooden club. Wherever the cudgel struck, an eye closed, a mouth grew silent, or an ugly, blackened welt formed on the creature's cloudy mass. Tentacles snaked around her arm and entwined themselves in her hair, trying to pull her closer to the large, fanged mouth that opened an arm's length before her.

"Sabak!" the woman cried. "I will avenge you. I will take your body through the portal when I slay these men."

The silly bardic tale again, the death knight thought. She thinks she is Kulchek, hammering at her foes.

The thing turned many of its eyes to Lord Soth. The watery orbs registered surprise, and the mouths babbled even louder. A thick, writhing tentacle ending in a clutch of pointed digits shot toward the death knight. Soth slashed the arm with his sword. The blow severed the tentacle cleanly but also sent a lightning bolt of pain from his injured wrist to his chest. The sword dropped from his hand with a clatter.

Again the thing studied Lord Soth. The death knight returned the clinical, appraising gaze. As he looked at the mass of eyes—some without pupils, some without irises—a notion took hold in his mind. Perhaps the bardic tale wasn't so silly after all.

He raised his hands. Although his right wrist fought against him, Soth wove an intricate arcane pattern in the air.

At a single word, a magical command as ancient as the world of Krynn itself, a brilliant light filled the room. The golden radiance was almost a physical thing, with weight and substance—rather like a deluge of clean, fresh water. Soth's never-blinking eyes smarted at the flash, but the magical light did not blind him. From the ear-splitting shriek that went up from the unearthly creature at the room's center, however, the death knight assumed its multitude of eyes had not proven as sturdy.

The creature stiffened, and its eyes became white, sightless orbs swimming in its liquid body. After the hundred-voiced scream died away, the mouths were silent for a moment. Then they began to whimper and mewl. That proved enough to break its hypnotic hold over Magda and Azrael.

The Vistani recovered first, blinking away the pain the spell had caused her eyes. She recoiled from the creature before her, but for only an instant. Gripping the cudgel, she struggled to her feet and swatted away the tentacles reaching for her. At the vigorous attack from the Vistani, the sightless thing edged away, positioning its bulk over Azrael.

A shout came from beneath the creature. "Bloody hells! Get this great mound of spit off me!" A horrible sound, like a dull cleaver slicing through raw meat, followed the cry. The thing lurched again, this time away from the dwarf.

Azrael lay on the floor, three of the creature's mouths still attached to his arm and shoulder. The fanged maws continued to work their teeth deeper into his flesh. It took all the werebeast's strength to pry the mouths apart. Magda moved to the dwarf's side and contributed a few well-placed blows.

Soth retrieved his sword, lifting it with his uninjured hand. He warily approached the gibbering thing, studying it as he did so. A thousand waving fingers protruded from the creature now, surrogate eyes searching the room for some escape route, keeping attackers at a distance. Mottled bruises dotted its smooth skin where Magda had struck it, and three puckered wounds marked where Azrael had torn the mouths from its side. One moment the creature appeared as a giant fringed mushroom suddenly pushed up from the filthy floor, the next it was a monstrous, spiky flatworm, slithering along the stones, seeking escape.

"The thing has no scent," Azrael said, wonderingly. "I would have smelled it when we entered the room, but it just doesn't have a scent." He kicked the mouths that lay on the floor. "Has quite a bite, though."

Magda helped Azrael to his feet, though she kept a wary eye on the creature. "Do you need help, my lord?" she asked of the death knight, who was moving in for an attack.

For a reply Soth stabbed the creature, burying his blade to the hilt. The sword thrust did little to harm the thing; like the injuries wrought by Azrael, the stab wound puckered closed almost the moment the steel left the flesh.

The thing gathered into a ball and slid toward a corner, its thin feelers sweeping over the death knight, trying to read his intentions. When Soth raised his sword to strike again, thick ropes ending with gaping mouths shot from the creature and wrenched the blade from his grasp. Before Magda or Azrael could take a step toward Soth, a single tentacle, this one as thick around as a jungle snake, encircled the death knight's waist and pulled him to the thing's side. The creature's milky flesh pushed up against the knight's armor. Pulsing skin filled the gaps in Soth's helmet, sealing out the air.

With his face pressed so close to the monster, Soth could see the ebb and flow of the thick ooze that made up its body, the play of filtered torchlight in its flesh as mouths opened and closed. At the center of the creature lay a lumpy mass, pale but darker than the matter around it.

Soth flexed his arms and snapped free of the dozens of ropy arms binding him. He drove his gauntleted left hand, held open like the tip of a boar-spear, deep into his attacker. The thing tried futilely to push him away, surprised that its attacker had not suffocated, but the death knight was too strong. His arm buried almost to the shoulder, Soth grabbed the pulpy mass that was the creature's brains and heart. The thing whimpered only once as Soth crushed the life from it, then it slumped to the floor.

When the death knight pulled himself free of the creature's limp form, he saw that Magda and Azrael were close by. They battered the thing savagely, stopping only when Soth held up a restraining hand.

The Vistani opened her mouth to speak, but a rush of unbearably hot air and the sudden roar of a massive fire superseded her questions. The wall opposite the room's single door had disappeared, and the gap where it had stood opened onto a vast sea of blue and gold flames. The three walked wordlessly to the edge of the stone floor and looked out. The heat forced Magda and Azrael to shield their faces with their hands; even Soth felt the inferno's warmth on his dead flesh.

The sea of fire lay hundreds, perhaps thousands of feet down, though pillars of twisting flame leaped into the black sky. The pillars spiraled higher and higher, finally diminishing into wisps of color and light. A whirlpool spun madly below the companions, a blot of red in the expanse of blue and gold. In the maelstrom's center yawned a circle as black as anything in the lowest depth of the Abyss.

"Th-this is the portal you're looking for?" Azrael gasped. "It don't look quite . . . safe to me."

"No," Soth said, almost in a sigh. "This is no portal."

Magda shook her head. "But the tales. Kulchek found a portal ringed in blue and gold flame. This *must* be it. The bones. The torches." She paused, then lifted the cudgel. "Even this. It's all too close to the tale to ignore."

"Then after you, by all means," Azrael growled, motioning to the brink with an open palm.

"Yes," came a smooth voice from the doorway on the other side of the room. "By all means, Magda, jump."

Strahd Von Zarovich stood framed by the door-jamb. His hands, clad in stylish kidskin gloves, lay folded over his chest in the fashion of corpses about to be put to rest. He wore the same finely cut clothes he'd worn the night Soth and Magda had arrived at Castle Ravenloft—the tight black jacket over a white shirt, black pants, dark leather boots, and a flowing cloak of ebony silk lined with a similar fabric colored red. A casual, almost amused look hung on Strahd's gaunt face, and his thin mouth was turned up in a mocking half-smile.

The Vistani looked into the count's dark eyes and saw sparks of anger, hints of the emotion the vampire lord's mask imperfectly concealed. Magda also saw her fate in those eyes—a slow death at Strahd's hands, a death that led to eternal life as one of the count's slaves.

She spun around and leaped from the precipice.

The air itself seemed to push down on her the moment she moved over the sea of fire. A horrible, abrupt sensation of vertigo made her head swim. Her eyes found the maelstrom spinning below, and she knew in that instant that Soth had been right. This was no portal.

In the same instant, the low collar of her dress bit into her chest. A pained gasp escaped Magda's lips, then she found herself thrust back into the room. She landed in a heap near the pile of bones at the room's center, the front of her dress torn slightly from straining against her weight. She dropped the cudgel, then marveled that she'd managed to hold on to it. Finally she looked to Soth.

The death knight stood on the very brink of the flaming abyss, watching her with his glowing, unreadable eyes. His left hand was still extended a little before him, the hand with which he'd plucked her from certain death. Azrael stood at the death knight's side. The werecreature crouched in a defensive stance, and his earth-brown eyes darted from Magda to Soth to Strahd.

"Too bad," the count said languidly, stepping into the room. "I would have enjoyed hearing her screams. Anyone clumsy enough to fall into the inferno catches fire long before they hit the flames." Gesturing at the open wall, the vampire continued. "The guardian you fought was here when I uncovered this place, too. When I killed it—"

"*You* killed it?" Azrael asked.

Strahd spared the werebadger a withering glance. "Yes, and if we stay here long enough, we will see it rise up yet again," he said. "When the guardian is slain, the wall opens. Perhaps it was a portal at one time, but not now. A few of my servants offered to . . . test this particular rumor some time ago. They came to a most painful end." He extended a slim hand to the woman.

When Magda shrank away from the offered hand, the count shrugged and turned his back on her. "Of course, I could have told you this was a ruse, Lord Soth, had you asked me." He faced the death knight again. This time the facade of amusement slipped away fully, revealing the anger seething underneath. "But, then, you spurned the hand of friendship I offered, as did this gypsy whore who follows you like a cur."

Lord Soth walked slowly to Magda's side. "Get up," he demanded coldly. Using the cudgel as a brace, she stood, though she never took her eyes from the vampire lord. Azrael, too, crept to the death knight, his extended claws scraping the ground as he loped forward.

"Servitude does not breed friendship, Count," Soth said. "You treated me like a lackey, an errand boy or hired murderer."

"And you are no man's lackey, eh, Soth? You believe you control your own fate?" the vampire lord asked. He smiled, a genuine smile of cruel amusement. "You will learn we are all lackeys of the dark powers that rule this place, chess pieces to be moved about and set against each other."

Soth curled his hands into fists. "Have you come to set yourself against me?"

"Us," Azrael said to the vampire lord. Magda held the ancient wooden club before her, an obvious statement of her agreement.

Strahd laughed. "Of course not," he replied. Bowing slightly and fanning his cape with one hand, he added, "I am here, Lord Soth, to call a truce to our little conflict and to offer myself to you as an ally."

"Fine," the death knight said. "Let us leave this place then. We'll find somewhere more suitable for . . . *allies* to discuss their plans."

Strahd bowed again, this time more fully. He headed for the door, saying, "I have an outpost nearby, a ruined tower. It will be perfect for just such a discussion."

Soth retrieved his sword and sheathed it, then followed the vampire toward the tunnel. Azrael quickly fell in beside the death knight and the Vistani.

Before he left the chamber, Lord Soth turned to the werecreature. "If you ever try to speak for me or amend my words again, I'll cut the tongue from your mouth before you can utter a cry of protest."

Azrael knew it would be foolish to answer, so he simply nodded and fell a few steps behind the death knight. In silence the trio made its way back through the tunnel, to the fork of the River Luna. The weight of dashed hopes hung on their shoulders like cloaks sodden with foul water.

 **TWELVE**

The young man's screams reverberated through the crumbling tower of Strahd's outpost on the outskirts of Barovia. The cries for pity became pleas for a quick death, growing more shrill with each passing moment. They filled the tower's chimneys like gusts of air and entered the midnight sky as little more than haunting moans. The few peasants who dwelt near the abandoned keep had heard far worse coming from the place, so they weren't unnerved. They were Barovians, after all, and such night-terrors were part of their lot in life. Those who heard the screaming merely checked the braces on their shutters and tried their best to fall asleep, thanking their gods that it wasn't them in the tower.

The unfortunate prisoner in the ruined keep prayed to his gods, too, but they did not—or could not—grant him a quick death. It was understood throughout the land, and perhaps even the heavens, that Strahd Von Zarovich seldom trafficked in merciful ends.

The vampire lord stood in a large hall on the tower's ground floor, his back to the fire burning cheerily in the hearth. He held one hand on the forehead of the captive, the other on Lord Soth's wounded arm.

The young man was a gypsy, a Vistani of Madame Girani's tribe and a cousin of Magda's. He tried again and again to shake the bone-white fingers from his brow, but each jerk of his head was weaker, less violent. With his arms tied painfully behind him and his torso and legs lashed to a heavy chair, the young man stood no chance of preventing the count from completing his enchantment.

For his part, Soth stood calmly, feeling the warm flow of the gypsy's life force seeping into his wrist. His hand flexed and his fingers spread of their own accord, as if the energy Strahd was draining from the Vistani was gifting his limb with an independent will. The death knight knew, however, that the necromantic spell the vampire lord cast did nothing but siphon the life from the mortal prisoner and transfer it to him. Soon the wounds he'd gained from the dragon's jaws would be healed completely. The muscle spasms were but an odd side-effect.

The look on the count's face told Soth that the vampire enjoyed the workings of this particular spell. Strahd's dark eyes rolled back and fluttered, showing only their whites. His pale cheeks flushed with color; his cruel mouth stretched into a wide smile of pleasure. The vampire's fangs had extended to their full length. The long canines gave the count's thin face a harsh, bestial cast. To a creature such as Strahd, who sustained himself on the life force of others, serving as a conduit for the transfer of such energy was a tantalizing, invigorating experience.

At last the screams faded to whimpers, then even those pitiable sounds stopped. The Vistani's handsome features changed as Soth watched; the youth's dark, piercing eyes grew vague and watery, his smooth face became pitted with pock marks and creased with wrinkles. The skin sagged over his cheeks and jaws like wet cloth, and a thin line of spittle slipped down his chin. When Strahd removed his hand from the prisoner's forehead, the Vistani slumped forward.

"Is he dead?" the death knight asked, rubbing an appraising hand over his healed wrist.

"Of course," Strahd replied. He pushed the Vistani's head up and studied his face. "He was the last of Girani's clan—apart from Magda, of course. When she's gone . . ." The vampire let the corpse's head loll forward again, then wiped his hands together, as if they'd been sullied by contact with the dead man.

Stiffly Lord Soth retrieved the battered vambrace that had covered his lower arm and the gauntlet that he'd worn on the injured hand. The metal of both pieces of armor showed the effects of the dragon's attack—the vambrace in the scratches and jagged-edged hole in its side, the gauntlet in its crushed joints and the small punctures pitting its surface. "I will go to the basement now and work on my armor," the death knight said.

"Not just yet, Lord Soth," Strahd replied. He gestured toward the only empty seats left in the hall—a pair of block chairs that bracketed the glowing hearth. "We should talk for a while. Besides, I can provide you with replacements for those from the tower's armory. No one has dared loot the place since I . . . evicted the previous tenant."

"I prefer to keep these," the death knight noted. "This armor is ancient, and over time it has become more a skin to me than this other." He held up his arm, and the withered flesh shone translucent, ghostly.

Taking a seat by the fire, Strahd nodded. "Of course, of course." Again he gestured to the other seat. When Soth finally relented and sat down, the vampire lord steepled his fingers. His long, dark nails were as sharp as Azrael's claws. "You have not asked me why I still seek you as an ally."

The death knight shrugged. "That seems obvious, Count. You hope to see Duke Gundar inconvenienced, if not slain outright. Now that I've proven my strength to you, it is clear I am the one to do this."

"Just so," the vampire admitted. "At first I was quite angry. Few dare to challenge me, let alone in my own home." Rolling his fingertips together, he added, "It's been quite a long time since anyone of such power entered my realm. Because of that, it was natural for me to underestimate your place in the domain's web of life."

Strahd stood and paced before the fire. "The dragon you destroyed is a rarity here, but not irreplaceable, and as far as Gundar's ambassador is concerned, you managed to trick him into cooperating with us."

"Pargat told me nothing before he died."

"But he told me *everything* when I conjured up his spirit," Strahd noted happily. "Gundar's monstrous son had cast a powerful spell over him, making it impossible for him to reveal any secrets to me, but it had power over him only while he was alive. I should have thought of that."

Strahd's dark eyes glittered in the firelight. "You proved yourself formidable . . . I readily admit that. I underestimated your power. To compensate you for that insult, I have healed your wounds and even forgiven you for your breach of hospitality."

"We start our dealings anew?"

"Just so," Strahd said, taking his seat again. "I know you seek a portal, a way out of these dark domains. I happen to know where one exists, as well as what rites need be performed to open the gate."

The death knight nodded. "Since this portal happens to stand in your foe's domain, it may be necessary for me to force him to see the urgency of my quest."

"We understand each other perfectly, Lord Soth." The vampire casually reached down and tossed a piece of wood onto the fire, though the blaze warmed neither of the beings who sat before it. "A fair exchange between allies. I give you the location of the portal. You do not restrain yourself from harming anyone who prevents you from reaching that gateway."

The conversation soon turned to Duke Gundar and the bloody history of the portal that lay within his home at Castle Hunadora. Like Strahd, the duke was a vampire, but he ruled his land through brute force, not through the subtle tactics of fear favored by the count. Barovians lived in dread of their mysterious lord—or, to be more precise, the boyar class of landholders who did Strahd's bidding, collected his taxes, and enforced his laws. The poor souls who dwelt in Gundarak feared not only the duke's army, composed largely of thugs and murderers, but the lord himself. Although they did not realize Gundar was a vampire, the people of Gundarak knew of his rampages across the countryside. His forays at the head of a mob of plundering soldiers had fueled many citizens' nightmares.

Those who lived under the long shadow of Castle Ravenloft worked hard to pay their taxes, all in the hope that they might never know what the ancient stone walls held; the men and women of Gundarak knew that, no matter what they did, they might end up a corpse suspended from Hunadora's blood-soaked battlements.

The story of Hunadora's portal was likewise

colored by violence. Hundreds of years past, the
duke's young son had quarreled with his sister in the
castle's main hall. Even then, the boy was a foul-
tempered reflection of his father, and the argument
ended with him bashing open his sister's skull. No
sooner had the girl's blood wet the stone floor than a
doorway of shimmering darkness appeared in the
room's center. Gundar and his son both tried to pass
through the gate, but a wall of crackling energy held
them back.

For more than a decade they preserved the girl's
corpse, using dark sorceries to make it bleed steadily. In this way they kept the portal open, but their experiments yielded the duke only disappointments.
While any not of the duke's bloodline could enter the
portal without hindrance, neither he nor his son
could pass through. At last Duke Gundar tossed his
daughter to the crows and let the gate close.

"The experiments with the gate left their mark on
Gundar's brat son, too," the count said, stretching his
legs as the tale came to an end. "Medraut is forever
trapped in a child's body. The scholars the duke con-
sulted claimed it had something to do with the ener-
gies the portal emitted."

"Yet the child-monster can be killed?"

"As far as anyone knows, yes. It is said that his
blood—or his father's—will open the portal again
when spilled in Hunadora's main hall."

For a time only the sound of the crackling fire
could be heard in the keep. Soth pondered what the
count had told him as the vampire lord sat content-
edly by the fireside, seeming to doze. Finally the
death knight stood. "I will leave in the morning,
Count."

"Splendid," Strahd exclaimed. The speed with
which he stood told Soth the count had been far from

asleep. "I have two final gifts to offer you. The first is advice."

The vampire lord moved to the room's single window and motioned for Soth to join him. "Once, long ago, Barovia was the only duchy in this netherworld," Strahd began. The death knight reached his side and glanced into the night. "The duchy was surrounded by a border of mist—the same mist that brought you here, Soth. As time went on, the mist carried strangers to my land. It was inevitable that, one day, someone would attempt to find his way back. A few travelers who entered the Misty Border were never seen again. Others simply left the mists in the duchy, reappearing far from where they'd entered."

Pointing to the south, the count continued. "That was true until a ghost of great power and great evil breached the Misty Border. When he walked into the mists, a new duchy formed, a land called Forlorn. The dark spirit, whose name has never been told, rules Forlorn . . . just as other powerful beings rule the domains that formed when they entered the Misty Border."

"You believe a new land would form if I entered this border?" Soth asked.

Nodding, Strahd turned away from the window. "Perhaps. And you would be trapped in that domain forever, just as I am a prisoner within the borders of Barovia." He poked the fire and watched the sparks rise up the chimney. "A stretch of the Misty Border edges Gundarak to the southeast of Castle Hunadora. Keep to the routes I will provide you, and you will be safe. Stray too far from my map and . . ."

The death knight needed no further explanation. "What is the other gift?"

The count looked into the fire. "Troops worthy of accompanying you through Gundar's lands."

"I have no need of men," Soth replied. "My thanks, but Azrael and Magda have proven to be somewhat useful. I plan to take only them with me into Gundarak."

Strahd frowned, and the look of consternation that crossed his face was sudden and severe. "I was hoping you would allow me to deal with the gypsy and the dwarf. Magda knows far more than I'm comfortable with, and the werecreature has been raiding my villages for some time, flouting my authority."

Soth gathered his damaged armor. "They are both pawns," he said. Turning his back on Strahd, the death knight headed for the basement and the tools that were stored there. "But they are *my* pawns, and I will not give them up without good cause. As an equal ally in this arrangement, I reserve that right. I'm sure you understand."

* * * * *

With the screaming finally at an end, Magda found it easier to work. Sighing, she pulled the brightly colored blanket a little tighter around her shoulders, then took a firm grip on the bone sewing needle and went about mending her tattered dress. The garment, which lay draped across her lap, had been a beautiful gown when Strahd had made a gift of it to her. After many days on the road and more than one terrifying encounter, it was little better than the homespun skirt the gypsy had been wearing on the night Soth had kidnapped her.

"Did you know him?" Azrael asked around a mouthful of bread. He pointed down, toward the room Soth and Strahd occupied. "The gypsy they have down there, I mean."

Magda squinted at the crude needle and threaded

it. After making a stitch or two in the dress's ragged hem, she looked up at the dwarf. "My tribe was very small. I knew everyone in it."

The clump of bread clutched in one hand, Azrael foraged through the basket at his side. Small wheels of cheese, loaves of bread, a few containers of preserved fruit and hardtack, and even two bottles of wine filled the straw basket to bursting. The dwarf pushed most of this aside, coming up at last with a cold leg of lamb. "You'll be the last one left soon . . . if you're not already."

"That matters little," she replied icily. "Apart from the old woman who led us, there was no one in the tribe who would have mourned me had I died before them—not even my brother." She went back to her sewing. "If I am the last, I will begin my own tribe."

The statement was made with little emotion, as if Magda had been speaking of the last meal she'd eaten or the weather from the previous day. With equanimity she held the dress up to the light of the single candle that lit the highest room in the tower. A skylight, its window long ago caved in by snow, augmented that feeble light with a wide pool of moonlight. The radiance cast a pale glow on the few boxes that made up the room's decor.

Satisfied with the stitchwork, Magda set about sewing the rest of the hem. After that, she would patch the few holes in the gown. It wouldn't be the type of dress to make men follow her with their eyes, but that didn't matter to her anymore. In her present circumstances, such concerns as romance or beauty seemed frivolous. One needn't worry about turning heads if keeping one's own was a matter left unresolved.

Azrael stuffed the last of the bread into his mouth. "You're not like the other Vistani I've run into," the dwarf mumbled absently. "Not that that's a bad thing, mind you. I mean, it's obvious you're not a spy for the count."

"Hardly," Magda replied, not looking up from her work.

Strahd's treatment of the woman on the way to the tower had been cold at best, openly contemptuous at times. When Azrael had noted that they were short on supplies, the count had led them on a detour to a lonely farmhouse near the fork of the River Luna. There Magda and the dwarf were ordered to present themselves as Strahd's agents. The peasants knew that anyone possessing the lord's seal had to be granted whatever they requested; all the pair had to do was ask for the food, clothing, and weapons they required. When Magda balked at the notion of taking food from people who likely had little to spare, Strahd flew into a rage. Only Soth's presence tempered the vampire's wild anger.

At last done with the repairs, Magda turned her back on the dwarf and shrugged the dress on over her shoulders. She let the blanket drop and smoothed the red cloth over the curve of her hips. When she turned around again, the dwarf was eyeing her lustily. She reached for the cudgel that lay at her feet.

"No need for that," the dwarf said quickly. "Sorry if you don't like the way I was looking at you, but . . . well, you are quite attractive for a human."

Magda left the weapon where it lay. After all, if Azrael threatened her, she always had her silver dagger close at hand. She'd moved it from her sack to her boot after the battle with the gibbering guardian; Vistani superstitions were clear on such matters. Only a fool ignored the prompting of such a warning.

Feeling secure, she packed her needle and thread

in her burlap sack. Along with a small loaf of bread and a jug of sweet cider, the sewing items were all she'd asked of the terrified old woman who lived in the cottage they visited. Azrael had demanded all the food he could carry, as well as blankets, a new tunic, and a pack for his new belongings.

The Vistani tossed the colorful but ill-gotten blanket she'd used to cover herself back to the were-creature. "Thank you for the compliment and the use of this."

"Why do you think the club's so special, if you don't mind me asking?" the dwarf asked without prelude. After Magda explained the tale of Kulchek the Wanderer, Azrael snorted. "If that was the cavern he visited, then his skull was probably stacked with the rest. The blob with all the eyes must have eaten him."

Magda refused to rise to the bait. "Strahd said the thing returns from the dead somehow after it is killed. What makes you think Kulchek didn't kill it before?"

"And the portal that was supposed to be there?"

The woman waved the question away with a flick of her hand. "Perhaps there was a portal there once, but the magic sustaining it fell away."

Momentarily rebuffed, the dwarf turned to rummage through the basket of food again. "Your great hero left his special club behind, eh? Doesn't seem likely to me. I mean, if it was magic, he'd have taken it with him."

Planting her hands on her hips, Magda said flatly, "You saw what the cudgel did to the guardian of the portal. Perhaps I should test it out on a shape-changer."

Azrael laughed, a growling sound that made Magda wonder if the dwarf again was transforming into his badger form. "Magic sticks'll do you no good against things like me," he said when the laughing fit had subsided. "Oh, maybe that cudgel's more than just a bit of wood, but don't rely on it."

Warming to the subject, Azrael got to his feet and straightened the brocatelle tunic he'd taken from the peasants. The heavy, colorful yarns that made up the garment lent the dwarf the look of a court jester. "Take the lout who ran into me on the road near Barovia village the other night," he began. "I hid in the bushes at the side of the road, waiting for an easy mark. When this boyar came riding along, I leaped out looking like a half-badger—teeth and claws and all that. Does he run? Does he draw a sword? No, he whips out this pendant and waves it at me."

A fit of laughter seized the dwarf, and he doubled over in mirth. " 'Oh,' I growls, 'don't do that no more. You'll make me hurt myself laughing at you.' "

Magda sat in shocked silence. In a daze, she rummaged through her small sack and withdrew the pendant she had sold to Herr Grest the night Soth had attacked her tribe. She'd told the boyar that the little piece of jewelry possessed the power to shield the person wearing it from creatures of the night. It's actual powers were much less impressive: It made the person wearing it invisible to mindless undead, creatures like zombies or living skeletons, things without free will or human intelligence.

"Hey, you've got one just like his," Azrael said, pointing at the drop of silver on the end of the chain.

"It's the *same* pendant," she corrected. "I got it from that boyar's kin. The villagers are blaming that murder on my tribe."

The dwarf chuckled. "They won't have many warm bodies to put on trial after Strahd gets through with your lot."

"I won't be one of them," the Vistani insisted as she slipped the pendant on. "Once we cross into Gundarak, there's no way I'm ever coming back to Barovia." She packed the rest of her belongings into her sack. "By the way, are you wearing that motley tunic all the way to Gundar's castle? His guards would see you coming ten leagues away."

"The count says there's some old armor in the basement." The dwarf picked at a loose thread of azure yarn. "I'll get a mail shirt and use this as padding."

"I wouldn't trust Strahd's word on anything," Magda murmured under her breath.

Azrael groaned. "But you trust Soth? At least Strahd is open about his plans. You can be sure he will do as he says." Spreading his arms wide, the dwarf added, "Do you know what this place used to be? The fortress of a local nobleman. When the noble stole tax money, the count had everyone in his household killed. Was it a surprise? Certainly not."

"What's your point?"

A wide smile played across Azrael's face, making his muttonchop sideburns bristle like whiskers. "A predictable person is a lot less dangerous than one who tosses surprises at you."

Magda slung her pack over her shoulder and took a last look around the musty tower room. "You're as good at giving advice and sharing your 'wisdom' as any Vistani fortune-teller I've ever met. Do you ever follow it yourself?"

Azrael didn't answer for a time. After he finished repacking his food, he noted, "If I followed half the advice I give, do you think I'd be here myself?"

*   *   *   *   *   *

Caradoc was finally growing accustomed to seeing the world at a tilt. His head still lolled on his shoulder, unsupported by his broken neck, but in the time since Soth had attacked him, the ghost had become less aware of the odd angle at which he viewed things. At times his mind compensated for the injury, straightening the landscape and the horizon he saw. Then there were the minutes and hours when Caradoc couldn't even walk because of the vertigo that gripped him, times when he couldn't tell up from down. Luckily, those attacks were growing less frequent, and the ghost was certain that, given time, his mind would adjust.

As he stood in the darkest shadows at the tower's base, Caradoc saw the world as he supposed it really was. The ancient two-story tower squatted atop a steep-sided mound like a dragon upon its hoard. For decades the tower had protected the hill and its owner, but even its sturdy walls had not been able to keep the count from exacting his ultimate revenge upon its master. Now the place was empty, save for the occasional wanderer who sought it out as ill-considered shelter from the Barovian night, and the rats that scurried openly along the ceiling timbers. Its few windows gaped darkly, like missing scales on a dragon's hide.

A dwarf and a woman walked from the tower into the chill predawn air. They deposited small packs at the doorway.

Soth's new minions, the ghost thought disdainfully.

A rusty shirt of chain mail hung well below the dwarf's waist; the motley tunic beneath it poked out at his shoulders and neck. The armor had obviously been meant for a human, but the dwarf seemed unaware how ludicrous he looked in it, much like a young squire pretending to be a knight. The dwarf's features instantly dispelled that image from Caradoc's mind. There was a feral glint in the dwarf's eyes, and his dark sideburns framed an upturned nose and wide mouth that looked as if they more properly belonged on an animal.

Clad in a gown of rich red fabric, hastily patched and with an uneven hem, the young woman appeared less threatening than the dwarf. Yet she carried herself with a confidence that unsettled the ghost. She was thin-waisted and lithe of frame, with the muscled legs of a dancer. The scratches criss-crossing those legs and the claw marks marring her shoulder told of a long, hard trek to the tower. The way she kept her gnarled cudgel close at hand revealed her wariness to sudden danger. Though her features were deceptively gentle—green eyes, full lips, and a soft chin—the ghost knew she must possess a reservoir of strength, for she had survived days of travel with Lord Soth and a harrowing escape from Castle Ravenloft.

"We'll be leaving any time now," the dwarf said, scuffing clumps of sod from the ground with his heavy boots. "I dare say the old count won't want to dally until the sun rises."

A brief moment of excitement passed through the ghost at the dwarf's disrespectful tone. If Strahd heard him, there would certainly be a confrontation, and Caradoc yearned to have an excuse to reveal himself and his new alliance to Lord Soth. Then he'll realize how foolish he was to mistreat me, the ghost concluded, clinging to the shadows.

Magda sat down on the steepest part of the hill, just before the gate. Next to her, an uneven and badly constructed stone stair rambled down the hill. "We can't be on our way too soon for me," she noted impatiently, tapping the ground with her club.

It wasn't long before the death knight and the vampire lord joined Soth's servants. Caradoc shrank back into the shadows, then into the tower wall itself, at the sight of the death knight. A memory of Soth's icy hands crushing his throat flashed in Caradoc's mind, and he shuddered. Perhaps this wasn't such a good time for a meeting.

"Although you do not agree with my assessment of your companions," Count Strahd said, "I will present you with special troops that you will undoubtedly find of some use on the journey through the duke's lands." Both Magda and Azrael glanced at the vampire, but he spared them not a word.

His hands raised over his head, Count Strahd bayed the words of a spell. Wolves echoed the sound from the woods ringing the tower, and bright moonlight rained down upon the hillside like a sudden downpour. Faces appeared in the white light, faces contorted in screams of agony. These swirled around the hill, then disappeared into the earth. The ground trembled in thirteen places along the slope. First one dirt-crusted hand clawed its way to the air, pushing aside dirt and grass, then another. Like some ghastly spring bloom, skeletal hands and arms slowly reached up toward the gibbous moon.

Magda gasped and crawled up the slope. Less than an arm's length from where she'd sat, a helmeted head had emerged from the ground. The skeleton pulled aside the earth from its chest with bony fingers, then sat up and proceeded to methodically free its legs. The hillside was awash with similar scenes—long-dead warriors, their armor hanging loosely upon rotting bones, responding to Strahd's call. Worms twisted and fell from the dirt between the skeletons' ribs, and pincered insects scuttled from beneath their helmets. At last, thirteen skeletal warriors stood on the hillside, their shallow graves at their feet, their battered swords in their hands.

"This should give you a fighting force worthy of a knight of your stature," Strahd said, gesturing to the grim host assembled there.

Caradoc shrank back into the castle wall even farther, until only his face lay outside the cold stone. The count was revealing too much! Soth had commanded thirteen such warriors on Krynn, and it seemed that Strahd was taunting him.

Soth nodded and gestured for Magda and Azrael to gather up their packs. "They will follow my commands?"

"As I said, they are my gift to you, Lord Soth," the vampire replied with a bow. "They once served the boyar who ruled this keep, and now they are yours to command." He paused and pointed to the west. "Beware of Duke Gundar's influence over them once you get close to his castle. Such mindless creatures are easily swayed to the side of a duchy's lord once they enter his province."

The death knight turned to the skeletal warriors. "Come," he said flatly and started down the stone steps. Magda and Azrael fell in behind him. The undead warriors shuffled into place, keeping a relentless pace behind their new master.

"May we never meet again," Lord Soth called from the edge of the forest.

The count raised his gloved hand in a casual salute. "Indeed," he said softly. "Let us hope."

Only after the death knight and his strange following had been swallowed by the forest did Caradoc emerge from his hiding place. The ghost floated tentatively toward the vampire lord, wringing his hands before him. "Forgive me, terrible lord, but by raising troops like those he commanded on Krynn, have you not revealed to Soth that you know more about him than you should?"

Strahd arched an eyebrow. "That was my intention, Caradoc. Soth did not miss the significance of my gift, and the question it will raise in his mind will help me. If he can't be sure what I know, he'll not be so quick to turn against me."

After studying the sky for a moment, Strahd turned away from the ghost. "Dawn is coming. I must away."

"Master," Caradoc cried. "I watched as you healed the death knight's arm. Might you heal my broken neck. I have been a faithful—"

Strahd faced his servant, the calm on his features and in his voice more terrible than any threat. "Don't be foolish, Caradoc. Be thankful Soth didn't discover your presence. I gladly would have let him destroy you, had you been careless enough to be seen."

The ghost fell to his knees and cast his eyes at the ground. "Forgive me. I thought—"

"You thought I might heal you. Put that thought out of your mind, Caradoc. It was the hope that you might be human and whole again that caused your problems with your last master—" Strahd gestured for the ghost to rise "—and I will not tolerate the repeat of such foolishness. Abandon all such hopes. You are a servant, and it is best for servants to be content with their lot in life."

The vampire lord closed his eyes, and a thin mist covered him. He blurred before Caradoc's eyes, then changed into the form of a monstrous bat. In an instant Strahd was flying through the night sky, hurrying back to Castle Ravenloft. The dawn was coming, and the box of earth that served as the vampire's protection from the sun's killing light beckoned him.

A bitterness welled up in Caradoc as he watched the bat fly to the east, but he knew Strahd was right. The ghost had nothing to offer, and the count would allow him to live only as long as he proved a complacent servant. Defeated, he set off for Castle Ravenloft. With luck he would be there by nightfall and ready to do Strahd's bidding when the vampire lord awoke and emerged from his coffin.

As he made the long journey through Barovia, Caradoc assuaged his bitterness with a single bleak thought: perhaps learning to exist without hope would be like learning to see the world with a broken neck. The trick was patience. With time, one could get used to almost anything.

 **THIRTEEN**

Carrion crows had picked most of the softer flesh from the naked corpse hanging at the road's edge. Its remaining skin looked as white as chalk in the midday sun, and it swung back and forth in the breeze. One of its legs was gone below the knee, taken by a wandering scavenger; its arms ended in ragged stumps. A sign hanging around the corpse's neck trumpeted the reason: Thief, it proclaimed in blocky, weatherworn letters.

"Welcome to Gundarak," Azrael snorted. He shook his head and glanced back at Soth.

The death knight stopped and signaled the thirteen skeletal warriors to do the same. No sign had marked the border between the duchies. The terrain was unchanged. Twisted oak and pine covered the foothills through which the party marched, just as it had in Barovia. "How can you tell we are in Gundar's domain?"

Jerking a thumb at the hanged man, the dwarf said, "That thing. Strahd's usually much more subtle with his victims. He's left a fair number of corpses scattered around the countryside in his day, mind you, but always for effect. You know, when villagers grumble about taxes, the count leaves a shopkeeper in the square at dawn, all his blood drained from him." Azrael faked a shiver. "Just enough carnage to scare the yokels."

Magda moved into the corpse's shadow, shielding her eyes from the bright sunshine as she looked up at it. "How is this any different?"

"Gundar and his thugs kill anyone and everyone who crosses 'em," Azrael replied. "We'll be seeing poor sots like him—" he, too, squinted up at the body "—or her, all the way to Castle Hunadora."

"You've traveled before in Gundarak?" Soth asked. "Why haven't you mentioned it before?"

"Oh, uh, hadn't I?" The dwarf laughed, though it was forced and unconvincing. "My apologies, mighty lord. I've roamed around so much that sometimes even I forget where I've been."

An awkward silence settled on the group. Azrael, aware of the probing eyes upon him, straightened his overlarge chain mail shirt and fidgeted with his sideburns. "I would have told you sooner or later, but I thought you might be suspicious. I lived here for a little while, but that was years ago."

Azrael grew more bold, even angry, when he saw the unspoken questions in the death knight's stance and the Vistani's face. "I was a thief just like this unlucky bastard. It was the only bloody way I could survive. See what Gundar does to criminals? That's why I left. Believe it or not, Barovia's a much better place to be. I mean, Strahd is dangerous and no doubt unbalanced, but Gundar is ten times the madman."

Soth signaled for the skeletal warriors to renew the march. He spared the dwarf a glance as he headed down the road again. "You have until the sun sets to reveal any other secrets you've kept hidden from me. I will decide then if you may continue with us."

Sighing, Azrael bowed his head and waited for the

shuffling undead soldiers to pass. When he looked up again, he saw Magda, still watching him from the other side of the road.

"If *you* don't trust me," the dwarf said, "you should run back to Barovia right now. After all, if I'm a spy, you and Soth'll never make it to the duke's castle. That's what you think, eh, Vistani? Maybe I work for Strahd? Or Gundar, perhaps?" He spit on the ground at her feet and turned to follow Soth.

"I will be watching you, Azrael," Magda called after the dwarf. "If you do anything suspicious, I'll bash your brains in while you sleep."

The dwarf stopped. When he looked at the young woman, his anger had gone and a toothy grin had split his face. "I've told you before, girl, don't threaten like that unless you intend to follow up on it." He took a few menacing steps toward Magda, and she raised her cudgel to strike. "That's better," he said smugly.

Chuckling, Azrael trundled after Soth. "By the way," he called over his shoulder, "I wouldn't stay too close to the corpse. Gundar's brat sometimes casts spells that keep 'em alive for a while after death. They're good at playing dead until something tasty gets close enough to grab."

The Vistani jumped sideways, away from the hanged thief, but the corpse did nothing but swing limply in the breeze. Hurrying after the others, Magda cursed the dwarf for his sick humor.

All along the twisting road through the foothills of Gundarak, bodies hung from the trees. More were lashed to boulders, with still others littered across the ground like fallen leaves. Most were labeled as thieves or traitors, but not all had signs around their necks. The duke's men were not particular about their victims; men and women, young and old, all dangled together.

Azrael was right—a few of the corpses were ensorcelled. The first of these they encountered hung from an ancient oak. A long piece of black rope suspended the corpse so that its feet almost brushed the ground, and, from the flesh remaining on the body, it was clear that once this had been a woman.

"She hasn't been here long," Azrael noted casually, eyeing her tattered dress. "The peasants strip the clothes from 'em within a day or two. Even rags like that aren't too meager to steal."

When one of the undead warriors jostled it, the female corpse began to thrash about on the end of its rope, as if the skeleton had awakened it. Cursing, the rag-clad body snatched the skeleton's helmet. With quickness that surprised everyone, it struck a powerful blow with the rusted helm. The skeleton's naked skull shattered, leaving a dark, jagged hole the size of a man's fist. The skeleton reached for its sword, but the corpse lashed out twice more.

Both blows sent fragments of bone spinning into the air. The second caved in the skeleton's eye sockets. Its skull yawning open, the undead warrior dropped its blade. The corpse wrapped its legs around the skeleton's rib cage and pulled the warrior toward it, shattering its right shoulder and crushing half its ribs.

The dozen remaining skeletons hacked the female corpse to bits, doing their fellow even more damage in the process. From then on, taking no chances, Soth had the twelve surviving undead knights attack every body they came across. A few corpses shouted curses and lashed out with fists or feet, but without the advantage of surprise, they were no match for the combined strength of the skeletal warriors.

"We wouldn't have to wait for the knights to hack

up all these bodies if we went through the woods," Magda complained irritably as they waited for the skeletons to silence another corpse that had been shrieking threateningly by the side of the road.

Azrael lay flat on his back in the middle of the road, arms spread out at his sides. From that undignified position, he mumbled his agreement. "Brilliant. I trust the forest. We'd be out of this sun then, too."

"We stay on the main road," Soth replied without taking his eyes from his skeletons as they slashed up the shrieking corpse. "Strahd gave me precise directions to Gundar's keep, directions that let us avoid any traps the duke may have set in the woods."

Magda moved in front of Soth and locked gazes with him. "My lord, you cannot trust Strahd. For all you know, this could be an elaborate plot to get revenge upon you for what you did at Castle Ravenloft."

"Perhaps that it so," the death knight allowed.

With a grunt, the dwarf sat up. "Then it's into the woods, is it?"

"No," Soth said. "We follow the count's directions."

Both Magda and Azrael gaped in disbelief. "Why?" the Vistani managed to ask.

"There is only one fact with which you need concern yourselves," the death knight rumbled. "I have chosen to follow Strahd's suggestions. There is no opening for debate."

Having finished with the latest corpse, the skeletons stood in the road, awaiting Soth's instructions. The death knight strode past the mindless undead, and they fell in after him. Side by side, Magda and Azrael watched Soth as he marched ahead.

"He's probably right," the dwarf noted. He slung his pack over a shoulder and shrugged his mail shirt into a more comfortable position. "I mean, we've encountered no foes on this road—none alive, anyway—and we are heading in the right direction."

That last comment fanned Magda's nagging suspicions. Her thoughts showed clearly in her dark expression. Azrael could not help but notice.

"Yes, I saw the castle once," he admitted, "but I was never inside. And, yes, I plan to tell Soth about it by sundown. I'm just waiting for a good time to tell him everything he might find the least bit interesting." He smirked. "My life has been more colorful than those Kulchek tales. No offense, but fairy-tale heroics always bore me to tears."

Without a word, Magda fell in behind the last of Soth's mindless soldiers. The undead knight shuffled along at a slow, steady pace, his armor clanking against bones, shoulders stooped and arms limp at his sides. Every step seemed a monumental task.

That must be what it's like to be undead, Magda realized suddenly. You want to rest, but you can't. You have to press on, toiling endlessly, just as you did when you were alive.

She edged closer to a skeleton and gazed at its strange visage. Although a battered bronze helmet covered much of its head, the dark sockets of its eyes were visible. They were empty, just as the knight's features lacked personality.

The undead warrior stepped sideways to avoid a large stone in the road, and ran straight into Magda. The Vistani knew that, though the skeleton had no eyes, it should be able to see as well as most living men. Her puzzlement deepened when it paused and scanned the road for whatever had caused its stumble; its eyes passed over the Vistani as if she weren't there.

"The medallion," came a voice from behind her.

Magda spun around at the sudden sound, her cudgel raised to strike. Azrael laughed. "They can't see you because of the medallion," he said. "You said so yourself." The dwarf shrugged. "I mean, that's what you told me, anyway. You could have been lying, I suppose, but we spies can usually tell when someone is bending the truth."

The Vistani smiled despite herself, though more from the absurdity of her situation than any genuine humor in it. In less than a half-cycle of the moon, she'd gone from a quiet, uneventful life among the Vistani to struggling to survive from day to day. Undead warriors and a werebadger were her traveling companions, creatures she'd heard about only in legends until Soth had appeared in camp. She even carried a weapon out of the tales she loved the most—for she truly believed the cudgel was none other than Kulchek's own Gard.

"Don't make light of my suspicions, Azrael," she said at last, though her voice held little anger. "You had questions about me when we first met, just because I am Vistani. I have proven myself, but you have not."

"You haven't proven yourself to me," Azrael replied bluntly. "Besides, I've never said I trusted you. I just have the good manners—even if I must point it out myself—not to bring it up every few hours."

They traveled for the rest of the afternoon in silence, stopping every now and then for the skeletons to deal with yet another body found along the road. Soth grew more distant from Magda and Azrael. He spent almost all of his time with the undead warriors. Once Magda even heard Soth talking to one of them, as if it might fully understand his words. The sight chilled her to the core.

By the time the sun touched the horizon to the

west, the road had begun to crawl up the slope of a
small mountain. Trees grew more sparse, then were
replaced by huge boulders as the predominant feature of the terrain. Fewer and fewer bodies dotted the
landscape as well. The relief anyone felt at that fact
was soon overcome by concern, for the going quickly became treacherous. Even the mindless skeletons, whose careful progress rarely faltered, slipped
on the loose gravel that covered the mountain road.

Only Soth and Azrael moved with ease. The rocky
landscape was not the dwarf's favorite, though, and
he trudged along with a sorrowful look on his face.
Magda wondered if the place made the dwarf
homesick—Soth had said that, back on his world,
dwarves lived deep underground in vast cities of
stone. She could not know that the place depressed
Azrael for the exact opposite reason.

"Can we stop for the night, mighty lord?" Azrael
asked, pausing to shake a stone from inside his boot.

Soth scanned the horizon. Massive chunks of
granite stood all around them, separated by only
winding, shadowy paths filled with gravel and pale
weeds. A pillar of white stone, flushed rosy red by the
setting sun, pushed above the jumble of granite
ahead. "We will stop at the base of that column," the
death knight replied. "It is a landmark Strahd mentioned in his directions."

Magda and Azrael hurried through the maze of
boulders, toward the white stone pillar, but it was farther away than it had first appeared to be. By the
time they reached the obelisk, the sun had disappeared, leaving Gundarak in the clutches of twilight.

The pillar was huge, as tall as any tree Magda had
ever come across in her travels with the Vistani. Perfectly smooth, its sides were covered with tiny runes.
As far as Magda could see in the gloaming, they ran

all the way up the column, but she could not understand any of the symbols. Around the column's base
lay a wide clearing, the ground hard but free of small
stones.

"Marble of some sort," Azrael noted. He tossed his
pack onto the ground and slumped against the pillar.
His mail shirt insulated him from the faint shudder
that slid up the marble, and the long day's march had
dulled his senses enough to make him deaf to the
faint magical hum, a signal that vibrated for miles in
all directions.

Lord Soth and the twelve remaining skeletons entered the clearing. "At sunrise, we will head north
from here, staying in the foothills of this mountain
and the one to the west of it," he said coldly. "The way
straight through the mountains is too difficult for
us."

Magda set her pack aside and began to scour the
area for firewood. "Not much to start a fire with." She
sighed, scanning the area through the growing darkness.

"No fire," the death knight said. "It would alert
everything within a day's march."

"That spoils the atmosphere for my life story a
bit," the dwarf noted sarcastically, "but we wouldn't
want Gundar himself charging up here to interrupt
me."

The others said nothing as the dwarf rubbed his
hands together, then cracked his knuckles. It was as
if he were about to arm wrestle someone in a tavern.

"The place where I come from looks a lot like the
land you see around you—boulders and rocks and
not much else," he began. "It's that way over much of
the surface, anyway. I'd only seen the surface a few
times, but that's more than most of my kind. No, the
others spent all their time in the cities, hammering

out weapons no one used and jewelry no one ever wore. Peace and humility were the rule in the city of Brigalaure, but they crafted the damned swords and rings anyway, just because it was important to *make* something. . . ."

* * * * *

Azrael's tale was as bloody a story as any Magda had ever heard, though, like most such stories, it started innocently enough.

His parents were crafters of modest income, and like all youths in the vast underground dwarven city of Brigalaure, Azrael was destined to learn one of their skills. He might have gained the lore of iron from his father, or the ability to cut rare stones into jewelry from his mother, but he was suited to neither type of work.

The pounding, the heat, and the stench of sweat in the iron forges made him sullen. His arm wasn't strong enough for the strenuous task of beating the metal into shape, and he lacked the stamina to tend the bellows or carry heavy burdens all day long. Still, his father possessed great patience; he decided to allow Azrael an apprenticeship of ten years to grow accustomed to the work.

For a dwarf of Brigalaure, who could expect to live for five hundred years or more, a decade should have been a brief enough time to learn a craft, but Azrael grew bored in less than twelve months. He spent each workday daydreaming, his mind lost in imagined exploration of the land above the city. Legends told of monstrous lizards—ones larger than any of the great winches the dwarves used to move stone—that ravaged anything standing in their way. This was the reason the dwarves had first moved underground, thousands upon thousands of years before Azrael's father had been born.

His father let his daydreaming go on day after day, even over the objections of his forge-mates, until Azrael's carelessness caused a fire. The youth was not bothered by the near-destruction of the smithy, and the plight of the apprentice who had been maimed in the blaze affected him even less. After all, the other young dwarf had taunted Azrael about his laziness.

His parents took his silence about the unfortunate accident as contrition, but they knew he could not return to the forge. Instead, young Azrael found himself in his mother's solitary workroom.

To his surprise, he liked this place even less than the ironworks—not because he'd expected to enjoy cutting jewels, but because he hated his father's work so vehemently. In the forges, he was one of three dozen apprentices. There no one seemed to notice if he disappeared for an hour or so. Just he and his mother occupied the small workshop, so she made certain his day was filled with tasks to help him learn the jewel cutter's craft. Polishing the finished stones, collecting up the chips of ruby and diamond, even sharpening the cutting tools—all these tasks required concentration; somehow, his mother knew that his heart was not in the effort, even before he realized it himself.

Azrael soon proved to be incompetent in his mother's craft as well. His short, stubby fingers worked against him in a profession calling for a delicate touch, and he refused to abandon his daydreams, even when handling the most precious of stones. Finally disaster struck. Azrael dropped a rare and fragile gem, and it fractured like glass. His mother, fed up with his incompetence and stunned by the thought of paying to replace the shattered stone, banished him from her workshop.

For the dwarves of Brigalaure, craft was status, and Azrael's failure made him an outcast. Without a trade he could not be considered an adult. He could earn no money, no place in society, no respect. No one would take him in as an apprentice, not after gossip about the forge fire and the shattered gem. As he stood outside his mother's workshop, her tirade still ringing in his ears, the young dwarf understood that he had failed definitively and that there was no place left to go. Brigalaure held nothing for him.

He packed his few belongings late that day without any idea of where he was to go. When his father confronted Azrael, demanding that he pay for the jewel he'd broken, a red swell of anger engulfed the young dwarf's soul. The moment his father turned his back, Azrael caved in his skull with a hammer.

His mother was next, then his brothers and sisters. Azrael didn't use the blood-spattered hammer on them, but his bare hands. While his fingers were too short for delicate craft work, they were blunt and strong enough for murder.

Because his sister had managed a shriek before he killed her, Azrael found a *politskara* at his door. Such watchmen spent their time breaking up feeble quarrels over who could craft the most perfect arrowhead, so this one was totally unprepared for the bloody sight that greeted him. Azrael almost got away, too, but the *politskara* had enough sense to call up a mob. The gathered fletchers and stoneworkers were enough to bring an end to the murderer's hope for escape.

What happened next was unclear in Azrael's mind. He was struck by an arrow fired from the crowd, and he had passed out as they closed in around him. He awoke in a dark tunnel, deep underground, banished, without food or light or any hope of finding his way back to Brigalaure. The citizens hadn't had the nerve to kill him.

A voice spoke to Azrael from the darkness, though it seemed to come from everywhere around him, even inside his head. It offered him life and power, but with the condition that he use that power to destroy the beautiful dwarven city. As the words of agreement left his mouth, sharp laughter filled the cavern and a terrible pain stabbed through Azrael's gut. He tumbled facedown onto the cold stone as his bones twisted. His head pounding, he screamed, and the sound that came from his mouth was like the yowling of a wounded beast.

He became a werecreature, part dwarf, part giant badger. With his newly heightened senses of smell and sight, he followed the trail left by his captors all the way back to the city. There he used the shadows to cloak his evil deeds. Over the next fifty years, he preyed upon those on the outskirts of Brigalaure, destroying homes and shops, killing those he found alone. Hundreds fell to his claws. The citizens of Brigalaure tried to hunt him down, but without success.

"I'd found my craft," Azrael noted proudly, leaning back against the white marble pillar. "And I was much better at it than any of 'em were at stopping me."

Despite herself, Magda was caught up in the tale. She sat close to the dwarf, leaning toward him in the darkness. By the pale moonlight she could just make out his face as he spoke.

"I was leading a hunting party through the labyrinth of tunnels I called home," the dwarf said, a look of wonder crossing his features. "I was hoping to separate one particularly fat baker from the rest—I hadn't eaten in a few days, you see. Anyway, I finally lured him away from the rest when, out of nowhere, this fog rises. One minute I'm wondering about the mist, the next I'm standing on the edge of a huge lake."

"In Barovia?" Soth asked. They were the first words the death knight had spoken since Azrael had begun his tale.

The dwarf shook his head. "No, in a grim place called Forlorn, to the south of here. The place is creepy—no people, no animals, just this big castle. Needless to say, I stayed well away from the castle."

The dwarf rummaged through his pack for a piece of bread but found nothing. He'd finished his share of the rations earlier that day. "Er, Magda, do you have anything I could eat? I seem to have supped the last of my supplies." When she tossed him an apple, he frowned at it as if she'd handed him something inedible, then shrugged and took a bite.

"That's when I came to Gundarak," he said. "I was only here for a couple of months. Not much good in preying upon villagers who have nothing worth stealing." He took another bite from the apple. "Besides, the peasants themselves are all skin and bone, nothing to sink your teeth into."

Closing her eyes, Magda turned away. Soth, however, seemed intrigued by the dwarf's tale. "Did you ever encounter the duke?" he asked.

"I've seen Castle Hunadora, but I never went inside," Azrael replied. "Lucky for me, I say. Just outside the place, I escaped from a dozen or so of his guards by jumping into the moat. They'd caught me sleeping in the woods and were bringing me in for 'questioning.' In most of the lands around here, that means torture."

At Soth's prompting, the dwarf went on to describe Gundar's castle, but his knowledge of the place consisted largely of details about the fetid moat that circled the estate. "I'm lucky I can hold my breath for a long time," he concluded. "The water is thick with sewage from the castle and the refuse from the experiments Gundar's son, Medraut, conducts in the dungeons."

A deep, liquid laughter filled the clearing. "You're right, Fej," they heard someone say, "it is a dwarf what set off the alarm. You can read them signals better'n anyone."

The sharp sound of steel striking flint echoed from the boulders, and two torches flared to life on opposite ends of the clearing. The skeletal warriors fanned out in a circle, but Magda had her cudgel at the ready before any of them could draw their swords. When the Vistani saw the two grotesque figures bathed by the light of the torches they carried, she couldn't suppress a gasp.

They were giants, standing twice Soth's height, but their features were horrific, their bodies misshapen. One had an eye that was twice the size of its mate. The mismatched pair rested below a brow lined with deep wrinkles, over a bulbous nose and a mouth that hung open like a gaping wound. The giant's teeth were missing from his lower jaw, and his gums had been scraped away from the bone by jagged upper teeth. One of the creature's arms jutted from his side, not his shoulder. A torn shirt covered his bulk, but he dragged a length of thick chain that ended in a studded iron weight.

The other giant was equally hideous. His features retained more humanity—apart from the piggish snout spread across his face—but large blisters dotted his skin from head to foot. These welts sprouted tufts of hair as red as any flame. He was hunchbacked but had managed to put together a motley collection of armor that protected much of his torso. He carried no weapon, but his hands were three times as large as they had any right to be. The giant flexed a fist as he stepped into the clearing.

"Awright, you lot," the first giant managed to say, his lower jaw moving little as he spoke, "you're coming with us. If you put down the weapons, we won't hurt you . . . much." Both giants laughed at that pitiful jest.

Magda's head swam. How had the giants managed to sneak up on them? They hardly looked capable of stealth. And what alarm had Azrael set off? She glanced at the pillar. The dwarf had been resting against it for much of the evening. Suspicions of treachery filled her mind again, but she hadn't long to dwell upon them.

A battle had begun.

An arm's length from the Vistani, Lord Soth moved his hands in the complex patterns of an incantation. The air before the hunchbacked giant suddenly filled with snow, then an ice wall appeared, stretching between two boulders. Barred from moving forward, the giant bellowed in rage.

Narrowing his overlarge eye at the death knight, the remaining giant advanced. He swung his crude flail, and the chain and steel weight swept across the ground, hissing like a scythe. Two skeletal warriors were caught by the blow. Their bones flew apart like shards of broken pottery.

Frantically Magda looked from Soth to Azrael. The giant was too close to allow the death knight the time to cast another spell, so Soth drew his sword. The undead warriors did the same. Azrael, however, backed toward the wall of ice. At the sight of the retreating dwarf, the Vistani cursed; there seemed little question now that Azrael was indeed a traitor.

Magda gripped her cudgel tightly and joined Soth against the flail-wielding giant. The thing had raised his weapon for another blow, but the death knight slashed him across the knee. As his leg buckled beneath him, he stumbled forward and the flail slipped from his hands. That didn't prevent him from swatting another of the skeletal warriors with his torch. The blow lifted the skeleton from the ground. It struck a boulder with a resounding, sickening snap of bones, then crumpled to the earth.

At the same time, a huge fist knocked a hole in the wall of ice. The second giant reached through the breach and grabbed Azrael. The dwarf, caught partway through his transformation into half-badger form, could do little but squirm and growl in the giant's grasp. With a grunt from his piggish snout, the hunchback tossed Azrael over his shoulder as if he were nothing but a discarded toy.

"Oi, Fej, give me a hand here," the first giant cried. He was on his knees, holding off five skeletons with his huge torch. His arms were covered with bloody slashes from the undead warriors' blades. His tunic hung about him in ribbons.

"Awright, Bilgaar. Stop yer whinin'." The hunchbacked giant had been busy climbing over the ice wall, and now he loped forward. At Soth's command, the skeletons broke off from the first battle and formed a line between Fej and his fellow, their swords bristling before them.

Bilgaar, the giant in front of Soth and Magda, braced a hand on his wounded knee and struggled to his feet. As he did so, the Vistani lashed out with her cudgel. Bilgaar tried to block the club with his torch, but all he received for the attempt was two broken fingers. "Aooww!" he howled. His torch spun from his hand and landed at the base of the pillar.

Magda raised Gard to strike again, but the giant shoved her aside. The Vistani tumbled to the ground. The action cost the giant dearly, though. Soth, taking advantage of the opening, chopped at Bilgaar's outstretched hand with a powerful two-handed swing. The death knight's blade severed the giant's hand from his wrist, and Bilgaar collapsed, clutching the bloody stump. Without hesitating, Soth drove his sword through the back of the giant's skull. After Bilgaar whimpered once, his gaping mouth closed and the life fled from his oddly paired eyes.

Fej was having a much easier time of it. A defeated skeleton lay unmoving at his feet, and the seven remaining ones were having a hard time scoring any hits through the giant's armor. One of the undead moved too close to Fej, and he used his huge fist to crush the skeleton into the ground.

The giant chuckled at the scattered bones, but that mirth was cut short by a bloodcurdling howl. Before Fej could spare a look behind him, Azrael leaped from a granite outcropping and landed on his hunched back. The werebeast had transformed fully into his half-badger form, and he looked none the worse from the giant's earlier attack. With daggerlike claws and teeth, he tore into Fej's throat.

The giant dropped his torch and tried to grab the werecreature. He screamed once before Azrael severed his vocal cords. Then the skeletal warriors closed in.

From the darkness between two boulders, Magda watched the skeletons and the werebadger tear the hunchbacked giant to bloody pieces. Soth, his back to her, studied the proceedings and cleaned his sword on a shred of Bilgaar's tunic. Azrael had joined the fight, she noted acidly, but only because we were winning. There was no doubt in her mind now: The dwarf had used the pillar to summon the giants. Whether he did so for Strahd or Gundar didn't matter; he was part of the trap.

This might be my last chance to escape, she decided. They are all too caught up in the slaughter to notice. Quietly Magda got to her feet and edged into the darkness.

"Six left," Soth noted grimly, counting the remaining skeletons. "And we are still days from Castle Hunadora."

Azrael, his muzzle and paws caked with gore, finally stood back from the dead giant. He scanned the clearing. "She's gone," he rumbled. "The Vistani bitch has run off!"

The death knight probed the night with his unblinking eyes. Azrael was correct. Magda had fled. "Can you find her?" he asked, something akin to disappointment in his voice.

Grinning ferally, the werebadger dropped his hands to the ground and sniffed the air. "Don't bother dispatching the skeletons," he said. "She's got a medallion that makes her invisible to 'em." That said, he disappeared into the maze of boulders, sniffing the gravel.

The moon had disappeared by the time Azrael returned, but he found Soth standing in exactly the same spot, in just the same position he had left him in earlier. The werecreature was in dwarf form again, and a large, swollen bruise covered the right side of his face. "She tricked me, mighty lord," he said humbly. "I followed her scent into a blind alley, but it was only her clothes. She'd left 'em there to draw me in." He bowed his head. "Before I could even turn around, she dropped off a boulder and hit me with that damned club. She knocked me out."

"Do not trouble yourself over it," Soth said after a

moment. "She has earned her freedom. Besides, she knows little that would be of value to our enemies."

Azrael gingerly touched his swollen face. "She could warn Gundar of your plan," he noted.

Soth roused himself from his reverie. "That is not like her," he replied. "She would put herself in great danger by contacting Gundar—if he is the madman he seems to be. That would be quite foolish, and Magda is no fool." He paused, pondering her disappearance. "Besides, these are not lands to be traveled alone. She will likely be dead by the time the moon rises again."

At the sight of the wounded dwarf, a smile came to Soth's lips. He pointed at the purpled bruise and added, "Though I wonder what creature might be strong enough to best her."

 **FOURTEEN**

The soft, rhythmic sobbing reminded Soth of the cooing of a dove. He looked up from the keep's account books, sparing his wife the briefest of glances. "If you cannot control yourself, go into another room, Isolde."

The elfmaid stopped crying and raised herself ponderously from the bed. Any movement was an effort these days—for she was far along with child—but Soth knew that the tears had not been caused by the strain of the pregnancy. A blue-black welt marred Isolde's perfect white cheek. Soth winced inwardly at the sight; she had deserved some punishment for her strident nagging, he reassured himself, but perhaps I struck her a bit too hard.

"I don't know how you can stand yourself anymore, Soth," she said as she reached the door.

The lord of Dargaard stood quickly, trembling with anger. The feeble remorse that had colored his thoughts a moment earlier was gone, replaced by a cold rage. With a curse, he snatched the leaded glass ink pot from the desk and hurled it at his wife. She ducked out of the room just as the glass hit the door. The ink splattered across the whitewashed walls, and a shower of tiny glass shards rained upon the floor.

The sharp sound, Soth mused, was like the laughter of the harlots who had occupied a cell near him in Palanthas's jail.

He tried to calm himself, but murder was all that he could think of. Caradoc had disposed of Lady Gadria. Perhaps he should do the same with Isolde. . . .

"Gods," Soth shouted, disgusted with the bloody thoughts, "have I fallen this far?"

The answer stared at him from across the room. Disheveled and scowling, Soth's image returned his gaze from the full-length mirror that had been the priest's wedding gift. The disgraced knight found himself drawn to that reflection, mesmerized by the man who stood before him.

His face was haggard and drawn, his blue eyes ringed by dark circles. Waves of unkempt hair hung to his shoulders. His mustache was similarly untrimmed. It framed his mouth but did not hide the split lip he'd gotten the previous night. Like the other men in the besieged keep, Soth drank even more than usual, wine being easier to come by than water after almost two months of captivity. After a long bout of drinking with his retainers, he'd slipped on an ice-slicked stone in the bailey and landed face-down on the frozen ground.

That was what his knights told him, at least. He didn't really remember.

Soth's shoulders were stooped from exhaustion. When he wasn't drinking, he was manning the walls. Not that the Solamnics could reach the keep's outer curtain; the gorge stood in their way, and any who attempted to lay the foundations for a bridge were driven off with arrows. However, each night the attackers catapulted flaming pitch into Dargaard. It took hours to put out the fires, but the flames always took another house or storage building or wagon before dying out.

Lord Soth knew that exhaustion and hunger and boredom were the besieging Solamnics' most valued allies; the knights under Sir Ratelif had been camped outside Dargaard's walls for weeks, but they had accomplished little if one tallied only the physical damage. In fact, with winter now hard upon the land, it seemed as if the keep would be able to wait out the siege. The lawful knights had established a blockade, however, and with each passing hour, Dargaard's supplies dwindled.

Disheartened, Soth reached for a cloth to cover the mirror. When his hand got close to the glass, he saw something that fanned his anger.

Blotches of ink covered his fingers like the marks of some horrid plague. Soth, loving adventure as much as he did, had never been one for keeping accounts and ledgers. That was what he paid Caradoc and others to do. In the last few weeks, however, he'd become obsessed with maintaining a careful record of their limited rations of food and drink. Now Soth rubbed his ink-stained fingers together, but the black marks wouldn't come off.

"They've forced me to become a clerk," he snarled, dropping the heavy cloth over the mirror.

He looked at his hands again. His fingers had spent more time wrapped around a mug of wine or a quill pen than a sword's hilt in the last month. Even though the Measure proscribed daily weapons exercise for all Knights of Solamnia, Soth had done very little in that regard since his trial in Palanthas. Nor was that the only ritual he'd abandoned. Upon joining the Order of the Sword, all knights fasted one day out of seven; Soth could not remember when he'd skipped a meal last, not by choice. He'd also failed to follow the Order's rules regarding drink and gambling and the chivalrous treatment of women.

These were all minor transgressions when compared to Soth's failure to worship his deities, those powers that watched over all Knights of Solamnia. Habbakuk, Kiri-Jolith, and especially Paladine protected the Order. It was the ideals these gods personified that drove each knight on to greater and greater deeds. Yet Soth had not visited the keep's chapel since the siege had begun. In fact, he had stopped praying to Paladine, patron of the Knights of the Rose, on the day he first made secret love to Isolde. Even the sacred vows he'd exchanged with the elf-maid on their wedding day had been said for the sake of convenience alone; if Paladine had heard them, it was not because Soth desired it.

The disgraced knight's first thought was to blame Isolde for his sorry state. Perhaps she had bewitched him somehow, turning him against the Code and the Measure. But he knew that wasn't true. She had pleaded with him almost daily from the start of the siege, begged him to raise his voice to the gods and ask for a quest. Only then might he make atonement for the sins he'd committed.

"Isolde!" he shouted, hurrying from the room. The sound of his voice echoed through the halls, but no one came running. Soth had stormed through the keep many times in the last few weeks, drunk and shouting for his wife; those in the castle knew better than to get in his way.

He found his wife straightening things in the nursery. Isolde started at his appearance, and Soth felt part of his soul wither at her fear. She was afraid of him.

"Please, Isolde," he said, falling to his knees. "Come to the chapel with me and pray. I want to be free of this burden."

She came to him then and held him close. When he looked at her face, he saw tears streaming down her cheeks, drops of purest silver against the dark bruise on her cheek. "Help me win my honor," he whispered, "and we will have our life, our old happiness, back again."

Hours passed, and Soth found himself in the keep's chapel, the smell of polished wood and the sharp smoke of burning tapers filling his mind. He focused on those smells and methodically closed his consciousness to everything else—the dots of light that swam in the blackness before his sealed eyes; the sound of Isolde's breathing as she knelt beside him; the rustle of the sacred tapestries; the bitter taste in his mouth. The discomfort in his back and knees from kneeling for so long and the dull ache of hunger in his stomach were more difficult to banish, but they, too, fell away from his thoughts.

Am I afraid to face my patron after so long, the blot of so many sins upon my soul? That was true, he realized, and with that realization he welcomed Paladine into his heart.

A meteor as large as a mountain streaked out of the blue sky. Soth felt its fire burning him, its heat turning his skin to char and ash. He tried to breathe, but smoke scorched his lungs, sending fingers of pain through his chest and throat. As the meteor got closer and the heat grew more intense, his vision blurred. Bubbling like boiling water, his eyes burst and ran down his blistered cheeks.

Then the meteor struck.

Only you can prevent this, something said inside Soth's mind. The voice was full of love and understanding, and it calmed his frantic thoughts. Such a voice could belong to only one being.

"Is this the hell that awaits me, Paladine?" Soth

managed to whisper through lips that an instant ago
had felt cracked and scorched. He opened his eyes
and found himself surrounded by pure white light.

*You were once a force for justice in Solamnia, Soth
of Dargaard, so I will give you a quest,* said the Father
of Good. *Yet know that your sins have been as great as
the things you once accomplished for my cause.
Therefore, the quest I will set for you will be greatly difficult. Only if you can turn yourself to the Good wholly
and irrevocably can you hope to win it.*

Another vision filled Soth's mind then—a crystal-
clear image of the Kingpriest of Istar, giving a speech
in celebration of a holy day. Framed by an arch of
purest alabaster, the kingpriest faced a milling
throng. With exaggerated movements, intended for
those at the back of the mob, he looked to the heavens and held his hands up. At first it appeared to
Soth that the kingpriest was preaching a sermon.
The vision focused on the kingpriest's face, and Soth
saw that he was raving like a lunatic. His hands
weren't held to the heavens in supplication; they
were thrust toward the gods like accusing fingers.

*Like you, Soth, the kingpriest has done much to
combat Evil in Ansalon,* Paladine said, his voice filled
with infinite sadness. *Now he has appointed himself
mediator between man and the gods. In his pride, he
and his thousands of followers will soon demand that
we guardians of Good give over to him the power to
eradicate all Evil.*

"I am to stop him from making this demand?"
Soth asked.

Paladine sighed.

*Yes. Go to Istar, Soth, and make the kingpriest stop.
He does not understand the Balance. By attempting to
bend such great forces to his will, he will destroy
everything for which he has worked.*

That the greatest god on Krynn would tell him of such an important quest stunned Soth, but he managed to say, "I will do all that you require of me, great Father of Good."

You will be redeemed, Soth of Dargaard, but it will cost you your life.

The vision of the kingpriest faded, but Paladine offered a warning. *Know that more depends upon your success than your honor, Soth. If the kingpriest cannot be swayed from his prideful course, all the gods— those who strive for Good and Evil and the balance of the two—will punish the world. The mountain will strike Istar, just as you saw it.*

Soth felt the pain of the thousands who would perish if that came to pass. The whole of Krynn would be changed—continents would shift, seas would boil red with blood, and countless lives would be snuffed out. The suffering of those left alive would be more horrible. The kingpriest alone—

If you fail, know that your fate will be more terrible than even that of the kingpriest, the Father of Good promised.

Soth found himself in the chapel once more. Isolde stared at him with wide, frightened eyes.

"I have my quest," Soth said. His face was flushed with righteous fervor. "I must leave for Istar right away. Paladine himself has given me the power to save all of Krynn."

* * * * *

"Paladine himself gave me the power," Soth said. "Paladine himself."

Azrael sat up and brushed the dirt and pine needles from his back. "What's that, mighty lord?" he asked softly. "Paladine gave you what power?"

For the first time in hours, the death knight stirred. "What do you presume to know of the god Paladine?" he rumbled.

The dwarf held up his hands before him. "Nothing. It's just that, well, you mumbled something about him just now. A god, you say?" Picking a tick from his leggings, he squished it between two blunt fingers. "I've never worshiped a god in my life, though I wonder sometimes if it wasn't some evil deity what gave me my powers—you know, just to create some chaos in the city." He snorted. "Funny, I haven't thought about that in years, not since before I landed in Forlorn."

Soth cocked his head. "There is something about this place that . . . *forces* memories to surface, ones that I'd thought long forgotten. I find it disturbing, though there seems to be no way to stop it."

What the death knight did not say was that his memories were growing more vivid with each passing day. Once he'd welcomed such visions, because they fired his emotions and staved off the numbness of eternal unlife. Now, however, they caused him unaccustomed anguish.

After rummaging futilely through his empty pack, Azrael tossed it aside. There was no more food or wine to be had. Even the supplies he'd taken from the unlucky wayfarer on the road yesterday were gone; Azrael wished now that he'd carved up more of the poor fellow's corpse.

"Some believe that dark powers rule over this place," the dwarf began. "They're not quite gods—or so the superstitious say—but they love to torment the poor souls who get stuck here. Maybe these memories are the dark gods tormenting you." He smiled. "Personally, I don't believe any faceless 'powers' have the least bit to do with anybody's plight here. As far as I'm concerned, I done this to myself. I think—"

The death knight turned away, ending the dwarf's rambling soliloquy. Since Magda's departure, three days past, Azrael had grown more and more open with Soth, as if he had been assured of his place at the death knight's side. Azrael's loquacity bored him at times, but Soth found that it kept him from wandering back to his past too frequently or, worse, dwelling upon futile thoughts of Kitiara. Besides, the dwarf was the only pawn he had left.

Soth had been forced to destroy the remaining skeletons himself. As they'd gotten closer to Gundar's castle, the mindless dead men grew more fractious, less willing to follow the death knight's commands. They never acted against Soth or Azrael, but they balked at orders.

Only yesterday, a large patrol of the duke's men had come close to overtaking Soth's party because the skeletons would not take cover until Azrael had forced them off the road. The death knight knew that it was simply a matter of time until they blundered into another patrol, spoiling what little hope he still had to approach Castle Hunadora undetected. With the dwarf's assistance, it had been no trouble for Soth to destroy half the skeletal warriors before they'd had a chance to react. The other three had put up a bit more of a fight, but neither Soth nor Azrael gained a significant wound in the brief struggle.

Now he and Azrael were camped at the edge of the pine forest that skirted two sides of Castle Hunadora's moat. Soth had decided that Gundar was a fool the moment he saw the castle; only an incompetent would let trees grow so close to his home. Even though the keep's moat was wide and its walls were high and well guarded, such cover would prove invaluable to a trained enemy. Indeed, Soth had been able to cloak himself in the forest's shadows and study Castle Hunadora for an entire day undisturbed.

The castle rested atop a manmade mound of earth, a gently sloping hill to its front, a steep, rocky precipice to its left. Thick pine forest grew to the rear and right of the keep, a perfect cover for a siege. Hunadora's walls were of dark stone, with lighter rock framing the arrow loops and crenelations. The main section of the castle was bordered by a square curtain, with small towers at the corners and in the middle of each wall. In turn, a wide moat filled with fetid water circled the walls, its dark surface broken occasionally by a bloated, white-skinned corpse or a pale tentacle slithering into the light.

Protected by the curtain and the moat, a massive tower and a large keep rose high into the sky. Two smaller buildings squatted nearby, their peaked roofs barely pushing above the battlements. Finally, the gatehouses and main portcullis jutted out from the curtain. This was where all welcome visitors to the castle entered, and on this particular day, a silent crowd of peasants milled in front of the gate, awaiting admittance. The ragged men and women glanced furtively at the bodies hanging from the gatehouses' roofs and the dark, inhuman shapes that moved between the crenelations, hidden from the setting sun.

"They're here to pay taxes," Azrael noted, following Soth's gaze. "The duke will keep 'em waiting all night if he has to. He lets two dozen into the gates at a time, so's his men can keep an eye on 'em."

"Then we will enter the keep now, while the soldiers are still busy with the rabble," Soth replied. He pointed to the stone curtain, where a half-submerged grate opened into the moat. "That is where we will enter. If what you've said about the child is true, his quarters are likely to be underground, where the screams of his victims will not arouse the others in the keep."

Azrael fidgeted, trying to think of the proper words for what he wanted to say. "Uh, mighty lord, it may not be, er, in our best interest to face Medraut in his laboratory. I've heard that he has artifacts of great power stored there, things he could use against us."

"We need the blood of either Gundar or his son to open the portal," Soth replied flatly. "Strahd tells me that the duke is a vampire. So unless you wish to hunt for his coffin yourself . . ."

Laughing nervously, Azrael moved to the edge of the trees. "Are we going to swim across?" he asked.

Soth did not reply. Instead, he grabbed the back of the dwarf's chain mail shirt and stepped into the darkness surrounding the trees. An instant later, he and Azrael emerged from the shadows inside the grate tunnel. The dwarf leaned back against the rusty grate. "Mmmm. You could have warned me."

Cold water swirled above Soth's knees, almost reaching Azrael's waist. It was colored by streaks of indigo and yellow and cerulean from the remnants of discarded potions. Fragments of parchment and half-burned figurines of wood floated against the grate's wide bars. Farther up the tunnel, small patches of flame covered the water where two cast-off chemicals had come together.

A large bottle containing a pink, spiderlike creature bumped against Azrael's hip. When he picked it up, the creature rammed itself against the glass, trying to get at the dwarf with its long legs and snaking tail. He snarled at the clutching thing, then pushed the bottle out through the grate. The glass bobbed in the moat, then a tentacle wrapped around it and pulled it under.

"Come," Soth said, ducking slightly to avoid the low, dripping ceiling.

Glowing lichen covered the walls above the waterline. Azrael waded cautiously behind the death knight. He was glad to have a little light to stop him from stumbling against the walls, but he wasn't all that certain he wanted to see what sloshed against him.

The worst part of the trip for Azrael was the smell. Although he pinched his nose, his heightened senses provided him with a clear report of the foul odors from the offal and refuse floating around him. "The first thing we'll want to do when we get through the portal is take a bath for a week," he grumbled. "Or have our noses chopped off." His voice reverberated up the tunnel.

"If you are not quiet," Soth replied, "I will perform that surgery right now."

After a time the tunnel sloped up, leaving the water behind. At first Azrael was glad to be out of the foul-smelling sewerage, but he soon decided that the drier part of the tunnel was no improvement. A dead giant's rib cage blocked the way at one point, and other, more disgusting things made it difficult for Azrael to struggle up the incline. Of course Soth managed it easily.

"Doesn't this place bother you, mighty one?" the dwarf whispered.

"It is not so unlike some I have seen in my travels," the death knight replied. "Besides, to me the world is not filled with the bright colors and sharp smells you sense. I only remember such things from long ago."

A circle of light appeared in the wall ahead, then laughter, high and shrill, filled the tunnel. Soth edged forward. The light came from a jagged hole, slimy with spilled potions and stinking from the old bits of flesh caught on the stones around its edges. Beyond lay a huge room filled with glassware and coils of metal, ancient skulls and the stuffed carcasses of unnatural creatures. Tables covered with beakers of rainbow-hued liquids stood in a dozen places around the floor. Musty shelves of books bound in leather or wood or more exotic fabric occupied two walls; cases holding collections of powders as well as rare items used in the casting of spells occupied the other two.

There seemed to be no door, no way into the room save the hole from which Soth now peered. Moreover, no torches or magical globes or any other source of light lined the walls, yet a clear yellow light filled the gigantic hall. The illumination was so complete that no shadows hung in the corners, not a single book or vial lay in darkness.

At the edge of this ordered chaos, very close to the entryway into the sewer, a boy sat upon a high stool. This had to be the duke's son, Medraut. He gazed into a glass-and-steel structure as wide and tall as a door. Level after level of doll-sized furniture and weapons rested between two thick plates of crystal, sprinkled with small holes; the use for these holes quickly became apparent. The boy lit pieces of paper with a nearby candle and stuffed them into the three lowest levels.

"You can't hide forever, little worms," Medraut said in a coarse voice. He rapped the glass with his little fingers. "Come out, come out. It's time to play."

As smoke filled the levels, things began to twitch about. Soth couldn't make them out at first, but as the figures scrambled up ladders to escape the smoke, he realized what was happening. Tiny humans! The captives shouted and cursed and shook their fists at the child, but that only made him laugh.

"The game for today is snakes and ladders," he said, taking a box from a table nearby. "Haderak, you survived this last time, so you needn't listen to the rules. The rest of you must pay close attention." Medraut slid a glove onto his hand and grabbed a handful of writhing snakes from the box. Standing atop the chair, he opened a small glass door. One by one, he dropped the snakes into the bizarre doll house. "Each time one of you gets eaten by a snake, I take a ladder away." Squinting at one figure, he added, "And you have to move forward, not backward, Costigan, you rotten cheater."

The last snake safely in the maze, he closed the door and settled down to watch. "If you manage to kill one of the snakes, like brave old Haderak, I'll put a ladder back." Folding his hands on his lap, he shrugged. "All right, then, off you go."

The figures scrambled for the tiny spears and swords that stood in racks on a few of the floors. Others hurried away from the snakes they knew would be crawling toward them. The smoke from the burning paper now filled the four lowest levels. "You can run, but you can't hide!" Medraut taunted, blocking the entrance to the lowest level with a glass slide.

Soth turned away, only to find Azrael shrugging out of his mail shirt. The death knight knew that the dwarf had to take off the mail before he transformed or the metal mesh would strangle him. Still, he cursed the werecreature's poor planning. The metal clinked and jingled. Luckily Medraut was too engrossed in his game to notice the sounds.

The death knight gestured for Azrael to follow him, then he took one final glance into the room and pushed through the opening. Medraut spun about on his stool the instant Soth entered the room. Although he was the size of a ten-year-old, no one could mistake the duke's son for a normal boy. His face was pocked from disease, and his teeth were mostly rotten. Running sores covered his bare, grimy legs. Above all, his eyes held a dangerous, maniacal glint.

"Another assassin from Daddy," Medraut said, leering like an old lecher. "Oh, how fun."

With lightning-quick hands, Soth formed a spell, but the duke's son was faster. Before the incantation could leave the death knight's lips, Medraut summoned his own sorcery. Soth's mind went blank. A tiny white whirlpool formed in the center of his consciousness, engulfing the words that would call forth the spell he had prepared. Then the vortex grew.

"Why is it you always interrupt my play time?" pouted the boy, jumping from the stool. He reached into his pocket and pulled out the materials he needed for another spell—a lodestone and a pinch of dust. "After I turn your arms to ash, I may shrink you down and put you in the maze with the others. Would you like that, Sir Assassin?"

Soth fought against the vortex with all his thoughts, filling it with anger and hatred. A memory of Kitiara, clad in a diaphanous gown, swam into view, and Soth bent his will to closing the whirlpool. His mind thus occupied, he heard Medraut's words only vaguely, through a fog. The same was true of the echoing yowl that rang from the sewers hard upon the boy's threat.

With a shriek, Azrael leaped from the hole. He was in half-badger form, his lips curled back from his white teeth in a frightening snarl. Instead of lashing out at Medraut with his claws, though, he struck the boy in the face with his chain mail shirt. The blow sent Medraut reeling backward, into the glass-and-steel maze. It wobbled, then fell over, slamming into a table full of scales and weights. Glass shattered and metal clattered on the stone floor.

Medraut struggled but for a moment with the heavy chain mesh shirt tangled around his head. That was enough time for Soth to overcome the spell. The vortex in the death knight's mind closed, without having done any real harm to his dark thoughts. As the boy tossed the shirt aside, Azrael's claws raked across his back. Hard on that blow, Soth cast his first spell. A gust of wind lifted the boy and blew him up toward the ceiling. Then, like a huge hand, it tossed him against a table of beakers and glass tubing. Shards of glass flew everywhere as the snakes and shrunken people darted for cover.

The boy came up smiling, trickles of blood running down his face from a dozen tiny cuts. "You are much better than the louts Daddy usually sends. This is almost fun." A wand appeared in his open hand, and he pointed it at Azrael.

The werebadger thought to dive out of the way, but the lightning bolt that erupted from the boy's wand struck him before his muscles translated that impulse into action. He saw the flash an instant before he felt the blow, but by then it was too late. By the time the roar of the attack deafened his ears, he'd been knocked through three tables. The stench of charred flesh and burning fur told Azrael that he was on fire.

The boy giggled and pointed the wand at Soth. Without warning, a man appeared between Medraut and the death knight. He wore a soldier's uniform—high leather boots, black pants, and a tight red jacket trimmed in white. A silver saber hung at his side, but Soth could tell immediately that the weapon was for show. The man's hands were coarse and callused, the hands of a butcher not a swordsman.

"Why, Daddy," Medraut cooed, "you've come to watch me finish off your assassins."

The duke might have been a handsome man once, but now he looked as much a beast as Azrael. His dark hair hung wildly around his head; his beard curled untrimmed around his chin and mouth. Eyebrows thick and matted ran together over his craggy nose, giving his features a perpetually angry cast. Fangs, white and long, protruded over a red tongue and lips. He was a vampire, too, but as unlike Strahd Von Zarovich as noon is to midnight.

"This is no agent of mine," the duke shouted, lunging at Soth. The death knight swatted away the vampire's grasping hands and locked his own mailed fingers around Gundar's throat.

"The master of Barovia sends his regards," Soth said, tightening his grip.

Medraut waved his hand, and the wand disappeared. "Well, well. An agent of the count." Righting his stool, the boy climbed atop it to watch the battle. "Daddy, I believe the nice man must be here for you."

With a curse, Gundar transformed to swirling mist in Soth's hands. The mist, in turn, slithered down to the floor and hid amidst the broken tables and scattered equipment. "Oh, bother," Medraut sighed as the death knight faced him once again.

A ball of fire streaked from Soth's hand, but a shield of blue light flashed into being in front of Medraut. The fireball struck the magical barrier and exploded, splashing liquid flame in a wide arc around the boy. A few of the tables began to burn and one mortar filled with yellow powder sizzled ominously.

Soth took a step forward, ready to bash in the monstrous child's skull if magic would not serve him, but a blow to his back sent him reeling. From where he lay against a toppled stack of spellbooks, the death knight saw Duke Gundar. The vampire lord crouched like a wolf, bloody spittle flecking his lips, a mad gleam shining in his eyes.

"Oh, Daddy, you've saved me," Medraut murmured, then fell into a fit of coarse laughter.

The boy's mirth continued as Soth and Gundar came together again. The two dead men locked inhumanly strong hands. Medraut was so caught up in the spectacle that he didn't notice the stealthy movement behind him. And when the smell of burned flesh reached his nose, it was too late.

Azrael, the left side of his body blackened and blistering, leaped onto Medraut's back. The boy tried to call a spell to mind, anything that would put some distance between him and the half-dwarf, half-badger thing, but the werecreature did not give him a chance. Held together by Azrael's claws, the two of them toppled to the floor. Medraut's scream was like that of a child waking from a bad dream; this nightmare was not banished so easily, however.

Gleefully Azrael tore out the boy's throat with his teeth, and the scream was drowned by a gurgling flow of blood.

At the sight of his son's grisly demise, fright played across Gundar's features. Then, oddly enough, the fear changed to a look of relief. Without a word, the duke again transformed to mist and slipped from Soth's grasp.

The death knight scanned the room with his unblinking eyes, but the duke was nowhere to be seen. "We have what we came for, Gundar!" he proclaimed. "Let us take the boy to your great hall and open the portal that lies there. If you try to stop us, you will share Medraut's fate."

Darkness enveloped the room, and Soth braced for an attack. None came. Instead, a section of a musty, crowded bookcase swung open, revealing a torchlit stairway. "Well," Azrael said, "that's a clear enough answer."

"Can you carry the child yourself?" Soth asked. He heard the werecreature grunt as he lifted the corpse.

"We'd better hurry, mighty one," Azrael noted, taking a careful step toward the doorway, broken glass crunching underfoot. "Or he won't have any blood left. It'll have all run down my tunic."

When they reached the hallway, the death knight noticed the effect of the lightning bolt upon Azrael. The fur on his left arm and the left side of his chest and face was gone, the skin underneath burned and cracked. His snout had split open; his left eye was closed. Azrael's arm and shoulder seemed to have suffered the most serious damage. His square, muscular shoulder was bent and twisted, and his arm hung limp at his side. His tunic was covered in blood, but that was from Medraut's wounds, not his.

"I'll be better in a couple of days," was Azrael's reply when he saw the death knight's gaze upon him. "Don't worry, mighty lord, I won't slow you down." As if to prove his point, he adjusted the corpse's weight on his good shoulder and trudged forward. A snarl of pain curled the werecreature's lip with each step.

They followed the tower staircase until they came to an open door. From there, a wide corridor ran straight into the castle's main building. Tattered banners, shields embossed with strange heraldic devices, and broken weapons lined this corridor, trophies taken from vanquished foes or symbols of ancient family victories. The hallway ended in a set of double doors. Detailed carvings depicting the castle's construction filled the doors' six huge panels.

Like the rest of the castle, the sumptuous main hall was devoid of people. The room was long, with an arched ceiling similar to those in some of the larger ancient temples Soth had seen on Krynn. Thousand-candled chandeliers hung in four places. On a sunny day, their light would be augmented by the stained glass windows that lined one side of the room; the growing darkness outside offered no light and obscured whatever scenes the windows might have held. The wall opposite the windows was lined with statues, all of them capturing Duke Gundar in some dramatic pose. Some were wrought in alabaster, others in jet, but they all showed the master of Gundarak as a heroic warrior.

Azrael shifted the corpse on his shoulder and glanced about nervously. "This has to be a trap."

Soth shook his head. "Most leaders who display statues celebrating their own heroism are cowards at base. The duke wants us to leave without doing any more damage."

The death knight walked to the center of the room. The story Strahd had told him made it easy to find the location; a large bloodstain, brown from age, marked the spot where Gundar's daughter had lain for years, her blood keeping the gateway open. There he took the corpse from Azrael and dropped it to the ground. As Medraut's blood flowed over the mark left at one time by his sister, a dark circle appeared in the air directly over the corpse. No light seemed to penetrate the blackness of the portal, and Soth could see nothing inside it.

"I come for you, my Kitiara," Soth whispered.

Without hesitation, the death knight stepped into the circle of darkness. Azrael gasped at his master's temerity, then gritted his teeth and followed him.

FIFTEEN

A dull blue light shone around Lord Soth. As the death knight watched, the sourceless light spread to a thin strip of ground, revealing a pathway that extended a dozen yards or so. Around this path lay darkness more profound than any he had ever seen.

Azrael appeared suddenly. He, too, was bathed in blue radiance. Crouching at the death knight's side, he muttered, "Black as Strahd's heart in here." He sniffed the air, testing for the scent of any hidden foe. The action only caused his charred nose to ache.

"Stay close," the death knight said. He started along the path, taking one slow, careful step after another. The werecreature pulled the tunic up to cover his wounded shoulder, then loped along after him. After they'd gone a few steps, an elaborate wrought iron gate appeared at the path's end.

"None shall pass unless they pay my toll," came a voice from the darkness. The words were thick with the promise of danger for those who disobeyed them.

Soth took another step toward the gate, and a figure slid from the darkness to block the way. The keeper of the gate seemed to be made entirely of shadow, though in silhouette she resembled a very tall woman or, perhaps, an elfmaid. Her arms and legs were long and slender, and she moved with practiced grace. Although the details of her features were hidden, the light from the gate revealed her profile when she moved. Long, flowing hair framed a face with high cheekbones, an aquiline nose, and full, pouting lips. She held her chin up, lending her stance an air of casual disdain.

The keeper had one exotic feature that was clear even though she was cloaked in darkness. A pair of twisting, branched horns rose from her head, much like a deer's, but more elegantly curved. The points on these horns looked as sharp as Azrael's claws.

"Go no farther," she warned, pointing at Soth.

The death knight traced an arcane pattern in the air, but when he spoke the word to trigger the spell, nothing happened.

"This is my realm, and your sorcery will not work here," the keeper explained. She extended a hand into the darkness beyond the path, then withdrew it. After a moment, a huge dog slunk into the light. Like the keeper, the hound was composed of shadow. It had the imposing form and flat skull of the mastiffs Soth had seen in some knights' castles on Krynn. Yet its stomach was shrunken from starvation; its skin barely hid its rib cage.

The keeper moved toward Soth and Azrael, the shadow mastiff at her side. "The toll for passing along my road is high, but all must pay it."

At that Soth drew his sword and lashed out at the keeper. The blade passed harmlessly through her, but the attack set the mastiff barking. The death knight sliced through the shadow woman again, and again the steel did her no harm.

Azrael backed up a few paces and looked frantically for the gate from which they had entered the shadow realm. "Mighty lord, perhaps we should go back."

"Never!" Soth shouted. "What is your price, keeper?"

The keeper bowed her head slightly. "You are a wise man. Even if you wished to, you could not leave before you paid my price. That is the rule of this place." She took another step toward Soth. The mastiff licked its chops noisily. "The cost of passing through my domain is your soul."

Laughing, the death knight sheathed his sword. "I forfeited my soul long ago, keeper," he said, then undid the straps holding his helmet in place and removed it. Patches of long blond hair hung from his scalp, dangling in places almost to his shoulders. His skin was parched, drawn tight against the bones beneath. Of his features, little could be seen; a shadow hid his nose and mouth. As he spoke, though, his white teeth flashed now and then from between his cracked lips. The darkness was greatest around his eyes, which were no longer human, but glowing orbs of orange light.

The death knight donned his helmet again and refastened the straps. "To gain my soul, you would have to travel to the home of my world's gods, to the domain of Chemosh, Lord of the Undead. Even then, you would likely find him unwilling to part with that prize."

After bowing her head, the keeper stood to one side of the narrow path. "You may pass," she said, gesturing Soth forward with one hand. The death knight moved down the path. When Azrael tried to follow, however, the keeper once again blocked the way. The mastiff began to bark anew.

"You are a strange creature, indeed," the shadow woman said to the wounded werebadger, "but a heart still beats in your chest. You must pay your toll."

"Will it hurt? Losing my soul, I mean?"

"I do not know. No one has ever paid the toll and lived to tell me about it," she explained impatiently. As she reached toward the dwarf with a long-fingered hand, she added, "Now, cease your prattle. It has been many years since anyone has passed along the path, and my hound and I have need of sustenance."

The death knight was standing behind the keeper, but it was clear he was not going to lift a hand to help Azrael. He was on his own. As the shadow woman's fingers drew closer to his chest, the werebadger stepped sideways, to the very edge of the lighted path.

"There is nothing to either side of the path," the keeper noted. She reached down and stroked the mastiff's broad skull. "If you leave the light, you will be lost in the darkness until I bring you out."

Azrael cursed and sprang forward, directly at the woman and the mastiff. Like Soth's blade, the were-badger's assault did the keeper no harm, but his powerfully muscled legs drove him into the heart of the shadow creature.

The next thing Azrael knew, he was engulfed in darkness, falling at an incredible speed toward some unseen doom. He screamed, but no sound came from his mouth. He flailed his arms and legs but could feel no movement other than the inexorable pull of gravity. In fact, he could no longer feel pain from his blasted shoulder. Perhaps, he realized with a shock, I'm dead.

He felt the touch of long, slender fingers against his shoulder, and his descent slowed. Next, a burst of blue light cut into his right eye like a needle; his left was still blind from the lightning bolt. A scream—his own, he noted with odd detachment—filled his ears, and the pain from his wounds throbbed to life. When his vision returned, Azrael found himself sprawled on the path. The keeper stood over him, her mastiff at her side. The dog had its mouth open, and ropes of dark saliva dripped from its jaws.

Azrael glanced down at his body. To his surprise, he had reverted back to his dwarven form. "W—What happened?" he gasped.

"You got a taste of what lies to either side of the path," the guardian said. "No more stalling, now. Give me your soul."

She thrust her fingers into the dwarf's chest. They felt like daggers of ice to Azrael, but the more he struggled against them, the more the coldness spread inside him. "It must be here!" the keeper cried. She buried her arm up to the elbow in his chest. At her side, the mastiff howled its hunger.

At last the shadow woman stood back. "I have never seen this," she said sadly. "You are living, yet you have no soul." The shadow mastiff slunk into the darkness to wait for another soul to fill its shriveled guts.

Shivering and gasping from her icy touch, Azrael stared at the keeper. "Im-m-m-agine that," he stuttered. He slapped his arms around his chest to bring the feeling back, then stopped. The keeper's touch had been painfully cold, but the numbness it had left behind was preferable to his burns.

Azrael staggered to his feet and looked up the path to the wrought iron gate. Soth was gone. "How long ago did he leave?" the dwarf wailed, rushing past the keeper. The death knight's disregard for him did not surprise Azrael. In fact, he expected callous treatment from such powerful beings. But he had not endured the long journey to be abandoned without a fight; Soth was obviously destined for great things, and Azrael wanted to be part of them.

She shrugged. "When you disappeared, he left without a word. Perhaps he thought you dead. You weren't gone very long, though, so he still might be near the other side of the portal."

The dwarf ran to the gate, but before he pushed it open, he glanced back to the shadow woman. "Where does this lead?" he asked.

The keeper stood on the verge of the darkness beyond the path, her slender form stooped in disappointment, her horned head dipped in sorrow. "I do not know," she whispered. "No one has ever returned to tell me, and I cannot leave this realm to find out for myself."

Azrael shoved the gate wide. It creaked open on stiff hinges, and a rush of warm air blew past the dwarf. As swiftly as the darkness had engulfed him earlier, he found himself in a deserted alley, standing in front of a toppled rain barrel. He looked in wonder into the barrel's mouth; he could see a faint image of the wrought iron gate in the water pooled inside. With the portal hidden this well, little wonder few people knew of its existence.

The water also reflected Azrael's features back at him, so that for the first time he saw the lightning bolt's effects. The sideburn and mustache were gone from the left side of his face, his left eye was closed tightly, and his shoulder was still hunched and twisted. His arm felt a little stronger, but the burns on his chest, side, and face hurt terribly. The loss of his hair bothered him more than the pain. By tomorrow, he would feel a lot better; his preternatural healing abilities were common to lycanthropes, from what he'd heard. For some reason, though, his hair took a long time to grow back.

When Azrael looked down at the sorry state of his brocatelle tunic—in tatters from the lightning bolt

and stained with Medraut's blood—he wished his
clothing would mend itself as quickly as his body. He
would simply have to steal something as soon as he
found Lord Soth.

The narrow alley in which the dwarf found himself
ran between two buildings, a bakery and a butcher
shop. The aromas of freshly baked bread and recently
slaughtered animals made the werebadger's stomach
growl. He pushed thoughts of food aside—as best he
could, at least—and studied his surroundings.

The walls framing the alley tilted together as they
rose higher, and the windows on the third stories
practically opened onto one another. Above that, the
buildings' roofs met, allowing only a trickle of sunlight through. In one direction, the alley led to a dead
end. In the other, it opened onto a busy marketplace.
Below each window, puddles dotted the unpaved
ground, stinking with garbage and the contents of
chamber pots. It was, in short, like the alleys in most
sizable towns—dark and dirty.

"Gods of light preserve us!" someone shouted
from the marketplace.

A woman's scream rang out, long and shrill, followed by exclamations of fright. They've spotted me,
Azrael decided, but when he looked toward the marketplace, he saw the commotion was caused by
something else.

He hurried to the alley's mouth and scanned the
frightened mob. Two hundred people crowded the
square, though many of them rushed toward the
wide thoroughfares leading away from the marketplace. Others pushed into the shops bordering the
square. Tents collapsed as men and women jostled
their supports. Carts were overturned, and baskets of
food were spilled, their contents flowing across the
dusty cobblestone square. Fletchers and bakers and

peddlers of all sorts of goods fled from the figure in ancient, blackened armor who stood in the market's center.

A wide grin crossed Azrael's face. The keeper of the portal had been correct: Lord Soth hadn't gone far.

The death knight lashed out at people indiscriminately. His sword carved a bloody furrow in one man's back, then he caved in another's skull with his mailed fist. A dozen or more corpses lay at his feet.

"Is this how he treats the people of Krynn?" the dwarf whispered. He looked at the crowd, but the reason for the death knight's fury did not present itself immediately. No one seemed to be challenging Soth, though one of the corpses did wear the garish uniform of a guardsman.

The sight of that uniform made Azrael's heart skip a beat. The blue jacket with gold buttons and epaulets; the black pants and high leather boots; the short, flat-topped hat with the black raven spreading its wings across its front—this soldier's garb was familiar to him. It belonged to the watch in the town of Vallaki. And if they were in Vallaki . . .

The dwarf shuddered. The reason for Soth's ravings crystallized in his mind.

The portal had returned them to the duchy of Barovia.

* * * * *

The Old Svalich Road remained strangely clear for the two days it took Soth and Azrael to march east from Vallaki to Castle Ravenloft. They both knew Strahd would hear about the slaughter the death knight had perpetrated in the quiet fishing town. Yet no one challenged their progress, even though the switchbacks and blind turns that allowed the road to climb the foothills of Mount Ghakis made it a perfect location for an ambush.

Of course, the wolves followed their every move from a distance, disappearing into the forest if Azrael tried to catch up with them. The death knight cared little about the beasts, though he knew they were conveying information back to the count. The dwarf found them a challenge, and he sometimes passed an hour stalking the wolves. While he was skilled as a hunter, they were beyond his abilities.

"Strahd will be expecting us, of course," Azrael said as he trudged along the road. "Do you have a surprise for him, mighty lord? I mean, if you don't mind me asking, of course." When Soth didn't reply, he shrugged and scanned the bushes for any sign of the wolves. The death knight had grown ominously silent since their return to Barovia. It was all Azrael could do to get him to speak four times in a day.

"I'm sure you do have a surprise for him," the dwarf said, more to himself than to his companion. He sighed, then scratched furiously at the peeling skin on his neck. A few thin ribbons came off under his fingernails, revealing new pink skin.

Few signs of the damage wrought by the lightning bolt remained on Azrael's body or face. The charred skin had been shed, and his shoulder had righted itself. His left eyelid drooped a little, but his sight seemed to have returned completely. The same was true of his sense of smell. Only his lip and jaw, as smooth and hairless as his pate, stood as reminders of the attack.

Azrael had stripped one of Soth's victims in the marketplace, replacing his bloodstained tunic and breeches with a new shirt and pants. Both were too large, but he used a razor he found in a man's pack to cut them to size. He'd also grabbed a mace from the fallen watchman, knowing as he did that the count would likely send skeletons or zombies after them. Such blunt weapons were effective for smashing their reanimated bones to dust. Now, with each short-legged step Azrael took, the mace tapped his thigh reassuringly.

They spotted the castle and the village of Barovia just before sundown, a fact Azrael took as a bad omen. "Uh, shouldn't we wait here until the sun rises again and Strahd is forced back to his coffin?" the dwarf asked tentatively.

"No," the death knight replied. "We will have to fight our way to the keep whether the sun or the moon shines down upon us. The sooner we begin this war, the sooner I will have Strahd's head adorning the gate of Castle Ravenloft."

The ring of poisonous fog that Strahd could raise around the village was nowhere to be seen, and the town itself appeared deserted from Soth's vantage; nothing moved in the streets, and the shops and marketplace were closed, even though there was still enough daylight to conduct business. That did not mean the count had failed to prepare a defense for his home, however.

A small army crowded before the rickety bridge, which Soth knew was the only way into the keep. "He has pressed the villagers into defending his home," Soth noted as he and Azrael started down the road.

"*Human* soldiers?" the dwarf scoffed. "This won't be much of a challenge."

But when the death knight and the werebadger reached the clearing, they saw that zombies made up the bulk of the army of two hundred, with a few skeletons and battle-scarred and fearless mortal mercenaries filling out the ranks. Gargoyles flapped over the crowd, goading the soldiers into position with whips of barbed steel. One of these officers left the ranks as Soth approached.

"My master sends his greetings, Lord Soth," it shouted as it flew toward the death knight. The gargoyle's slate-gray wings took on a red tint in the light of the setting sun. Its face was long, with a chin that jutted out like a sharpened dagger. Its body was so rounded that it appeared almost soft. Soth knew better; such creatures always had skin as hard as stone.

Landing gently before Soth, the gargoyle kneeled and bowed his head. "My master has heard of your return to the duchy, noble lord, but he knows not the reason for your anger."

The death knight faced the messenger. "I have nothing to say to you, lackey. My words are for Strahd alone."

Standing, the gargoyle nodded. "Know this, then, Lord Soth. My master has sealed the keep with his sorcery. You cannot enter by walking through the shadows." He gestured at the assembled army. "You can gain entrance only by passing across the bridge, and we are charged to prevent this."

"Then the doom of these troops is sealed," Soth replied.

After bowing again, the gargoyle flapped back over the army. He crossed over the bridge and entered the keep's courtyard to inform the count of the death knight's words. The commanders shouted final orders, and the army shuffled forward.

Azrael cupped the mace in his hand. He wished he'd remembered to take the mail shirt from Gundar's castle, but he brushed that thought aside. Weapons of steel or iron could do him little harm; he regenerated too quickly from the wounds they caused for them to present any serious threat. Only

weapons created by magic or blades wrought from
silver were a real danger, and it didn't look like the
zombies and skeletons carried such precious arms.

"One-hundred-to-one," the dwarf said, grinning up
at the death knight. "Just enough to make it interesting."

Soth turned. "I won out over greater odds when I
was a mortal knight on Krynn," he replied. "And I did
not possess the powers I have now."

The army had closed to a dozen yards. The zombies were unarmed, though Soth remembered how
difficult they had been to defeat when he faced them
on his first night in Barovia. The skeletons and the
few humans wielded a variety of weapons—swords,
axes, even flails and pole arms. Yet he did not draw
his own blade, not yet at least.

With a quick movement of his hand and a softly
spoken command, Soth called a swarm of flaming
stones into existence. The meteors were the size of
the death knight's fist, and when they hit the front
rank, they burned holes through whatever they
struck—flesh, armor, or bone.

A skeleton, its skull shattered, dropped to one
knee. The zombies behind it trampled it beneath
their stumbling advance. Rag-clad dead men caught
fire, and their attempts to put out the magical flames
simply spread the fire to their hands and arms. They
fell, too, though their fellows dodged the flaming
corpses. In all of this, the undead soldiers made no
sound. The battle was far from silent, though. The
human sell-swords screamed as they died and the
gargoyles continued to shout their commands.

Soldiers shambled forward to replace the thirty
destroyed by the sorcerous attack, and the death
knight drew his sword, its blade dark in the growing
twilight.

The first soldier to get within striking distance fell to Azrael's mace. The dwarf howled his victory as the skeleton dropped to the ground, its spine crushed, its rib cage split apart. It was soon joined by a human; Soth had almost severed his head from his neck. But the cry of victory died on Azrael's lips when he saw a glint of silver. A mercenary, scars zigzagging his cheeks, stepped toward the dwarf. In one hand he held a silver long sword, in the other a dagger glowing with a faint aura of magic.

* * * * *

"After he prayed to Paladine, Soth received a quest," Caradoc reported. "He was to go to the city of Istar and stop the kingpriest from demanding the power to eradicate all evil on Krynn."

Strahd Von Zarovich steepled his fingers. "Go on," he purred. This was the third time the ghost had repeated the tale of Soth's curse for the vampire lord, and he had finally discovered a useful theme in the story.

"That very night, the knights who were besieging Dargaard Keep fell under some sort of spell, a magical sleep that allowed Soth to sneak past them undetected," Caradoc continued. "He rode for days toward Istar, but the thirteen elven women who had revealed his dalliance with Isolde to the Knights' Council stopped him on the road. They intimated Isolde had been unfaithful to him, that the son she was carrying was not his child at all, but the bastard of one of his 'loyal' retainers."

The vampire smiled. "And Lord Soth turned away from his sacred quest to confront his wife." He stood and paced the study, his agitation playing across his features. "He was a man of strong passions, eh,

Caradoc?"

"He told me Paladine had granted him a very clear vision of what would happen if he failed to stop the kingpriest," the ghost explained. "He said he knew the gods would punish the kingpriest's pride by hurling a mountain at Istar. In his vision he felt the fire engulf the city, heard the screams of the dying."

Strahd took a seat at a writing desk at the room's edge. "But he returned to Dargaard to accuse his wife of infidelity."

The ghost nodded awkwardly, his head resting on his shoulder. "And when he died that day, his curse encompassed everyone who had served him faithfully. His knights became mindless skeletons, and I . . ." He raised his hands and looked down at his transparent form. "Soth's passions brought him low in the end, but I should not have been doomed with him."

The vampire lord considered the ghost's words for a moment. As he did, something the blind mystic had written on the day Soth and Caradoc had been drawn into Barovia came to his mind: *Boarhound and boar, master and servant; do not hope to break the pattern. Honor it instead.*

The obscure warning became clear to him at last.

Taking a quill pen and a piece of parchment from the desk, Strahd scribbled a hasty note. "I want you to memorize this message and deliver it to Lord Soth."

Frightened, the ghost tried to stammer a plea, but the words simply wouldn't pass his lips. Seeing his servant's distress, the count held up one gloved hand. "I will extend the magical wards that make the castle safe from his sorcery to the gatehouses bracketing the bridge. As long as you go no farther than those towers, you will be safe from him."

Caradoc started to object, but the count laid the paper upon the desk. "I would like the death knight to hear these words from your lips before the moon rises. You have my word that you will be safe. Do you doubt that I will uphold that promise?"

"Of course not, master. I—I will do anything you ask of me," Caradoc said, bowing his head as the vampire left the room.

The gargoyle to whom Strahd had assigned the dangerous task of greeting Soth at the clearing was waiting for the count in the hallway. "The battle is going badly, master," it reported. "The death knight and the werebeast have slain almost half the soldiers you raised, though they have taken few wounds themselves."

Closing the door to the study, Strahd nodded. "The battle is not going badly, Iagus. It is proceeding just as I expected. If the army falls to under fifty, I will raise new troops from the graveyard on the outskirts of the village. Soth has no chance of crossing the bridge."

Strahd started down the hallway. Over his shoulder he said, "In a few moments, Caradoc will leave to deliver a message to Lord Soth. Follow him and report to me everything that happens." He hurried away to a room high in one of the towers.

It was a small cell with no windows and only a single door reinforced with iron. The door opened at a word from the vampire lord. A pair of torches bracketing the jamb flared to life of their own accord as he entered the room. Unlike much of the rest of Castle Ravenloft, no dust covered the shelves lining the walls and floor, no cracks snaked up the stone blocks. Even the torches burned without smoke. The wall behind their flames was free of soot.

Tapestries decorated with elaborate designs of interlocking rings and geometric patterns hung upon three walls. The ceiling, too, was covered with a mesmerizing fresco of swirling lines and colors. Two pieces of furniture stood in the cell: a three-legged stool and a large table with a clear glass top.

The count positioned the stool before one of the tapestries and sat down. As he did so, two of the table's legs elongated so that the glass faced him. Gundar does hate it so when I contact him this way, the vampire noted to himself, then forced a grave mask over his mirth. He closed his eyes and pictured the unkempt ruler of Gundarak in his mind.

"You have some nerve contacting me now, you bastard!" Gundar shouted. Strahd opened his eyes and looked into the glass. There the duke stood, redfaced and snarling.

The lord of Barovia knew he appeared as nothing more than a ghostly, disembodied head to Gundar, a head surrounded by the mesmerizing patterns of the tapestry behind him. Anyone who stared at those patterns for too long found themselves hypnotized.

Gundar had dealt with Strahd enough times to know better. He focused his eyes on the count, not the tapestry, as he said, "You'll pay for Medraut's death, Strahd."

"The creatures who killed your son are not my servants, I assure you. The werebadger is a renegade, a murderer, and the death knight is far too powerful to serve either you or me." The count did his best to look concerned. "In fact, they are besieging my castle right now. The portal took them from your hall to an alley in the village of Vallaki. The death knight blames me for this."

Tugging at his curling black beard, Gundar narrowed his eyes. "You admit they found out about the portal from you?"

"Of course," the count replied, "though I only dealt with the death knight. The other is his lackey." He leaned forward. "But let us be honest here, eh, Gundar? I had hoped the death knight would create a little havoc in your keep. If he killed your son, so much the better, but I knew he was not powerful enough to harm you—not seriously anyway."

The duke uttered a string of foul curses, and Strahd held up one hand. "If the death knight had come to you first," he noted coldly, "you would have turned him against me. It's rather like murdering the envoys we send to each other."

"This isn't the same as murdering ambassadors," the duke bellowed. "That monstrous werebeast tore poor Medraut's throat out. Someone must pay my blood-price for this," he warned. "I want restitution."

Strahd laughed. "The werebeast should ask *you* for payment, Duke. You were terrified of that little brat. If you could have, you would have killed him yourself years ago."

Slowly Gundar turned his back to Strahd, and silence fell upon both men. When the duke faced the ghostly image again, a look of worry, almost of fear, hung upon his features. "The death knight fought me to a standstill," he said gravely. "Here, in my own castle!"

"That is why I am contacting you," Strahd explained. "This death knight—Lord Soth, is his name—has proven himself to be a threat to *both* Barovia and Gundarak. As I said, he is fighting against my minions as we speak, trying to batter his way into my home." The count smiled, revealing his fangs. "I can rid us of him, but I will need your help."

Again Gundar paused, then he asked, "What do you need me to do?"

* * * * * *

Soth and Azrael fought back-to-back. The corpses and bones piled around them served to slow down the assault, and they added to that grim barricade with almost every stroke of Soth's blade, every swing of Azrael's mace. Both had taken blows from the attackers, but the death knight's armor saved him from all but the most powerful strike and the dwarf's amazing powers of regeneration helped him shrug off most wounds. Only the scarred mercenary had scored palpable hits against the werebadger time and again; his silver sword and ensorcelled dagger dug deeply into Azrael's shoulder and leg. The dwarf had not been able to strike back at the human, for he attacked whenever Azrael was caught up in a struggle with a zombie or skeleton. Then he faded back into the press.

The zombies proved to be the most difficult foe, as Soth had expected. Their limbs continued to fight even after being sliced from their torsos. Azrael now clutched a burning branch in one hand, and set the creatures on fire whenever a chance presented itself. Flames seemed to be the best way to stop the shambling undead, for their ragged clothing and desiccated flesh caught fire quite readily.

Azrael had just set another zombie on fire when the half-dozen gargoyles that flapped overhead shouted a retreat. "Back to the bridge," they cried, snapping their wire whips against the zombies' backs.

Soth did not allow the soldiers to break off without paying a price. He cut two mercenaries down as they fled and bashed in a skeleton's rictus grin with the pommel of his sword. As the remainder of Strahd's army backed toward the bridge, Soth studied the battlefield, waiting for some new and more deadly opponent.

"Greetings, Lord Soth," came a voice from one of the crumbling gatehouses slouching to either side of the bridge. "I bear a message from my master, Count Strahd Von Zarovich."

The familiar voice startled Soth, and his sword slipped from his fingers when he saw Caradoc standing atop the gatehouse. The ghost's head still lolled upon his shoulder as he hovered uncertainly, half hidden behind a crenelation. "The count sends his regrets that he cannot deliver the message himself, but has asked me to inform you that he will come to parley with you when the moon reaches it zenith."

"Caradoc," the death knight whispered, unable to believe his eyes. "You traitorous cur!" He staggered a step forward and pointed. A bolt of light flashed from his hand and sped toward the ghost, but before it reached the tower, it struck an invisible wall, a powerful shield against magic that Strahd had erected around the castle. The beam dissipated in a dazzling burst of reds and golds.

It took Caradoc a moment to find his voice. Strahd had kept his word; the death knight could not reach him. "My master's message to you is this: 'I regret you have not left Barovia, but your treatment of my subjects in Vallaki and your attack on my home cannot be pardoned. If you break off your hostilities now, I may find mercy for you.' "

Azrael kicked one of the corpses littering the field. "Mercy? He's the one cowering inside his castle, and he's offering *us* mercy?"

"His message for you is different, dwarf," Caradoc replied. "I am to say that you are doomed."

His fists held before him, Soth rushed forward a few steps. The army pressed together to hold him back, but he stopped before he reached the front rank. "You cannot hide from me forever, Caradoc," he shouted. His rage burned within him, as hot as the fires that had robbed him of his life.

The ghost leaned out over the crenelations. "You will never defeat Strahd." He laughed and gestured toward his broken neck. "This is the best you could do against me, and I'm the least of his servants."

So caught up in the joy of taunting the death knight was Caradoc that he did not notice the soft shimmer in the air above Soth's head.

"I robbed you of Kitiara," the ghost shouted, "and you expect to outwit Strahd? The medallion was hidden in my skeleton in the tower at Dargaard. You practically stepped on it when you scattered my bones. It's still there, but you'll never reach it. She is out of your grasp forever."

A huge fist appeared above Soth, glowing with a fierce red luminescence. The death knight raised his gauntleted hand over his head, and the radiant fist he had formed rose higher. When it was level with the top of the gatehouse, Soth pounded the air before him; the fist mirrored that action and slammed into the invisible shield.

"You . . . will . . . never . . . escape!" the death knight shouted. The fist struck the barrier with each word, sending peals of thunder rolling through the clear night sky. Lines of blue light snaked across the air like cracks in plaster, and the gatehouse quaked to its foundation.

Caradoc needed no more prompting. He fled back to the keep, Soth's shouts and the ominous rumble of magical thunder filling his ears. Relief washed over him when he saw Strahd framed by the castle's entryway.

"You seem to have angered him," the count said

smoothly. "That's quite unfortunate."

Caradoc's relief turned to fear when he saw the cold glint in the vampire's eyes, the calculating way in which Strahd was studying him. "Master, I—"

Strahd shook his head, silencing the plea before it left the ghost's mouth. "I'm afraid you are no longer welcome at Castle Ravenloft, Caradoc," the vampire lord said. "I want you to leave immediately."

SIXTEEN

The magical fist Soth wielded against the barrier protecting Castle Ravenloft struck one final blow, then faded. The invisible wall had withstood the death knight's furious attack; though it had cracked many times, the snaking lines of blue had healed after each blow, never widening into a full breach. The last thunderous report reverberated from the castle's outer curtain of stone and into the crevasse that gaped before the front gate, then silence fell upon the clearing.

Strahd's army stood in formation before the bridge. The zombies, skeletons, and human mercenaries had originally outnumbered Soth and Azrael one-hundred-to-one, but their number had been halved in the first assault. A few of the soldiers had intellect enough to understand their peril. They prayed to whatever dark gods they worshiped that Strahd would not order them to attack again. They did not wish to share the fate of the mangled corpses that littered the field.

Whistling tunelessly, Azrael took advantage of the lull in the fighting and made his way across the battlefield. He set fire to the twitching remains of the zombies and battered anything that tried to move.

Whenever he came across a human mercenary, he would rifle the dead man's pockets, taking whatever coins or trinkets he found. Having completed his rounds, the dwarf moved to Soth's side.

The death knight stared at the gatehouse where Caradoc had stood, taunting him. "He will not escape me," Soth repeated softly. "I cannot let his treachery go unpunished."

Azrael was about to ask the death knight how he intended to get at the ghost, seeing as Strahd's defenses were standing up quite well to their assault, but movement in the enemy ranks silenced him. The gargoyles who commanded the mob suddenly took to the air, cracking their whips. At the savage prompting, the dead men and sell-swords parted into two groups, leaving open a wide path directly to the bridge. Soth took a single step toward the gap, then stopped.

A cloud of mist was swirling across the bridge. As Soth watched, the cloud stopped midway, took the shape of a man, and solidified into the vampire lord of Barovia, Strahd Von Zarovich.

"Where is Caradoc?" the death knight shouted.

Strahd's hands were clasped behind his back. He wore a white shirt with billowing sleeves, its buttons undone partway down his chest. His black pants were lightly wrinkled and his high boots scuffed. Soth knew the count's appearance was a carefully considered facade, meant to give the impression that he had been caught unprepared by the attack on his home.

Glancing to the left and right, Strahd eyed his remaining troops. The zombies and skeletons stared blankly at the count; the humans averted their eyes. "You may return to the keep," he told them.

As the soldiers shuffled across the bridge, Soth

stormed forward. "You have much to account for, Strahd," he rumbled.

Strahd cocked his head. "I have *nothing* to account for," he replied without emotion. "I told you all I knew about the portal. If it did not take you back to Krynn, I am hardly to blame."

"And Caradoc?" Soth asked. He was close enough to Strahd now that the vampire could smell the bitter scent of blood on the death knight's blade and armor. "You told me he died entering your home, remember? He is my servant. I want him released to me immediately."

"The ghost *was* your servant, Lord Soth," the vampire corrected. "He came to me seeking sanctuary. Since there are no churches to speak of in Barovia, I feel it is my responsibility to take such unfortunates into my care. Caradoc swore an oath of loyalty to me, and I consider him one of my own household now."

"Then I will tear your household apart until I find him," Soth said, stepping past the count. Strahd did not attempt to stop him as he headed toward the keep.

Gesturing to the castle, the count said, "You will not find Caradoc there, Soth. You frightened him so badly with your show of force that he fled."

Strahd suddenly turned to Azrael. The dwarf was only a few paces behind the count, his mace gripped tightly in his hands. Before the dwarf could utter a single word, he found himself paralyzed. "You are fortunate, cur. I have a dozen spells that would have taken your miserable life instead of freezing your limbs."

Although his features were locked in a snarl, Azrael's brown eyes showed his fear and surprise quite clearly.

The count faced Soth again, a complacent smirk twisting his thin lips. "I will not hold you accountable for the mistakes of those who serve you. Do not hold a grudge against me because you have an old score to settle with a servant of mine."

The death knight looked back at Strahd. The vampire was standing over the paralyzed dwarf, tracing with one finger the wounds Azrael had gained during the battle.

"Once," Strahd noted casually, "when I was a soldier, I was forced to eat raw meat. It was the only food we could find, you see, and we couldn't start a fire because the enemy would have spotted our camp." He licked Azrael's blood from his finger and gritted his teeth. "I never thought I would live to enjoy it so much."

Soth walked back to Strahd. "Where is he?" he asked. When the vampire continued to prod Azrael's wounds, the death knight grabbed his wrist. "Where did Caradoc go?"

Narrowing his eyes until they were dark slits, Strahd licked his lips. "If Magda was still with you, I would demand a trade—her life for the ghost's. The dwarf is not worth so much." He wrenched his hand from Soth's grasp and pointed at Azrael. "You will need him to find your errant seneschal."

The count paced a few steps from Soth, then straightened the cuff of his shirt. "Caradoc fled the castle and is heading for the portal to Gundarak. Perhaps he is hoping to gain Gundar's aid against you, but I suspect the good duke fears you enough that he would never harbor someone you seek."

"Then he intends to find the Misty Border," Soth concluded. "He hopes the mists will deposit him somewhere far from me. And if I follow him . . ."

Strahd nodded. "As I explained to you before you

left for Gundarak, Lord Soth, any creature of darkness takes a great risk by entering the Misty Border. If he is powerful enough, a new duchy forms around him, trapping him there forever."

Soth did not hesitate. "Free Azrael," he said. "We must be on our way."

The count did as the death knight requested, but the instant the dwarf was free of the enchantment, he flew to Soth's side. "Mighty lord, I could hear what was being said. This is a trap. Strahd is hoping you get caught in the Misty Border."

"Of course," Soth replied. "Where else would Caradoc have heard about the portal or the Misty Border?" He turned to the count. "I assume you have cut a deal with Gundar to keep the way clear for us from Castle Hunadora to the border?"

A smile on his lips, Strahd bowed. "Just so, Lord Soth. You are most perceptive."

Azrael was stunned. Instead of a bloody battle, the conflict between the death knight and the vampire had become a chillingly polite exchange of words.

"Go to the portal in Vallaki," the count said to the dwarf. "You will find the ghost's trail there. I'm certain you will be able to track him."

Without another word, Soth headed back up the road, along the circuitous route he had taken from the fishing village. Azrael hurried after him. The dwarf stole a look at Strahd over his shoulder just before he rounded a bend and trees blocked his view of the castle; the count stood bathed in moonlight, his arms folded over his chest.

"Do not worry, Azrael," Soth said coldly as they hurried through the night. "We will deal with the ghost now since he may elude us if we delay too long. Strahd has no such road for escape; he is trapped in Barovia forever, and even if it takes a thousand years, I will make him pay."

In the clearing before Castle Ravenloft, Strahd's own thoughts mirrored the death knight's. He knew Caradoc had provided him with a way to turn aside Soth's anger, but only for a little while. Sooner or later, the death knight would return to seek his revenge.

As he crossed the bridge to the keep, Strahd noted with some satisfaction that he had discovered much about Soth from the story of his doom. The fallen knight was a being of great passion, with a damning concern for loyalty. He had abandoned a gods-given quest to punish a wife he feared unfaithful; why shouldn't he forego an escape from the netherworld to destroy a faithless servant?

Yes, Strahd decided as he passed into the crumbling halls of Castle Ravenloft, a man's form may change, but his heart remains the same forever— whether it beats in his chest or not.

* * * * *

The sun hung poised on the horizon, a huge red disc against a darkening sky. It was a guidepost by which Caradoc found his way southeast from Castle Hunadora toward the Misty Border. Strahd had told him that the border offered the only chance he had to escape Lord Soth. The ghost didn't trust the count, but he had no choice in this matter. If Strahd was lying, he was doomed. If not, he just might avoid the death knight's wrath.

Caradoc didn't need to look over his shoulder to know that Soth and Azrael were close behind him. He'd passed through the portal to Gundar's keep, then through the tent village outside Hunadora, but the death knight had stayed on his trail. For days— he'd lost track of how many—he had plunged through endless miles of mountainous forest. No matter how fast he moved, the death knight and the werecreature kept pace with him. And in the last few hours, they'd come close to capturing him several times.

Something snarled to the ghost's left, and he glanced into the ravine that had been parallel to his path since noon. Things were moving in the caves that dotted the gorge, things that watched him with four pairs of small, bright eyes.

"If you want some solid food," he shouted into the ravine, "there is a dwarf and a dead man following me."

The creatures blinked, then disappeared into their various dens. It was worth a try, the ghost told himself.

"Your desperation is pitiful," said a hollow voice from behind Caradoc. The ghost spun around to see Soth emerge from the shadow of a boulder a hundred yards back. His unblinking orange eyes flickered ominously in the growing twilight. "Stop now, and I will destroy you quickly."

The death knight stepped into the boulder's shadow again and vanished, but Caradoc didn't wait to see where he would come out. Swiftly he dropped into the ground, sliding easily into the hard-packed earth. He had evaded the death knight this way many times in the last few hours. It was only useful as an emergency escape measure, though. Caradoc could see nothing beneath the ground, so he lost his way each time he hid there.

After a while, the ghost surfaced. Cautiously he poked his head up and surveyed the area from inside a fallen tree. Cursing and prodding the ground with his sword, the death knight was hunting for Caradoc in the spot where he had disappeared into the earth.

The ghost smiled with relief; he had lost his pursuer again, at least for a little while.

"There you are, you coward," a voice said, and a mace passed harmlessly through the ghost's head. He looked up to see Azrael standing over him, ready to strike again.

Attacks with mundane weapons had no effect upon the ghost's noncorporeal form, but Caradoc knew that he could harm a mortal creature, even an unnatural one like Azrael. Before the dwarf could shout an alarm to Lord Soth, the ghost shot from the ground. He rushed past Azrael, raking his ethereal hands through the dwarf's face as he went. The pain was so great that it made Azrael collapse to his knees, gasping and unable to cry out. The ghost's touch had left the chill of the grave upon him. His face and skull ached as if he'd been stabbed with ten barbed daggers, and the newly grown stubble of his sideburns and mustache turned as white as newly fallen snow.

The dwarf's agony bought Caradoc some much-needed time. Without the werecreature's tracking ability, the death knight could not follow the ghost's trail as quickly. Moreover, clouds were beginning to roll in. With luck, they would blanket the moon. Without that orb's light, there would be no shadows Soth could use for travel. He would be slowed to his walking pace.

The sun sank in the west, and the velvet darkness of night replaced the muted colors of twilight. A cavern in the gorge belched forth a thousand bats. The little rodents fell screeching through the air, hunting for their sustenance. Caradoc envied the creatures their freedom as they darted overhead through the cloud-choked sky.

Without the sun or moon to guide him, the ghost

found himself slowing his pace, too. Even if he had been able to see the constellations through the clouds, he wasn't familiar enough with Gundarak's stars to navigate by them. Fear tugged at his mind, filling his thoughts with wild imaginings. Each tree seemed capable of hiding Soth or Azrael. Each sound in the darkness—the distant yowl of a night-hunting cat, the hiss of leaves rustling in the cool air, the babbling of the river that ran at the ravine's bottom—seemed to warn Caradoc of the doom awaiting him at the death knight's hands.

And so it went through the long night. Caradoc kept the ravine to his left as he hurried on. At first he traveled close to the edge of the gorge, but a gnarled branch thrust up from the slope looked so much like a hand reaching up to grab him that he chose to move farther into the woods. Perhaps the branch was a warning, he told himself, suddenly convinced that the land itself was pointing out ways in which Soth could lay an ambush.

Like the clouds blotting out the moonlight, Caradoc's fear choked off his senses and muddled his thinking. So many things in the night terrified the ghost that his mind began to turn on itself, blocking out the sudden noises of animals on the prowl or wind through the trees. Soon only the void that awaited undead creatures who were destroyed yawned horribly in his mind. The sights and smells of the forest around him paled before this apocalyptic sight.

Caradoc didn't notice when the first bands of pale blue and gold appeared on the eastern horizon, the harbingers of the dawn. Nor did he notice the thin fog that clung to the ground beneath his feet as he raced blindly through a copse of pine. Even if he had seen the fog, he probably would not have realized that he had finally reached the outskirts of the Misty

Border. As the sun pushed its way into the sky and shadows began to fall around the trees, Caradoc knew only one thing: he had to keep running, because the death knight was behind him.

He was wrong.

From the shadow of a gnarled pine in front of the ghost, a gauntleted hand appeared. The ice-cold fingers reached for Caradoc's throat but only caught him by the hair. "I have you at last," Soth rumbled.

The death knight stepped fully from the shadows and lifted Caradoc from the ground by the hair. The pain and the shock snapped the ghost from his numbness, but there was little he could do. Viciously Soth slapped him across the face with the back of his hand, then twice more. "The sun will set again before I am done with you," the death knight said.

"Mighty lord!" Azrael shouted, rushing through the trees. "The mists are rising!"

The dwarf was correct. In the growing light of the new day, swirls of white fog curled around the tree trunks like huge snakes. Smaller tendrils of the stuff wound around Soth's legs, almost to his knees. The fog covered the shadows and muted the daylight.

"Quickly," Azrael said. "Kill him! We might still escape from here!" There was panic in the dwarf's voice, and not just from the threat of the Misty Border. He could see himself in the ghost's place.

Caradoc struggled against Soth's grip, but the death knight clamped his other hand around the ghost's throat. His orange eyes flickered as he tightened his grip.

"You will . . . never . . . have . . . Kitiara," the ghost managed to gasp through the pain.

Soth laughed. "You are hardly in a position to deny me anything, traitor."

The doomed ghost did not, could not, hope for a

better afterlife, but in the instant before he died for a second time, Caradoc saw the mist rising up around Lord Soth. He knew then that revenge had cost the death knight everything. It was enough.

The mist billowed around the death knight in the same instant Caradoc died, his body slipping through Soth's fingers like fine sand. As it had in Dargaard Keep, the mist filled Soth's world, blinding him and deafening him. The sun, Azrael, the copse of trees—all were blotted out, as if they'd never really been there at all. For the briefest moment, he dared to hope that the mist would clear and he would find himself back on Krynn, in the burned-out throne room of Dargaard Keep.

A figure appeared in the fog. He was clad from head to toe in shining armor patterned with roses and kingfishers, the symbols of the Order of the Rose. A sash, a token from the woman he championed, girded his waist. The sash was the blue of a clear spring sky, and it matched the color of the eyes that gazed out of his helmet.

Soth tensed at the sight of the knight. The man moved with an easy, confident step, which told the death knight he faced a seasoned warrior. Only one used to the battlefield could move gracefully in heavy plate armor. Yet hope also flared to life in Soth's mind; the presence of a knight of the Order meant he had found his way to Krynn!

"Follow me," the knight said, his voice clear and steady and full of resolve. "I have come to rescue you." He turned and strode into the mist.

Soth followed but took only a few steps before the blanket of fog lifted. He and the silver-clad knight stood next to a busy road. The broad way passed through the thriving tent city that sprawled outside the walls of a castle. Hundreds of knights and priests and merchants bustled toward the keep, and its open drawbridge and gates welcomed them all. The keep was wrought from rose-red stone, its main tower ending in a twisted cap much like an unopened rosebud. Pennants of blue and gold and white fluttered in the wind, and the sound of music and laughter came to Soth's ears.

"Dargaard Keep!" the death knight said. His mind reeled at the sight of his ancient home.

The mysterious knight stepped forward. "Yes, Soth," he said happily. "While Dargaard was never like this, it could be. You can make it so."

A woman came to the knight's side then. She was thin, with the graceful step of an elf. Her long golden hair hung loose, cascading over her shoulders like warm sunlight. A veil concealed her face, but her eyes shone with beauty and serenity. "My lord," she said, bowing slightly.

The silver-clad knight removed his helmet so that he could kiss the woman, and Soth gasped. The face was his own, as it had been long, long ago. His golden curls framed his features like a halo, and his mustache was neatly trimmed. His blue eyes shone with wisdom and peace, things Soth had lost many years before his death. Those eyes bored into the death knight like a cold spike as he pulled the veil away from his wife's face and kissed her.

Isolde! The elfmaid, too, was as she had been before the siege, before the Cataclysm. As she embraced her husband, a smile of joy lit up her face.

The death knight drew his sword. "What sorcery is this?"

"No sorcery at all," Isolde said kindly. "This is a world where you completed the quest given you by the Father of Good. And since you saved Krynn from the wrath of the gods, these people—" she spread her arms wide in a gesture that encompassed Dargaard and the tent city "—have come to our home to share in your glory. Many in Ansalon honor you as the greatest of the Knights of Solamnia. Some say you will outshine Huma Dragonbane in your lifetime."

"Bah," Soth rumbled. "This is all just an illusion, and a poor one at that. Paladine told me that I would have to sacrifice my life to stop the kingpriest." Yet something in the scene spread before him called to Soth, kindled long-abandoned speculations within his mind. He had been a great knight once, capable of any feat. If the gods presented another chance . . .

Isolde smiled sweetly at him. "Yes, Soth. The gods of Good are forgiving. To have this, to have me again, all you need to do is kneel before your new home and swear to protect it."

"Prove you are worthy of your new palace," the mortal Soth said. "Bow down to the gods of Good."

The demand stirred a wave of anger in the death knight's mind, a black wave that washed over the budding hopes for a new life and drowned them. "I bow before no one," he replied. He stepped toward Isolde. "Is this some test, woman? Some part of the curse you leveled against me that is coming to pass only now?"

The elfmaid shrank back from the death knight, but contempt, not fear, colored her features. "You have always said that your damnation is your own doing, Soth. This is no different."

A feral smile crossed the dead man's lips. "You are correct, of course."

He lashed out, and his sword went deep into Isolde's shoulder, splashing a gout of blood across her white dress. She cried out in a voice like a newborn's as she crumpled to the ground. "And your doom has always been your own doing, fair Isolde."

A bright blade clashed against the death knight's bloodstained one. Soth looked up at himself; the noble knight's face was twisted in righteous fury. "Pray that she still lives, fallen one. If you kill in this place, you are damned forever."

The two exchanged blows, but neither dealt his opponent a wound. Their swords clanged and sparked as they met between the evenly matched foes. All the while, Isolde's blood soaked the ground beneath her still form. The crowd stopped on the road and pointed, their faces masked with horror. The passing knights drew their weapons, but they could not interfere; such was the way of the Order. A few women moved tentatively forward to tend to Isolde's wounds, but they were driven back by the fury of the conflict.

At last one young knight did rush forward, having just come upon the battle. "Mother!" the youth cried, tears streaming down his face.

Peradur, the son of Soth and Isolde, was fair of skin, with hair so blond that it was almost white. A look of piety and resolve made his features appear hard for one who'd lived only sixteen years, but his eyes reflected the goodness of his heart. Like his father, the boy wore the armor of a Knight of Solamnia. The metal was painted pure white, and holy symbols of the gods of Good were its only decorations.

Trembling, Peradur removed his gauntlets and laid his hands over his mother's wound. A faint glow radiated from the youth's fingers as he cast his tearing eyes to the heavens. The bloody wound closed beneath his touch, and his mother slumped into a healing sleep.

The death knight and his foe came together, so close that the dead man could smell the warm breath of the other through the slits in his helmet. The mortal Soth drew his mouth into a hard line and said, "You still have a chance, fallen one. Lay down your sword."

The death knight shoved his foe away and looked from the distorted reflection of himself to the youth—his son. Their armor was perfectly kept, their swords glinting like razors in the sunlight. Just as he radiated the chill of undeath, the cold of the Abyss, they were cloaked in an invisible aura of vitality and strength. They were models of knightly virtue, men whose goodness shone in their faces and their deeds.

He hated them with all his unbeating heart.

With a cry of anger, the death knight grabbed his opponent's sword with his free hand. The blade squealed against his metal gauntlet, but he only tightened his grip on it. With strength no mortal knight could match, he wrenched the blade from his foe and tossed it aside.

Instead of diving for the sword, the silver-clad knight got down on his knees before the death knight. He looked up at him with hope-filled eyes. "You have bested me in combat," he said. "I will name you the victor if you bow down and give thanks for your power."

Though he knew this was all some sort of test, some way for the keepers of the Misty Border to decide if he was worthy of a domain, Soth never considered heeding the words of his goodly reflection. Instead, he raised his hand and uttered a word of magic that would surely end the conflict.

Dark fingers of energy snaked from Lord Soth's fingers toward the silver-clad knight. Before they hit their target, though, Peradur threw himself in front of the blast. His speed was amazing, all the more so for his armor. The youth took the attack full in the chest, the black bands staining his white armor and blotting out the holy symbols painted there. The energy insinuated itself through the hole hammered into Peradur's breastplate and found the boy's noble heart. As the fingers seized that heart, he cried out, not in fear or pain, but in a humble, reverential plea to Paladine.

Tears in his eyes for his wounded wife and dead child, the mortal Soth cradled the youth in his arms. "You have lost," he said to the death knight. "Thus you have made your new domain."

Most of the crowd bowed their heads and turned away, becoming pale and insubstantial as they scattered into the tent city. Likewise, the bustling tent city became silent and ghostly, fading before the death knight's eyes. Clerics came forward to bear Isolde and Peradur away, while thirteen knights—Sir Mikel and the others who had followed Soth in the time before the Cataclysm—surrounded their silver-clad lord and consoled him. They walked in slow procession toward the rose-red walls of Dargaard Keep.

As the small group entered the keep, a pall fell over the land. Even Soth felt the chill that swept around him, breaking up the misty images of the tent city, scouring the rocky ground clear of signs of habitation or commerce. Then, as if shrugging on clothes of mourning, Dargaard Keep itself grew dark. Its rosy walls became black and crumbling. The pennants disappeared from the towers, and the sounds of music and laughter were replaced by the mournful keening of banshees.

The death knight glanced up into the night sky that spread suddenly over the ruined keep. What he saw there told him that he was not back on Krynn, though the castle looming before him resembled Dargaard. Only one moon hung in the velvet-black heavens: Nuitari, the orb of evil magic. Had he been on Krynn, Lunitari and Solinari—the red and the white moons—would certainly have been there to represent the Balance.

Azrael stood in the middle of the ancient rutted road, shaking his head. "What happened? You disappeared into the fog, and next thing I know, I'm standing here." He gestured to the sky. "The whole day's gone, too! Are we in Krynn, then? Is this Dargaard Keep?"

"No," Soth replied wearily. "This is not Dargaard Keep. We are home, but not on Krynn."

The death knight walked slowly into the castle. No sooner had he entered the keep itself than the banshees began to wail the song of his damnation. The wicked tale was longer now, and everyone in Barovia, Gundarak, and the other duchies that made up the netherworld heard it clearly. Soth walked in their nightmares that evening and for many nights to come.

 **EPILOGUE**

The years passed slowly for Lord Soth. He named his new castle Nedragaard—ancient Solamnic for "not Dargaard"—because it was very much like his keep on Krynn, but dissimilar enough that he never passed a day without finding some small discrepancy. Most were minor—intact doors where ruined ones should have hung, walkways that were a few paces short of their original length—but for a creature who needed no sleep, who had paced through every hallway, every room in his home on Krynn for three and a half centuries, each inconsistency clashed painfully with his memories.

There were other, more striking differences, too. Thirteen skeletal warriors walked the halls of Nedragaard Keep, the thirteen loyal retainers who had served Soth on Krynn, yet they did not man the posts they'd held when they died. They roamed the keep freely, watching for trespassers that never came.

The banshees had come to Nedragaard, but somehow their memories had been warped. They no longer told Soth's tale in exactly the same way each night, but instead forgot verses or added events that had never occurred. This infuriated the death knight. No matter how much he chastised them or how many times he flew into a violent rage at their imperfect telling, the banshees never sang his history the same way twice.

The past had been the only consolation left to the death knight; the pain caused by memories was the only thing that could goad his sleeping senses and emotions into a semblance of humanity. Now the past was thrust violently into Soth's consciousness with each step he took through the flawed halls of his home, each fractured verse from the banshees' lips; the constant pain caused by those memories and the longing he felt for the things he had lost no longer stirred his senses, but deadened them.

So it was that Lord Soth sat, numb to the cold wind that blew into the throne room, past the sagging main doors. He did not hear the tread of iron-soled boots across the stone floor or the keening of the banshees. And it wasn't until Azrael was kneeling before the death knight's worm-eaten throne that Soth noticed he had entered the hall.

"What do you have to report, seneschal?" Soth asked, his voice hollow, devoid of emotions.

The dwarf stood. He was clad in breeches dirty from a long trek and chain mail stained by rain and sweat. A silk doublet hung in shreds over his mail shirt. The black rose on its front presented a stark contrast to the dwarf's bone-white mustache and muttonchop sideburns. "I am sorry, mighty lord," he began tentatively. "I can find no sign of the Vistani camp."

Soth sighed. In the past few months, rumors had come to him of a small band of Vistani traveling through his domain. Their leader was a woman who claimed to possess an artifact of some power—the cudgel of the hero, Kulchek the Wanderer. The gypsies earned their bread by telling tales to the domain's scattered tribes of elves. Most of these concerned Soth, or a doomed silver-clad knight who seemed very much like the lord of Nedragaard Keep. Soth did not doubt that Magda had somehow survived to form this band; the story the Vistani told of the brave knight who had rescued their leader from the wyrm guarding Castle Ravenloft was proof enough for him.

"And the other?" Soth prompted. He tightened his grip on the ancient throne, and the wood cracked beneath his grip.

"The dark-haired woman with the crooked smile roams the hills as well," Azrael reported. "The elves say she calls herself Kitiara. She claims that she was your doom, that you followed her voice into the mist that brought you here."

Soth pounded the throne with a mailed fist. "I want you to have anyone spreading that rumor killed!" he shouted. "I forged my own doom. I am the cause of my damnation."

The death knight had repeated those words quite often in the last few years, but he knew they were a lie. There were things of darkness that had power far greater than his. He was lord of Nedragaard Keep and master of a duchy even larger than Barovia. But the elves called Soth's domain Sithicus, an Elvish term that meant "land of specters." Although he would never admit it, Soth knew the name was a fitting one for his kingdom of shadows.